D0267687

FILE ON A DIPLOMAT

"Love is a form of metaphysical enquiry"

LAWRENCE DURRELL

ANDRÉ BRINK

File on a Diplomat

Translated by André Brink

LONGMANS

LONGMANS GREEN AND CO LTD
48 Grosvenor Street, London W1
*Associated companies, branches and representatives
thoughout the world*

Copyright © in English Translation
Central News Agency Ltd. 1964
First published in Afrikaans in 1963 by
Human and Rousseau (Edms) Bpk.
This Edition first published 1967

This novel was first published
in the Republic of South Africa
in both Afrikaans and English, as
THE AMBASSADOR

Printed in Great Britain by
Lowe & Brydone (Printers) Ltd, London

FOR INGRID

CONTENTS

NOTE

Reference to specific Ministers, and to Government and Embassy officials in Paris, South Africa and elsewhere, was inevitable in a novel of this nature. It must be emphasised, however, that only these offices, *per se*, have any factual existence: the characters acting in these offices are entirely fictitious and have no relation whatsoever to present or past incumbents of such posts, or to any other persons, living or dead.

THIRD SECRETARY

I have decided to report the Ambassador to Head Office in
Pretoria.

People like Anna Smith – and possibly even Koos Joubert –
would find various personal motives for such a procedure: egoism,
thwarted ambition, wounded pride, anything. I leave it to them.
But Anna has a passionate admiration for the Ambassador and
Koos is much too obtuse to see what is happening under his very
eyes, let alone react to it. I presume Douglas Masters, in turn,
would be able to cite arguments from Satow or Nicholson to
prove why a Third Secretary should not adopt this line of action.
But I am firmly convinced that I have no choice left. It would
be a flagrant neglect of duty to allow the present state of affairs to
continue, especially now that such delicate negotiations with the
French Government are in progress.

I do not intend to deny that my action is free from all personal
considerations. But I do deny emphatically that it is prompted
by antagonism, envy or hate. The only personal motives involved (I must stress this) are sincere disgust, and my deep-
seated loathing of hypocrisy. I don't think I would have lifted a
finger if the present Ambassador's predecessor, Jan Theunissen,
had been involved – that is, if anybody could imagine Theunissen
in a situation like this. For Theunissen never tried to hide his
essential humanity. But today I am confronted with Ambassador
Van Heerden: the efficient automaton, the imposing man-of-
influence, and probably the most outstanding diplomat that has
represented South Africa in many years. Not the slightest error or
negligence is tolerated in the Embassy, for the simple reason that
he himself never errs or neglects anything. I have often heard even
diplomats from other missions refer to him with the greatest
respect, and sometimes with awe. Bonnard of the French Foreign
Service recently said quite openly that Paul van Heerden was the
only reason why there was still some respect for the South African
point of view in Paris.

This, then, is His Excellency. And then he fools about with that
little bitch, Nicolette Alford, while his wife is away on holiday in
Italy: he who poses as virtue itself, as integrity incarnate, he who,

only three days ago, humiliated me in public at the Doyen's reception in the Hôtel de Ville.

He spends his nights in the rue de Condé. And by day he is God Almighty.

I have, naturally, studied the records to see what happened in similar situations in the past. In 1957 Peter Williams, at that stage a mere cadet, accused the chargé d'affaires in Buenos Aires of fraud. Four years previously Vincent Johnstone accused his Ambassador in Berne of carelessness with classified official documents. Before that there had been other cases, of course, but I need not go into all of them. I also know that both Williams and Johnstone were summarily transferred back to Headquarters in Pretoria. As a matter of fact, Johnstone is still there. The Department has a highly efficient way of isolating such officials in musty little offices where they spend their time drawing up unimportant memoranda or initialling circulars. Williams was transferred to an obscure outpost; he resigned recently. I am, consequently, only too well aware of the implications of my action. But I happen to know that in both these cases I have just referred to there existed considerable suspicion about the motives that prompted the accusations, whereas my conscience is clear. I am confident that I can give such a convincing reason for my intended action that no shadow can rest on my future career as a diplomat. And that future is very important to me. I had promised that to myself even before I joined the Corps. I have seen enough of frustration and careers ending up in cul-de-sacs. Even my father will have to admit, eventually, that I have reached the top – in spite of all his sarcasm in the past when that very future came to be discussed.

Perhaps I can rationalise this past now that I am here. But I wouldn't like to think too much about my youth. It is of no importance in the present situation. That is, it may have some psychological significance in explaining why I am what I am, but I resent sorting out my personal life in public the way Anna Smith does with so much relish and preferably in the presence of His Excellency. Besides, psychology so easily becomes a mere formula. I can remember, for example, how at the age of fifteen I had a long series of interviews with a psychologist in Pretoria who had to find out why I was such a "difficult" child. I quite enjoyed the diagnostic tests. But I still remember very acutely the shock, the loathing, with which I accidentally discovered his final report reducing me to a "case history." (*Case 325: Keyter, Stephen Wilhelm.*) The particulars about my father ("*51; teacher; dominating*

2

personality; regards son as weakling") and my mother (*"38; gentle and somewhat reticent; tends to be moody"*); all the clever references to *"intelligence above average"*, to *"neurosis"*, *"impulsiveness"*, *"emotional repression"*, *"mother-fixation"*; the disgusting phrase, *"masturbation since early puberty"*; and finally the prosaic revelation of everything he had hypocritically cajoled out of me: how, as a small boy, I had been terrified to sleep alone; how I had often gone to lie with my mother at night; how my father had gradually come to accept this – except on Sunday nights; how I could never understand this, until one Sunday night I had gone to spy on them. (*"Traumatic experience"*.) Q.E.D. It was all so smug, so neatly formulated, so adequate – and, God, so relative.

One might just as well rely on a second possibility, which would certainly be no less improbable than the first: Nicolette curled up in an armchair here in my apartment in the rue Jacques-Dulud, her shoes kicked off, her feet tucked under her, her fair hair loosely hanging round her shoulders, while she reads slowly and deliberately from a woman's journal what the stars have to say about me:

"People born under the sign of Gemini possess a double personality, so that they are continually at war with themselves. Of all people they are the most difficult to understand. On the one hand they are extremely amiable, on the other hand they can be hypercritical. They usually make excellent diplomats." (She smiles with the funny little curl at the left corner of her mouth, and says quietly, without looking up: "Budding young diplomat!" before she resumes her reading.) *"They are always active, and yearn for what they cannot find. Therefore one should never try to bind them to their promises, or expect them to act consistently: not because they are dishonest, but because to them every moment exists as a separate entity in time, and because they continually switch from impulsiveness to rationalisation."*

"And what about yourself?" I ask her.

"Scorpio. October 21 to November 20." Her hair forms untidy wisps across her eyes as she leans forward to continue reading: *"Until their twentieth birthday these people are usually chaste and religious. Then they often suddenly change to the opposite extreme. Some of the greatest saints were born under this sign. They are good fighters, yet they abhor violence, therefore they usually assume the rôle of pacifists. Sex plays an important part in their lives."*

"And do you really believe it all?"

"That's what the stars say." As if that is sufficient in itself.

If I think back to my youth, there is only one day that returns to my mind – without any conscious effort on my part to sort it out or determine its importance. It must have been a Monday morning, because I felt ill. (I used to get headaches every Sunday night.) Therefore I felt irritated when my mother called me back from the front door and sent me to put on a clean shirt. Mine – a white one with fine blue stripes – had a dirty rim round the collar. I grumbled. We had an unpleasant argument. When I left for school I slammed the door behind me. And when I came back that afternoon, she was dead. My father explained that she had tried to clean his revolver.

2

Winter set in early this year. Autumn was hardly a separate season; merely a morbid prelude to the coming cold, with something sinister and oppressive about it, as if the city found itself on the edge of a winter which would make it hard and narrow and bitter. Perhaps we will not even be allowed the mercy of snow: everything is just gradually reduced to rigidity, to the nakedness of black tree skeletons in the Bois de Boulogne just beyond these grey rooftops of the boulevard des Sablons.

Among the monotonous buildings one sees the branching veins and nerves of the city in all its shameless anatomy, an X-ray photo, stripped of illusion. Paris. Perhaps that was, from the very outset, the most unnerving experience of all: that I could never escape from the mere awareness of 'the city'. It is so much more than a backdrop or an inevitable assortment of buildings and people. It has always had something of a life of its own which is larger and more fateful than the sum of all the smaller destinies within it. Sometimes I think, reluctantly, that the city has acted as a catalyst for all that has happened and is still happening. It is a law of nature, a law of heredity, a parental body; and we, existing inside it, are the swarming chromosomes alive with genes. Even my standing here at the window (the panes opaque because of the excessive heating inside), sorting out arguments and motives for the report I have to draw up, could never take place without this deep awareness of the city organism outside. It may seem that I am isolated, far removed from that life outside and under my window – it is always easier to look at outer darkness through a glass pane – yet it is unavoidably all around me, in my very inside. The few who furtively, dartingly risk it outside, belong to another species – and yet they are fatefully part of me.

There are hardly any pedestrians under the branched trees. The men who, a little while ago, came back from playing *boules* in the parks (it is Sunday), squat and plump in their overcoats and bérets, are now standing against the counter of the bistro on the corner, talking, gesticulating, drinking red wine and hot grog. From time to time one of them ducks out into the drizzle and disappears in the direction of the metro station in the avenue de Neuilly. An old clochard is leaning against the railing of the narrow strip of garden directly under my window, shivering and pathetic in the cold. Nobody else, only motor cars. There are no prostitutes in this quarter. Fine. They upset me. I can't stand them. Nowadays, when I come across one of them, I address her before her soothing voice can disturb me. "How much will you pay me if I come along?" I ask her. It usually works. In the beginning, when I arrived here two years ago and was still living in the impossibly expensive hotel in the avenue Wagram where the Embassy had booked a room for me, I paid much more attention to them and even made special excursions to the boulevard Sebastopol, Montparnasse, and the environs of Pigalle.

It was Koos Joubert who saw to my 'initiation'. Koos should have become a farmer, not a diplomat. He is incongruous in any sophisticated surroundings. "I'll open your eyes for you," he offered. "It's high time you saw a bit of life." That was my first Sunday in Paris, and actually, I felt grateful towards him for the opportunity of getting away from my anonymous hotel room. We had dinner together, in the Avenue des Ternes if I remember correctly: he and his timid little wife and myself. Afterwards, "the men" would set out on their own expedition (accompanied by a wink and boisterous laughter); Marlene could take a taxi home – Koos couldn't be bothered.

A few streets away from the Place Pigalle we entered a small, dimly lit nightclub: it seemed as if Koos knew exactly where he wanted to go. It was evidently not a club with a very select clientèle. Inside it was smoky, and cold, and rather dirty; and the nude girls on the stage were inexperienced and clumsy, a few of them openly afraid.

"This is just a little refresher," Koos said, abundantly sure of himself. "Come along. Now we're going to the real thing. It's bloody expensive, but your eyes will pop out."

He negotiated with a porter at the red entrance of another club,

5

winking knowingly in my direction, and without moving a finger the stranger conjured up two women on the pavement next to us. They didn't look too bad on the surface and in the dim light. But once in the drab little 'hotel' room, with their furs removed and their scars and wrinkles revealed, it was as if everything – they, us, the bed, the room – suddenly became unbearably tired, unbearably old. I have only a very vague memory of their wrestling, of the dirty green bedspread covered with old stains, of the wriggling of etiolated flesh and ludicrous patches of moss – and, finally, of the cool, smooth rim of the washbasin under my twitching hands while I stood retching behind the screen with the large pink roses. I heard a crow squawk. The bare bulb on the ceiling became a cyclops eye mocking my burning retinas. Afterwards all possible shades of emotion broke loose inside me: humiliation, anger, resentment, shame, bitterness. But at that moment, standing there, convulsed, there was only one senseless thought turning over and over in my mind: *It is Sunday night. It is Sunday night again. Paris or Lydenburg, it is Sunday night!*

Of course Koos would never forget it. It was no use trying to oppose myself to it. After all, he was Second Secretary while I was still a mere cadet. I would just have to learn to accept and face it.

Since then I preferred to look for this sort of 'entertainment' on my own, but I always remained a spectator only, fascinated against my will by the rhythmic dance of shadows on drawn curtains visible from the pavement; until, one night, a redhead with merciless eyes planted herself in front of me and started shouting insults while a throng of curious, amused spectators formed a circle round us. I walked away madly, blindly. On the next corner a short, plump creature approached me from a dark niche and grasped my arm, whispering hoarsely. For a moment I stood frozen with disgust and uncertainty. She leaned back against the dirty wall and stared at me through drooping eyelids, with no expression whatsoever on her face. Above her red head, in high, uneven letters a fanatic had written: *Love thy neighbour as thys—.* The rest was a whitish, dirty smudge. Underneath was an obscene drawing and the word *merde.* And past her passionless back forbidding black letters proclaimed: *Défense d'afficher. Loi du 29 Juillet 1881.* Three yards away, on the edge of the pavement, was a round disk fixed to a pole, with the inscription: *Défense de stationner.* The entire city, like my distant youth, had suddenly become a jungle of prohibitions.

"How about it?" she insisted.

I clenched my teeth and murmured: "Come."

6

She took my hand as if I was a child going to a circus – or to the bathroom, for a hiding. In this false camaraderie we passed some staring strollers, entered one of the numerous shady 'hotels' of the quarter and went up to a bleak little room where someone had obviously tried to straighten the crumpled bedspread just before our arrival. I remained inert, watching her while she prepared herself. All the time I angrily tried to persuade myself that I really *wanted* to do it; that there was nothing else I *could* do. With all the hate and resentment, and possibly even fear, this situation had always inspired in me, it also held me with morbid, hypnotic fascination as if this was an opportunity for avenging something. And now it had become unavoidable.

With banal invitation, but her eyes hard and cynical, she came to me and first demanded her fee, carefully counted the notes, slipped them under her suspenders (which she never took off) and said: "Well, come on. I'm in a hurry."

I was impotent. She laughed at me, and at last left me, humming an idiotic little tune, and went to the door where she started a conversation with someone, blurting out all the humiliating details of our encounter while I was still dressing clumsily and numbly.

Later that night I was sitting on the edge of the bath in my apartment, aware of my skinny white body and the ridiculous appearance of a man without clothes; and I thought, confusedly: God, I'm revolting. I come from a past of Sunday nights and I am still caught in that spell. Nothing will ever release me. And I want to be. And I don't want to be. Or should I try to be 'philosophical' and decide: the Tree of Knowledge bears shrivelled fruit; and sometime or another one has to taste them? It brings no revelation of angels or devils, and there is no god who, lately, looks for offenders in the evening breeze. Perhaps this very fact is the greatest disillusionment of all. Adam and Eve could at least expect punishment; and in this way they could – albeit masochistically – achieve something. But if there is no punishment because there has never been any sin to start with, one can only feel duped.

On a somewhat different level there was the New Year's Eve party in Douglas Masters' apartment in the boulevard Malesherbes: the refined decadence of the 'cultured'. The only memory I really have of that night is Jill. I never heard her surname. I think she was a mannequin, in London or somewhere, and probably she was brought there by one of the British diplomats – Masters has many friends from their set. She had make-up plastered all over her; and she was sophisticated, suave, and on heat, wearing the sort of black velvet dress which, in front, reaches chastely up to her throat but, at the back, forms a parabole down to her hips. With a much too long cigarette holder in the one hand and an olive between the thumb and forefinger of the other, she took part in exaggeratedly refined little conversations, interspersed – more and more frequently as the night wore on – by wild rock-n-roll or cha-cha-cha movements which caused her to pull up her close-fitting dress so high that the lace of her only piece of underclothing showed. At one stage I was refilling her glass while she hung round my neck, blabbing a series of moist coital suggestions in my left ear. I danced with her. Later she just disappeared. I went to look for her. When I opened one door I found myself in the Masters' bedroom where a huge French double bed stood in the corner, next to a high ornamental vase. The vase had a terrifying appearance, representing a man with an open skull from which monstrous birds were pecking the brains; on one side was a screaming cross-eyed devil half hidden by fig leaves. On the bed I noticed bits and pieces of clothing, blankets, movements, a stranger, and Jill. I closed the door and left. A few hours later somebody discovered that the vase had been broken inexplicably.

And then, Nicolette. It is neither by chance nor through any bitterness on my part that this discussion of whores and hetaerae has to wind up with her. For what else could she be, essentially? Oh I know: she created an altogether different impression on the surface. But what was she *really*? Scheming and deliberate in everything she did; entirely unscrupulous; self-sufficient, much too sure of herself, and loose; with a certain semblance of passion which could deliberately be turned on or shut off as the occasion demanded. Eating, and talking, and copulating Nicolette apparently regarded as synonymous actions, all of them equally unavoidable, equally ludicrous, equally senseless. (But even that was a mere pretence, for under the surface there was a complete lack of passion, almost an antipathy to passion, a sort of cynicism which was meant to wound anybody who dared to probe her secret.) If there did exist any causal relation between these actions, it led from talking to sex, and from sex to eating (or buying clothes, or any other component of 'life'). That was her only hierarchy.

In the beginning, of course, I was not aware of this. In the beginning she was only a fairly attractive slender girl who came into my office in the Embassy basement in connection with a lost passport. She wore dark blue sunglasses, a flimsy scarf round her fair hair, a blouse with one button missing, a skirt and open sandals. There was an almost professorial air about her, especially when she removed the sunglasses with something myopic about the way in which she blinked against the first glaring light. Apart from that: something virginal? Also, perhaps – although the mere thought is ridiculous – something prudish? And, unquestionably, something very *banal,* although I realise exactly how inadequate and even wrong this may sound in words.

It is difficult to describe this impression, even more so because I am steeped in constipated officialese. Words are too formal, and certainly too smug, too polished for recording primary impressions. Perhaps I could illustrate this with a seemingly silly example: while I was at university the men students one night caught a bucketful of frogs and took them to a women's hostel where a frog was shoved under each white cup. These wild, bewildered, amphibious frogs so completely out of their element under the demure, prim porcelain cups – that is the sort of thing I would like to formulate. And then, of course, the shrieks the next morning when the cups were turned round – because of these *things,* and their slipperiness, their jumpiness – that is what I would like to achieve: but in the end one is left with only the cup in one's hands, all appetite for breakfast gone.

As far as Nicolette is concerned, therefore, not only that first morning but afterwards also, I shall have to rely on approximations, on possibilities, on 'impressions' – the impression, for instance, one gets with some women: of a bare body under the clothes.

She had no perfect figure. There was something boyish about her, a certain angularity of elbows and knees, and her breasts were small. And then there was this nonchalance, as if the loss of a passport really wasn't worth so much trouble at all. To my consternation it appeared that she had, in fact, lost it several months earlier and that she would never even have taken the trouble of reporting it had she not needed it to have her *Carte de séjour* renewed by the police.

"Have you been here for a long time then?" I asked.

The corner of her mouth barely moved. It was only after some time that she apparently realised that I had asked a question. She removed the end of her sunglasses from her mouth, smiled, and said: "I beg your pardon?"

"I asked whether you have been living in Paris for a long time."

"Mais oui." The French came so spontaneously that I doubt

9

whether she herself had even become aware of the change of language.

"How long?"

"Must you know all this to give me a new passport?"

"I merely asked." I felt irritable. The rest of the interview was very formal. She had to make a declaration to the *mairie* in her quarter and bring back a receipt before I could do anything about the matter. She left, with a vague promise to come back later.

I suppose, thinking back to it now, that it was this very hint of friction between us at our first meeting which brought her memory back to me so often during the week that followed, as if that trivial incident implied a challenge of some sort. I must add that I would have been extremely susceptible to it at that stage. It was July, eight months after my arrival in Paris, and the oppressive, sticky heat made one much more excitable than normally. At four o'clock in the morning the streets were white with light; it was nine o'clock in the evening before the sunset finally quivered in the slimy water of the Seine. There was a restlessness in the blood which urgently needed an outlet. My single life was becoming too much for me. It was really a most disturbing experience. And then, suddenly, Nicolette was there. In the course of the week following her first visit she gradually assumed a very definite shape in my mind, and became the expression of my deep need.

But when at last she reappeared – just as nonchalantly as before, and almost dishevelled – it was almost a shock. For all of a sudden she was so vastly different from the provocative woman of my week's feverish thoughts. In fact, she was almost too ordinary in appearance, too composed. And, I think, too direct, too blatant, without the element of suggestion and mystery of other girls: she made the impression, not of a woman, but of *femina*, a positive and disturbing affirmation of body and limbs – and it seemed as if she was completely unaware of it all.

She sat down before I could invite her to do so, opened her straw bag and started fiddling around in it while I waited for the slip of paper with outstretched hand. But when her hand finally emerged, it held only an empty blue cigarette box.

"Hm," she said. "Empty." But I was quite sure that she had known that long before she said it. "Have you got one for me?"

I picked up my own box from the desk and held it out to her. She took one, glanced at the South African trade mark, and said: "Thanks." Then she leisurely blew out the smoke. One of her open sandals hung loosely from a big toe. She sat watching it intently as if it was some acrobatic performance. There was no brassière under her blouse.

"Did you bring the receipt from the *mairie*?" I asked formally, after quite some time.

"The receipt. Of course." She fumbled in the straw bag again, brought out a rather crumpled bit of paper which she carefully straightened out on her knee before giving it to me. "Here you are."

While I was filling out the required form, I became conscious of her eyes watching me. I quickly looked up with the express purpose of embarrassing her, but her eyes (strange eyes, intensely green) stared at me without the slightest wavering.

"What do you do for a living?" I asked to conceal my own embarrassment.

"Model." And, almost as an afterthought: "At Dior's."

That was quite unexpected.

"You're lucky!"

"I suppose so." She carefully stamped out her cigarette in the ashtray. "I used to attend classes at the Beaux Arts."

"And when are you going back to South Africa?"

Once again that peculiar little curling of her lip. "Let's cut out the questions. I want to go."

I felt like a child who had just been scolded. "Shall I get in touch with you when the passport is ready?" I asked quickly. "I could phone you at Dior's."

"It's not necessary. I'll call for it."

She went to the door. Something like panic surged up in me. Suppose she left – and never came back? There was such an ephemeral quality about her. And I could no longer bear the summer alone.

"By the way – ," I began.

She had just put on her sunglasses again and now moved them to her forehead to look at me, waiting.

"I wonder whether you would like to have dinner with me sometime." How atrociously formal!

Without any hesitation she said, "Yes, thank you."

"Tonight?"

She nodded.

"Could I come to fetch you? Where do you live?"

"I've got an apartment in Neuilly."

"So have I. Then –"

"But I have to come to the city first," she added quickly. "I have a singing lesson. You could meet me in the Champs-Élysées, in the *Café Étoile*. I'll wait at a table on the terrace."

11

"Eightish?"

"Fine." And then she was out, with a swing of her green skirt, passing through the typists' office to the reading room. There she probably sat down to page through some magazines, because it was fully half an hour before I saw her legs pass my window as she walked across the cobbled courtyard. (My office being in the basement all I usually see of visitors is from the waist downwards.) She had slim hips, I noticed – as if it was a momentous discovery – and there was a hint of calf muscles on her slender brown legs.

In the shadow of the opposite wall where the courtyard narrows into the short driveway leading past the official residence to the front door in the Avenue Hocke, the concierge stood looking at her for a long time after she had disappeared from my range of vision. Only after the front door had banged, did Lebon touch his tie, wink to himself and go to unlock the garage door so that the chauffeur, Farnham, could pull out the official Austin. I picked up my telephone and asked the switchboard girl to reserve a table in an exclusive little restaurant in the rue Boissy d'Anglas. Then I looked back to the particulars on the form in front of me. VAN/SURNAME: *Alford*. VOORNAME/CHRISTIAN NAMES: *Nicolette*. OUDERDOM/AGE: *23*. Meaningless statistics. Even the photos she had brought with her for the new passport looked impersonal and stern. What did she really mean to me? Nothing but this: it was summer; she was young; she had immediately said "Yes" to what I had asked – and to what had been left unpronounced behind the formal words. (The frog in the porcelain cup?)

For a moment I felt aversion. After all, I was so unprepared, so damned inexperienced! But not entirely. For I had read a lot after my first failures here in Paris. Henry Miller. Frank Harris. De Sade. Apollinaire. And all the anonymous little books in green or beige covers. I had everything neatly catalogued on paper, and in my mind. And at eight o'clock all the disparate details would, for the first time, be assembled in a coherent pattern.

But by a quarter past eight there was still no sign of her at the *Étoile*. I could feel the premonitions of a dangerous mood. I was determined not to be on the losing end again. The aperitif on my little round table was left untouched. Uninvited, the spectacle of life was streaming past me on sidewalk and street. The city on promenade. Or rather, the whole round world, for there was more German, English, American and Scandinavian to be heard than French; and in the midst of all this, stranger and more re-

12

jected than ever before, was I sitting at the little red island of my rickety table. I often sat on that terrace, and I used to enjoy it, but now it had become unbearable, as if I suddenly found myself naked in front of all those people with all my disillusioned intentions exposed like an exhibit in a distasteful criminal case. I never saw her coming, although I kept looking for her. The first I knew of her presence, was when she said next to me: "Oh, here you are."

"Where on earth have you been so long?" I felt annoyed and relieved at the same time.

"Am I late?"

"Thirty-five minutes."

"Oh."

And that was all she said about the whole affair. Not that she seemed rude; actually I think it just never appeared to her that any apology or explanation might be required.

She wanted to drink something (a martini) but I refused, not without some deliberate stubbornness. We had to get to the restaurant first. If we waited any longer, we might lose our table.

A little way lower down, near the metro station, we found a taxi and swerved into the stream of traffic down towards the Place de la Concorde, and turned left into the little street where the restaurant awaited us with open glass doors. I had no idea of what might happen in the course of the next few hours, and I concealed my uncertainty under a slightly resentful reserve. But while we were still in the taxi she already started talking as if we had known each other for years. Talked about her singing lessons; commented endlessly on all the latest creations of fashion she had tried on that day and on the prospects for the autumn parade – trivialities which would normally irritate me but to which I unexpectedly found myself listening, slightly amused, thankful, and almost with joy, because it made everything so much easier. It was only when the haughty headwaiter handed us the large, handwritten menus that she became quiet for a few moments, looking up at him, smiling pertly, and said, quite unnecessarily: "Merci." His professional dignity became slightly mollified. That was only the beginning of what, in the course of that long evening, would develop into a shameless flirtation: without anything deliberate, but none the less embarassing to me.

"What a handsome man," she said with conviction after I had given our order, looking back at him over her shoulder.

"Who?"

"The waiter."

"He's too old for you," I said disparagingly.

"I adore older men. The young ones are so – " She looked at me, for a few moments we considered each other's expression, then she shrugged her shoulders and laughed. "Well, I still like him. And he's got beautiful hands. Let me see yours? I think a man's hands are tremendously important. Even more important than his eyes. I like this sort of menu with all its curls and swirls. Do you think each one is written separately? It's quite impossible to read them, but they're gorgeous. And as expensive as hell, but I suppose you Embassy people get a lot of money. If I earned as much as that, I would get up at half past four in the morning – in summer, of course – to see the sun rise (at what time *does* it rise?) and then go back to bed and sleep till noon and have a bath until two. And I'd buy all the clothes I saw, everything which I now have to show to other people. There was one heavenly dress today: all golden, made of straw, raffia, it looked as if it had been woven by hand, just one long sheath, with a wide brown belt and an antique clasp, and brown amber earrings and a large chunk of amber on a thin gold chain, but I think turquoise would also go well with it. How do you like the earrings I'm wearing tonight? They come from the Monoprix but I think they look quite expensive if one doesn't know. Here comes the *melon glacé.* Just watch his hands when he puts it on the table. I hope it's really *glacé.* But I suppose it will be, in a place like this. You must come here very often, I noticed that the man at the door recognised you. And you should have seen the shoes that went with it. You'd never think any foot could get in there. Fortunately mine are quite narrow – " She glanced down, round the corner of the table, and for one moment I was afraid that she might take off her shoe to show me her foot. – "Now have you seen his hands? I wonder whether he's really French? Merci, Monsieur. It's a pity your knuckles are too big. You should tan a bit, you know, you're much too pale. I usually go down to the bottom path along the Seine to tan during the lunch hour. There are hordes of people doing it, more or less everybody from *Samaritaine,* because they're right up against the river, of course. God, but it makes one lazy! It is *glacé,* I see, and fresh too. Of course you could do it under Notre-Dame too, on the Île, but there one is stampeded by tourists and there are so many clochards. Stinking to high heaven. But usually I like them. I think I'll go to live under a bridge myself one day when I'm old and worn out. A bridge near Notre-Dame, then I can always hear the booming of the bells, how many tons does the big one weigh? It's like the voice of God the Father. And those crazy little flags on the towers. One only needs an old drum

14

for coals, then one could live quite comfortably. One ought to find something like that at Les Halles, if one gets up early enough. Have you ever had onion soup among the vegetable boxes? But it must be in winter. Else you could buy chestnuts and throw them from one hand to the other until they're cool enough to be eaten. But chestnuts always make me feel sad. Oh well, I suppose you're a clochard you haven't got much of a choice. Here he comes with the snails. *Formidable, monsieur!* I wonder where he lives. I'd love it to live on the Île Saint-Louis, but they say it's only for the rich. What on earth would rich people be doing on an island? And near the bells too? Not that one can really hear them so well. It's usually only the hoarse bleating of the cargo boats. Most of them come from Normandy. The men always look so angry and stern. I was in Brittany once. During Holy Week, in Saint-Malo. All I can still remember is the one night on the old city wall when the waves broke right over it and drenched all my clothes with spray. I was soaked to the skin and my teeth chattered so much I couldn't get a word out when I got back to the room at last, long after midnight. And Jean-Paul complained that my whole body tasted of salt. Yes, please, fill my glass. What is it?"

"Pouilly-Fuissé. Who is Jean-Paul?"

"An artist, I think. Used to be. I didn't know him very well. Only a week or so."

There were many more questions I wanted to ask, but she was already talking again. She stopped only once to gulp down some wine and she was in such a hurry that she choked. At that moment the waiter reappeared. Nicolette emptied her glass, leant back in her chair, watching him intently all the time he was serving the *canard à l'orange,* and then started complimenting him again. This time he lingered round her chair a little longer than was necessary. Her cheeks were flushed and because of the stuffiness inside there were a few fine strands of hair clinging to her cheeks. She was talking less now, and eating more, almost as if she was afraid that the plate might be taken away before she had finished. She made no protest when I refilled her glass. All the time I sat looking at her, with the impression of staring through a one-way window so that she remained completely unaware of my presence. As if she was an object, not herself.

"I suppose I'm talking too much," she mumbled unexpectedly, her mouth still stuffed with food.

"Of course not. I enjoy listening to you. Anything you say." I was somewhat surprised at my own words.

"Who would have thought, ten years ago, that I'd be here tonight?" she said, whimsically, holding the wine glass in her two cupped hands and looking at her own reflection or at the shivering circles of light on the surface.

"What do you mean?"

"Have you never heard of Cinderella?" There was a touch of nervousness in her voice. Her cheeks were more flushed than before. And then she blurted out a long confession, leaning forward and putting her hand on my wrist. It was all so personal that I felt ill at ease. She only interrupted herself to order a *flan*, and afterwards two *petits suisses* and coffee. She was apparently driven by some strange force to unburden herself of everything: a miserable youth of rejection and rebellion, even maltreatment: an orphan youth, bitter and utterly joyless. This, then, was the complement of the lightheartedness she had formerly revealed. And I thought despairingly: something had gone wrong; somewhere we had taken the wrong turning; we had to get away from there.

I beckoned the waiter and paid the bill. Her head was hanging – she was feeling dejected after the long confession – but I noticed that her eyes were watching the notes I counted into the plate. And once again there was that little curling corner of her mouth: an expression which caused me to wonder rather uneasily whether she was really sitting there, fretting, a desolate nymph looking at her reflection in a pool under brooding thunderclouds – or whether she was, in fact, mocking me, playing with me (but what sort of game?).

The waiter brought my change and I counted off his tip. At the last moment she interrupted, saying: "Wait!", took a few extra pieces from my hand and put them on the plate; then she laughed up at him with the cheapest sort of coquetry. He smiled significantly and pulled out her chair. She put her hand out towards him. He hesitated a moment, then accepted it courteously. A woman in a tight evening dress behind us leant over to whisper something in her companion's ear. I quickly came round the table, took Nicolette's arm in a much stronger grip than was necessary and led her to the vestiaire for her shawl. She forced me to give the attendant a preposterous tip before we could, at last, pass through the double glass doors with the embossed motif.

"What's the matter with you?" I asked crossly.

"Why?" She was fanning her throat with a folded tissue. "Isn't it terribly hot?" There were tiny points of perspiration on her forehead.

It must have been the wine – among other things. But the whole situation had unexpectedly reached a dangerous, thin borderline where everything could easily go wrong and thwart all my careful calculations.

"Come," I said, as indulgently as possible. "We should find a taxi at the Madeleine. We could do with some exercise."

She walked next to me, humming something, but still somewhat tense.

"You shouldn't have told me everything," I tried to reach her secret self. "Now it makes you feel guilty to think that I know all about it."

"You mean *you* feel guilty." She didn't even turn her head.

I knew exactly how clumsy and melodramatic it would sound, but I simply had to say it: "I'm glad you told me, Nicolette. Perhaps it has opened a door between us."

She began to laugh, not quietly, but as if she was convulsed by a joke which she knew was rather off-colour.

I had only one hope left: that we would get home as soon as possible. There I might have more control over the circumstances and recreate the 'atmosphere' that had seemed possible earlier in the evening.

When we reached the taxi rank she asked over her shoulder: "Where are we going?"

"I thought – " I started tactfully.

"Let's go to Montmartre. I want to have a look at the city."

"But it's late."

"Then I'm going alone."

The taxi driver was placidly watching us in his mirror. I could see his unshaven face and sardonic eyes. "All right," I said.

The narrow streets of Montmartre were crammed with people. By the time we reached the last steep incline of the rue Lepic, we had to crawl along at a snail's pace. On the Place du Tertre we got out and were carried along to the terrace of the Sacré-Coeur by the steady stream of people. Strollers, tourists, holiday makers; accompanied by a babel of hawkers and vendors swarming like flies around the crowd. Gnarled old women with bunches of flowers or dolls or the *France-Soir*; lanky boys with nuts and sweets and rattles and other noisy toys; ice cream vendors; and the vulture-like 'artists' who insist every five yards on drawing your portrait. And, of course, Nicolette's vanity could not resist this temptation. For ten minutes I had to wait patiently on the edge of the street while she was posing tranquilly, with flushed cheeks and intense eyes, in the middle of a curious, admiring circle of spectators. Without any embarrassment she stood there until he had finished, then held the drawing at arm's length and handed it to me over the craning necks between us, so that all eyes turned round to stare at me. I paid five francs for the drawing. It was not a bad resemblance after all, although it certainly wasn't Nicolette – but how could anybody capture her on paper? – and then I got her away from there as quickly as possible.

She wanted to have a cold drink in the square. By this time her negative mood had passed and she seemed to be revived by the breath of air on the hilltop. She still wasn't as gay as before. It was something stronger, more difficult to determine: an obscure ecstasy, revealing itself in gusts and spurts.

The whole square was a fun fair of parasols, green tables and chairs, scurrying waiters, boisterous teenagers and milling, jostling strollers. From various cafés came deafening, dissonant music. And while we were drinking our cold drinks a rubbery young scoundrel in tight-fitting pants and an open shirt moved past the tables with a guitar, trying to sing, leering through his long forelock at anything that appeared vaguely feminine. Nicolette's enthusiasm was, of course, aroused immediately. And within five minutes he was at our table, *on* our table, strutting and prancing, her laughing eyes following every ripple of his young male body. And when he tentatively strummed the notes of one particular 'hit' tune, she immediately started humming to his accompaniment. I still don't know how it happened; inexplicably she was no longer with me, she was dancing with him, joined by a few other couples. At first they milled round the tables, then moved farther away to the cobbled street obstructing the traffic. She had taken off her shoes. Her piled up hair slowly tumbled down and fell loosely round her shoulders. It was a disconcerting dance, an overt expression of sensuality, an affirmation of youthful sex, with invitations and reactions, parodies and variations. I could not move a finger, I was soaked with perspiration. I could feel my shirt clinging to my back. My unsmoked cigarette burnt my fingers. I absentmindedly let it drop and clasped the end of the green table until I felt my fingers go numb. I could not – would not – comprehend. I know now that all the time (which actually could not have been more than fifteen minutes) I sat there transfixed in an unbearable state of hate and fear.

At last I did react; and thank God I could do it with outward calm. I got up, moved past the first dancers, took her arm, and said: "Come." She obeyed without objection. I realised that the wine and the luxury, the long confession and the heat and the primitive music had stirred up her passion. And this acute awareness of her almost unbearable excitement had inevitably kindled a reaction in myself. We had to get back to my apartment.

Holding her hand I went urgently in search of a taxi, but there was not one to be found. Halfway to the Sacré-Coeur terrace she said: "Let's go down to the metro. It's much more companionable."

I have an intense dislike for the dirty metro, but I didn't want to oppose her. So we went down the steep steps to the smoky bustle of boulevards, nightclubs, sidewalk stalls and cafés below. We were halfway before she realised that she was still carrying her shoes in her hand. She was complaining of aching feet by the time we reached Pigalle and entered the rancid, sticky atmosphere of the metro.

"Are you quite sure we shouldn't take a taxi? We'll easily find one here."

She merely shook her tousled head and stood waiting for me on the other side of the ticket office while I bought a carnet. I handed two to the shapeless blue woman at the little green gate and gave the other eight to Nicolette: "You may have them. I never use the damn things."

She smiled her thanks as if the spontaneity of this little gesture meant more to her than the premeditated luxury of the expensive meal.

We had to wait a long time before the train burst out of its tunnel and came to a standstill at the dirty platform. For the first few stations there were no seats and we had to lean against the sticky chromium poles. There was a fat woman with nodding head and gaping mouth bobbing up and down on one of the narrow brown benches; workmen in crumpled overalls, with day-old beards and greasy, long-read newspapers, sat staring at Nicolette with lecherous eyes. By the time we reached Villiers where we could at last sit down, the depressing effect of this subterranean atmosphere had already begun.

At Étoile we had to change to the Neuilly line. At the first exit she stopped, surprised but resigned, and asked tonelessly: "But where are we going?"

"You're tired," I said evasively, conscious of my own drowsiness. "So I thought you might like a last cup of coffee in my apartment – "

She looked at me but I could not interpret the dull expression in her eyes. At last she nodded. She was paler than before.

And when we went further a young couple took seats opposite us, weighed down by the sort of fatigue which – I presume –

c

19

succeeds the hour of passion, when there is nothing else to do but continue the languid mime of the game of love. Only the gestures were left, the indolent movement of old brown weeds in a quiet sea. There was something unreal in their behaviour: a grotesque commentary on human relationships, and on us. It oppressed me; and I felt resentful *because* of it.

When we finally reached Les Sablons the heat and fatigue had almost physical weight; at the exit, above, one became unpleasantly aware of cold perspiration on one's face.

We walked in silence to the rue Jacques-Dulud and crossed the street to my building.

She was a few yards ahead of me and stood waiting for me at the front door, swinging her handbag behind her back. I pressed the button to open the door's electrical latch, and we went in. Inside it was silent, with the city suddenly removed from us like an old snakeskin. The staircase quietly wound its way upward, the narrow strip of carpet like an endless red tapeworm with shiny stripes marking the segments.

"It looks quite smart," she commented.

She went up first. I became conscious, once again, of the moving muscles in her calves. It was a tiresome climb, four storeys high. I unlocked my door, switched on the light inside and allowed her to pass.

When I closed the door behind me she said, her back still turned to me: "Well, now you've got what you wanted."

"What do you mean?" I asked, uneasily.

"Surely this is what you had in mind all evening?"

"Is there anything wrong with it?"

"No. But why did you really want me to come?"

"To have some coffee. I've said so – "

"It'll be very nice." With her narrow back still towards me, she walked into the room to inspect the decorations on the opposite wall: a straw mat, a few odds and ends of African beadwork, a small Pierneef etching.

"Why must you people carry South Africa with you wherever you go?" she asked. "Are you afraid – it might get lost somewhere?"

I decided, perhaps wrongly, to ignore the remark, and went to my minute kitchen to put on the percolator. I purposely remained there much longer than was necessary, to allow her some time to acclimatise. She was only feeling a bit ill at ease, I convinced myself. Everything had been so perfect on the square. I just had to find the correct approach –

20

When I finally returned to the living-room she lay comfortably stretched out on the mohair bedspread covering the divan, with her shoes kicked off. It was almost a shock seeing her. I hesitated, controlled my voice, and went over to the radiogram: "Shall I put on a record?"

She turned her head to look at me. After a moment she replied evenly: "If you want to."

"Anything in particular?"

"Anything."

I deliberately selected something light and sentimental. She didn't move. After a while I went back to the kitchen. I was busy pouring the coffee when the radiogram was abruptly switched off.

"Don't you like it?" I called.

She didn't even bother to answer.

When I took in the coffee, she was half-sitting, half-lying on the bed, propped up against a cushion.

"It's all balls," she said, helping herself to four teaspoons of sugar. "All this sighing about love. Slobbering in the moonlight. Why are men so damned dishonest?"

"Dishonest?"

"Why do you choose sweet little songs, why do you invite one for dinner, why do you make coffee, why do you keep on playing with one? Couldn't you say straight out what you want? Why don't you go and find yourself a tart? What makes you think *I* am one?"

She leant her head against the wall and burst out laughing, with an edge of hysteria in her attitude, spilling her coffee on my beautiful new bedspread.

I angrily put down the tray. "Nicolette, I swear – !"

She stopped laughing, but her eyes were still smouldering. "And now he's angry. He thinks someone has promised him a sweetie and taken it away again!"

I violently caught her arm.

"Leave me alone!" She swung her legs from the bed and stood up. The cup was overturned. "Is *this* the sweetie you wanted –?" With one angry jerk she had opened the zip behind her back and stripped the upper half of her dress from her shoulders. Wordless, trembling, she stood before me. Without her dress she seemed smaller, younger, thinner. There was even a hint of ribs. And cupped in the shells of her brassière were her small breasts, soft and protected and private. I desired her, and hated her, and pitied her, all at the same time. But when I made the slightest

21

movement towards her, she quickly turned away, with her back to me, and zipped up her dress, put on her shoes, pulled her fingers through her hair, took her handbag and left. The door was closed quite calmly behind her. I couldn't decide whether I should follow her or let her go. But the decision was soon taken from me, when less than five minutes later she knocked again.

Although I knew it couldn't be anybody else, it was still a surprise to find her there. She was pale, but quite composed.

"I haven't got any money for the taxi," she said.

I wanted to explain, even to plead with her; but all I could do was nod and take out a note. Then I hesitated and offered to go with her. At first she refused – emphatically – but after a while she acquiesced. In the narrow sidelane next to the boulevard I opened a taxi door and helped her to get in.

"Are you sure you'll be all right?"

"Of course. Now you must go."

"I want to see you off."

"No. You must go straight away."

I realised it would be wiser to obey; so I said good-bye and walked away. When I reached the corner I heard a door slam and turned round. She was on her way to the metro, fifty yards further. Immediately I started following her, but I soon came to a standstill. It was too late already. Without glancing back (although she surely must have expected me to follow her) she went down the metro steps and disappeared. It was a complete mystery. There is no metro line to any other part of Neuilly, where she had said she lived: where could she be going? And why did she come back for money if she already had eight metro tickets in her handbag?

Sleep did not come easily that night. I couldn't explain my own feelings. I was humiliated and angry; my most urgent need had been thwarted. And yet this very need had lost its overwhelming importance.

The next morning I telephoned Dior's.

"Alford? Nicolette Alford?" the person repeated. "But we've never had anybody with that name here."

3

This will never do. I knew I would get lost in Nicolette again as soon as I allowed memories of her to come back. It was in July of last year that it all started; today is the fourth of December. In the course of these eighteen months we have come to know each other – that, I suppose, is what it would be termed in superficial conversations. True knowledge, however, remained a fiction. (As did biblical 'knowledge'. Except once, that is, but that was such a disillusioning, wretched business that it could only be recognized by the fact that two bodies were involved.) It would be possible to describe every one of our meetings in just as much détail – sometimes in more – as that first evening; and every time it would end with the same question mark, the same experience of incompleteness. Not that there was anything 'mysterious' about her as I would have liked to believe in the beginning, but because she deliberately told so many lies.

The first time I saw her again after her inexplicable disappearance – it was about ten days later, when she came to collect the passport – I referred specifically to it.

"Where have you been all this time?"

"Busy."

"Still at Dior's?"

"Yes."

"I tried to get in touch with you there," I said carefully, emphatically, leaning forward to study her reaction. "But they have never heard your name."

"So what?" She didn't bat an eyelid. "Why do you have to know everything about me?"

"And all the other things you told me?"

"Don't you believe me?"

It was impossible to carry on a conversation like this. I gradually came to suspect that the lengthy confession about her unhappy orphan childhood had also been a figment of her fertile imagination. Sometimes she told me other stories in its place, always equally seriously and confidentially. I still don't know what the truth is. But I doubt whether she is doing anything so melodramatic as trying to escape from her past. I suppose the simple explanation is that it just doesn't make any difference to her which of her stories is true, consequently she can't understand that it might matter to anybody else. (Or am I wrong? Why do I really care about her truth? What difference could it possibly make?)

Sometimes we went out; often we spent our evenings in my apartment. Once or twice she even tried to mend my clothes – sewing on shirt buttons with red cotton – but it didn't quite succeed. A few times she tried to cook for us. She insisted on preparing the most expensive dishes. Once the chicken was almost

23

edible; more often than not it had to be deposited, solemnly and without comment, in one of the grey rubbish bins at the bottom of the staircase.

Towards October last year I spent two weeks' holiday in the Loire Valley. She offered to look after the apartment during my absence. When I returned a day earlier than expected, I hardly recognised the place. There was no empty chair: they were all stacked with make-up, stockings, open suitcases, women's journals, underclothes or unwashed cups and glasses. The carpet was rolled up against the wall, the bed was a confusion of sheets and blankets and pillows. It was drizzling outside and the heater was turned on full blast. (The electricity bill at the end of that month amounted to seven hundred and twenty francs.) It was quite obvious that she had held a series of extravagant parties during my absence; and this suspicion was confirmed by an ill-tempered neighbour and the concierge. Nicolette, of course, denied it point-blank. But perhaps she had a more subtle way of admitting her guilt: the extraordinary zeal with which she helped me tidy up the apartment.

My other memories of these eighteen months are rather confused. There were always quarrels. She could drive me mad the way she would excite me, and invite me, and challenge me – only to evade me, laughingly, in the end. But while I was furiously shouting all sorts of insults at her, she would coolly shrug her shoulders and say: "Oh balls." Or: "Did you know there was a button missing from your coat?"

Once she suddenly got it into her head that she had to refine her education. She wanted to get acquainted with the great philosophers. With some kind of perverse amusement I brought her the most bulky and awe-inspiring volume I could find in the whole American Library: a scholarly review of philosophy from Socrates to Albert Camus. For three weeks I hardly ever saw her. She studiously worked through every page of that impossible book – and then mislaid it, so that I had to buy the library a new copy. She never referred to it with a single word, not even when I pointedly asked her about it.

Sometimes she would just disappear, evaporate. It was different from the first time, when I had merely lost track of her because she had lied about where she lived and worked, since by then I often visited her in her tiny apartment – first near the Porte d'Auteuil, afterwards a few streets away from the Place des Vosges, and eventually in the rue de Condé. On these occasions even her concierge knew nothing of her whereabouts. Afterwards it would appear that she had either been "busy" in another part of Paris, or roamed somewhere in the country, usually all by herself. Once, I know, she went on a pilgrimage to Chartres, with thousands of students, because she often referred to it. (Unless that, too, was a hallucination.) Cathedrals apparently held a peculiar fascination for her: that, at least, was what she pretended.

Why didn't I banish her from my life earlier? That is one of those delicate questions touching on so many hidden motives. The main reason why I held on to her, I think, was that I believed (or hoped) that sometime or other I would still manage to have my way with her, to succeed with her where, with others, I had so often failed. And at last it did happen, as I have already intimated. It was an evening towards the end of September this year, when the first ominous signs of autumn had already become visible. She came to my apartment to have a bath. (There was nothing unusual about that, except that she used to come during office hours, when I was away; about once a week. Her own little apartment in the rue de Condé has no bathroom.) She arrived early, with her bathing things in a string bag which she casually threw down on the divan. We started talking: the sort of cul-de-sac conversation we so often had. And, as usual, it soon touched on our 'affair'. I accused her of being whimsical and petulant. Why should she always keep me on a string, playing an inscrutable little game, and always keep out of reach? After all, I knew exactly who and what she was – that she never tried to hide her numerous flirtations with other men. "Or do they perhaps pay you enough?" It was the first time I had dared to ask such a direct question.

She flared up.

"I suppose I can do what I like," she said. "Nobody has ever paid me to do anything I did not *want* to do."

In a rush of anger I pulled a few notes from my pocket (there was at least one of a hundred francs among them) and threw them on her lap.

"Well, take this! Is that what you want?"

She said nothing. She picked up the notes, straightened them, arranged them in a neat little pile and put them on the oblong tea table with an ashtray on top. Then she got up and went to the bathroom. I heard her opening the taps and waited for her to come back, because she had left the door open. But before I realised what was happening, she was already in the bath.

Then followed one of those silly, childish scenes which seem highly enjoyable while they last, but later leave one with a nasty aftertaste. I stood on the living room side of the open door, threatening, playfully and with a touch of bravado, to come in.

"Well, why don't you?"

"You won't be so sure of yourself if I do."

"You're scared."

Should I? Dare I? Suppose she meant it? Suppose she *didn't* mean it – ? On the other side of the door the water was gaily splashing over the sides of the bath. Greedily, self-consciously, I pressed my burning face against the slit on the side of the hinges trying desperately to see something inside.

I was still standing there, leaning forward, when she non-chalantly skipped out of the bath, darted past me, naked and glistening, and took up the soap and towel from her string bag on the divan. Her wet hair formed dark strings down her shoulders. Before I could properly react, she was back in the bathroom; this time she locked the door between us. Foolishly I turned away and went to light a cigarette. Before I had finished smoking it she opened the door and came back: fully clothed, but her hair still wet. She went to sit on the bed, and started rubbing her hair with the damp towel. I stood looking at her, then stubbed out my cigarette very slowly and emphatically and went over to her. For a short while she went on drying her hair with quick, nervous movements, then gave it up and, with the wet towel still in her hands, looked up at me: anxiously? mockingly? derisively? She probably realised that this time it would be useless to resist.

It was over very quickly. She lay without moving, all the time, her eyes closed, her eyelids unmoving, passive, altogether passionless. I should have expected it. Apparently such women are often frigid.

But at least she had to do *something* by way of reaction! Silence would drive me mad.

"Well?" I said when I got up. "You can't say you didn't ask for it." I felt aggressive.

"No," she answered quietly, pulling down her dress over her knees. I noticed, accidentally, that she was wearing a piece of scarlet underclothing, something cheap and vulgar, a banal joke emphasising the senselessness of what had just happened.

"Why don't you say anything?" I insisted.

"What should I say? Compliment you on your performance?" She laughed quietly and started rubbing her hair as if nothing had happened. "Big boy!" Her breathing was still slightly irregular.

I clasped my hand, then turned round to fasten my buttons

26

with my back to her, fully aware of how ludicrous it must all seem. And very soon she did burst out laughing, exactly as I had foreseen and feared.

"You yourself haven't got very much to boast about!" I snarled.

"No." She got up from the crumpled bedspread and went to the bathroom. "You could make us some coffee. We are cold, both of us."

The bathroom door was locked. The taps were opened as before. And there were thin skins on the coffee cups by the time she finally came back, quite composed, clean, her hair tidily brushed. We were silent while we drank. Afterwards she got up, took her string bag, glanced at me, lifted the ashtray from the table and picked up the notes. She rolled them into a tiny square and slipped them under her bra.

"Nicolette – "

"Good-night, Stephen."

I saw her going down the spiral staircase, each storey narrower than the previous, until, small and distant, she went past the rubbish bins and disappeared into the street.

4

Some fortunate cadets are sent overseas very soon. But I was in Pretoria for two and a half years before I was finally transferred to Paris. Not that I regret it. It gave me the opportunity of being very thoroughly trained in more than one section of the Service, of passing all the necessary examinations, and – which is important – of getting acquainted with several men in senior positions: something which could always prove extremely useful. After only one month in Paris I was promoted to Third Secretary – six weeks before Peter Marais in Berne, who is really my senior, but who took longer to pass his examinations. The main disadvantage of this state of affairs was that after the considerable time in Pretoria, where I had become accustomed to a familiar, secure way of life, I felt completely stranded in this bustling city with the Embassy the only island where one could still enjoy the precarious sense of security caused by the presence of compatriots.

It is not a very imposing building. Seen from the Avenue Hoche it is nothing but a large brown door with a shiny copper plaque inscribed in three languages; with the exception of public holidays there is not even a South African flag to distinguish it from all the equally large, equally brown doors in the same avenue. Immediately inside the main entrance a few stairs on the left lead downwards to the quarters of the concierge, Lebon, followed a few yards farther on by the broad staircase to the front door of the official residence; then the short driveway widens into the small cobbled courtyard on the opposite side of which one enters the double glass doors of the office building. From the reading room, which also serves as foyer, a door on the left gives access to the typists' office in the basement, followed by my own; on the right a dark staircase leads up to the Registry Department, and the offices of the other Third Secretary, the Second Secretary, and the First Secretary; the last door is that of the Ambassador's own large and stately office. On the top floor are the three attachés (Military, Cultural, and Commercial), their respective secretaries and the official translator. Everything is rather cramped, the narrow corridors are ill-lit, and one is eternally surrounded by the musty smell of old books.

Naturally, I got acquainted with the other staff members very soon: in the Embassy, at a few informal receptions, and especially at a cocktail party Jaap Mouton had organised to welcome me in Paris. At that time he was still the other Third Secretary, and amiable fellow who has since been transferred to Cologne. He was succeeded by Theo Harrington, something of a windbag who is much too conscious of his attraction for women despite the fact that he is already married to a beautiful, reserved young girl; but he undoubtedly has a flair for his work. Koos Joubert, the Second Secretary, has already been mentioned: a typecast 'Boer' and a fanatical supporter of government policy. As a matter of fact, we have had quite a few brushes on this very subject. "How the hell could you represent a government you don't support?" he argued. "I am an Afrikaner, man. The moment my government goes, I go too. In the meantime I'm a Boer diplomat: if anybody gets in my way, he is trampled underfoot." In reply, I could only counter with the statement: "I serve each successive government with equal fidelity and equal contempt." But this is not altogether true, of course. It would be more accurate to apply this philosophy to Douglas Masters, the First Secretary, who is correctness incarnate; to him, everything forms part of a never-ending game, a shrewd battle of wits and calculation. Yet I doubt whether he would ever become a great diplomat. His personality is really that of an exceptionally brilliant administrator who is as fastidious as an old woman. Compared to his philosophy mine would rather be: this career is a means to an end, not an end in itself.

The end being to arrive at the top. I think it would be too facile to interpret this as a reaction to my father's contempt. It would be more accurate to judge it as something positive, as a firm conviction that the only person who 'means' something is he who proves himself master of every single situation as well as of the decisive test. Survival of the fittest? Perhaps. Zarathustra? In the final analysis, yes.

Koos' colourless, mousey little wife usually stays at home to look after her numerous children. But Masters' Sylvia is the exact opposite. She likes to talk about "fabulous Paree", in spite of the fact that she does not care a damn about the city. Her mornings are spent in bed: she seldom rises before noon. In the afternoon she goes out to "tea". Two Spanish servants take care of the household. Her son is at a private school in England. Sylvia is attactive, I suppose, but spiritually she is anaemic, and sexually she is as exciting as a wet newspaper. It would be in the interests of my career to get married sooner or later, but God forbid that I choose a wife like Sylvia.

The three Attachés I meet very seldom. Two of them, anyway. I doubt whether Colonel Kotzé has any close friends: he is much too caught up in the web of his military past and in the pathos of his present paper work. As for the Commercial Attaché, Verster, he usually hides behind his thick glasses and has no reality apart from his home and his work. Victor le Roux, however, soon became a close friend of mine, probably because he is the only other bachelor on the staff. Victor is interested in writing, although he is something of a dilettante and rather effeminate; but in a small company he often proves himself a delightful causeur. We have spent many long nights arguing about philosophy, art, religion, or sex.

Then there is Anna Smith: She used to be a teacher, but then she got married and after two years her husband eloped with another woman – who would blame him? – and she ended up in the Foreign Service. Anna is tall, decidedly ugly, and lean; and she regards herself as "a connoisseur of the stage". Paris went to her head. She has her hair done at Alexandre's, she dines in Maxim's, she mixes with the "right" people. She likes to regard herself as one of the "younger set", although her ideas tend to move in an extremely narrow circle. (Move? They *stand*, in the tradition of Luther.) She has "unseverable bonds" with her people, her language, and her church – she is a Methodist. All new South Africans in Paris are sheltered under her wings – a fate I myself could not escape. But we quarrelled on my very first

Sunday in Paris when she wanted to take me to her church. I made it very clear that I had no intention of using every irrelevant little mystery or guilty feeling to "lift mine eyes unto the hills", living on the responsibility of a convenient fiction.

"But how on earth could you exist without God?" she gasped.

"I manage to get along extremely well. I decided, once and for all, that I was going to have my life here and now and that I would never rely on the illusion of a 'hereafter'."

She nevertheless promised to pray for me.

And then there were Their Excellencies, at that time Jan Theunissen and his wife. He was a relic from a previous order and, as often happens, had been moved higher and higher by the inscrutable turning of the diplomatic wheel simply because no single mission could bear his general inefficiency for very long; and so, at last, his huge amiable backside had come to rest on this plush chair. He had a liking for me from the very beginning, prompted, I think, by two motives: firstly, I listened sympathetically (!) to his detailed daily exposition of his main concern – that he was not adequately appreciated by the government because he had been a supporter of its predecessor; and secondly, I shared a box of South African grapes with him which I received shortly after my arrival in Paris. He blatantly favoured me, much to the indignation of Masters' predecessor, Prinsloo. Much important and highly confidential work, which normally would never be entrusted to a Third Secretary, was left entirely to my own discretion. Towards the end of his career in Paris if often happened that I was responsible for correspondence on extremely delicate subjects while he never even glanced at the letters I wrote or received. And when protocol demanded his personal signature he would barely scan the typewritten sheets before signing his name at the bottom in his grand, antiquated handwriting.

"There's only one way for a young diplomat to learn the ropes," he used to say. "He must do the work himself." Both of us knew that it was a euphemism; the truth behind his words was that his suspicion about the government's attitude towards him had long ago paralysed his energy and enthusiasm.

As far as official conduct was concerned, I felt nothing but contempt for him. The same applied to his wife, who would make her appearance at the most solemn occasions wearing an idiotic old hat covered with frills and flowers and lace and gilt hatpins. But judged solely as *people* they were one of the most charming and sincere couples I have ever come across.

It is not without reason that I reminisce about the Theunissens, in spite of the fact that they left Paris a whole year ago when, to the heartfelt relief of the government, he could finally be pensioned. I do so because I want to emphasise the enormous difference between them and their successors. Or, more accurately, between old Jan Theunissen and Ambassador Van Heerden.

We were all impressed by the new man's appearance. By that time we had already heard about his exceptional reputation at the missions in Vienna, where he had already been an Ambassador, and New York, where he had represented South Africa at U.N.O. When the doors of the Boeing were opened at Orly and the passengers came down the gangway, anybody would have recognised him immediately, even if he had not waited until the very last in order to be taken to the special V.I.P. reception lounge. He was not taller than the average, but broad-shouldered and powerfully built, with greying hair, a strong nose, unwavering eyes, remarkably healthy white teeth – in fact, meriting all the clichés usually employed to describe such a person.

On his third day in the Embassy he dialled me from his office and asked me to come up to him. I finished the file on which I was working – as I had been accustomed to do in Theunissen's time – and then mounted the stairs to the first floor. He barely glanced up as I entered, and continued writing. I waited for two whole minutes, following the leisurely circle of the red second-hand on the large clock opposite his desk.

"Have I kept you waiting, Keyter?" he asked suddenly, without looking up.

"I beg your pardon, Mr. Ambassador?" I was taken by surprise. "No. Of course not."

He smiled faintly. "Of course I have. For two minutes. On the other hand it took you seven minutes to climb one flight of stairs."

I opened my mouth to answer, but he stopped me with an almost imperceptible gesture of his right hand which was still resting on the paper. Neither of us has ever referred to that incident since. It has never been necessary. And I suppose I deserved it.

He took a letter from a pile at his elbow, weighted down by a small bronze statuette, and asked: "Did you write this?"

I recognised it immediately. It was my latest letter to the Minister's secretary in Pretoria in connection with certain negotiations with the Banque de France.

"Yes, Mr. Ambassador," I answered readily. "I sent it up in your basket to be signed."

He was holding my letter in both hands, looking at me quite kindly. "Don't you think you should consult either Mr. Masters or myself before entering into correspondence of such a delicate nature?"

I could feel blood surging into my face. "But, Mr. Ambassador, I've been engaged in this correspondence for more than a month already –"

"Then, perhaps, it is time the matter was solved. In future no letters of a contentious nature will be written on behalf of any senior official without his, or my, specific instruction and approval. As far as this particular matter is concerned, I shall deal with it personally." He folded the letter, calmly tore it up, crumpled the bits in his strong hand and dropped them into the wastepaper basket. Then he said: "That will be all, thank you, Keyter."

There were other, similar, incidents in the course of the first month. Gradually it dawned upon my disconcerted mind that all the liberty and initiative Theunissen had allowed me were now being relentlessly suppressed. Even trivialities like using official paper for private correspondence were prohibited. I suppose all these things would fall under the heading of minor irregularities, yet they happen, as a matter of course, in practically all Embassies, as in all State Departments. The result was that a disturbing and unnecessary impression of authority was created. And as could be expected it affected me much more than the others who had not enjoyed old Theunissen's confidence to the same extent. To crown everything, I was, at the end of the first month, transferred from my ordinary duties in the political section to consular affairs, which are obviously much more tedious than composing and deciphering code telegrams, summarising confidential memoranda, or being involved in correspondence on delicate and intricate matters of state.

What made it so hard to stomach, was that one had to concede that the Ambassador had every right to do as he did and that he was infinitely more than just a competent administrator. In diplomatic circles he was generally regarded as a man of considerable stature; and within two months of his arrival in Paris there was an appreciable change in the attitude of members of other delegations towards us. But whereas Theunissen had never been a diplomat, only a human being, it is wellnigh impossible to imagine His Excellency ever acting in a private capacity. One is confronted with the simple fact that he does not lead two lives – official, and private – like all other diplomats. He can be most charming and affable at receptions, but one soon discovers that even his charm and apparant warmth are the devices of an experienced man who knows exactly what he wants and – which is more important –

how to get it. I do not mean that he "passes himself off" as an official being, hiding his true personality behind this public face: what makes it so disturbing is that he really *is* the man he appears to be. For instance, I cannot picture him in any intimate situation with a woman, not even with his own wife, let alone with Nicolette – but I'll come to that in due course.

The Ambassador's wife, Erika, arrived a week after His Excellency in the company of her daughter. She must be very much younger than him, probably between forty and fifty, and it is evident that she must once have possessed what is termed "classical beauty". Even now she still reveals the sort of grace which is improved rather than diminished by age. And yet, if one comes upon her unexpectedly, one is sometimes startled by the weariness in her eyes.

She immediately set about organising a dinner party to meet all the members of staff, even the typists; and she is, without doubt, the best hostess I have ever come across. The way in which her daughter, Annette, mingled with the guests, starting up brilliant, superficial conversations as she went, suggested that she, too, had from an early age been primed for such a life.

After that first dinner the staff members were often invited, in twos or fours, to the official residence. At these occasions the atmosphere was always formal, yet pleasant and stimulating.

It is very difficult, at this stage, to determine why I started paying any attention to Annette. The fact that my affair with Nicolette had again entered one of its periodic lulls, might have contributed to it. But I think a more feasible explanation would be that it suddenly occurred to me that, through Annette, I might compensate to some extent for the futility of the inferior position to which her father had relegated me. He had absolute power over me, but if I could win Annette I need not be at the losing end; or even if I did, it would not mean so much, balanced against the satisfaction and perhaps the malicious joy of knowing that I was having an affair with his daughter. Moreover, she was very young – eighteen – and obviously inexperienced, so that it should not have been too difficult to seduce her. And above all, there was something so challenging about her youthful self-assurance, her cool, protected virginity, that one simply had to find out what she really was like behind that mask.

I took her out a few times. And I must confess that she surprised me: the moment she was taken from her mother's presence she revealed facets of rebellion, will-power and spontaneous enthusiasm which no one would ever have suspected in that attractive little social robot.

And then, late one evening, we were together in my apartment, tired and relaxed. I offered her a pillow so that she could lean back more easily and while I stood bent over her I suddenly thought: Tonight she wouldn't resist. She smiled drowsily and said: "I should be going home, you know."

"No." I closed my hands on her shoulders. It frightened her. I started kissing her. She tried to struggle loose and kept on repeating: "Don't. Don't. Don't."

I was surprised by her resistance and determination. I simply had to succeed. For if I failed, she would tell them about it at home and then the Ambassador – I started to panic. My hands fell from her shoulders.

She was standing, her back rigid, pressed against the wall, panting, shocked, confused.

"I – am sorry," I stammered.

"Take me home. Take me home immediately." She tried to brush away her ruffled hair. Finally she regained her composure and said jeeringly: "Why don't you have a glass of cold milk first? It might cool you off."

That was the final humiliation. I went to the door and said, without looking back: "Come." We were silent all the way to the Embassy. I desperately wanted to plead with her, to grasp her hands and beg her not to tell anybody about it. But I couldn't. And at the same time I felt furious about the failure.

I didn't sleep that night. For days I lived in agony. Nothing happened. I gradually relaxed. She hadn't told them. She would not tell. And everything returned to normal. But deep inside me, behind the customary surface of things, there remained a scar and the cancer of fear.

I did not anticipate that Her Excellency would enter into the picture. Towards the end of February – a month after the incident in my apartment – she unexpectedly telephoned me to my office and asked me to accompany her and Annette to an Anouilh play in the *Gaïté-Montparnasse:* they had received complimentary tickets but her husband would be occupied that night and they did not want to go alone.

I dared not refuse, although I had already seen the play. The whole affair was much too delicate for any rashness. And I suppose I should have felt "honoured". I had no idea what to expect. But the evening was most successful, without any hitch, and Annette did not reveal the slightest trace of resentment or antagonism. After the performance Her Excellency insisted that I have a cup of coffee with them at home. The situation was again threatening to become dangerous. But the moment we entered the official residence Annette excused herself, with the threadbare pretence of a headache. (I must admit that she was looking slightly pale.)

Her mother hesitated, then said: "I am sorry. I hope my company won't be too much of a burden for you."

"On the contrary," I assured her.

She did not answer, but it was evident that she could see through my superficial courtesy.

The servant brought a tray with cups which my hostess arranged herself before pouring the coffee. Under the impersonal white lamplight I could see the fatigue she no longer cared to hide behind her make-up, an expression almost of pathos, of emptiness and of experiences beyond my limited horizon. (But was that what I saw then – or are these only my thoughts in retrospect?)

For a little while we carried on the usual meaningless little conversation about how we liked Paris, about South Africa, French customs, and the latest gossip in the newspapers.

Then, right in the middle of a sentence – she was talking about the prospects of an early spring, I think – she suddenly put down her cup and asked: "Why must we do this?"

I didn't immediately realise what she meant and sat waiting for an explanation.

"Are we really interested in the weather, Stephen? Is it really so tremendously important that we can't find *anything* else to talk about?" I had noticed before that she would sometimes become overwrought, but it was much more obvious now than on any previous occasion, probably because there was nobody else present. It also struck me how she, just like Annette, became a totally different person when she was alone, as if they were two loving but poisonous plants which had never been meant to grow together, but which now, fatally, found themselves in a situation where there was nothing else they could rely on. (And how did the Ambassador fit into this context?)

"We could talk about anything else," I said obligingly.

"Yes. I could tell you about the clothes I've ordered for Annette and myself. Or you could tell me about the latest film you have seen." She no longer tried to hide her bitterness. "God, how bored you must feel, Stephen!" She leant back and with a quick, jerky movement pulled open the curtain behind her. I could see the movement of her breasts in the light and was surprised by their persistent youthfulness. "And there's the city, the whole teeming city. Five million people, behind light or dark windows, engaged in the process of living. Does it matter whether they do it gracefully or perversely? Even the clochards sleeping on metro grilles have their own way of living. They are aware of the heat coming up from below, and of the cold night wind above them. They can *feel*. They are outside. They are part of something. And here we are – look at us – shut in by our four walls, safely protected against this strange spectacle, life, of which we have heard, but which we hardly know." For a moment she rested her head on her shoulder. Her hands were clutched, one of them on her knee, the other still holding the half-opened curtain. Then she turned her head back to me and there was a hint of a smile round her mouth. "You must forgive me. I didn't mean to talk about 'us'. It's only an illusion, making it easier to bear. Shall we make it – a 'royal we'? But you mustn't stay, Stephen. You are terribly bored." It seemed as if she wanted to say something else and only waited to see what my reaction would be.

"What makes you think I am?" I asked mechanically.

"I know." She allowed her head to fall back and for a moment the shadows softened her weariness and suggested the beauty of her youth: the delicate nose, and the full mouth, and the firm, stubborn line of her jaw, and the challenge in her eyes. Then she moved her head back into the light. She was no longer speaking directly to me: "You are young; one of these days you'll be getting married. And then? Then you'll become a true diplomat. You'll be promoted and promoted. For how long? And then, one day? One day you'll suddenly discover that only one thing has happened – you're no longer young." She got up and went to a graceful antique cabinet, opened the door and asked: "Would you like something stronger than coffee?"

I wasn't feeling like it but I did not want to disappoint her, and she poured whisky for us both.

"Santé."

She emptied hers very quickly.

"Why do you pretend to be old?" I asked after a while. "Surely that's not true. Not you."

She smiled. "You shouldn't be so ready with compliments, Stephen. It becomes a habit. So many things become habits. Staying alive, for instance." She went back to the cabinet, refilled her glass, then walked across to the window and with a firm, decisive movement, closed the curtain. "And then there's Annette," she said – but it was more like a question.

36

For a moment I was paralysed with shock. Then I asked, as neutrally as possible: "What do you mean?"

"Oh my God, Stephen." She quickly emptied her glass and shrugged her shoulders. "I don't know what happened between you that night – "

"Nothing!" I protested, much too emphatically. "Did she say – ?"

"She said nothing. And you needn't apologise. You don't understand what I mean. I assume you wanted to 'teach' her something. I suppose it's a good thing. And I suppose it's necessary – sooner or later. I don't know. She's very young."

Relieved, I did not answer. And she went on: "I was still awake when she came back. She knew that, but she went past to her own room and never said a word. Before that she used to confide in me. You see, we've always tried to be friends rather than mother and daughter. And it's rather disconcerting to discover quite suddenly that as she is growing up and coming nearer to me, she is really becoming farther and farther removed from me than ever before."

She turned towards the cabinet again.

"You shouldn't drink any more," I said. I had no idea what on earth prompted the temerity of the remark.

But she only looked at me and nodded. "I shouldn't. You're quite right. But what the hell?" She sniffed derisively. Then, quickly, contradictorily: "I am not old, Stephen. I don't want to be old."

"You must not – exaggerate what had happened." It took a great effort to sound normal and composed. "Perhaps you should give her an opportunity of finding her own way."

"Do you blame me for wanting to protect her?"

"No. But one forgets so easily that everybody has a right to his own life. Annette. And you yourself."

She did not react immediately. I realised that we had reached a crisis. After a while she said: "It seems you've got answers for everything." There was something derogatory in her remark; but also something complaisant which relieved me.

Very shortly afterwards I rose to leave. She accompanied me to the front door, once again the immaculate hostess. But when I was on the point of going out she suddenly laid her hands on my arm and said: "I am glad you came here tonight, Stephen." The phrase had suddenly lost its customary formality.

And once again I became aware, acutely aware, of the fact that she was not only Her Excellency, but also, and very significantly, a woman. I wanted to tell her that, but it would sound either presumptious or clumsy. And, to tell the truth, I was unnerved by my own discovery. It was too acute, too dangerous. Yet I have a suspicion that she could guess my thoughts.

In the course of the next few months we often saw each other at receptions, parties and other social functions; two or three times I was even invited to the official residence, but on these occasions one of my colleagues usually accompanied me, as if she wanted to make special arrangements to avoid any embarassing situations. On the surface our relationship was completely formal. This, however, was nothing but a courteous camouflage of what the French would term *sympathie*. It was safer for both of us that way. But I think we both had a presentiment that it must sooner or later come to a head – however little we might have wished it.

In May the Ambassador had to attend a conference in Brussels. Victor had home leave and was back in South Africa so that I was the only bachelor on the staff. Consequently, I suppose, it was quite natural that he should casually ask me one morning, as I was passing through the reading-room to my office, whether I would care to sleep in the official residence during his absence "to keep an eye on everything". Yet I could not help wondering whether it had been his own idea or hers. And if it was hers: what were her motives? I would have preferred not to go, but it was impossible to refuse. And the next afternoon after work I rather reluctantly bundled a few of my things into a suitcase and took up my abode in the official residence.

But my apprehension, it appeared, had been groundless. I was treated like a royal guest; Annette was always in our company; once or twice other people were invited. She seemed to be doing her utmost not only to save me any embarassment but to make my visit as pleasant and natural as possible. That, at least, was what happened until the very last night.

Using the pretext of a "date" I had dinner at Valentin's in the rue Marbeuf and afterwards went to the rue de Condé. Nicolette was at home, but the evening soon proved to be a repetition of the now customary pattern of trivialities, leading up to the inevitable refusal and the equally inevitable quarrel. It was, if anything, even more violent than usual because the preceding week had, in spite of all appearances, subtly taxed my nerves. At eleven o'clock I was back at the Embassy, irritated, depressed and resentful. I parked in the narrow sidelane next to the avenue

Hoche, pressed Lebon's bell and went into the official residence. It looked as if everybody was in bed already. But as I went past the large reception hall downstairs, Her Excellency softly called: "Is that you, Stephen?"

She was sitting at one of the long empty tables, smoking. I don't know whether she had staged the scene intentionally to create an impression of forlornness (she has a remarkable, intuitive – but somewhat melodramatic? – talent for acting).

"Did you enjoy your evening?" It was the obvious question to ask, but I sensed a deeper meaning in her attitude.

"Not much." I was in no mood for a conversation.

"A girl? Or do I sound like an inquisitive old woman?" She must have known very well that she was looking even younger than usual.

"It's no secret," I answered courteously. "And nothing unusual either, I think."

"Of course not. There must be many girls – " She (intentionally?) left the sentence incomplete.

"Unfortunately not." Against my will I was being drawn into the situation. "It seems I have an exceptional talent for repelling people rather than attracting them."

"You're bitter, Stephen."

"I suppose I have reason to be."

It is very difficult to reconstruct the rest of the scene. I can remember how one part of me felt cool, cerebral resentment towards her uninvited meddling. At the same time, I suspect, I experienced an inevitable masochistic desire to lick my wounds in public. (Is it an innate urge in man that drives one to confession? Is this the substance of all religion?) Added to my other feelings was an acute awareness of our seclusion in that huge baroque hall; of the empty semi-darkness around us; and of her warmth, maturity, sympathy, which made me feel unreasonably young and wronged and yearning, but without the self-consciousness which so often overcomes me in the presence of younger women. I sat down next to her and told her everything about Nicolette, a wandering, incoherent confession of the most intimate details. It reached back to my past: the series of disillusionments I had experienced in Paris; my youth, my parents, and the endless row of Sunday nights following my father's long, solemn prayer at the supper table, with darkness surrounding our single illuminated room; the whole paradox of disgust and desire, of repulsion and longing. The evening dissolved into night over us. And then it all ended in an unexpected, unavoidable embrace in which there

39

was nothing of mother and child: there was too much distress in it, and desire, and fulfilment and physical awareness.

There was a silent agreement about the whole affair, of which we were conscious even while we were still calmly sipping our liqueur from exquisite crystal glasses: neither of us would ever, with word or gesture, refer to what had happened. Because that would immediately define and limit it. Its true value, after all, was the very fact that we dared not formulate it, for fear that it would then destroy itself. And therefore, after we had finished our liqueur, we merely put down our glasses and got up to go to our bedrooms; and I said: "Good-night, Erika."

I lay awake for a long time, thinking. There was no question of anything as simple as "guilt." I simply tried to sort out what had happened; and I was aware of the irony of it all – first, the humiliating episode with the daughter; then, unexpectedly, this contact with the mother. It was all so impossibly complicated. And yet it could all be reduced to a single question: "What would happen if the Ambassador found out about it – ?" It was, naturally, a purely hypothetical question: it was unthinkable that he *might* learn the truth.

But this very fact slowly but surely turned his presence into a never-ending threat: not because he knew, but because he could come to know. And because, apart from and in spite of all our personal actions, he held my entire fate in his hands.

This phase of my relationship with Erika lasted for a very long time without giving rise to either anxiety or particular happiness. There was no attempt to rationalise; yet (or perhaps *because* of this) it was a period of harmony and inner peace. And there was only one further episode of any importance, drawing its meaning from the very fact that it marked the end of this period of contentment, and made everything infinitely more complex.

It happened seven weeks ago, towards the middle of October, on a bleak, windy evening. At about ten o'clock there was a knock on my door. Nicolette? It would be her first visit since our miserable, memorable evening of bath and bed, three weeks before. I hurried to the door. It was Erika, leaning against the doorpost. She wasn't drunk, but she had evidently had too much to drink. It was quite a shock to see her venture outside the Embassy in this state. I was aware of this weakness in her, of course, but usually it was strictly confined to the official residence.

"Are you – occupied?"

I shook my head and allowed her to come in.

"Awful evening," I said.

"Awful? Yes. I've forgotten my cigarettes at home. Have you got any?" She was trembling while I offered her a light. At last she said: "I was feeling rather lonesome. Paul is at the British Embassy. Annette has gone out with a student."

The conversation dragged. We were both irritated by its superficiality, but it was one of those occasions when one gets caught in a whirlpool and can't get out of it. She smoked four or five cigarettes. The last one, almost untouched, was left lying on the edge of an ashtray while she absently followed its lazy line of smoke.

"Have you got anything to drink?" she asked bluntly.

"Should you?"

She uttered a short, rough laugh: "I know. I'm smoking too much. I'm drinking too much. But I can assure you there's nothing else of which I'm doing too much."

The cigarette on the ashtray was still smoking and smoking.

Suddenly: "I went to see the doctor. At long last."

"The doctor? But why? I didn't realise – "

"I only wanted to make sure. It's so easy to start imagining things. Or do you think I am like Anna Smith, going to a doctor every three weeks because that is the only opportunity she has of being legitimately touched by a man?"

"What is the matter then?" I purposely ignored her last remark.

"There was nothing tangible. I just couldn't go on like this. I am upset by everything that happens. I suppose I only wanted him to set my mind at rest."

"Well – ?"

"It seems an operation is necessary. Quite urgently too."

"But why?"

Her eyes never looked away from mine. "I won't be a woman any more, that's all," she said cruelly. And then she added (it was the only time I have ever seen her completely lose her self-control): "Spayed like a cat."

"Erika, for God's sake – !"

Then, for the first time, she gave way to the hysteria which had been threatening for so long. She cried herself out in my arms. There was nothing I could say or think which would make it easier for either of us; I could only stroke her hair and arms. Finally she calmed down, but she did not move. That was the most intimate contact I have ever had with any woman: that monologue which followed. It was very confused, troubled by

41

the after-effects of the shock which still had to be absorbed. Loneliness. Frustration. The loss of contact with Annette.

" – I don't *know* her any more. She is always going out with men I have never even met. I know that she is desperately unhappy, but she refuses to come to me for help. It can't go on like this. It has become unbearable for both of us."

And later: "It is easy for *you* to be here, away from your country and your people. One becomes blasé. But there is something in me, these days, which urges me to go back. I know there is nothing to keep me there. But there's nothing here either. I have no ties with anything, I am drifting, I don't know where I'm going or what is happening to me. I doubt whether you would understand this, Stephen. And yet you are the only one I could come to."

"But how could I help you? It is so impossible – in our position. Think of – "

"I know," she said, almost rudely, and got up.

That was the very first time either of us had touched upon it with words. And immediately, as I had foreseen all along, everything was tangible, discernible, definable: an almost cheap little affair.

She did not reproach me; but I know that on that moment I failed her. (Is this a deadly fate I have to carry with me? Must it always come to this?)

"I must be looking like a scarecrow," she said, trying to sound nonchalant, playful. "Do you think there's anything that could be salvaged?" And with that she went to the bathroom.

When she returned she said almost casually: "I've decided – just now – to go on holiday. Annette must come with me. Perhaps that will clear up something. I don't think so. But I must try."

"Where?"

"Italy," she answered, as if it had been decided long ago. "It's warm there. I have always hated cold and here winter is setting in early this year. Everything is getting cold, everything, everything!"

(Three weeks before, in this very room: "We are cold, both of us.")

On our way to the door I asked: "How long will you be away?"

"Don't know. I won't be tied to any programme. Shall we call it a pilgrimage?" And then, mocking from the open door: "You see: I'm becoming sentimental. In my old age."

I kissed her, or she me. It was like a question which had to be left unanswered. And then she went away.

5

I must return to my report. And I must emphasise that I need not rely on conjecture – which would, after all, carry no weight with the Minister – but solely on verifiable facts.

Unfortunately there is no means of determining exactly when the Ambassador's flirtation with Nicolette started. There are various indications, I think, that it had been going on for quite some time before it first came to my notice; it would seem to date, therefore, from a period prior to Erika's departure. However, since I intend to confine myself to facts only, I shall have to begin with my discovery on the afternoon of 6th November. I am quite sure of this date, because it was the day just after the party in my apartment when I had finally broken with Nicolette.

The party – It was her very first visit to me since our wretched little adventure. I had been to her a few times but it had not turned out very successfully. Actually I was quite surprised about her acceptance of the invitation, but by that time I had become used to her unpredictable changes of mood; moreover, in all the time I had known her she had never missed a party.

Even though there were far too many people in my cramped little apartment the evening was a success. I suppose we were all inclined to abandon ourselves fatalistically to any form of enjoyment – eating, drinking, making merry, not knowing what the morrow would hold in store for us. Because it was an ominous moment for South Africa after the unexpected turn the strike near Cape Town had taken the previous day. The strike itself had been threatening for a long time, originating, as usual, in a triviality blown up out of all proportions. But it was different from similar incidents in the past in that, this time, it was not confined to threats and counter-threats; very soon dangerous tension was building up between the strikers in their township and the police cordon drawn around it. At one stage it had very nearly resulted in an open clash. There were rumours that the inhabitants of neighbouring African areas would also go on strike to prove their sympathy with the original group. Troops were sent to reinforce the police. The most banal incident – an arrest for a contravention of the pass laws; the scolding of a noisy drunk – could have devastating consequences. And when the threatening situation had nearly reached its climax some of the leaders of the resistance movement had dispatched telegrams to the representatives of various Afro-Asian countries at U.N.O. demanding immediate aid. The whole affair had suddenly become a dangerous international dispute.

We had to rely on the reports in Parisian newspapers, and on the ominous news flashes transmitted irregularly by the Hell-schreiber of the Information Service. For twenty-four hours a day somebody had to be stationed at the Embassy in case the Post Office telephoned to inform us of the arrival of an urgent telegram from Headquarters. The Ambassador himself was in his office for almost sixteen hours a day. The previous night it had been my turn. Which was all the more reason why I wanted to enjoy my one night's pleasure as much as possible.

But Nicolette evaded me, which was not very difficult among so many people. At the same time she was extremely provocative in her tight-fitting jersey-cloth dress. (Didn't she feel the cold, I wondered? For outside it was rainy, and there was a chill wind.) It was almost eleven o'clock before I could find her alone for the first time. She was in the small kitchen, looking for potato chips when I came in to rinse a few glasses.

"Why are you trying to hide from me?"

"You're imagining things." But she was already on her way to the door.

I was angered by her aloofness and caught her arm.

"Let me go, Stephen!" she said fiercely. "You're drunk." (Which was a lie.) And then she slapped me.

Had we been alone in the apartment I would have slapped her too. But any moment some of my guests might enter the kitchen, and a scandal of that nature could easily reach the ears of the Ambassador. (Always this damned "professional conduct" that has to be respected!)

She made use of my momentary indecision to wrench her arm from my grip and rushed to the front door. It slammed behind her. I was standing in the kitchen, my fists clenched, forcing my-self to keep calm. Uppermost in my mind was one single thought: that had been the last straw; that was the end.

Although none of my guests made any reference to Nicolette's precipitated departure, it had a marked effect on the atmosphere and despite well-meant efforts by several of them nothing could dispel the feeling of uneasiness and vague suspicion. By midnight I was left alone among the filled ashtrays and the dirty glasses.

Inside the room was grey with smoke; outside the cold rain was shivering against the panes.

That, then, was the night of 5th November. And it was at three o'clock the next afternoon that I saw Nicolette in the Embassy. I was on my way downstairs to my own office, coming from an interview with the Ambassador. She passed me near the bottom of the stairs. I greeted her stiffly. She ignored me. But that was not the reason why I stopped. It was the Ambassador's jacket which she was carrying, carelessly draped over a shoulder. There could be no doubt: anyone on the staff would immediately have recognised the dark blue material with thin grey stripes. I stood motionless on the bottom step watching her go up to the first floor, where she went past the Registry Office towards the Ambassador's.

It was not until I was back at my own desk that I was struck by the full implications of the incident. I thought of Erika. Perhaps the scene I had just witnessed suggested one of the reasons for her hypertension during the last few weeks before her departure? I was dismayed by the cold-bloodedness of it all. While she was travelling in Italy in her state of nervous depression he apparently had no qualms – To think that *he* could act like that, this formidable diplomat who always insisted that protocol be obeyed in the smallest detail! Carrying on with Nicolette of all people! Was that the reason for her aggressive attitude towards me the previous night?

However difficult it was, I decided to shut the whole incident out of my mind. It would be most unwise to become involved in it.

But less than a week later, on Monday 12th November – I made a note of the date – I was in the reading-room discussing a new procedure with the messengers, when she, once again, entered the double glass doors. She hesitated for a moment, then smiled haughtily and came past me, going up the stairs with a self-consciously challenging air about her. I watched the teasing movement of her dress round her legs until she disappeared out of sight. She didn't even bother to have her presence announced, as is expected of even the most important visitors. She simply went up to his office – and she did it quite openly. I gave the messengers their last few instructions and went back to my own office.

I didn't get much work done during the rest of that day. And towards closing time I decided that I would make it my business to discover the whole truth. I had no particular aim in mind. But it was imperative, I felt, that I *knew*.

For altogether four days, starting that very evening, I kept a close watch on all Nicolette's movements – but without success. When I arrived in the rue de Condé on the first evening, after work, she was not at home. (From the rue de l'Odéon, at the back of her building, one can see her window high up on the fifth floor.) I had dinner near by and loitered around until eleven, but there was no sign of her. I was too tired to wait any longer. For although the tension in South Africa had eased after talks between the strike leaders and Government representatives, we were still flooded with work caused by the episode – interviews with members of the press and with various industrialists who had capital investments in South Africa, negotiations with the French Government in connection with support in the Security Council against efforts by the Afro-Asians to exploit the situation.

On the second evening I had been waiting near her front door for about half an hour when she made her appearance and set out in the direction of the boulevard Saint-Germain. I followed her to the metro, but in the hustle and bustle of the peak hour I soon lost her. All I could see was that she took a train to the Porte d'Orléans, which didn't mean anything, since she could easily change to a different line on another station. The only fact that could be deduced from it, was that that particular line did not lead to anywhere near the Embassy. I went home, but towards eleven o'clock a sudden inspiration took me back to the rue de l'Odéon where I could see light in her window. I mounted the dilapidated old staircase and went to listen at her door. There were voices inside, but it was impossible to recognise them as the middle door, between the tiny entrance lobby and her room, must have been closed as well. I went outside and resumed my vigil. After a while her light went out, but nobody left the building. I was still no nearer to a discovery. I had to restrain myself from going upstairs and knocking on her door. The mere thought of what might be happening inside, made me feel feverish. But I had to remain uninvolved. So I left her building and came back to my apartment to sleep. The next day the Ambassador told me that during my absence he had telephoned me a few times in connection with an urgent memorandum. It seemed – unless it was a ruse – that I had been on the wrong scent anyway.

The third night brought an unexpected, disconcerting discovery which, however, had no immediate connection with the matter I was investigating. At about seven o'clock I followed her at a safe distance while she threaded her way through the labyrinth of streets in her quarter. In the rue Hautefeuille she was joined by a young stranger. It was evident that they had an appointment; and just as evident that she was late. He must have been a student and I doubt whether I would recognise him if I ever met him again. They had dinner in a cheap restaurant (the Acropole in the rue de l'École de Médicine) and afterwards returned to her apartment together. I was prepared for a repetition of the previous night's activities, but much to my surprise it was barely nine o'clock before the young man left by himself and went off in the direction of the Luxembourg Gardens. I quickly went round to the rue de l'Odéon; her light was still on. What could that mean? That she was expecting a second visitor? That they had quarrelled? Or simply that she was planning to stay at home the rest of the evening? After a while it seemed as if the latter was the most probable. But shortly after ten she came out by the front door and started walking briskly in the direction of the metro. This time I made sure that I wouldn't lose her again. I was fatalistically prepared for a hitch: the ticket woman might shut the little green gate between us if a train happened to arrive at the wrong moment; or Nicolette might recognise me, although I tried to hide behind an open *France-Soir*. It was rather risky to travel with her in the same coach, but it would be too easy to lose her if I did not. Fortunately she didn't seem to be in the least interested in her immediate surroundings. It was an endless journey. Cité, Châtelet, and onwards. We passed every possible correspondence station as far as Barbès-Rochechouart. There, a few seconds before the doors slammed shut, she quickly jumped up and stepped out on the platform. I followed just in time. She was walking towards the Porte Dauphine platform. For the first time it dawned on me what our destination might be. It settled in my stomach, a numb, paralysing heaviness. My God, I thought, not *that*. Be loose, Nicolette, be unscrupulous, be a bitch: but not *that*!

For a moment there returned a flicker of hope when we passed Pigalle. But even before we reached Place Blanche I could see that we were nearing our destination. She got up and stood at the door, waiting, her narrow hands holding the shiny handle, her forehead pressed against the glass so that she could stare at the sides of the tunnel, a child standing at a shop window. (But surely there was nothing to look at here?)

After the dull heat and the heavy odour of garlic in the metro, the cold outside came almost as a shock. It had started to rain while we were inside. People were scurrying past, crouching under umbrellas or in thick coat collars. There was the monotonous swishing sound of motor tyres on wet tar. But Nicolette did not hesitate for a moment. It was obvious that she knew her way. We

47

went down the rue Blanche, then turned into a dark, narrow street; and suddenly in the darkness between two lampposts, she was just – gone. I stopped in my tracks. Cold raindrops were trickling down my collar into my neck. Then, in the shadows next to me, something moved and a husky voice whispered: "*Chéri* –?" Almost violently I shrugged the white claw from my arm and hurried on. Between two buildings I noticed a narrow alley. That accounted for her disappearance. I looked around. It didn't look very safe to venture in there alone. Ten yards further on there was an entrance to a sixth-rate strip-club with a thick-set porter in red uniform standing next to it, watching me like a vulture. On both sides of the entrance were the customary illuminated frames with photos of girls in various stages of undress.

"Excellent show, sir," the man said. "The best in Paris. Come in and have a look for yourself. There's nowhere else you could see it at this price."

I hesitated, then hurriedly paid him his fee and entered the dingy little hole, feeling my way to one of the empty tables. It was no bigger than a smallish living-room. Everything was musty, and decorated as cheaply and tastelessly as possible. A waiter brought me some champagne which I didn't want and which cost an exorbitant price. A loudspeaker blared forth nerve-racking, ear-shattering music. It lasted for ten minutes, while five or six other clients were ushered in – all of them male, and all middle-aged. At the bar counter against the back wall several plump prostitutes were sitting like hens on a perch, cackling and whispering, and consuming large glasses of alcohol. At eleven o'clock the "show" started. Clumsy, vulgar capers; second-hand costumes, probably bought for next to nothing on the fleamarket; a complete lack of rhythm and co-ordination. After about half an hour a greasy master of ceremonies announced the "star" of the performance. The fabulous, spectacular, unique, sexy Lulu – or something to that effect.

A variety of coloured ostrich feathers made their appearance on the stage. And in the middle of the bundle, like the heart of a flower, was Nicolette, with sensual red lips, heavily painted eyelids and a blonde wig. The rest of her item could be predicted: the feathers disappeared one by one until she moved about wearing nothing but a tiny, glittering *cache-sexe*. She didn't dance too badly, although it was nothing remarkable. The light changed monotonously into all the colours of the rainbow. The music grew wilder. She was breathing heavily as if she wasn't used to so much exertion. For the first time I could look at her quite detachedly, impersonally, judging her as nothing but a body: her long arms, her small, firm breasts, pointed upwards as if two bees were perching on them, her slightly angular hips and slim legs. Was it possible that she could really be reduced to this? But if so, what was the source of my melancholy? It was uncalled for, because *she* revealed no trace of shame or embarrassment. On the contrary: her attitude suggested undisguised contempt of that assortment of impotent old men gaping at her; uncompromising rebellion against that smoky little hall; and the absolute liberty of one who knows that she belongs to nobody but herself. And *they* were still believing in the illusion, I thought with bitter amusement: they were adding up her limbs and that which was concealed by the little triangle, determining the measure of its ecstasy. But I – I had already found the solution to her little sum; I knew all too well the coldness of her answer. *Quod erat demonstrandum.*

But why did I get up then, why did I flee when she jumped from her low stage and came dancing to the tables? It was not that I could no longer bear it, or because I was afraid; and certainly not because I wanted to save her any embarrassment. Perhaps it was, I must confess, because I found it impossible that she might know about *me,* and that I would know that she knew.

In the taxi on my way back to where I had left my car, I purposely tried not to think of anything immediately connected with what I had witnessed. The only rather irrelevant question in my mind was: "How much would she get for such a performance?" There was, of course, the possibility that her night would not end with the show. Many of these wretched places specially cater for interested clients afterwards –

But why should I feel concerned about it? She probably enjoyed it. There was nothing between us. The only thing that really mattered was: should it become known that the Ambassador was associating with that type of person, the situation would be even more inflammable than I had anticipated.

And so four evenings had been fruitless. Then it appeared to me that I had been approaching the whole matter from the wrong end: it was not Nicolette who had to be followed, but the Ambassador himself. It would naturally be more dangerous; and it was much more humiliating. Should she find out about my activities, I could still justify myself. Confronted with him it would be impossible.

Yet even my new procedure seemed to lead me nowhere. On the first evening the Ambassador stayed at home. The next evening he attended an official dinner and went home directly afterwards; the third evening he once again went straight back to the avenue Hoche after a visit to the Australian Ambassador.

But late on Sunday afternoon, 18th November, he took the first suspicious step. From where I had been parked on the opposite side of the avenue I saw him leave through the main entrance. Without any hesitation he started walking towards the Place de l'Étoile. I turned the ignition key and slowly followed him until I could see him get into a taxi. Following a nimble taxi-driver through the streets of Paris would be unwise, and probably impossible. I could only hope that my assumption had been correct, and try to reach the rue de Condé as quickly as I could. The traffic was not very heavy, but the street lights were already burning in the falling dusk, making it extremely difficult to see. Once across the Pont de la Concorde it became easier because one could almost blindly follow the bright yellow lights of the boulevard Saint-Germain.

I first went round to see whether her light was on. But the window was dark. That in itself did not prove anything. Neither did the sudden appearance of her light five minutes later. I took in my position on the corner of the rue Saint-Sulpice, leaning against a wall, waiting. Every five minutes I made sure, from the rue de Condé, that her light was still on. It was almost an hour later, just as I was returning from one of these expeditions, when I suddenly saw her approaching from the direction of the boulevard, strolling leisurely, eating *frites* from a greasy paper bag. Had I been watching the wrong window all the time? I quickly darted back to the rue de l'Odéon. Impossible. Would that mean that the Ambassador had all this time been waiting in her room? But how did he get in – supposing it was he – unless he had a key of his own? It seemed that my bit of sleuthing was at last leading to something worth while. But I experienced no particular feeling of pleasure: only a suggestion of nausea when I thought about the possible discovery awaiting me, knowing very well that it would inevitably draw myself into the affair. And I did not want to become involved. Yet I doubt whether there was, at that moment, any choice left. The very knowledge of what was going on would get me entangled. And this knowledge I had to have.

It was almost seven o'clock before the front door of the building was opened. I slipped round the corner and pressed myself against the wall. Yet it was not until they had reached the opposite side of the Carrefour de l'Odéon that I could recognise the Ambassador beyond all doubt, walking next to her carefree girlish figure.

That was more than enough incriminating evidence for my purpose. But I could not leave it at that: I had to make even more sure. It was impossible to venture into such a delicate affair before dispelling every possible shadow of doubt. (And I must emphasise again that at that stage I had no conscious intention of drawing up a report.)

On Friday, 23rd November he visited her again. It was about 8 p.m. Like the previous time I had been waiting on the corner of the rue Saint-Sulpice. It was raining; and this might have contributed to the fact that at a given moment (without having come to anything as clearly formulated as a "decision") I crossed the street and pressed the button at the main entrance. It was a beautiful if somewhat decayed old door, decorated with charming designs which must have been the work of an outstanding wood sculptor: apples, grapes, a faun and a nymph. Once inside in the musty entrance-hall I realised, and accepted, for the first time that I was on my way to her. I mounted the crumbling staircase very slowly, because only every second landing was dimly illuminated by a bare bulb hanging from the ceiling. Besides, the time switch did not function properly so that the light regularly went out when one was less than halfway between two landings. Then one had to feel one's way, groping along the walls with their loose shreds of plaster, until one found another switch. Here and there I stumbled over broken steps; but by that time I knew how to avoid most of these snares.

I must have waited outside her door for at least five minutes. One couldn't hear anything inside. I could feel the skin tighten on my temples and cheeks. (Were they – ?) Then I knocked. There was no answer. I knocked again.

After a while I heard a shuffling. And then, barefoot, and in her underclothes, she appeared on the doorstep. She had closed the middle door behind her. Her hair was hanging loose. She drew in her breath sharply when she recognised me.

"What do you want?"

"I just thought I'd drop in."

"We've seen enough of each other."

"Are you perhaps entertaining – another visitor?"

"No."

"Why can't I come in then?"

"Because I don't want you to."

I suppose I could have forced the door open, but why should

E
51

I? I had already discovered enough. But there was one thing I could not resist: just before I turned away I looked straight into her eyes, and said: "You're playing with fire, Nicolette." She came out behind me as I was going down, and stopped at the railing of her landing. I suspected that she was feeling worried about what I had said, but I did not look up at her, on purpose. Yet I couldn't tell whether I had scored a victory or suffered a defeat.

I went back to my watch-post. And as I had foreseen, the Ambassador left her building very soon afterwards. He remained standing in front of the large door for quite some time, looking up as if he was expecting to see her somewhere above him, then, probably remembering that her window was on the other side of the building, started walking in my direction. (I had stepped back round the corner.) On the Carrefour he stopped again, then hesitated, and changed his direction, walking briskly towards the boulevard Saint-Michel. And there, ten minutes later, I stepped up behind him where he was sitting inside the glass partition of a café terrace, and said:

"Good evening, Mr. Ambassador. I wasn't expecting to find you here."

He was obviously disturbed by my sudden appearance, but he nevertheless invited me to sit down. In the course of the next fifteen minutes, while he was drinking his coffee and I my grog, I asked all my meticulously prepared questions: "Do you often come in this part of the city?" "It's a nasty evening to be outside, isn't it?" Et cetera. I drew immense enjoyment from this game of hide-and-seek. It might not be very "noble" of me to admit it, but at least it is honest; and how much of human activity is truly noble in the final analysis? We are not a noble species. That was the first time in all our close contact that I was holding the whip-hand, and it made me feel strangely elated, and free. Not that he gave the slightest hint of having been caught on the wrong foot. He was too much of a diplomat for that. And to my "innocent" questions he replied very adroitly that he was bent on a systematic exploration of the whole city; and that he enjoyed being outside in rainy weather. ("One gets stifled in the office.") At last we caught a taxi and went back together. After dropping him at the Embassy I asked the driver to take me back to the rue Monsieur-le-Prince where I had parked my car.

And still I did nothing with all the knowledge I had acquired, and which was lying so heavily on my mind. To tell the truth, I found myself caught in a whirlpool where I couldn't get out, however much I wanted to. And less than a week later (on Wednesday night, the 28th) the next sheet of evidence was added to my file. There was a reception at the Embassy that night, given by the Military Attaché. The usual boring sort of chattering round cocktail glasses. But among the guests, suddenly, I recognised: Miss Nicolette Alford. I had never before seen her at any diplomatic reception. That in itself, of course, had no significance. But I was positive that her sudden interest – after she had so often expressed quite bluntly her intense dislike of all official functions – could not be innocent. And where would the Embassy all of a sudden have found her address to send her an invitation after she had always steered clear of such things? I resolved to keep an eye on her. But halfway through the evening I was annexed by the wife of a French general and by the time she finally moved on to her next victim, Nicolette was nowhere to be seen. I looked everywhere, thinking that she might just have disappeared temporarily among the guests. But there was no trace of her. As soon as protocol allowed, I too departed.

The concierge, Lebon, was at his post at the main entrance, slightly ruffled, as usual. (One gets the impression, whenever one sees him, that he has just been in bed with a woman.) I stepped into the street, when suddenly a thought struck me and I turned back to him.

"Have you seen Miss Alford leave, Lebon?"

"Alford?"

I described her briefly.

He gave a knowing smile, suggesting that he knew much more about her than I, and answered that he hadn't noticed her. She could perhaps have left in the company of some of the other guests, but he wasn't sure.

The next morning just before tea he came into my office. I was in no mood for his gossiping. (He knows everything about everybody.)

"Yes, Lebon?" I asked curtly. "What's the matter?"

"You inquired about Miss Alford last night." His small eyes were gleaming behind his glasses.

"What about her?"

"She didn't leave before much later, sir."

"Oh." I made no effort to hide my disappointment.

"Very much later." He leaned over the desk towards me, supporting himself on his hands, and added softly: "It was three o'clock, to be exact."

I immediately started questioning him, but he had nothing in-

53

teresting to add. Not that I needed any more information. "Information," "evidence," "proof" – I had more than enough of everything; too much, as a matter of fact. But enough or too much *for what*? Even at that late moment I still had no definite aim or plan. Until Lebon made his appearance in my office that morning it had been, as I have emphatically pointed out, a collection of impressions as an end in itself. The only difference his added bit of information made, was that I now became very acutely aware of the sheer weight, the burden, the ballast of everything that had come to light. It was no feeling of guilt, merely a state of dejection, of uneasiness, of weariness; and I knew that I could not bear it much longer. I wondered pointedly: what was he aiming at? Where was I moving to? Where, and how, could I get rid of everything?

Under ordinary ("normal") circumstances the incident at the reception of the Doyen of the Diplomatic Corps, held in the Hôtel de Ville on Friday night, 30th November, would have caused a mere ripple on the surface. But happening, as it did, at that specific moment, it proved to be the bottleneck through which the quiet river passed into unmanageable rapids.

It was a miserable day. The city's centuries were resting heavily on her. In the early morning, while I was walking along the pavement towards the Embassy, through the sad and weary fog, an undertaker's bus came past, with little formal rows of mourning people inside. Because of the fog the traffic moved along almost soundlessly, which made everything seem unreal: a macabre journey across the waters of death, with the greyish-black buildings on either side of the street resembling the steep charred banks of the Styx. An inexplicable misère, a cafard, an illness with a thousand names was aching in my breast. In the course of the day my state of mind was aggravated by a hundred minor pinpricks. There was a typist who made a few mistakes in preparing a report for which the Ambassador was waiting, so that I was blamed for it. There was Anna Smith who came downstairs and for almost an hour shared *her* miseries with me. There was the visiting wife of a South African M.P. who took up another hour of my time with a sarcastic tirade about the inefficiency of "certain" officials, which would certainly be brought to the Minister's attention. And added to all this: a ceaseless, gnawing, sinus ache throbbing in my nose and eyes and forehead.

In the afternoon an important file was mislaid and in the process of looking for it I unexpectedly, and unpreparedly, came upon the sheet of paper on which, the very first day, I had jotted

54

down a few particulars in connection with Nicolette's lost passport. There were eighteen months between me and that distant day. And what had I done during those eighteen months? What had I achieved? I was overwhelmed by the futility of the whole affair, of everything. It was as if, for one moment, I could look at myself with merciless objectivity. And what I discovered was a nightmare: a small white creature in a small dark room with nothing but a locked door and a keyhole; and a whole life devoted to staring through that keyhole because in the room itself there is nothing to be seen. But outside only a bedroom is visible, a bed. And the only thing this little creature does, the only thing it could possibly do, is to put a feverish red eye against the keyhole and stare at an endless series of intimate, perverse scenes on the bed, all of them variations of the same original one. The little creature loathes it and is continually shouting all sorts of obscenities at the silent, panting puppets on the bed, but they cannot hear it because no sound comes through the keyhole. And it is impossible to plug the keyhole, for then the little creature would suffocate in its own room. It would like to break open the door, but outside the bedroom it is eternally dark and the little creature is afraid of darkness.

I was aware of an unendurable desire inside me to be with Nicolette; for a moment I even decided that I would go to her immediately after work. But then I analysed my motives and tried to determine, beforehand, the outcome of such a visit – and decided against it. What would I say to her? That I wanted her? She would scoff at me, or ridicule my desire. And, which was more important, I suddenly wondered whether it would be true: *did* I want her? Or did I merely want to hurt her, by assuring her that I "knew everything"? But what about it? She would say: "So what?" and then she would find out how I had discovered it all; and I could well imagine how she would react to this variation on the keyhole theme. Perhaps I would have liked to say in her face: "Now I know what you are. An ordinary little stripteaser in a dingy nightclub." But would that surprise or upset her? And why would I *want* to upset her? And so on. And the only result of all these fretful thoughts was that my headache became worse.

When I left the Embassy at half-past five it was dark already. I came straight home, poured myself a stiff brandy and sat down on a corner of the divan. Stephen Keyter, Third Secretary, budding young diplomat, miserable bloody failure: prosit. There was little traffic outside. It is a quiet street. In this neighbourhood people shut themselves in behind their walls. Floor upon floor, building upon building, block upon block – it suddenly became a terrifying thought – all these similar doors, these similar windows. And God, all those people inside, teeming, squirming, breeding. In Imperial Rome, in long-lost Babylon, there had already been such buildings. And it was still going on, going on: moving and talking and eating and copulating. Generation after generation, sex, sex. And *homo sum* – I refilled my glass and arranged the pillows against the wall so that I could lean back. I was drinking too much, I thought. Those had been Erika's words too – or something similar, anyway. And now she, like her words, was gone; looking for a place where it would be warm. A "pilgrimage" she had called it, cynically. Was there any essential difference between her action and Nicolette's game of ring-a-rosy round the bed? Both boiled down to self-deception, a bit of make-believe in order to keep on moving, keep the circulation going, warding off the final cold, a pathetic dance of incantation to the long dead gods. One away on a little mecca journey; the other, one of Aphrodite's perfunctory hetaerae. (And how long did it go on? Until the tired heart stopped all by itself, or until, some day, one decided to "clean" one's husband's revolver, ignoring one's children?) And in between (or remote, apart?), was I. What about my own little pilgrimage, not towards "eternity" but towards ambassadorial status in twenty years or slightly more? But at least I was living within reasonable, and calculable, limits; I wasn't trying to exorcise anything; I was existing beyond illusion. I didn't know whether that was more hopeless or less than any other way of living. But then, did it really matter?

I put down my empty glass, got up and went to dress for the reception. Had it been possible to find a pretext, however flimsy, I would have stayed away. But since it was impossible, I dressed in the way expected of me, swallowed a few tablets which would make no difference to my headache, entrenched myself in an overcoat and went down to my car.

There were a few hundred people in the imposing hall with the crystal candelabras and the baroque tapestries on the walls. It made the impression of a festive occasion but one soon discovers that all this brilliance is merely a camouflage for collective boredom. The next day the Press would make its customary references to "chicness", "splendour" and "distinguished guests" with photos of the few most obtrusive women and the few most exorbitant dresses; but all this forms part of a lustre which is visible from the outside only. Not that it has no strange fascination of its own, sometimes. It is a challenge to be as adroit at the game as possible; it is a ballet of gestures, words and relationships. At times its effect becomes almost narcotic, a cosy shelter. Few other situations can impress one so deeply with a realisation of being delicately integrated with a huge organism, with an existence in which all meaning is derived from the whole. It becomes more than a denial of individuality: it utterly *dissolves* individuality, discards it, in favour of a form of symbiosis from which all "lower passions" are miraculously excluded. But on that evening it only irritated me, as a result of either the morose self-analysis that had preceded it, or the few neat brandies. I executed the necessary, correct actions and even contributed to a few conversations, but I felt isolated from the whole. Unfortunately there was no way out of my misery: I had to stay there until the Ambassador left. And since it was the first important gathering of all diplomats in Paris after the trouble in South Africa four weeks before, he could be expected to avail himself of the opportunity to explain to as many people as possible the "real state of affairs". Fortunately I managed to steer clear of similar conversations during the first half of the evening. But suddenly a conceited young secretary of the Indian Embassy, with whom I had often argued for hours on end, said something like: "This is only the beginning for the South Africans." Then he turned round superciliously as if he had not been aware of my presence until that moment, and added sweetly: "Or doesn't our friend Mr. Keyter agree?"

On any other evening I would have either tactfully stepped out of the situation or discussed the matter with professional patience and impartiality. But on that particular night I was in no mood for this hypocritical little game.

"I don't care a damn what you think," I said curtly. "Do you think your prejudiced opinion could make any difference to the matter?"

He reacted with imperturbable correctness. After that initial outburst I also stayed within the bounds of courtesy; but I suppose I spoke slightly louder and more excitedly than I should have. And I forgot, temporarily, that it was my duty as the youngest member of the staff (Harrington being away on home leave) to attend to the Ambassador, should he require anything.

So I was caught unawares when His Excellency suddenly appeared next to me, nodded courteously but impersonally to the other people in the group, and very calmly said: "I am sorry to interrupt, Keyter, but I just remembered that there may be a telegram tonight in connection with the Prime Minister's statement in Cape Town. Could you please go to the Embassy and hold the fort until I come?" He spoke in English so that the bystanders who were either curious or ill-mannered enough to listen would understand what he said. But neither they nor I could have any doubt as to what the true reason for his intervention had been. What His Excellency really meant was: "Please remove yourself from here as soon as possible."

I tried not to bat an eyelid and answered: "Certainly, Mr. Ambassador," said good-night to the circle of younger diplomats and departed as unobtrusively as possible.

The strange thing about it all was that I felt no anger on my way back to the Embassy. There was literally no single thought in my mind. And even while for three long fruitless hours I sat waiting in my office I was conscious of no resentment. Although I must admit that I was trying on purpose to refrain from thinking.

Therefore I could greet him almost with detachment when he arrived very late that evening and asked, apparently friendly: "No telegram?"

"No, Mr. Ambassador." My eyes did not move away from his.

"I suppose you realise that you were guilty of most unprofessional conduct tonight."

I made no answer.

"I have no idea of what you actually said," he went on. "I trust you had enough responsibility not to say anything which might harm the delegation. But your mere manner of speaking was something I will not tolerate again."

"I am sorry, Mr. Ambassador," I said, because that was what was expected of me.

"Under normal circumstances your behaviour would warrant a report to Headquarters." His grey eyes were unyielding. "I shall not do so this time. But in future you must realise that your conduct will be very closely watched."

That was the end of the interview, except for the words he added at the front door: "I have a very high estimation of your abilities, Keyter. If it hadn't been for that I would not have taken such a serious view of what happened tonight."

A few minutes later I was back in my own apartment. I made no effort to rationalise the matter. And yet, quite illogically, I knew: this was the point towards everything had been moving. Perhaps it was a good thing that it had been reached. It could not go on drifting much longer.

Had I started on my report that night, or even the following day, formally accusing the Ambassador of misconduct, it would have been impossible to judge properly and without resentment. But now I have had enough time to reflect and to sort everything out. I can see it all with almost terrifying clarity. And yesterday there arrived a telegram from the Minister of Foreign Affairs instructing that earlier, tentative negotiations with the French Government in connection with the purchase of arms must be intensified. The recent troubles in South Africa will naturally be a complicating factor in the matter. And should the Ambassador's personal conduct, at this stage, cast any reflection on his integrity, everything could end in failure. That is the crux of the matter. That, and the necessity of bringing an end to the hypocrisy of his double life.

There is nothing else I can or dare do. I considered discussing the matter with Masters, but I could tell beforehand what the outcome would be: either everything would be hushed up and a sword suspended above my future, or he will act on his own initiative and leave me in the dark. That is something I could not face. It is the first time in my life that I have an opportunity like this.

The Apostle could rely on faith, hope and love to illuminate the darkness of his night. I have no faith in faith, and little hope of hope. And of love I seem to know nothing. I have one thing: my report. I have failed in everything else. But not in this.

CHRONICLE

1

It was at the end of an official day that she came to him.

From all corners of Europe, it seemed, and from the distant country in the south, invisible rays were converging on that solid stinkwood desk, that telephone, that memorandum block, that firm, neat hand. The previous day, 4th November, had brought the news of the unexpected turn in the Cape Town strike. The Hellschreiber's reports were, necessarily, short, cursory, and often cryptic. The evening papers splashed it on their front pages, exactly like the previous occasion in 1960, sensationally illustrated with photos of the strike leaders and the police cordon round the township. The situation was said to be "under control", but as far as the Press was concerned, it was still only the beginning. There were references to "imminent clash", "blood bath", "racialism", "second Sharpeville".

Special representatives of all the leading French papers were instructed to leave for South Africa within the shortest possible time. All these journalists had to be closely screened before visas could be issued to them. Because of the delicacy of the situation every case had to be investigated by the Ambassador personally before recommendations could be made to the Department of Internal Affairs in Pretoria. Even before the Embassy was opened to the public on the morning of the 5th representatives of right and leftist groups had already gathered in front of the main entrance: the leftists to protest, the rights to offer their services and sympathy. There were rumours of a full-scale demonstration by students from African countries in the avenue Hoche that afternoon. The police had to be contacted beforehand to arrange for a protective cordon round the block.

Urgent cablegrams had to be composed for transmission to London and Pretoria: the first in connection with uniformity of procedure, the latter an urgent request for full particulars and instructions. For twenty-four hours after the beginning of the strike the South African Government was still too busy studying the situation to send any official interpretation to foreign missions. In the course of that day there were a visit from a representative of the French Department of Foreign Affairs; a personal inquiry from the British Ambassador; telegrams from Rome and The Hague; deputations from firms with considerable investments in South Africa. Each one insisted on the importance of his business. Each required personal reassurance.

The Ambassador showed no outward signs of irritation or uncertainty. He did all his work systematically, gave audience to all his numerous visitors, calmed the nervousness or belligerence of others. He had the advantage of thirty years' experience in the Service, which enabled him to discard all superficialities in grasping the essence of matters and in formulating his opinions. Yet it was impossible to rely purely on intuition for an indeterminable period. Moreover, he was not the type of person to be satisfied with warding off attacks: he believed in positive, convincing action. But such action was dependent on the full facts of the situation. This had become an even more urgent necessity since the announcement of the telegrams sent by the strike leaders to Afro-Asian representatives at U.N.O.

Shortly after lunch the first telegram arrived. It was decoded without delay and brought to him. Obviously it was the Minister's own work, judging from the pompousness of the message: something the Ambassador had never been able to stomach so that he had often, and in no uncertain terms, expressed the opinion that the Minister needed some sound diplomatic training; on a few occasions it had already resulted in some tension between them. The telegram summarised the Minister's interpretation of the events and suggested some general lines of action to be adopted by the heads of delegations abroad.

The second telegram reached the Embassy at half past three. It was short and to the point (drawn up by the Minister's Secretary): *Immediately request interview with French Foreign Minister in effort to keep Afro-Asian proposal out of Security Council.* Half an hour later, after the Ambassador had already instructed Masters to make an appointment with the French Minister, the third telegram was delivered, containing extensive instructions in connection with the interview that was on hand. The Ambassador withdrew into his office and immediately set to work on a memorandum for the interview.

Even though the Afro-Asian reaction might have been anticipated from the very beginning, it added considerable danger to an already dangerous affair. Should these countries succeed with their drastic resolution in the Council – and the circumstances seemed to favour such a result – the consequences could be fatal.

At seven o'clock, while the Ambassador was still working on his memorandum, the First Secretary, Masters, entered with a telegram from London which had just been decoded:

Trafalgar Square flooded by demonstrators. Public opinion so roused that British P.M. could not conceivably weaken tottering party by supporting South Africa at U.N.O. Cable from Washington announces that State Secretary tactfully refused our Embassy's first effort to arrange interview.

For a moment the Ambassador brooded over the transcript, then looked up at Masters with the shadow of a smile on his face. "In other words – ?" he said.

The Secretary nodded anxiously. "In other words, everything depends upon your visit to the Quai d'Orsay tomorrow."

The Ambassador made no answer. He got up and locked away his documents. "I don't think there will be any more messages tonight, Masters," he said, dropping his keys into his pocket. "You may as well go home."

They went downstairs together. At the entrance to the official residence Masters said good-bye and left. The Ambassador went inside for dinner.

But before eight o'clock he was back in his office in the dark, desolate Embassy, working out the details of the next day's interview. Nothing could be left to chance. And in spite of the deep sense of futility he had to overcome, because there seemed to be so little chance of success, he was conscious, sitting there at his desk, working slowly and with unrelenting concentration, of a feeling almost of power, of indispensability. It was a form of ecstasy, but muted ecstasy, canalised ingenuously into argument after argument, paragraph after paragraph. It was a test, a challenge: himself against all the world – an almost heroic struggle, alone in his isolated, illuminated office in that dark building. Each word that was formed in black letters on the white paper under his hand was a tiny act of creation against nothingness and meaninglessness. He was not thinking of his country or his people while he sat there working, nor of an almost fictitious Minister in Pretoria. These things so soon faded into abstractions, were so soon reduced to captions in newspapers, in unreal Hellschreiber messages that made their appearance out of the invisible ether, in esoteric telegrams decoded in good faith without any possibility of proving their authenticity; "government", "country", "nation" so soon became components of a god manifesting himself in official instructions which could neither be traced back to any origin, nor be used as evidence of its existence. And he found it impossible to react to such a fiction – except in so much as all reactions tended to be come reflexive. What he did was done because he could not conceive of any other form of existence, because that was his only way of self-expression, and of self-realisation.

He was oblivious of the passing time. It could have been anywhere between ten o'clock and midnight when he heard the light sound outside his office. He looked up, annoyed. Who would visit him at that time of the night? One of his staff? That was rather improbable. Lebon? But the concierge never set foot in his office unless he was expressly summoned, and even then he would come grudgingly. For a moment he felt anxiety. But he had too much confidence in himself to yield to it. He shut away his memorandum in a drawer and leant back against the padded back of his high, heavy chair, closing his eyes, tired. It had been a long day, and he had been in the centre of everything. Now he was only conscious of a vague, throbbing headache and burning eyes.

Then the door moved. He opened his eyes but made no other movement.

And out of the dark corridor she suddenly made her appearance, blinking her eyes in the light: the strange girl with the loose, ruffled, wet, blonde hair, her clothes dripping wet, her hands – slender hands with short nails, like a boy's – pale against the lapel of her expensive, wet, inadequate overcoat.

When she saw him, she quickly wiped the loose strands of hair from her forehead and eyes and said: "You must take me home, please."

He got up courteously, as was his habit, but he did not reply; he seemed to be waiting for an explanation.

"I know you're terribly busy," she continued. "But I was – with a friend on the other side of the Porte Maillot, and he threw me out, and I have no money to go home."

"Where do you live?"

"Rue de Condé." She must have noticed his questioning eyes, for she quickly added: "In the Latin Quarter, near the Odéon."

"I see. It's quite a distance."

"When the weather's fine –" She shrugged her thin shoulders, her teeth lightly chatterng. "But now it's raining."

"Yes, I see." In spite of himself, there was a tiny smile round his mouth, because of her unexpected, incongruous presence in his busy, important world.

"It doesn't usually form part of my duties," he said seriously, but his eyes were amused.

"I'm not asking for any favour!" she answered angrily. "I'll pay you back – later." Her lips twitched cynically. "Or tonight, if you insist." For a moment he was unaware of the hidden meaning in her words, because it was so entirely unexpected. Her cold fingers were already touching the buttons and the much too small buttonholes of her wet coat. She glanced at him. For a moment neither of them moved on the thick, expensive carpet. Behind her he could see the darkness hovering in the passage. She tried to wring loose the first button.

"Don't!" he said laconically.

Her hands were unmoving again. With a shock he realised how her wet clothes were clinging to her.

"Come," he said calmly, with an effort. "We shall find you a taxi."

She shook back her light hair with a quick, decisive movement, and went out into the darkness, ahead of him.

"And who is your heartless friend?" he asked, trying to sound playful, less depressed.

"Why do you want to know?" There was no resentment in her voice: it was a mere question.

"You need not tell me if you don't want to. Actually I suppose it was a stupid question. There are five million Frenchmen in Paris."

"He's not French." When they reached the reading-room at the bottom of the stairs, dimly illuminated by a single light, she added: "Stephen Keyter."

"I see." His voice was still calm and unwavering, but his next words revealed the change inside him: "If you'll wait in the reading-room I shall pull out the car."

"But –"

"It's safer and cheaper than a taxi." He even managed to smile. She sat down on the arm of an upholstered chair. He went out to Lebon's quarters, his head bent to ward off the rain. The concierge was in his kitchen, reading.

"Please open the front door, Lebon," he said. "I am going out in my car."

"Yes, sir." Lebon was the only person who ever called him "Sir", instead of "Mr. Ambassador".

While the concierge was unbolting the large door the Ambassador pulled out the car. As soon as the concierge had disappeared downstairs again he opened the door for the wet girl; she got in with sophisticated gracefulness, pulling down her dress meticulously to cover her knees. They reversed into the narrow side-lane outside, waited for an opening in the traffic and then steered to the opposite side of the avenue Hoche.

F   67

"You'll have to show me the way," said the Ambassador, almost kindly. "I am not quite sure that I know it."

She nodded. Alternating segments of light and shade slid across her face. There was something about her which touched almost forgotten memories in him: an unconscious gesture, a little curl in the corner of her mouth, something indeterminable. It worried him. But she was looking straight ahead, apparently quite unaware of his searching eyes.

"I hope Keyter didn't cause you any embarrassment," he said when they moved into the Champs-Elysées from the Place de l'Étoile. "I'll certainly give him a talking to."

"Why?" she asked. "All men are like that. Weren't you?" She was looking at him now, leisurely studying his face.

"Perhaps," he answered, his expression inscrutable, wisely refraining from any further remarks.

At the Place de la Concorde she forgot to show him the way and they had already reached the Tuilerie Gardens when she suddenly called out: "Stop!"

He slammed the brakes. There was an angry burst of hooting behind him and a car came flashing past, missing them by inches.

"Must we turn back?" he asked.

"No. We can go stright on. At the Place du Châtelet you could turn right and drive across the island."

"You seem to know the city very well."

"I've been here long enough."

"Alone?"

"I'm over twenty-one." She said it with a hint of bravado which made him smile.

The wipers were buzzing monotonously, sweeping away the raindrops. The sound became an almost acute presence while they had to wait for the traffic lights opposite the Pont du Caroussel, as if both of them were trying to find something irrelevant on which to concentrate. What was there to talk about, after all? There were so many years and worlds dividing them.

When the lights changed to green, he said: "Things are looking bad in South Africa."

"Why?"

"Don't you know about the strike?" He glanced at her sharply.

"No."

"But all the papers – "

"I don't read newspapers. Besides: does it really matter? We aren't there now."

"I'm afraid I cannot shrug it off as easily as all that," he said sternly, yet not without amusement.

"Of course," she admitted. "I suppose such things matter for you."

He tried to judge the meaning of her words, wondering why she had said them almost as if she felt sorry for him. But the only thing he could find in her was her neutral coolness which belied the suggestion of naïvety he had so often sensed in her remarks.

"Turn right here," she reminded him – in time.

The river was a lazy, oily movement in the darkness somewhere below the lights on the bridge. Leaning against a lamp post, surrounded by a thin, glowing net of rain, a woman stood looking into the night.

"Tomorrow, or the day after, her body will be fished from the river," said the strange girl next to him. Her hands were restless in her lap.

"What makes you think so?"

"It's the river that does it to one, especially when it's dark. She is much too alone there. And it's raining."

"You're too young to be so morbid," he soothed her – glancing, however into his rearview mirror to catch sight of the woman again. But she had disappeared in the dark rain beyond the head-lights following them. "How do you know that she's not merely waiting for somebody?"

"You don't know Paris very well, do you?"

That was true. Immediately after his arrival, a year before, he had spent a week on daily trips through the city with Masters, visiting all the major monuments and attractions, trying to form a general idea of the whole. But, with the exception of a few Sunday afternoons in the Louvre, there had been very little time for that since so that, apart from certain set routes to other Embassies he knew very little of the city. It was confined to a continuous low noise behind buildings, an awareness of people and traffic, and – sometimes – a view of the Eiffel Tower's tentacles of light moving in the night's dark sky.

They had to wait for another set of lights on the opposite side of the Pont Saint-Michel. Ahead of them, like a broad channel, stretched the endless, wet, illuminated boulevard. He knew it by sight. But on either side there was only a vague suggestion of hundreds of streets and alleys, straight or crooked, bewildered, caught among the high buildings, a new Court of Miracles of which he knew nothing. On one of the trips with Masters he had

69

briefly visited the Quarter, but now it was just a confused memory; moreover his visit had taken place in bright autumn sun. Now it was night, and almost frightening, with all the jumbled lines of light reflected, upside down, in the shimmering streets. And yet this was her world, these very streets where he felt so ill at ease. For the first time since his arrival in Paris he experienced the city as something strange, something with its own uncontrollable existence beyond the confines of his daily horizon.

And while his own assurance dwindled, hers was growing. She was talking more easily and freely than before, she was less elusive, she revealed less cynicism.

"You are cold," he said once, when his eyes caught her unawares.

"It doesn't matter. I like the cold. You must turn here. No, it's a one-way. Try the next street." Her words became more and more effortless, giving birth to themselves: "It's a pity we don't have more snow in Paris. Last year there wasn't a single flake. But the first year I was here it started early in December. I can remember one afternoon when I was sitting on a bench in the Luxembourg Gardens – it was quite late already, just before the gates were closed. It wasn't in the opening in the middle – you know, where the pond is – but among the trees. They were pitch-black, with white lines of snow on all the branches, clean, clear lines, just like Japanese drawings on rice paper. I was sitting there without moving, with the snow quietly sifting down on my hair and my lap, until I was all white, I almost forgot that I was there. And an old clochard came to sit next to me – I doubt whether he'd even noticed me, I was sitting so quietly – and he opened a canvas bag and took out a bottle of wine. Red wine, cheap wine, heavy and dark red, beautiful in the snow. He pressed off the cork with his thumb and started drinking with slow, long gulps, breathing little white clouds. And I suddenly felt an unbearable desire to drink with him, and I asked him whether he would mind if I took a few gulps from his bottle. I think he got quite a fright when he noticed that there was somebody sitting next to him. He only said: *"Salope!"* and went on drinking. It was as if he was having Mass all by himself while the whole world, and he, and I, were getting whiter and whiter. And then I left and went to a bistro in the rue Vavin, and there I stood at the counter and drank my own glass of cheap, red, heavy wine, but it was different. And when I came outside again, the gates were closed and I had to walk right round to get back to where I lived. The snow was no longer falling, and the world looked different, dark and unfriendly, and I was feeling like the poor man who was thrown out because he had no wedding garment, so that he had to lie outside in the dark, whimpering and gnashing his teeth. It must be terrible: always being outside in the dark, whimpering and gnashing one's teeth. We've gone too far now. You'll have to turn here."

They swerved into dark, narrow sidestreets. She seemed to know every turning; but she evidently did not take one-way streets into account, so that they had to make impossible detours. But nothing troubled her serenity.

"I suppose it seems silly," she said after a while – and he could only guess that she was referring to what she had said earlier. "But I think what really frightened me was that ever since I was very small I've always had one particular nightmare: I dream I'm standing outside a large garden or a dark building, with all the gates and doors closed, so that I have to go on walking round and round it, crying, without ever finding a place where I could enter. Now you can follow the rue Saint-Sulpice as far as the Carrefour de l'Odéon. Look how it's raining! It's getting worse, I think. Do you think it means anything if one keeps on dreaming the same thing over and over again?"

"They probably tried to frighten you with that story when you were a child," he said soothingly.

She was staring in front of her, pensive. Then she asked: "Did you know they always use white wine for Mass, and not red? I wonder why?"

"Why would that bother you?"

"I think it's very important that it should be red. After all, it is changed into blood. Is it really?" She began to recite monotonously to herself: "*Da nobis per huius aquae et vini mysterium* – I don't know the rest. But it sounds beautiful. Don't you think so? *Per huius aquae et vini mysterium* –"

"Are you a Catholic?" he asked, surprised.

"No!" she answered quickly. "Here we are. It's my door over there, the one with the woodcutting." She opened the car door.

"You can't go across the street in this rain," he said sternly. "You'll catch a cold. Take my jacket."

"It's not necessary."

"Take it." He resolutely placed it round her shoulders, and opened his door.

"Don't," she said. "Why should both of us get wet?" But she lingered for a moment, then jumped out, quickly took off her shoes and darted across the slippery street, barefoot, with his jacket over her head. At the entrace she pressed the latch button,

71

leaned against the heavy door with her whole body to force it open, then turned round to him, shouted "Thank you!" and waved an impulsive, playful kiss. The door closed behind her with a heavy bang.

2

With a wry little smile the Ambassador remained outside in the car for a few minutes, watching the windows of the façade above the door. But no light went on.

Then he shifted the gear-lever into position and carefully started to find his way back. More than once he ended up against one-way streets or cul-de-sacs, but finally he reached a broad traffic stream along the left bank of the Seine, which he followed until he could cross the river with a bridge that looked vaguely familiar.

And with that, he thought, the little episode, the little intermezzo in his busy day, had come to an end. There was not even a sign that it had ever taken place. What had it been to him? Some relaxation, perhaps; and, undoubtedly, a change from the day's extraordinary bustle. Nothing more. And yet he was aware of a faint echo lingering in his mind, an ancient memory he could not trace. And all the time he had the impression that she was no stranger, really – although he did not even know her name. (And she had taken his jacket with her –!)

He must have been very near the Trocadéro when he suddenly found a name for his vague, uneasy memory:

Gillian.

And now that he had found it, he could not understand what resemblance there was between her and that night's stranger. Gillian had been dark. Gillian had been shorter. He could think of a hundred differences separating them – much to his surprise, because there were so many years between him and that past to which Gillian had belonged. It was the first time in all those years that he had recalled anything specific about her, although it had inevitably happened (less and less frequently, though) that he would unexpectedly recognise a swinging dress in a crowd, or a laugh, or the way in which a girl stopped in front of a shop mirror to touch her hair: absurd little nothings which would cause him to know, or wonder, suddenly: *Gillian* – ? But it had never been more than these fleeting moments. He had never dared allow it to be more. He had too consciously shut it out of his mind until, at last, it stayed away by itself.

72

But now it had returned: that distant Cape Town night, tired with old wind, the streets desolate, the mountain a heavy, inert mass, the sea an invisible threat in the dark. He was on his way back to his flat, it was late, almost midnight; and he was in a hurry because he felt exhausted. Suddenly, in one of the higher streets, a nonchalant shadow started moving from a dark pavement straight across his way, driven on by the wind, bent sideways by a heavy trunk. His brakes screeched among the silent buildings; fortunately there was no other traffic at that hour. When he came to a standstill almost on the right hand side of the street, and furiously turned down his window, the shadow was caught in his headlights and transformed into a woman. A girl, rather, with windswept hair and a large overcoat.

She stood panic-stricken next to her huge trunk.

"I – I'm sorry. I honestly didn't hear the car –"

He got out. There was something defensive in her attitude when he approached her, but he ignored it. Afterwards he realised that she had obviously been crying shortly before, and he decided that that must have been the reason for her antagonism.

"Where on earth are you going this time of the night?" he asked, still a bit shaky after the shock. "Aren't you afraid alone?"

She shrugged. Her hair kept on flowing, blowing in the wind.

He offered her a lift. She shook her head violently. But he paid no attention to her, bent over and picked up the trunk. For a moment it seemed as if she would resist, then she resigned herself to the inevitable and followed him to the car.

"Perhaps you could drop me at the station –"

"Right. Get in." At that moment it did not strike him as unusual.

They drove on in silence. She was sitting in a tight little bundle against the door on her side, as far away from him as possible, sucking a few strands of hair. Once or twice he looked in her direction, but he couldn't make up his mind and turned his head away again without saying a word.

It was only after he had dropped her and her trunk at the station and noticed the suspicious stare of a railway constable that he asked her: "On what train are you leaving at this time of the night?"

"I can wait here until tomorrow."

"But where are you *going?*" He felt anger stirring inside him, thinking of the important case he had to defend the next morning. (At that time he was an attorney.) He needed a good rest.

"I'm leaving," she answered. "Does it matter where to? I just want to get away."

"Do your people know about it?" he insisted, realising how very young she was.

"My father died yesterday."

He was quite put off by this matter-of-fact statement. "I'm sorry," he mumbled. "I didn't realise –" Then he noticed that she wasn't even listening to him.

"Could you find me a place to stay then?" she interrupted his apologies.

"I'll try. Come, get in again."

But the hotels were dark and nobody wanted to open.

"Have you really got nowhere to go?" he asked in despair when his third effort proved useless.

"I don't want to be at home alone."

"I didn't mean to –" He was groping for words that would soothe her. "I'm terribly sorry. I realise how miserable you must be feeling."

"Oh for God's sake stop it!" she flared up. "Have you ever thought of the possibility that I could be *glad* that he died?"

He did not attempt an answer. He tried another hotel. There was no reaction to his ringing.

"Couldn't you give me a bed for tonight?" she asked, exhausted and irritated. "I don't take up so much space."

He hesitated.

He could see the cynical expression in her eyes. "You're afraid," she accused him coolly. "Of course, I suppose it's 'not done'." And then, almost with disgust: "My God, I'm not asking you to sleep with me!"

She pushed open the door and tried to get out. He quickly made up his mind. He went over to her side and said: "Get in."

"I didn't ask you for a lift. It was you who insisted."

He kept calm, but he almost forcibly helped her back into the car. She wrenched herself free from his hands and started to cry; but she did not resist when he closed the door.

And while she was lying back against the seat, sobbing unrestrainedly, he swung the car round to Sea Point and took her to his flat. There was nothing he could give her, except a cup of strong black coffee. She took it in her small cupped hands and emptied it slowly without looking up at him once. Then she pressed back her dark hair with an irritated, tired gesture, wiped her eyes with her hands, got up and asked politely: "Where can I sleep?"

He gave up his bed for her and went to sleep on the couch in the living-room. Or rather: he lay down, for he could not sleep; and

74

for many hours he lay staring into the darkness listening to her occasional movements in the bedroom next door. Once he heard her sigh. And he kept on wondering about her, and about where she had come from, about her smouldering eyes and her quick reactions, about her frailness, about her future – and about theirs.

For he had foreseen correctly: it had been no mere chance meeting which would end the next morning. That was only the beginning of a storm which, eventually, would break down all his fixities, all his certainties. It was the first, the *only*, reckless deed of his entire exemplary life.

He reached the Place de l'Étoile and went round to the avenue Hoche.

His momentary confusion was past. There could not possibly be any consequences of this night's episode. And Gillian's return to his thoughts could, at the utmost, cause a short period of anxiety and then pass. He was no longer twenty-five, but fifty-six; no longer a young attorney, but an Ambassador: and he was engaged in important work. This night's strange girl was only one of the hundred thousand or more of her like in Paris. In herself, she was of no importance; even among others of her generation she might be in no way memorable. And it would be even more so in *his* life of important people, important decisions, important circles within circles.

Immediately after the B.B.C. building he stopped in front of the Embassy and went to press the bell. He heard hasty shuffling footsteps, and then Lebon was standing in the doorway with his creased jacket, the fine purple veins around his eyes and nose outlined mercilessly by the sharp light.

3

The Ambassador left his car in the courtyard and while the concierge drove it into the garage and locked up for the night, he hurried back to the office building, shivering without his jacket. At two o'clock the light was still shining from his window across the delicate web of rain outside. Gradually all noises faded from his immediate surroundings, but he remained conscious of a dull sound board in the background: like an ocean, but more urgent. And it disturbed his concentration, because he had never been aware of it before. It was a consciousness not only of sound, but of the light and darkness of the entire city, of alleys and avenues, brilliant étalages and sad crumbled walls, of strangers and natives, of people like himself – and people like the young child who had appeared unasked from the anonymous mass; and he was aware, above all, of the memory she had stirred up in him, the way in which a ripple in a pool would cause a bubble to rise upwards from a swaying root or leaf. One who slept; and one who – was asleep. It was time he, too, went to bed. There was an ache behind his tired eyes. He got up, meticulously arranged his papers on the desk, locked up the others, put off the light and went slowly downstairs in the darkness. He locked the front door behind him, stepped out in the light drizzle and quickly crossed the courtyard to the official residence.

Inside it was large and silent. The servants had gone to bed long ago. On his way to the staircase he passed formal arched doorways, antique wall ornaments, and the dull glimmering of candelabras surrounded by darkness. When he reached the top he stood still for a moment as if he was wondering: Erika –? But then he realised: Erika was far away, she was in Italy. Unsmiling, he proceeded to his room. Erika would be far away even if she had been here. Why should he find the silence so disturbing tonight? She had had her separate bedroom for many years, as he had his. He could not even remember exactly how it had happened the first time. In the end an incident like that lost all its intrinsic value and became merely another obvious step in a journey that had no remembered beginning. First there would be the experience of the bed as a habit, followed by an hour's lying awake with the inevitable question: Why? Wasn't the whole business really very ordinary, and, perhaps, slightly humiliating? Then, gradually, the tempo would slack down and be reduced to a friendly cohabitation without the sordidness of sex: the senseless little ritual of preparation, spasm, bathroom, and sleep. It would be a consolation if he could convince himself that it had been different once, perhaps before Annette's birth. But it was hardly more than formal assurance. Could it be that their marriage had become a habit even before it had been consummated, for the simple reason that it had always been taken for granted by everybody that they would choose each other? That was what had been expected of them. It would satisfy their parents. It could promote the Afrikaner cause. His father: Afrikaans school principal in Johannesburg, energetic cultural leader in a time before concepts like "language" and "nation" had become mere slogans. Hers: one of the first among his people to force himself into the foreground of industrial development. What could be more obvious than that this particular boy and this girl had been "meant" for each other? It was "divine providence" as much as was the future of the nation.

The only thing that had ever come between them and this ideal, had been Gillian. But Erika, and her parents, and his, had never even known about her. Erika might have suspected it. How else would she have explained his sudden departure to Europe only six months before their planned wedding? (Not that the date had ever been consciously chosen; that, also, had been "destiny".) He had been away for eighteen months; he had *lived* for eighteen months. And then he had returned, to take up, once again, all the ties he had so readily shaken off, to marry Erika, and join the Diplomatic Corps.

And now, at last, he was here, in Paris. This was the summit. He had fulfilled everybody's expectations: his relatives', his Government's, Erika's, and even his own.

But, as usual, there was no time to abandon himself to the free flow of his thoughts. The few hours of sleep ahead of him were much too precious. He undressed, got into the bed, and put off the light. While he was gradually submerged by sleep, he watched a lazy interplay of water images. The white circle of light on his desk. A face framed in blonde hair, with raindrops on the cheeks – but he could not recognise it because it continually changed into other faces, until it faded away. A garden – it was like a memory, but not his own – and somebody wandering round and round it in the dark. A station scene. A city; cities; people –

At six o'clock he woke up. Outside it was still dark, but it was a darkness alive with sound and movement. He turned on the light, took a bath, shaved, dressed and went outside. It was still overcast but the rain had stopped. His footsteps echoed from the walls of the courtyard while he walked to the office building. For a moment he stood still to enjoy the cool darkness; then he unlocked the front door, went up to his office and started arranging his papers in the impersonal light. At eight o'clock he went down for breakfast. Immediately afterwards, before the staff arrived, he was back at his desk, working on the documents he had put aside the previous day while the memorandum had been drawn up.

Anna Smith was the first to arrive. Still wearing her coat and hat she appeared in his doorway, irritatingly apologetic, to ask whether there had been any new reports. He reassured her.

"I get so upset when I see what people are saying about our country, Mr. Ambassador. If only one could *do* something – "

He nodded formally and asked: "Is there anything else, Mrs. Smith?"

"Actually there is, Mr. Ambassador. But I don't know whether

I should bother you with it. You see, it's a rather – difficult matter. But I *do* think you ought to know."

"Well?" he asked patiently.

"It's one of the messengers, Mr. Ambassador. The younger one who was appointed last month. Pierre."

"Wouldn't it be better to discuss matters concerning the staff with Mr. Masters, Mrs. Smith?" he asked politely.

"Yes, Mr. Ambassador. But it's not an ordinary matter. It's rather difficult to explain. You see, I heard that Pierre – well, how shall I put it? – that he – that's what I *heard* anyway – with *men*, you understand, Mr. Ambassador? Unlike other boys who go out with girls. I mean – "

"Do you think it affects his work as a messenger?" he asked calmly.

"Oh no, not at all, it's just –"

"In other words, you have no complaint about his work?"

"No, Mr. Ambassador."

He folded his hands on the desk. "In that case, Mrs. Smith, I suppose we should allow him to lead the sort of private life he prefers, don't you think so?"

She blushed. "Of course," she said precipitately. "Please, Mr. Ambassador, I don't want you to think that – "

"I can assure you that I am not thinking that at all, Mrs. Smith."

She went out to the Registry Department. He resumed his own work. At five past nine, according to his custom, he went downstairs to make sure that nobody was late for work. At the very moment when he reached the reading-room on his way to the basement offices, Keyter opened the front door, hesitated, mumbled a quick good-morning and an apology – but from the expression in the dark eyes burning in his thin face it was evident that he did not mean a word of what he said.

The Ambassador turned round and went upstairs again, aware of Keyter's stare following him. Ambition, he thought. That in itself could be commendable. But in Keyter it was something unhealthy: he had too much of it; it could become fanaticism. There was only one remedy: it had to be forced into a clearly defined channel and be continually tempered. That was the only way to become a diplomat; he knew that from his own experience. Keyter often reminded him of his youth. But he had been more calculated, more systematic, more consistent, realising that the fulfilment of the smallest duties eventually added up to success. Keyter had more impulsiveness, a sort of restlessness which apparently found no outlet. He should find himself a good, doting wife. This thought suddenly reminded the Ambassador of his strange guest the previous night. Keyter had thrown her out, she had told him. He frowned. Could it be that the Third Secretary was too extravagent in his ways? It was conceivable that he would lead either an ascetic or a debauched life.

He set to work again, summoning the First Secretary for more particulars concerning negotiations with the French Ministry of Aviation, knowing that, as usual, Masters would know every-thing by heart. If only the man could handle large wholes the way he dealt with intricate details he would have a brilliant diplomatic career ahead of him.

At ten minutes to eleven he got up; and almost as if he was embarking on just another of his day's numerous ordinary duties, he put his memorandum in an attaché case and went downstairs to where the chauffeur, Farnham, had already parked the official car. Farnham touched his cap when the Ambassador got in and received a short "Good morning" for an answer. Nothing else was exchanged between them on their way to the Quai d'Orsay. When they reached the Ministry of Foreign Affairs, the Ambassador ordered laconically: "Please wait here." Then he went up the broad steps to the front door.

The interview started formally, an almost purely intellectual action. The Minister, strictly neutral, sat listening, his cheekbone supported by an immaculate hand with a narrow golden ring on one finger; his eyes were expressionless.

At last he calmly reminded the Ambassador of France's considerable international responsibilities which might have more importance than matters which did not directly concern the Government.

That marked the transition to the more subtle game: references to relations and actions in the past and the implications of these matters for the future; and finally, as had so often happened before, the Ambassador was required to provide a delicate exposition of policy, of race relations, of motives and goals. When the interview was closed there was no perceptible hint of any positive result. Except for a thin smile round the Minister's mouth and a cryptic good-bye: "I appreciate your exposition. I should like to get in touch with you again."

But this in itself suggested a possibility of success, and the Ambassador knew exactly how to react to such nuances. When he got back into the black Austin his face was almost completely relaxed.

Shortly after his return to the office, Koos Joubert made his appearance with a few letters. But without much beating about the bush he stated the real cause for his visit: "I hope you succeeded in convincing the Minister, Mr. Ambassador?"

"He has to consult with his Government first."

"Well, I hope they've got more sense in them than the damned English and Americans," Joubert said angrily. "It's high time th's bloody lot of blacks at U.N.O. get a trouncing they won't forget quickly.

"We hope they can be checked, Mr. Joubert," said the Ambassador.

A few minutes after Joubert had left, he locked away his documents and left in the official car to have lunch with the British Ambassador.

When he returned at about half-past two the day's press cuttings, prepared by Victor le Roux, were already waiting on his desk. He was still glancing through them when Keyter entered with a draft letter.

The Ambassador quickly scanned it, nodded, and said: "Thank you, Keyter." Then, almost complaisantly, he added: "It is very well formulated."

Keyter showed no reaction. As often in the past the Ambassador became almost unpleasantly aware of the young man's exceptionally long thin hands.

Then he was left alone again. But it lasted for barely five minutes, when there was a soft knock on his door. Before he could answer, it was opened and suddenly, just like the previous night, she was standing in his office with her wry, absent, cynical little smile and her green eyes and (he had not noticed it before) the almost imperceptible touch of her small breasts against the large jersey. She seemed taller than he had thought the night before. Long, slender legs. All this he noticed in passing, while he was waiting, with a touch of irritation, for her to explain the reason for her visit.

"You are busy again," she said, as if she was surprised by it.

"Unfortunately *everybody* cannot loaf about."

"It's a pity," said the girl. "The streets are alive today." She came nearer, although she had not been invited. "I've brought back your jacket." She removed it from her left shoulder and hung it over the back of the chair opposite the desk.

He could feel his hands pressing hard against the dark wood in front of him.

80

"You should not have brought it back like this," he said with sudden anger. "Do you realise – ?"

"Why not?"

Could her naïveté be real, or was it a pose? It made no difference to him. He was adamant that this irresponsible young girl would not be allowed to have her way.

"I would have sent for the jacket," he said sternly. "It was quite unnecessary for you to bring it back."

"But I had to," she answered simply. "I had to come and thank you for last night – that you didn't throw me out like he did. One can't sleep on a metro grille when it's raining. Besides, it's not very safe for a girl."

"That never entered the picture," he said curtly, as if he was scolding his own daughter. But he remembered how she had seemed quite willing to "pay" him for the favour last night, and he felt a stir of nausea in him. Therefore he tried to divert her attention (and his own) by asking: "Why didn't you ask one of the messengers to announce your visit?"

"Should I?" She laughed. "You're so angry today." Then she came past him to the window and peered curiously at the scene outside. "It's a rather depressing view you have from here," she commented, with her back turned to him. "Only the little court-yard and high walls. It looks like a prison. And did you realise how stuffy it's in here when one comes in from the outside?"

"Usually I am much too busy to pay attention to tiny inconveniences which cannot be avoided."

"Oh, I'm sorry," she said, quite sincerely. "I must be disturbing you. Is it very important work you're doing?"

"It is."

She came past his desk again, stopping in front of a calendar with a colourful South African scene and said: "How lovely!" Her green eyes looked up at him. "You must enjoy working in this beautiful office?"

He made no answer.

She turned to the door, lingering for a while at the chair to arrange a fold in his jacket, and looked back at him: "You're a very good man," she said. "Good-bye."

He tried to come from behind the desk so that he could open the door for her, but she was out already. He could hear no footsteps. *A girl steps lightly on the ground* – There must be a poem with such a line, he thought; only it would express it more poetically than the mere statement of fact he recollected. She was gone; and here he was left with the sober knowledge that she

81

had been with him, a minute ago, in spite of his opposition, his irritation, his work, and his warning.

A sudden impulse sent him back to the window. Through the glass he stared into an ambiguous world: the "rather depressing view" of the courtyard, and the linear reflection of his office interior with its one burning light. And which of these two, he suddenly wondered, would be the more real? Or were they both schematic representations of something which could be repeated to infinity? The door of the reading-room slammed and a moment later she crossed the slippery cobbled courtyard, moving gaily through his thoughts and through both scenes in the window pane. Lebon appeared at the corner of the driveway the moment before she disappeared from sight. The Ambassador could see him lift his beret, followed by an inaudible remark. She replied, and laughed, and went her way.

The Ambassador returned to the orderly certainty of his office. The large Persian carpet which obediently absorbed all sounds. The paintings on the colourless walls: a Pierneef; a Maggie Laubscher; a Wenning water-colour. The solid, imposing desk with a Van Wouw statuette on one of the far corners. The rows of books behind glass doors. The heavy easy chairs upholstered in dark leather (with a jacket casually hanging over the back of one of them). Imposing simplicity; the practical elegance of unchallenged authority.

He picked up the calendar which had caught her eye, staring absently at the rows of dates, down and across, each one an adequate summary of the day's experience, arranged in the conventional chain of chronology. Time suddenly checked, caught in figures: the expression, in black (and sometimes red) on white, of what was happening, of what was past; and of what was still waiting in the future to be past in turn, one day.

Here and there he noticed a pencil tick next to a date.

The 22nd October: Erika and Annette at the Gare de Lyon, half an hour too early for their train to the south. It was only about eight o'clock, but the cloudy autumn weather created the impression of an hour that had lost its way very deep into the night.

"You needn't wait," Erika insisted. "We can manage quite easily."

"I'm not in a hurry."

They strolled up and down along the endless dirty platform with nothing to talk about. A train crammed with soldiers was on the point of leaving. Here and there little boisterous groups were leaning through windows, singing, shouting, whistling at passing women. Others were sitting passively among their bundles on the floor of the narrow corridors, staring into the void. Leaning against a lamp post a young couple were saying good-bye, their bodies passionately, shamelessly pressed together.

Annette laughed nervously and tried to glance back at them. Erika made a disparaging remark about the "disgusting public spectacle".

"They're young," he objected patiently without knowing why he found it necessary to defend them.

"Does that make any difference?" she asked, displeased.

"I don't suppose so."

Then a bell rang. In the distance a loudspeaker voice started crackling; raucous and inhuman. The young soldier forced his way into the train, wriggling like a worm. The girl was standing on the platform, sobbing her heart out. And the minute hand of the station clock continued its short, jerky jumps from minute to minute.

Shortly afterwards their train pulled up next to the platform.

"I hope you'll have good weather," he said formally.

"We shall. As long as we can have a rest. If only we could have gone home."

"Home?"

"South Africa." She quickly glanced at him, then away. "I'm tired of strangers, Paul."

"After thirty years you should be accustomed to our sort of life."

"On the contrary, after thirty years I have suddenly discovered that I am *not* accustomed to it. And it came as an unpleasant surprise."

"What are you trying to say, Erika?"

She shook her head. "I don't know. It's just – that I am looking for something. I don't know whether Italy will help. We have reached a dead end, Paul."

"It was you who always wanted this life."

"Blame it on me, then."

Perhaps he had never before realised so acutely how much of a stranger she was to him; how impenetrable she had become. And yet they were supposed to have been "happy"!

The train would be leaving at any moment.

"Is there anything else we still have to discuss before you go?" he asked.

"Is there anything we have ever had to discuss?"

G

"But what is the matter, Erika?" Perplexed, he clasped her hand in his.

The train jerked. He kissed her hastily, touched Annette's cheek with his lips, and was left behind while they disappeared to the south, into the night.

Resolutely he put the calendar back on the desk. There was no time for such thoughts. He still had to draw up a code telegram to be dispatched to Pretoria, as well as an extensive report on the morning's interview.

As he went back to his chair, he remembered with a wry smile: *"You are a very good man –"* He wondered what she could have meant; and why – this uninvited child whose name he did not even know.

4

He was not prepared for it that she would come again. There was no reason to anticipate it, nor, in a weaker moment, to hope for it. During the week following her second appearance, he occasionally remembered her (it was unavoidable), usually in the form of a question or a smile, at most as an episode. Perhaps he sometimes felt vaguely regretful that it had all been so ephemeral, but he had never expected it to turn out otherwise. And when he did think of her – usually when he was alone in the large house, late at night – it was confined to: *What would her name be? What was she doing all alone in Paris?*

On Sunday 11th November he was unexpectedly summoned to the French Ministry of Foreign Affairs. It was a short interview, but it yielded gratifying results. France could not see her way open to veto the matter in the Security Council, but the Government was prepared to intervene behind the scenes to temper the Afro-Asian proposal, mainly because a dangerous outburst in the Cape Town troubles had been averted.

The next morning, while he was writing his new report – having given special instructions to be left undisturbed – there was a knock on his door and somebody entered. She.

He immediately got up to reprimand her severely about this new breach of his express instructions. At the same time he had been caught so unawares, after a week in which she had often occupied his thoughts, that he was speechless for a moment.

"Good morning," she said. (Was she teasing him?) And when

84

she reached the chair where, the last time, she had left the jacket, she asked: "May I sit down?" Without waiting for his permission she sat down, and prudishly arranged her dress. "I know you are very busy," she said. "But I have come for business."

She needed money, she explained frankly. In that case she should consult the consular secretary, he answered. Besides, the Embassy could only offer assistance in the most urgent cases, usually to send destitute South Africans back home. But, she insisted, her landlady had threatened to throw her out unless she managed to pay part of her long due rent before tomorrow. And she couldn't get any money before Friday. Where did she work? At a night-club. He scowled, and she quickly explained that she sang, and that it was a very respectable place, even though they paid her such a miserable salary.

"Go to the consular office anyway," he closed the discussion, firmly. "They will treat the case on its merits. And for the last time: if you ever come back again, you are to ask a messenger to announce your visit."

She ignored his last words. "If I go to the consul I'll only get entangled in a new lot of forms. That's why I came to you. I thought – "

"Young lady," he said severely, coming round the desk. "This is not the sort of thing I would like to encourage. But for this once I shall give you a hundred francs."

"I didn't come here to beg!" she protested with unexpected vehemence.

"I did not mean to insult you," he answered. "But if I lent it to you it would give you a pretext for coming back again."

"And I should rather stay away because I embarrass you?"

He went to her, irritated, but somewhat confused as well. "My dear child – ," he said soothingly.

"I'm not a child." Her voice was stubborn, but no longer biting. "What is your name?"

Her first reaction was to look at him with suspicion, on the defence. When she finally answered, it was so quickly that she had to repeat her name before he could catch it.

With the utmost patience he tried to overcome her resentment, emphasising that without rules and regulations everything would become anarchy. She merely uttered a short, derisive laugh. And, very reluctantly, he had to admit that she would probably be stifled by his disciplined form of life. (Like Gillian – ?) He nevertheless tried to represent it as acceptably as possible. But right in the middle of his explanation she interrupted him (without any in-

85

tention of being rude) saying: "You shouldn't wear this tie with your suit. It's much too gloomy."

"I won't do it again," he answered with the hint of a smile, but sighing.

"And now could I have my money, please?"

He handed her the note. "Will it be enough?"

She nodded, undid the top button of her jersey and slipped it under her brassière.

"I shall come to listen to you in your nightclub one day," he promised, trying to sound lighthearted.

Her green eyes were mocking.

"Where is the club?" he asked.

"Oh, you'll never find it," she said lightly, on her way to the door. "Good-bye. And thank you very much."

"Good-bye, Nicolette."

Once again he was left with the impression that she had – perhaps – just been playing another game in which he was always the loser. Nobody else had ever robbed him of a hundred francs so easily. An now he had to return to the report which would, once again, prove his brilliance as a diplomat. The Government should never instruct him to open negotiations with one Nicolette Alford, he decided wryly.

These twenty minutes had wrought a subtle change in the whole affair. He was forced to admit this, even though it was, perhaps impossible to rationalise its meaning. There was only a suggestion that a breach had been opened in the walls of his fortress. But why? Because she had succeeded in making him feel guilty about his conduct? But surely that was senseless. And he had expressly warned her not to come again; she would obey, this time. But, after all, it was no longer necessary for her to return. She had left her name; and an impression; and an open door – into the unknown.

It vexed him to admit this vulnerability in himself; and he tried to compensate by acting curtly and harshly towards his staff, even towards Masters with whom he had always been on an extremely good footing. But Masters ascribed his attitude to a natural reaction after the exceptional success of his negotiations and refused to be upset by it.

5

That night he deliberately tried to sort it all out. For it was annoying, it was impossible, that the appearance of an obstinate young waif could make any difference to himself and his way of life. Admittedly, she was not impressed, like everybody else in his surroundings, by his status or his personality; and, whether unconsciously or on purpose, she paid no attention to his instructions and the rules of the Embassy. But that in itself was no reason why she should be anything more than a disquieting memory. He had to conclude that what really upset him, had nothing to do with her personally. The only reason why she had to some extent disturbed the regular flow of his life was that she had revived his recollection of Gillian. And even that was senseless. Gillian belonged to the past; she had been the sole folly of his life. But then: it had been the sort of folly which gradually acquired its own *raison d'être* and became indispensable –

The whole episode had lasted for less than two months: from the night she had been blown into his motor-car until he finally left by boat with all the money he had saved for his wedding. Her father, whose death had led to their first meeting, had been a pastor of some sect or other. She had always refused to talk about him. He had never before come across such intense hatred in any person. From the few bitter remarks that sometimes escaped her, he deduced that she had had a very harsh childhood. The pastor's religion had consisted mainly of fire and brimstone, so that as a child her nights had often been a foretaste of hell. Her whole life had become a seething concentration of terror and hate. Once she had tried to run away. Her father, almost driven to despair, promised that he would never force his will on her again, or punish her in his highly efficacious manner. (For the most trivial offence or hint of "vanity" she was first punished – as if his religious fanaticism contained a dangerous streak of sadism – and then subjected to hours of Scripture reading and passionate prayer on behalf of her "sinful, damned soul".) And then he died, without any warning, before his fiftieth year. A heart attack, it seemed. And suddenly she was free, terrifyingly free: a freedom which she directed against everything and everybody. "I want to live, live, live, live, *live*!" she cried one night. "Don't you understand? No, you won't. Not you with your obedient little bourgeois soul. But you can't keep *me* from doing it. Nothing can. I'll do everything, anything. Even if I have to land in hell for it. As long as I *deserve* it!"

It was a fanatic, fantastic existence, a burning desire to live, so positive that it transcended the limits of everyday life into a dimension where everything existed as its own paradox: thus her passion for life, for saying "*Yes*" to life, found its expression, in practice, in a devastating denial of all appearances, all conventional values, and consequently all forms of "civilised" life – something which, in the end, had to consume herself as well as everybody who was close to her.

And it was this girl he had come to love. For forty days. The duration of the Flood. The time between Resurrection and Ascension. Everything in which he had believed, everything which had seemed certain and self-evident, she took away from him, until he was left in utter despair. And then she, the succubus, laughed at him, mocked him because he did not dare follow her on her way of destruction.

Yet, at the same time she was a child who knew nothing of "the world". Often she was dismayed by her own discoveries; but she could never turn back, because she was too proud and too passionate. She had to "try" everything –

He forcibly interrupted his thoughts, refusing to recall the particulars of that past. There could be no sense, no use in it now, after all these years.

– And in between her outbursts there had been islands of silence and happiness. She would cry over a sad story. She would nurse a wounded dove; she would bring little plants from the mountain and nurture them at home; she would knit a tea-cosy for an old man who lived alone. She could be infinitely patient with children; and she often went to the Gardens to play with them – and with the squirrels. At times she could sit down at the piano and play serenely for hours on end.

But after a pious *All things bright and beautiful* she could, without warning, start thundering away madly until at last she would slam down the lid, sobbing hysterically. There had been moments when he thought she must be mentally unbalanced; yet he knew that that was not the case. She was just not equal to the passion in her frail body. And he had been unable to give her what she needed so desperately.

After those forty days, he left. For eighteen months he lived in Europe, trying to get rid of all the pent-up emotions she had turned loose in him. Then, one day, he received a letter from an acquaintance, not even a friend, containing the casual sentence: *"I suppose you have heard that the girl with whom you went out for some time, Gillian, I think, recently died in Durban?"* The next day he set out on the first stage of his return voyage to South Africa.

The next week was a jigsaw puzzle of activities. Until, one night, sitting in his office, thinking of her first appearance out of the darkness, listening for her footsteps as if he was expecting her again, he thought: it was impossible to go on like this. He had to go to her, just once, to find out more about her, to talk quietly and without hurry, to shake off the illusions she had awakened in him. Because he wanted to get rid of Gillian – and of her, this stranger, Nicolette; even if he had to treat her deliberately as a child. His mind made up, he felt more at ease, as if a burden had been removed from him.

But the Friday night there was a dinner party at the Dutch Embassy. Saturday night he had an important interview with the Australian chargé d'affaires. And it was Sunday evening before, with a feeling of sudden liberation, he could finally walk up the avenue Hoche, take a taxi in the avenue Wagram and go to the rue de Condé. There he paid the driver, allowing him to keep the change from the ten franc note, and went to the door where she had entered the first night. For a moment he inspected it atten-tively, almost with amusement: that dilapidated entrance to a long lost paradise. When he finally pushed open the solid door, he was aware of an unusual resignation inside him, as if he suddenly realised very clearly exactly where he was, and what he was doing; as if, with that gesture, he was abandoning many things, including hope; thinking, almost fatalistically: Come what may –

He turned on the light in the lobby. There were five or six grey, dented rubbish bins standing in a row underneath the melancholy post boxes on the wall. One of these had no name on it, so he presumed it was Nicolette's, apparently on the fifth floor, for there were names for the other four. He looked up at the crooked old staircase. Then the light went out. He scowled, felt his way along the wall until he found the time switch again, and then knocked on the concierge's glass door. But there was no answer, so he started climbing the stairs. The second landing had no bulb, causing him to stumble a few times over broken steps. There was a musty odour of food and ages of human activity. It was the Ambassador's first experience of one of these old build-ings and he almost decided to turn back. When the light failed for the second time, he actually stopped for a moment; but then he took out his cigarette lighter and made up his mind to con-tinue, after all. On the fifth landing he pressed the time switch again. There were two doors, the one on the right bearing a dirty name card: *Mme Cosson*. The one on the left was anonymous. He went to it, considered his decision for the last time, and pressed the button. To his surprise the bell rang both inside and on Mme Cosson's side. And it was she who eventually opened, a slovenly old hag in a loose dressing gown, with dishevelled hair.

"What do you want?" she asked.

"Isn't Miss Alford at home?" inquired the Ambassador coolly.

The old woman giggled. "No," she said. "But I don't think she'll be away long. Not that one can really tell, of course."

"Thank you." He turned back.

"I'll open up for you," she offered, taking a bunch of keys from her gown pocket.

"It is not necessary," said the Ambassador. "I could come back later."

But without paying any attention to him she shuffled across the landing and unlocked the grey door. "There," she said. "Now you can wait inside."

He was still wondering whether he shouldn't rather leave, resenting the old hag's presumptuousness. But where would he go? Home?

"Thank you," he said curtly and went inside. There was a minuscule lobby with two doors, the first leading to a kitchenette with slanting walls and ceiling. He noticed a chair in front of the stove, but it seemed univiting and cold. The second door took him into her bedroom. He stopped on the threshold, feeling guilty, an intruder, and yet it intrigued him. The room was in an incredible mess. The narrow, uncomfortable single bed (coir-mattress, worn out and bumpy) was unmade, one piece of pyjamas lying on the pillow, the other on the threadbare mat next to the bed. A length of string with a number of knots was put up between the open wardrobe and the window, with two pairs of nylons, a slip, a brassière, three diminutive panties and a man's shirt hanging from it. On the back of the chair was a wet towel. There was a table with a bright check cloth, containing a heap of illustrated women's journals (old numbers of previous years mostly, probably bought second-hand at a bouquiniste), a portable radio, a shoe, unwashed dishes and plates, lipstick and an attractive little reading lamp. On top of the open wardrobe was a trunk; on the floor was another, open, filled with crumpled clothes, as if this was only a temporary residence. On the walls were a few pictures cut from magazines. Above the bed he noticed, to his surprise, a small cross, slightly weather-beaten, but still a beautiful piece of woodcarving. On the floor, next to a wicker chair, was a cheap record player and some records, most of them without sleeves. On the chair itself lay a flute.

He leisurely went from one thing to another; and, losing the uneasy feeling of being an impostor, he began to scrutinise everything with great care, as if he hoped to find a key to the strange girl living in this confusion. But everything remained remote, isolated, without life or special meaning. It became an almost passionate urge in him to penetrate the surface of these things, to use them as symbols which would reveal to him the meaning of this girl-life so entirely different from his own orderly existence. And at the same time he felt guilty, as if he was paging through a stranger's diary.

As he was trying to find some heat at the cold radiator, he heard a key turning in the lock of the front door. A moment later she entered, her hair hanging loosely round her shoulders.

"Oh," she said, not at all surprised. "It's you. Good evening." She crumpled a paper bag, wiped her greasy fingers on it and dropped it into a cardboard box in the corner next to the table. "Have you been waiting for a long time?" She carefully sucked off her fingers.

"It doesn't matter," he said. "I wasn't busy tonight."

"Ouch." She was shivering and came over to the heater. "It's cold. I don't know what I'm going to do this winter. These things never warm a room properly. One really needs a fireplace." She turned the knob. "Why didn't you switch it on?"

"I didn't know whether you would be coming back."

She remained standing there until a faint suggestion of warmth started radiating into the room. Then she quickly pulled the crumpled blankets over the bed.

"Did old Cochon open the door for you?"

He nodded, and smiled: Cochon.

She sat down on the bed, pulled in her legs under her and draped a blanket round her shoulders.

"Why did you come here?" she asked frankly.

He was at a complete loss for words and could only shrug his shoulders. "I – I just felt like it."

There was a little twitch in the corner of her mouth.

"You shouldn't live in a room like this," he changed the subject.

"Why?" she asked, surprised.

"It's dilapidated. It's falling to pieces. Surely you can't be happy here."

"You are accustomed to other things, I suppose," she said soberly.

He felt irritated. "But are you sure I can't help you?"

"With what?"

"Anything. Money – "

"I'm not for sale."

He could feel a throbbing in his temples. "I never insinuated that you were. What makes you think – "

"You're a man." She smiled blithely. "Men always want to help. They themselves believe firmly that they are unselfish. Then, just when one is properly entangled, they suddenly want their reward."

Her words deepened his fatigue and made him more painfully aware of the distance between them.

"Don't you realise that I want to help you because I believe you *need* it, because I feel sorry for you?"

"Sorry?" There was no suspicion in her voice, only surprise. "Why on earth would anybody feel sorry for me?"

"I don't think you have a very easy life."

She rested her chin on her drawn-up knees, and with that familiar little twitch of her lips, staring fixedly at the window, she said: "I was born on a Wednesday."

"What on earth has that got to do with it?" he asked, perplexed.

She didn't look at him. She only recited, to herself, the old jingle:

> *"Monday's child is fair of face.*
> *Tuesday's child is full of grace.*
> *Wednesday's child is full of woe – "*

He made no answer. The warmth was silently breathing through the room, a lazy, almost imperceptible movement, yet undeniably there. And gradually he became conscious of it, and she too, realising that it was now warmer inside than outside, behind the window, and that there was a precious if vulnerable presence of consolation and compassion in the light. And their conversation was flowing more easily, without hidden motives behind every sentence, without asking too many questions or expecting too many answers. There was no necessity for that any more. Later, in the cold outside, it would return; but now, here, together, he sitting at the foot-end of the bed and she in the middle, they were content. The growing warmth caused her to shake the blanket from her; later she even unbuttoned her thick jersey over her blouse; but she made no other movement and remained sitting with her head on her knees and her hands resting on her bare feet. Unusual

92

hands, he noticed, with a slight unevenness in her fingers, and with very short nails; and her feet were small, quite narrow for their length, but not bony. She was young, more than child, almost woman. Never in his life had he been so near to the strange invisible world of a girl. But was it really she alone, he wondered, who stirred up these thoughts in him, or would the same have happened to him in the presence of any other person of her sex and age? This sudden doubt caused him to recoil a little.

"What do you really *do* in Paris?" he asked.

"Nothing in particular." For a moment she was distant again, looking attentively at her toes. "In the beginning, four years ago, I did many things, here, there, everywhere, just to stay alive. Then it became winter. I had no money left. One morning I sold my overcoat. It was terribly cold. I thought I'd get at least five or six thousand francs for it. But the bloody swindler paid me only fifteen hundred. Old francs, of course. I bought me a *baguette*. And then somebody snatched my purse and ran away. I tried to follow him, but he had disappeared. So I went on, eating my bread, and walking, walking, walking, just to keep warm. At last I was so tired that I couldn't care any more. I sat down in the Luxembourg Gardens among the winter trees. I could feel my body becoming colder and colder. At first it was awful. but later I got sleepy and I thought if only I could fall asleep I would never wake up again. Then somebody came to sit down next to me. A student. His clothes were rather threadbare but at least he wasn't cold. He started talking to me. I can't even remember all the things I answered. Then he proposed something You know – ? At first I shook my head, I was too cold for anything. But he kept on. So I said: 'All right, if you buy me food and keep me with you all night.' He laughed and helped me to get up and took me with him. I never even asked his name." She closed her hands serenely round her feet. He could feel tiny pinpricks of perspiration on his forehead, cold against the warmth of the room. She laughed softly, at and to herself. Started to hum something. Then stopped, as if she had forgotten the tune. And he listened to her while she piously recited: *"Agnus Dei, qui tollis peccata mundi, miserere nobis."* She pulled back her hands, folded her arms round her knees to support her head, and became a praying embryo. *"Agnus Dei, qui tollis peccata mundi, dona nobis pacem."*

"Nicolette!" he said, almost sternly.

She lifted her dishevelled fair head and looked at him with large, innocent eyes. "What is it?"

"What are you doing?"

"Nothing." She swung her legs over the side of the bed, started rubbing the numbness from her thigh muscles for a while, then held her dress above her knees, looking critically first at her legs and then at him as if she expected a comment. But when he remained silent, she merely laughed, wriggled her feet into her shoes, arranged her dress and said: "Would you like some coffee?"

He nodded absently, trying to decide which of her quicksilver moods had been serious, and which pretence; or was he merely too old and stolid to adapt himself to all her changes?

He could hear the hissing of the gas stove in the kitchenette and the sound of running water, of teaspoons and cups. And all the time he remained where he was, looking benevolently at the confusion in the little room which now formed a harmonious whole, as if a catalyst had appeared to assemble all the disparate elements.

"Oh, damn!" he heard her exlaim. All the noises stopped.

She appeared in the doorway. "There's no more coffee."

"Well, shall we go to a café?" he suggested, smiling at her.

"Oh yes! But I'll have to tidy up." A minute later she called from the kitchen: "Will you bring me my lipstick, please?"

He remembered having noticed it on the table, picked it up and took it to where she was standing at the washbasin in front of a tiny mirror. He stood watching the smooth movements of her young arms while, with lifted elbows, she was arranging her hair. He had to wait for some time before she took the lipstick and started pulling faces in the mirror. He turned round considerately, intending to go out, but she uttered a sound which seemed to mean: "Stay!" And, reluctantly, he obeyed, watching the strange spectacle as if he had never seen it before. (When had he, in fact, seen it last? Annette and Erika always locked the bathroom) She seemed to perform the movements of a dance; but it undeniably suggested vanity, and it was also funny, and at the same time tremendously serious; above all, it had a magical quality: it was no mere series of moments, but a ritual.

At last she turned round to him, waiting.

"You look beautiful," he said with the courtesy that had become a habit; but there was a new meaning in his formal compliment.

She smiled, with mocking eyes. Then they went out together; and he watched, with surprise, the graceful way in which she went down those crumbled steps.

"Where are we going?" he asked when they came outside. "You'll have to show the way."

She chose a street into the labyrinth.

94

"Have you had dinner already?" he suddenly asked.

"*Frites.*"

"Then we'll go to a restaurant," he decided firmly.

Afterwards he would never again have found his way to the little restaurant where she had taken him that night. All the time he was conscious only of strange, narrow streets and the high lines of the rooftops. The restaurant had room for no more than four tables, covered with sheets of paper on which, afterwards, the *patron* scribbled their bill. There were a few other clients, probably students, arguing in a corner. But the only thing that really mattered was Nicolette; and he sat watching her as if she were a strange, amusing little animal which he could study with scientific impartiality while she was consuming incredible quantities of food without for a moment interrupting her conversation.

He was aware, also, of himself, sitting opposite her in that quaint little restaurant, wondering, bemused: How had it happened that he came there tonight? What was he doing there? What would happen if an acquaintance would find him there? Everything had an air of unreality, even of impossibility. At first he was so much upset by it that he would have preferred to get up and escape from there, back to his familiar world. But in the growing geniality caused by the warmth of the heavy, cheap wine he remained, looking at her, listening to her, while she was buzzing on and on like a friendly insect, eating, occasionally greeting somebody who entered or went out. Keep on talking, he thought drowsily: keep on talking, talking, keep on all night, never stop, allow this moment to *last*.

But in spite of all his subtle efforts to urge her to order more and more food so that they could stay longer, she finally leant back and, with an expression of complete satisfaction, called: "Garçon! L'addition, s'il vous plaît!"

Five minutes later they were back on the cold pavement in the dark. She was walking next to him with complete familiarity and trust, her hand holding his arm, singing:

> "*Au clair de la lune, mon ami Pierrot,*
> *Prête-moi ta plume, pour écrire un mot.*
> *Ma chandelle est morte, je n'ai plus de feu;*
> *Ouvre-moi la porte, pour l'amour de Dieu –*"

He listened absently, only partly aware of it all, conscious of the paralysing weight of the coming parting.

When they came near her front door, she slipped away from him, darted ahead of him, pressed the button, laughed. He fol-

95

lowed leisurely and opened the heavy door for her. He almost
hoped that she would invite him to come in – knowing very well
that he would have to refuse even if she did.

"Thank you," she said, slightly out of breath. "It was a wonderful dinner."

"I should thank *you*." In spite of the annoying formality of his
words he was very sincere. "I've suddenly discovered that I have
been living in Paris blindfolded."

"Oh, I'll show you the city," she promised, as if it had long
been decided between them. Then she lifted herself on her toes,
chastely touched his mouth with her cool, soft lips, and went inside. Holding the railing of the old staircase she waved at him
and started climbing. Without moving he stood listening to her
humming voice:

> *"Au clair de la lune, Pierrot répondit:*
> *Je n'ai pas de plume, je suis dans mon lit.*
> *Va chez la voisine, je crois qu'elle y est,*
> *Car dans sa cuisine on bat le briquet."*

The rest was inaudible.

7

"Oh, I'm *so* glad to see you, Mr. Ambassador!" Sylvia Masters
approached him with outstretched, limp right hand, a large car-
buncle of a ring gleaming on one finger, a heavy bracelet on her
wrist. "We feel so guilty luring you away from your work, but it's
such a *special* occasion."

She was acting as hostess to Victor le Roux's party, charmingly
welcoming the guests at the front door of the luxury apartment
in the boulevard Haussman.

The Ambassador nodded briefly and greeted her politely, over-
conscious of her obscenely bare, white arms. She was wearing a
light pink dress which did not go very well with her reddish hair.
But she regularly bought all her clothes in London and displayed
a characteristically British lack of taste. Why would he find it so
particularly offensive tonight? That – and the gaudy necklace
round her thin white neck, and the large earrings flickering with
every movement of her head.

"Mr. Le Roux was rather secretive about tonight," he said
with superficial interest. "Is there anything up his sleeve?" (What
he really thought was: *Couldn't she wear a tighter brassière?*)

"It's a secret," she giggled. "A big surprise. Come, you *must*
have something to drink. What would you like?"

He followed her into the large, imposing apartment with its high walls, decorated ceiling and well-kept Empire furniture; the longest wall of the living-room was covered with two luxurious tapestries. On the far side of the room was a large ornamental mantelpiece crowned with a dry arrangement of proteas and other South African flowers – Victor le Roux's own work.

There were not many people, about eighteen or twenty. The Ambassador found his way among them, stopping occasionally for a short conversation, gracefully obeying all the rules of courtesy. More than once he became aware of Sylvia again. Excellent hostess, after all. He had seen her a few times at the Embassy – something of which he strongly disapproved – and had noticed how very different she looked during the day-time: usually wearing tweeds, with a greyish listlessness in her eyes. But on evenings like this they seemed to revive, as if expensive lights had been specially switched on in them. This was her only true element, he thought. He had often noticed something similar in Erika. Yet Erika was altogether different. She had an innate charm, and immaculate taste. Perhaps even too immaculate. He smiled absently into his glass while his mouth mechanically continued the conversation in which he was involved. He remembered how, during the first years of their married life, he had sometimes noticed a hint of uncertainty in her. But she had soon acquired a polish, so much so that he often had to admire her self-assurance, her quiet sophistication. At home, withdrawn from the public eye, she would often be untidy. She tended to smoke too much. And drink too, he suspected. Although nobody would ever notice it on a party. He sighed, wondering where she would be tonight

(And: *she*? She, in her dilapidated old building, and her sad little room, with her young eyes, light-years removed from this apartment with the splendour of ancient luxury.)

While he was listening – apparently with intense interest – to the wife of the British Cultural Attaché, somebody (Masters) clapped his hands and the voices died down, except that of Anna Smith who was finishing a sentence, followed by a boisterous laugh.

"Ladies and gentlemen – !" Masters was a polished speaker equipped with admirable dry humour. And while he was making his announcement with deliberate pompousness and prolixity, the audience listened with due attention and polite smiles.

" – Mr. Le Roux has indulged in a bit of poetic licence – or would it be licentiousness?" (They laughed.) He held a slim green volume above his head and revealed the secret: Victor had published a collection of his impressions of Paris, illustrated by himself.

97

Everybody started exclaiming and laughing (as was expected of them), pressing nearer to see and to congratulate. Sylvia flung her etiolated arms round Victor's neck, and kissed him. He was quite defenceless in her embrace, grinning with embarrassment, his blonde forelock plastered to his perspiring forehead, his glasses large and dusty under the lamplight.

And then, the inevitable: *For he's a jolly good fellow* (which Anna Smith and Koos Joubert sang in Afrikaans).

The Ambassador did not immediately step into the cheerful bustle. Only afterwards, unobtrusively, did he approach Le Roux to express his congratulations. And then he returned to the Embassy.

Victor's book. The severe line of his mouth slackened into an almost wry smile. Thirty years ago he, too, had been playing with such possibilities: during the eighteen months before his wedding, here, in Europe – in London and the South of France. He had filled hundreds of pages, typing away like a man possessed in his tiny rooms in Chelsea or Padstow or Arles, until, in the early hours, the neighbours would start hammering on the walls. Perhaps it had been a way of ridding his system of Gillian. But the reason had been less important than his passion, than the mere necessity of finding expression. He had published a few articles in magazines to stay alive; but his real work – an uncompleted novel – never left his drawer.

It had been eighteen months of chastity. The women he'd known had been mere companions, satellites on the periphery. All his energy had gone into the growing pile of typewritten pages on his table. In the occasional interludes he allowed himself he travelled extensively, accompanied by a few close friends. It was all part of an orgy, a ritual of purification.

As the novel neared completion he started making plans for the future. If it succeeded – and he was confident it would – he would make writing his life. He would keep on *living*.

But it turned out differently.

After his marriage he still wrote something occasionally, but the novel was left untouched. Where would he find the time? He was so inspired by his career that he could no longer get away from it. Gradually it became his sole form of living and expression. A conditioned identity? Perhaps. But then, it was an existence like any other. He doubted, now, whether he had ever had any real "talent". It had been nothing but an urge.

Why did he allow all these things to come back to him tonight? Or was he getting old – ? He sniffed. He should work more and allow himself less time for recalling irrelevant memories.

8

Erika wrote—
Here in Rome the weather is slightly cool, but it is still sunny.
For a few days Annette felt like exploring the ruins – I ask you!
– but most of the time we are shopping in the Via Veneto and
the streets near the Piazza di Espagna. What else can we do –
even though we never get up before eleven in the morning? Last
night we had dinner in a restaurant in the Via Marche with the
Kriges. I suppose you remember them: we met them on our last
home leave. The night before there was a party at the Ambassa-
dor's residence. Tonight we are going to a nightclub. And to-
morrow there is another party at one of the Italian Ministries. I
am not sure yet whether I want to go. Annette has met a young
man in the Italian Foreign Service and is accompanying him
wherever he goes, preferably without me. I suppose I should let
her have her own way. There is still a strange gap between us.
She is desperately looking for something: what it is, I don't know;
neither does she, I think. Is it something peculiar to a young girl,
or does everybody experience it at some stage or another? Do you
think it is merely an urge to free oneself from authority? I can
still remember how I rebelled against my existence during those
eighteen months before our wedding when you were in Europe
and it seemed as if everything had gone to pieces. One's demands
are so absolute when one is young. I even, melodramatically,
considered suicide. (My God, what does a mere child know of
life and death? It seems to me it is only now that I am gradually
beginning to learn the meaning of these things.) Or else I wanted
to marry the first man who turned up, preferably a marriage that
would shock my parents. Everything had to be so proper for them.
(So "comme il faut", I suppose I should say nowadays, to be in
vogue.) But every time it looked as though there was a chance of
escape, I shrank back. I was so scared. How bourgeois of me! It
is so easy to make-believe, to play the little game. Yet it becomes
more and more difficult to play at "people"! Perhaps one's imagi-
nation disappears as one grows up. Anything, as long as one
need not think.
   My thoughts are wandering, I'm sorry. It is time for my bath.
Tonight I am wearing one of my new, rather decolleté dresses;
just an experiment to see whether I could still shock myself. Ann-
ette has been dressing this last hour. Have you ever noticed how
beautiful she really is? But what does it matter, after all? One of
these days she'll get married – to her Italian or to one of his

successors – and then? Is that the only thing being beautiful
could be bait for?

You mustn't work too hard. And yet, what else would you do
if you did not work? Has it always been like this? I cannot
remember that it was ever different. Love, Erika.

9

It was a lonely week. The evenings following Le Roux's party
were miraculously free. Usually the Ambassador welcomed these
opportunities for finishing work that had fallen into arrears, or
for reading the latest publications on international politics. But at
present there was silence, an isolation, a feeling of being lost in
immense space, which made him restless. When he was working in
his office he turned on the lights in the passage and the reading-
room as well to create an illusion of life, whereas normally he
would strongly disapprove of wasting electricity.

While, on the Friday night, he was studying a book on Anglo-
French relations, he suddenly heard a woman laughing somewhere in the basement. It was so vague that he was not even sure
that he had really heard it. Lebon's wife perhaps? But he had
seen her go out earlier in the evening. So it was probably a mis-
tress. The thought was extraordinarily painful to him. He closed
the book resolutely and got up: tonight he would commit the
unforgiveable crime of going to one of the luxury cinemas in the
Champs-Élysées. He put on his coat and went out. It was raining, pleasantly cool after the overheated residence. Because he so
seldom walked he forgot to take the short-cut along the rue de
Tilsitt and landed at the Place de l'Êtoile. The rain was coming
down more steadily. He pulled his hat down over his forehead,
measuring the distance to the nearest cinema. He would be
drenched before he reached it. And then, almost without consciously making a decision, he turned round to the avenue Wagram, opened a taxi door and jumped in. A few raindrops trickled
down his neck.

"Rue de Condé," he said, wondering whether it could really be
as easy as this – ?

When he reached the fifth floor of her building, slightly out of
breath because he had mounted too quickly, the light on that
landing was also missing. Fortunately he had taken the precau-
tion of using his cigarette lighter to guide him up the old stair-

case. For a few minutes he stood outside her door to regain his breath, then lifted his hand and knocked, realising the finality of his gesture, but aware, also, of the challenge in it: as if the momentary contact of his knuckles with the scaly wood was an affirmation of his rebellion against loneliness, silence, protocol and fate.

For a long time all was silent, and he was just wondering whether he should turn back or ring the bell for the old land-lady to open Nicolette's door like the last time, when the little bolt clicked inside and the door was opened. He had not heard any footsteps, but it was understandable for she was barefoot. Her hair fell over her shoulders, loose and fair; and she was wearing nothing but a halfslip and a brassière. There was no surprise in her eyes. She stepped aside to allow him to come in.

The Ambassador hesitated; then he entered without looking at her.

"You should have dressed first," he said.

"I was just going to wash my hair."

"Even so. It's not proper." He was irritated by his inability to handle the situation, and this prompted him to ask suspiciously: "Or were you expecting someone else?" (Why did he say that? He had not come there to quarrel!)

"No," she answered quite frankly. "Would you like to sit on the chair in the kitchen while I'm busy?"

"Take your time." He turned away and went to her bedroom. She shrugged her smooth shoulders and danced into the kitchen with a gay swing of her halfslip. He could hear water running. She started humming something he didn't know.

He removed a few things from the table and sat down on one corner. In spite of himself he listened to the sounds coming from the kitchen, then took out a cigarette and lit it. As he sat smoking, his thoughts seemed to become clearer. Relaxed, his eyes moved through the room. There was the same pleasant confusion on the bed, chair, table and wardrobe as before. On the bed lay a heap of newly ironed clothes.

Was there something deliberately taunting in her attitude to-wards him? It could hardly be, for she had not been expecting him here tonight. And yet – Her voice grew louder, interrupting his thoughts. A thinnish, unformed voice. It could not be a very distinguished night-club where she sang. He stubbed out his cigar-ette in the lid of a drinking chocolate tin.

She stopped singing in between two bars, calling: "Hell, it's raining, isn't it?"

"Yes."

The song went on.

A minute later: "Why did you come?"

"To visit you."

"Oh."

She remained in the kitchenette for fully half an hour before she returned, rubbing her hair with a gaily coloured towel. Without tidying anything, she went to sit down on top of the heap of clothes on the bed, folding her pretty feet under her.

Question, answer; question, answer.

He was waiting for the magic word to be uttered which would suddenly change everything, making an end to the futility of this superficial little game, but she seemed to derive a perverse pleasure from going on like that indefinitely. She was in a negative mood, cynical at times, remote; and yet her words were contradicted by the mixture of conscious and unconscious invitation in her attitude – as if she was playing another game with herself, her mouth repeating the phrases of a play while her body and thoughts were occupied by freer things.

Then came the knock. They both heard it. She shook her damp hair from her face, and unfolded her long legs. He made no movement, but his whole body was tense.

When she reached the middle door he ordered sternly: "Put on your clothes first."

"Why?"

He quickly went to the bed, picked up a crumpled dress and pressed it in her hands. "I want you to dress properly before you go out."

She was standing right in front of him, almost touching him, her eyes shallow and angry. Then, with a quick movement, she darted away from him, through the middle door, kicking it shut behind her with a bare foot, and went to open the front door. He followed her. But when his hand touched the knob of the middle door he realised in what a compromising situation he would be trapped if her visitor saw him there, and his hand dropped. He could hear her talking to a man at the front door, but it was impossible to distinguish anything. For a moment he glanced round him frantically, went over to the window, hoping that it would offer some means of escape; but underneath the ornamental railing of the tiny balcony there was only the perpendicular, wet, grey wall of her building, five storeys high. The Ambassador turned back. The voices at the front door were silent, but Nicolette was not coming back. He waited for another minute, listening intently, his hand trembling slightly on the door-knob; then he quickly flung it open. The front door was ajar. At the rails of the staircase, a whitish silhouette against the dark, her frail figure was leaning over, looking down.

"Nicolette."

She turned round.

"Come back."

She leisurely came towards him, dancing coquettishly on the tips of her toes. He clutched her arm and pulled her inside, slamming the door behind them. She went to the middle of her room before she turned round to face him, folding her arms so that her chin could rest in a cupped hand.

"Who was it?" he asked.

"Wouldn't you like to know!" she mocked.

"Who was it?"

She went past him and sat down on a corner of the bed. "Somebody who loves me very much," she said with a theatrical air. "Somebody who wanted to sleep with me."

His forehead was aching. "How long do you intend to go on living like this?"

"Just as long as I like." There was a dangerous edge in her voice.

"Put on your clothes," he ordered. "You've been prancing around naked long enough!"

"I don't dress in front of men."

For a moment he felt like slapping her as one would an impertinent child. Then he turned his back on her and remained standing, unmoving, waiting.

She uttered a short laugh. But after a while she yielded, selected a jersey and a skirt from the mess on the bed, and started dressing.

"Naked!" he could hear her say. "One isn't naked when one hasn't got any clothes on." Her voice became deeper. "You are naked when the man you love holds you against him and turns you round with your back to him, and passes his arms under yours, and puts his hands on you, and talks to you, and lets his hands stray farther, and back again, talking all the time, very softly, talking. Then you are naked even if you are wearing a thick overcoat."

"Have you finished?" he asked. He was breathing heavily.

"Long ago."

He turned back. She was leaning over to reach under the bed, coming up with two nylons. Slowly, almost lazily, she started

103

putting one on. After she had fastened it, she stretched out both her legs and asked: "Do you like my legs? Or are they too thin?"

He did not answer.

She put on the second stocking, then got up, arranged her skirt, and moved her expressionless green eyes to his. "I think you are impotent," she said, with the suggestion of a derisive pout of her lower lip.

He looked at her; then away. "You are – young," he said.

He walked past her, outside, closing the door behind him. In the darkness of the top landing he hesitated, half turned back and touched the door-knob, knowing that she was inside, waiting. He closed his eyes. Then, slowly, he went to the staircase and starting feeling his way cautiously with his feet.

When he came outside, there was a short lull in the rain. He began to walk towards the nearest taxi rank, but the thought of his home, empty and formal, made him change his mind and he turned right, in the direction where he expected to find the boulevard Saint-Michel. He felt a need of other people, even strangers, preferably strangers. He selected the brightest, busiest café, where a large crowd was compressed round small round tables in a steaming terrace. For ten minutes he stood patiently waiting for an empty seat; then he sat down at a table and ordered coffee from an irritated, perspiring waiter. It became unbearably hot in his thick overcoat but there was no room to take it off.

When he looked up once, Keyter was standing beside him. It caused a momentary tingling of shock, followed by profound, inexplicable relief.

"Please sit down," he said, almost eagerly.

The Third Secretary, he noticed, was quite astonished to find him there; and it gave the Ambassador a feeling of satisfaction, indeed of amusement. (If only Keyter knew – !)

"Do you often come to this part of the city?" the young man asked.

"Sometimes." His expression remained unchanged, but he was inwardly smiling, accepting his own challenge, playing a game with himself. "I'm trying to explore the whole city systematically." *(I have been visiting a young girl. A little bitch. A beautiful young little bitch.)*

"But it's such a nasty evening to be outside, isn't it?"

There was something Mephistophelean about the pale young man, thought the Ambassador: it was almost as if he was trying to make the most ordinary questions and remarks sound sinister.

"One gets stifled in the office. The rain is quite a pleasant change." *(She said I was impotent. She thinks her legs are too thin. Do you know how beautiful they are, Keyter? What would your reaction be if I suddenly told you – ? But you know it already, because you had thrown her out that night, before she came to me. You are a cynic, Keyter, and you are trying very hard to look sophisticated, but you are really so very young –)*

At last they went back together in a taxi. The Ambassador got out in the avenue Hoche; Keyter proceeded to Neuilly. But instead of pressing Lebon's bell, the Ambassador turned back and, in spite of the rain, went to the Champs-Élysées where he once more entered a crowded café. But this time he did not order coffee.

10.

It was final, it was the end, and he resigned himself to the inevitable, forcing himself not to think about it again. Going back to her was impossible, utterly impossible. Yet it was without any desire to offer her a challenge – on the contrary, it was with a measure of irony – that, somewhat guiltily, he personally sent her a formal invitation to the Military Attaché's reception in the official residence. Therefore he was caught completely unawares when, that Wednesday evening, he saw her enter the door of the reception hall. With calm dignity she handed her card to the porter who announced her, then formally greeted the Military Attaché and his wife, and entered into the crowd. He was involved in a conversation with an important member of the French General Staff when she came past him, nodded coolly, and murmured: "Good evening, your Excellency."

He greeted her and, noticing the General's questioning, wise expression, explained: "Some student or other, I presume."

"I see." The Frenchman threw a last, comprehensive glance in her direction, sweeping his eyes from her slim back down to her ankles, and resumed the conversation.

The Ambassador was conscious of a new excitement inside him. He very effectively kept it under control, but he knew that the evening had suddenly become lighter. And behind the flow of the conversation with the General he was wondering why she had come, after all. Could it be interpreted as a subtle counter-challenge she wished to offer?

An hour later, however, she was gone. He had never seen her

leave, but there were so many guests that she could easily have slipped out unnoticed.

From that moment the reception seemed to drag on endlessly. Even after most of the guests had left a few conversations continued stubbornly. And finally the Ambassador dutifully invited the Military Attaché and his wife to a last drink in a private lounge.

It was fairly late by the time he was left alone at the front door, tired and with a dull headache. But there was still work to be done and he crossed the courtyard to the office building. Until half-past eleven he worked methodically and with forced concentration on a report requested by the French Foreign Minister, before he locked away all the important documents. In the cool courtyard he lingered for a few minutes, looking up at the low clouds reflecting, dully and wearily, the city lights; then he entered the house, and went upstairs to his room.

It was almost imperceptible; yet the moment he reached the landing on top of the stairs he became aware of a scent, warmth, a presence. He stood quite still, trying to find an explanation for it. Erika's door was ajar. He crossed the thick carpet and switched on the light in her room. It was empty. But the scent was more obvious here than on the landing. Perhaps one of the servants had been here. To make quite sure he also went to Annette's room, wondering with a tired smile: "The three little bears – ?" Everything appeared impersonal and tidy; yet there was the same intangible impression that everything was not quite as it should be. He shrugged, closed Annette's door behind him, and went to his own room.

Her fair head moved on the pillow when he put on the light. One shoe was lying on the edge of the bed; the other had fallen on the floor. Except for that she was fully clothed, but crumpled and rolled up like a hedgehog on the expensive damask-cloth.

He remained on the threshold, his hand on the button. She groaned softly, and stirred. Then she lifted her tousled head, blinking at the light and at him, mumbled something, and fell back on the pillow.

The Ambassador went to the bed, removed the shoe and put it, neatly, next to the one on the floor.

"I'm cold," she sighed sleepily.

He brought a warm dressing-gown from behind the door, spread it over her, made sure that she was tucked in properly, and then put off the light. There was only a faint glow from the landing visible through the open door. He heard her heave a deep sigh; then she relaxed and started breathing quietly, evenly. He sat down on the uncomfortable straight-backed chair at the bedside. She was merely a vague shadow on the blue bedspread, her hair a dark mass on the white pillow. And there was her breath, sweet breath, and a scent, and mercy; a mere child, a child. God, he thought, he was becoming sentimental. Soon he would have tears in his eyes. But it was dark, and that was a good thing. And it was silent. Only she was breathing, alive on his bed, sleeping, a shadow in the shadows. He had been with his child, just like this, once when she was two years old, and ill, so that he had to sit up with her, for Erika was tired. And in the night he gave her water, and sat next to her, and tucked in the blankets round her small shoulders, and looked at her little blonde head moving restlessly on the pillow, and he tried to hum without much melody: Sleep, sleep, my little one; sleep, sleep, my little one. Outside was the wind and the restless trees. Outside, tonight, was the city, the winter city, with late pedestrians and cars and the never-ending convulsions of its tired grey heart. And once with Gillian, after they had been in the sea, that one, single time, it was cold, and it was raining, and she had always been so frail, but she would never listen; he was numb with cold, but she, with her blue bathing costume, kept on, ahead of him, into the waves, through light white foam and blue-grey hills of water under the glistening rain; she was possessed by something, by a sensual ecstasy of nature, singularly alive in the sea, with her white limbs and the blue costume and the wet strands of hair on her cheeks; and finally he forcibly brought her back to the desolate beach under the heavy hulk of the mountain and the green port jackson trees, she was shivering, blueish with cold, slender, but she was laughing, laughing, her head thrown back, and she stripped the costume from her and stood in front of him with the mat glistening of a wet pearl, and she needed the heat of his body, which he dared not refuse, which he dared not refuse any longer, which he no longer wanted to refuse; it was the first time, it was the *only* time, lying on the sand among the wet green shrubs, and there was fine white sand on her shoulders when they got up, and in his mouth was the salt taste of tears and the sea; they rubbed each other dry, shivering, sometimes laughing, and then they went back to drink something hot, brandy or something; but the doctor had to be called, it was pneumonia, and nobody thought she would ever come out of it alive, but she did; and he was sitting up at her bedside, aware of her nearness and her frailty, and once she put out her hand and laughed softly and whispered: "I'm glad, I'm not sorry. I'm glad." And then she fell asleep and did not die.

And so the night grew old and young around them, marked off in neat segments by the mute, melodious chimes of a clock somewhere in the large house; there were long lines of sound caused by the traffic outside in the boulevards, streets and alleys under the cloudy sky; but all the time he remained conscious of her, and of her hair, and of her breathing; and once or twice he got up, after she had stirred, to tuck in the warm gown round her shoulders.

It was past two when he realised that she was awake, lying without moving, her body tense, as if she was trying to find out where she was.

"Nicolette?" he asked.

She quickly sat up, the gown clutched to her throat like a blanket.

He got up and went to put on the light. She blinked, started sweeping her hair back over her shoulders, and then smiled slowly, as if she meant to apologise but first wanted to judge his attitude.

"I felt so tired," she said at last. "It must be very late?"

He went to the door. "I shall go and make us some coffee. The bathroom is next door, if you want to comb your hair."

She smiled, and nodded. Ten minutes later he heard her coming down the stairs. They did not speak. But when she was finally sitting in a large arm-chair, holding her cup in both hands (like Gillian), she remarked quite naturally: "You and your wife sleep in separate rooms."

"Yes."

Her eyes were scrutinising him over the edge of her cup, but she made no comment.

"The third room is my daughter's."

"I know."

He frowned, questioningly.

"I saw her clothes in her cupboard," she explained, without a hint of shame.

"They're away on holiday, in Italy."

"And now you are all alone in this big house."

With a single nod he admitted everything.

"I must go home," she said. "What time is it?"

"Almost three o'clock. Must you?"

It was an unnecessary question, and her only response was to get up, arrange her black shawl round her shoulders and take up her evening bag from the chair.

"It's a lovely dress," he remarked quietly.

"Yes, it is." There was a quick little smile on her tired lips.

"I shall take you home."

"It's not necessary."

"You can't be outside alone at this time of the night."

"It wouldn't be the first time."

He shook his head and went out with her, opened the front door himself and pulled out the car. It was very quiet while they drove along the empty streets with their rows of yellow lights, back to where she lived.

"Good night," she said, as he opened her heavy door for her.

"Good night."

They did not touch each other.

He stood waiting in the lobby until she reached the first floor. Then he went back to his car and returned to the Embassy. As he bolted the front door the sleepy, dazed concierge made his appearance. Behind him there was shallow, yellowish light in one of the windows. Without looking at him directly, the Ambassador said good-night, entered the official residence and went up to his room where his bed still revealed the pattern of her small body.

11

The following weeks were exceptionally busy, even more so because of the new series of negotiations in connection with the South African arms deal. At first the Ambassador had several private interviews with the French Foreign Minister; then, during the subsequent discussions with the War Minister, he was assisted by the Military Attaché, Colonel Kotzé. Convincing arguments had to be found and adequate security offered. The recent troubles in South Africa had ended peacefully, the French Ministers insisted, but what would happen in the case of new clashes? Apart from this, the U.N.O. affair still required attention; there was a confidential report in connection with a Communist congress in Paris that had been attended by some prominent Africans from the Republic; there were negotiations with a group of influential French politicians who intended visiting South Africa personally in order to examine the situation.

Only once could he get away from his urgent business to visit Nicolette, and then she was not at home; as he had no desire to talk to the landlady, he returned, disappointed – and yet, in a way, relieved because of what had happened, or because of what had *not* happened. A few days later he nevertheless repeated the visit. She was out again, but when he left, he met her downstairs and went to a bistro with her to have hot chocolate.

And that was the meagre balance sheet of almost three weeks. Yet all the time the Ambassador could sense that he was now part of a strange, irresistible movement which had started, unnoticed, somewhere in the past and was now moving into the future. Its destination was unpredictable; and to try to resist it was unwise. For everything was tentative, a prismatic collection of possibilities, all of them latent, and so delicate that an imprudent word or gesture would disturb the balance. That balance had been achieved the night she had slept in his bed – which, itself, was the result of everything preceding it – and it had its existence beyond themselves: they could not improve it; they could only, if indiscreet, disturb it. And so he was doing his work, and she was going her secret way through the Minoan labyrinth of the old city. He was continually aware of her; and she, presumably, of him. But it was all dormant in a layer of symbols and free associations beyond the conscious world.

It lasted until Tuesday, 18th December.

12

It was an ordinary long white official envelope with the embossed coat-of-arms of the Republic on the back.

It was addressed simply to *The Ambassador* and marked: *Strictly Personal and Confidential.*

Inside was another envelope with the legend: *Top Secret.*

It contained a letter from the Foreign Minister on a foolscap page, and eight typed quarto sheets.

His Honour explained, with almost ingratiating formality, that the report (attached hereto) was brought to the attention of the Ambassador for scrutiny and comment as soon as possible. He felt convinced that the Ambassador would be able to furnish an explanation which would speedily bring this unpleasant and presumably unwarranted matter to a satisfactory close. He would like to emphasize that the Department was regarding the conduct of the Third Secretary in question in an extremely serious light; and it could be anticipated that as soon as the Ambassador's expected commentary was received immediate steps would be taken accordingly.

The hands holding the white sheet did not move. The Ambassador's only reaction was an almost imperceptible pouting of his lower lip. He calmly and deliberately removed the paper clip, put the letter on the desk and leisurely read through the report. There was no expression on his face. Merely a slight movement of the eyebrows when, for the first time, he came cross the phrase: *Miss Nicolette Alford, a South African girl of questionable morality.*

Finally he replaced the letter, locked the document in his safe, and methodically studied his other mail. When he had finished, he summoned Anna Smith to dictate a few letters. After she had left, he asked Masters to come to his office for a discussion of the First Secretary's report on the proposed extension of the present Embassy building. He suggested a few minor changes in Masters' text before handing back the report for its final redaction. At half-past twelve he left in the official car for an important business lunch in the rue du Faubourg Saint-Honoré. Shortly after two o'clock he was back in his office to give audience to a leading French editor. Then he signed the letters Anna Smith had typed, drafted another of his own, gave her a few new instructions, and at exactly half-past three he picked up the telephone and asked Keyter to come up to his office.

A few minutes later the young secretary was standing in front of the stinkwood desk, unsuspecting, waiting, antagonistic, with one hand resting on the back of a chair.

That was where she had left the jacket. *Corpus delicti* number one. For a moment everything in him threatened to break into confusion so that he had to clench his hands on the chair's arm rests. Then, quite composed, he said: "I have received a report from the Minister."

"Mr. Ambassador?"

"Or rather, a transcript of a report. With your signature on it."

Now he was quite calm, watching attentively, with almost scientific interest, the two red spots gradually appearing on the young man's pale cheeks. On the wall opposite the window the clock was meticulously ticking off the seconds.

"Mr. Ambassador, I – You must realise that I merely did what I considered my duty. I have a very great respect for you. It was just that I thought the reputation of the entire – "

"I have already studied your motivation in the report, Keyter. I am pleased to hear that the reputation of the Foreign Service is so important to you." He moved into a more comfortable position, leaning slightly backwards, his fingers pressed together. "Now

111

perhaps we could dispense with the official trappings. Would you care to tell me why you *really* did it?"

"But Mr. Ambassador, don't you believe that – "

This, the Ambassador thought, this was hate; this was how it looked.

"In other words you acted according to your sincere conviction. What a pity you did not consider discussing the matter with me, or with Mr. Masters, before you acted. Was it necessary to disregard protocol?"

"It was urgent."

"I appreciate that. For surely nothing else would have induced you to compromise your whole career." He courteously inclined his head. "That will be all, thank you, Keyter."

"Mr. Ambassador – " He remained standing, with the two red blotches of anger on his cheeks and something smouldering in his almost colourless eyes; and – perhaps? – with a hint of doubt as well. But he left his sentence incomplete. Turning round abruptly he opened the door to leave.

"Keyter."

Obviously struggling to maintain his composure the Third Secretary looked back.

"Why did you throw Nicolette out of your apartment that night?"

Suddenly there were tears behind the young man's eyelashes. His lips were twitching; then he quickly went out and closed the door with a short, furious click.

It was silent in the large office.

The Ambassador got up and went to the heavy safe against the wall next to the glass book case. Only then, his hands clutching the smooth, cold corner of the safe, did he abandon his pose of calm. It had been his last display of power. To what end? To deliver a final blow to a man already driven to despair, while he himself was convulsing?

But God, God: not *this!*

He was perspiring. He turned round to face the office, *his* office, lifting his arms as if he wanted to protect everything with them; then they fell limply back to his sides.

"The wretched, irresponsible fool – ! "

He restrained his passion. The whole situation was humiliating enough as it was. He could only make it more humiliating, more vulgar by losing his temper. It was all so childish really. Surely he had enough confidence in his own ability to crush the matter quickly and efficiently.

He unlocked the safe and took the report back to his desk. For an hour he forced himself to work on a draft commentary. Then he neatly folded up all the written pages and burnt them to ashes in his waste-paper basket. How could he be expected to explain everything in smug, smooth terms? – *Your Honour, she was tired and she was sleeping, untouched, on my bed and I covered her with my dressing gown and sat up next to her until she awakened – Your Honour, I was waiting in her room while she was washing her hair and afterwards she said I was impotent and I left – Your Honour –*

It made him feel sick to reduce everything, in this way, to language, to statements, to self-defence.

And yet: suppose he did not do it?

He started again, but with the same result. Long after the rest of the staff had left, he burnt the last few pages, locked up the document again and went out. The cold darkness was burning his overheated face and body. He went to the main entrance, barely nodded at Lebon, crossed the street and proceeded to a restaurant in the avenue Wagram.

But before the last dish he had ordered could be served, he called the waiter, paid his bill, leaving an exorbitant tip, and went out. A fine drizzle had started.

And now: "home"?

No. When he reached the main entrance he turned away towards the Champs-Élysées. He could not face the isolation of his familiar fortress tonight. But he was also irritated by people; he felt hounded by them. He went on walking until the drizzle became so urgent that he hurried to the middle of the street, got into a taxi and ordered the driver to take him to the Latin Quarter. He stopped at the Odéon, not wanting the driver to discover his destination (why not?), and from there he walked to the old, carved door in the rue de Condé, which, even though he had been there so seldom, had suddenly become more familiar to him than the entrance to his own house.

There was no answer to his knock on her door. He waited for five minutes. She *had* to be there. She could not be away tonight. But she was. Somewhere in the teeming city, and not to be found.

He slowly went downstairs, and round to the rue de l'Odéon, his eyes searching for her bedroom window high up under the line of the roof. It was dark. He started walking to the Luxembourg Gardens, then back again, upstairs to her door. There was still no answer; and under her door there was still no line of light.

It was imperative that he see her. For this was the point to which everything had been moving. He should have foreseen it, yet it had caught him unawares. And now there was only one thing he could do: he must find her, talk to her, make an end to everything. The whole report was based on a misrepresentation. He was innocent. Before the next morning the very appearance and suggestion of guilt had to be eliminated, even if he had to wait for an hour, or hours.

He calmly pressed the bell. Almost immediately the landlady's door was opened behind him and the segment of a face appeared in the slit.

"Could you tell me where Miss Alford is?" he asked. "I must see her. It is a matter or urgency."

The door was opened wider. No, she did not know. If she had to find out where the girl was going every single time she went out there would not be time for anything else. But she could open up again if Monsieur would care to wait –

He shook his head, but when she had already started closing the door he changed his mind and said: "All right. If you please."

In the small bedroom he wandered about aimlessly, restlessly, feeling cornered, no longer sure whether he should have come in at all. Then his eyes were arrested by a movement in a window across the street, one floor lower than Nicolette's. At first it was the mere movement in itself which held his attention – the mercy of having something, *anything,* on which he could focus his thoughts, even the meaningless gestures of a stranger in a strange room: it suddenly seemed immeasurably significant to be standing there, half hidden by the curtain, observing without being observed, as if, for the first time in his life, he was really a spectator of the strange phenomenon, *man.* A man in a red dressing gown, sitting on a bed reading a newspaper; getting up to fetch some cigarettes across the room; returning; resuming his reading. A woman appearing from the mysterious interior of the building, wearing a short black tunic; undressing in front of the window, watched, silently, by the man. She was pregnant. The man put down his paper and came to her. She undid his gown. They turned back to the bed. And because of the distance all this was happening in dead silence, without words, a perfunctory Punch and Judy show with unselfconscious exhibitionism; and yet it suggested a form of very primitive life, something which could be expressed and satisfied by elementary movements and gestures.

The Ambassador turned away. He would have liked to be reassured about the banality of the scene, but he was forced to admit, however reluctantly, that he had been moved by it, that it had

114

instilled in him a vague anxiety which made it impossible to stay in that little room. And so he went out quickly, closing the door behind him. Lifeless, in alternate light and darkness, the five flights of stairs stretched downwards before his feet. When, at last, he reached the Carrefour, he deliberately chose the smallest, darkest streets. Soon he found himself in sinister little alleys which, a month ago, had not even existed in his mind. Narrow lanes with the odour of waste water, urine and rotten vegetables; disintegrating, crooked buildings supported, here and there, by ugly buttresses; stray cats; a tattered old clochard, tired and drunk, stumbling behind a child's pram containing all his earthly possessions; unexpected groups of students in dirty doorways, arguing and gesticulating, surrealist figures with burning eyes, pale faces and dishevelled dark beards; the noise of laughing, dancing and fighting from Chinese or North African caves and bistros dark with smoke; the wailing of a child being beaten somewhere in the dark. And all this was *her* world. An unreal, grotesque, fantastic world where pedestrians were shuffling past in the rain, bodiless and without any definite outlines; where occasional lamp posts were crowned by round spheres of light which did not seem to shine outwards and could not penetrate the darkness; a world which caused him to wonder whether he himself was real, whether he had ever been real. He walked on slowly, trying, it seemed, to select from all those unrelated things elements of her, explanations for her. He became a middle-aged traveller lost in a strange wood. And he thought, incredulously, how until recently Paris had been nothing to him but a name printed on top of a sheet of official paper, a set routine, particular routes, and a specified assortment of people.

After many detours, which more than once caused him to loose his way, he arrived back in the little street at the back of her building. Her window was still dark. This time he was not alarmed. The city itself had caught him in its grip. He resumed his wandering along another half-dark street, turned left, and strayed into a new labyrinth, until a broad stream of traffic suddenly opened up in front of him, with the dark, soundless Seine beyond. He crossed over to the pavement on the riverside, climbed up the steps of an old wooden bridge and went to lean across the rails. Twenty yards away from him, invisible in the dark, a clochard was playing a rickety old barrel-organ. Now and then, in a raucous voice, he would sing a few loose snatches of the melancholy tunes turned out by his organ. But eventually the singing and the music stopped; perhaps he had fallen asleep, perhaps he had left. Only the lazy movement of the river was continuing far below, with languid leaden ripples of light. All sounds were muted in the thin drizzle of rain.

He stood there thinking, remembering an impossible, distant night, and her words: " – *That's what the river does to one –*" But the memory was incomplete, merely a vague feeling of unrest. "*Tomorrow they'll be fishing her body from the river.*" Why did one do it, he wondered? What would make *her* do it, if she were driven to it? It came as a shock to him. For it did not seem altogether improbable that she might one day attempt it. There was that intangible melancholy in her – She was a stranger to him; he did not know her. But whom *did* he know? His wife, his own daughter? He kept staring out across the river. Would it mean that, against his own will and wish, he had simply become conditioned by his work, his way of life, until he could exist in only one sphere of thought and reflexes? That all other actions had been reduced deliberately to what was useful, practical, efficient, banished from consciousness, repressed merely because there had never been any time or desire to interpret or recreate experience? The pattern, the orderliness, the prescribed actions, protocol: everything that had always been so indubitably secure, so utterly reliable, because they were the formulae in which all human relationships had been catalogued and summarised. And why not? With complete detachment he decided: he had simply lost the faculty to *feel*. But was that so much of a loss? It was his sudden isolation here in the darkness, in the rain, above the moving water, that prompted these gloomy thoughts. Perhaps he was not leading anything like a "full" or a "complete" life: but it was all he *had*. He could not forsake it and start anew. He had no wish to. He was satisfied with what he had, and determined to retain it, come what may.

He resumed his journey, wandering through street after street; but now he regularly returned to the river as if it magnetised him.

Satisfied –? He was Ambassador. He was fifty-six. He had reached the summit. He could go no further. But suddenly he found the thought as suffocating as the back streets through which he was wandering. Yet why should it disturb him? He had always known that this day would come. Sooner or later one inevitably reached a point where all possibilities were fulfilled. And then one merely had to accept it, mark time, continue. But for how long? He might be transferred, one day, to London or Washington, but that was hardly relevant. It would mean a slight change of milieu: the nucleus would be the same. Letters and telegrams from an invisible Government. Instructions. Negotiations. Reports. Recep-

116

tions. Conversations. Official functions. It was his chosen life. He had entered into it with open eyes.

On a little square near the river, next to the dark mass of a statue in one corner, a windblown couple were trying to repair their broken-down scooter. The girl – light hair, large coat, narrow jeans – was holding a torch while the boy was working on the carburettor. There was a small line of tension between her eyes, and her teeth were chattering. They were oblivious of everything around them: completely isolated from the whole world in their unimportant little crisis. But they were *together*. And he was wandering through the streets, alone. Where was Nicolette? Where Erika and Annette, where Gillian, where anybody, anybody in the world? His bewilderment drove him past restaurants and bistros where invisible people had taken refuge behind steaming windows, until he reached the island, the heavy blunt towers of Notre-Dame. In his thoughts were words and unconnected phrases from Erika's last letter, three days ago. She would not be home for Christmas. Perhaps she would stay in Italy for another month, or longer. (*"What does it matter whether I am here or there? What does it matter whether I am, or not?"*)

Was it inevitable, then, was it something fatal, this solitude of his? Of Erika? Of everybody? Was it impossible to escape being caught in the mere *process* of living – of moving, eating, working – until all contact with others had ended?

He followed the little street beside Notre-Dame and crossed over to the Île Saint-Louis.

Keep walking, he thought. Keep moving your arms; talk aloud if you must. It would be nothing but a body moving and uttering sounds; something had disappeared from it. He was playing a part; playing a wanderer; playing an ambassador, delegated from death into this peculiar life – and all the time he was *aware* that he was playing. How could he escape from it? By returning to the few confused, insane, fanatic weeks with Gillian? But that would be absurd. It was not a matter of people or time, present or past; it was a matter of himself.

He went to lean over the stone wall of the little island, staring towards the back of the cathedral. And he felt almost resigned while he thought: once in his life, in the battle against Gillian, there had been an experience of agony, which made him think that it could never become any worse; there had been a new agony, during his eighteen months of self-imposed exile; and another, like a final conclusion, when he had to accept the fact that his child would never be to him what he had hoped her to become. Each

117

time he had thought: this was terrible, this was unbearable, this was the final crisis. But tonight's agony was more subtle, worse than ever before: the discovery that he could be *satisfied* with a life like his – the acquiescence in a pattern, the acceptance of a system, the resignation to a predestined existence. In reality he had long ago ceased to *be,* not only for himself, but for his Minister, his Government, his country. He could be cast aside and replaced and the work would go on as usual; perhaps, at times, less smoothly, and not always quite so spectacularly; but the brute force of the large machine, into which everything was integrated, would have enough momentum to carry on.

And yet, and yet: he *had* nothing else!

It was very late already. He had to return to Nicolette. Now it was even more urgent than before. It was she who, that night, had stepped from the outer darkness into his life to set everything in motion.

On his way he came past a huge building in which a few offices were still illuminated. At one desk a grey-haired man was sitting, leaning forward, writing, isolated in the sterile circle of his reading-light. And to the Ambassador the man at the desk was no stranger, but himself, sitting there, remote from the rain and the night, working, hour after hour, night after night, day after day, caught in a monotonous eternity; and he felt the urge to shout: "Come outside!" But he knew that the man would not even hear him, so he bent his tired shoulders and continued on his way.

The moisture was penetrating his thick overcoat. He was walking more slowly than before; weary; saddened by memories. It was not even a moment of choice, he thought – it was much more final. It was, very simply, a confrontation with his own nothingness.

She had not yet returned. Where in this wild city could she be? He was much too tired to resume his aimless wandering. On the floor of her landing, in the dark, he sat down, resting his back against the dirty wall. He would wait. Perhaps she would come soon. Perhaps she would never come. But he had to wait, whatever happened; it was the only thing he had left to do.

He had to untie himself. From her. From their few precious hours of being together. But was it possible to disentangle oneself from anything, ever? His whole life had been a gathering of bonds. A wife; a child; a household; and all the manifold bonds of his career. Nothing had ever happened accidentally, nothing had ever been forced on him; and there was nothing he would willingly discard. It was this very fact, that he had desired these bonds, and was still wanting them, which held him, irremediably caught. For

118

what would there be beyond his familiar existence? Gillian had desperately tried to break loose, to become free, to *be*. Nicolette was free already, but her liberty bewildered him; she was dancing too lightly through this dangerous world; she was too elusive, and too untouched, too ephemeral.

He must have dozed for a while. But his burning thoughts were continued in his dreams: He was wandering through strange streets, round and round a closed park, and all his efforts to enter were in vain. Then he awakened and thought, angrily, that it had been *her* dream, it did not belong to him. Unless, on this moment, she was dreaming of him. She – or someone. And if the sleeper were awakened, the dream would end as well, and *he* would end, like Tweedledum or Tweedledee.

At half-past one he heard the front door slam downstairs, far away; and the few landings with electric bulbs were illuminated. He heard voices. Someone laughed. She. A man answered. He could hear them leisurely climbing the stairs, singing. At first it was nothing but a tune, of which the words had been lost somewhere in his memory:

Au clair de la lune –

Then a burst of helpless laughter, and the little song started all over again. When they reached the third floor, the words went on:

Au clair de la lune, Pierrot répondit:
Je n'ai pas de plume, je suis dans mon lit –

By the time they started climbing the stairs to the fourth floor their mirth was becoming boisterous:

Au clair de la lune, l'aimable Lubin
Frappe chez la brune; elle répond soudain:
Qui frappe de la sorte? Il dit à son tour:
Ouvrez votre porte, pour le Dieu d'amour.

At the beginning of the fifth flight of stairs they struck up the last verse. Somewhere a door was opened and a sleepy voice shouted at them to shut up. But they only laughed, and went on singing as they mounted:

Au clair de la lune, on n'y voit qu'un peu.
On chercha la plume, on chercha du feu.
En cherchant d'la sorte, je n'sais c'qu'on trouva,
Mais j'sais que la porte sur eux se ferma.

Her companion – young, tall, lean, probably a student – reached the landing first and stood waiting, leaning drunkenly against the wall, while she was fumbling with her keys. At last the door swung open. She turned round, laughing. Theatrically, gaily, with slow emphasis, they repeated the last line as they went in:

119

Mais j'sais que la porte sur eux se ferma.

The Ambassador remained sitting on the dark landing without moving. Why had his headache become so unbearable? She had every right to be leading her own life.

After a long time he got up and went to her door. There he stopped, helpless. He looked back at the staircase. It was a dark void. He heard her laugh inside, far away. He had to go. What was he doing here? But he made no movement. From time to time he could still hear her distant laugh, languid and content. His head was throbbing. He was wet with perspiration.

It was almost three o'clock when at last he turned away from her door. From inside, from afar, from the deep, secret world of her room, he could hear the sound of quiet voices. He took out his cigarette lighter and set out on the long journey to the lobby downstairs, thinking, for no apparent reason, of the scene he had witnessed earlier that night, in the window across the street. He angrily shook his head, as if that would help to rid himself of it.

Exhausted, he arrived downstairs and sat down on one of the rubbish bins near the entrance. Now only a limitless desolation was left in him, all thoughts gone. He looked up. From the sky-light, very high up, came a faint glow of light. The rest was darkness. For fifteen minutes he remained sitting, simply because he had no courage to leave and to hear the front door slam behind him.

Then, suddenly, voices came bubbling from her room; and a few minutes later he heard her visitor's footsteps coming down. He did not move. The young stranger passed within a few feet of him, a tired, relaxed smile on his face, his hair dishevelled. Without even glancing at the Ambassador he went to the door, struggled with the latch for a moment, cursed, and disappeared.

The Ambassador got up and, once again using his cigarette lighter, started climbing the stairs, very slowly, but with determination. He had no thought left.

He knocked on her door. There was a slight movement inside, but no answer.

He knocked again.

"Who is it?" she asked softly, afraid.

"Open the door, Nicolette!"

The latch clicked and she peeped out. "What do you want?" she asked sleepily. "It's late already." She yawned, covering her mouth with her hand. The blanket she held round her, slipped from one of her shoulders.

He forced his way past her and went straight to her room. It was warm inside. More than the warmth of the radiator: it had a physical, human quality about it. The bed was crumpled, the pillow deeply indented. Her coat and dress were hanging over a chair, her underclothes lying in a bundle on the floor near the bed.

His hands were clenched tightly.

"Why did you do it?" he asked through his teeth.

"I haven't done anything. I was asleep."

"That's a lie!" His jaws were tense. "I was outside all the time."

"Oh." She looked neither ashamed nor surprised.

He took a step nearer. There were tiny dots jingling in front of his tired eyes. Then he grabbed a corner of the blanket she was clutching to her shoulders and jerked it away from her. She made no move.

"Little bitch!"

She was waiting patiently for the inevitable to happen.

His anger, his hours of waiting, his rebellion, his disillusionment, everything that was crumbling around him – it all suddenly broke loose in him; and it was all directed against *her,* this girl who was so quietly standing there in front of him, naked, as if it was quite natural to her. His hands were violently, jerkily fumbling with his clothes; he caught her right arm in a painful grip, threw her back on the bed, forcibly took possession of her. But force was not necessary, for she offered no resistance and was lying with her eyes closed, and a small twitch of pain round her mouth, her teeth biting into her lower lip.

Immediately after the momentary spasm he knew how derisive he had been; he brusquely freed himself of her and remained sitting on the edge of the bed. Now there was nothing left. He had made an incredible mess of everything. In the window opposite him he was mercilessly revealed to himself against a background of nocturnal darkness: a middle-aged man with greying hair and a hint of flabbiness round his middle, a naked blob of protoplasm ridiculously posed on the edge of a bed in an ugly, chaotic little room, his face contorted. He pressed his head into his hands, trying to wipe out his own image

Unmoving, slightly tense, she was still lying behind him. And only after a very long time did he feel the touch of her small boyish hand on his shoulder, and her hair against his back.

"You are unhappy," she said.

She pushed her back up against the wall, moved a pillow in behind her and allowed him to lie backwards with his head on her lap. His eyes were still tightly closed, humiliated, disillusioned, hopeless, while her cool hand was stroking his warm face.

"What has happened?" she asked.

He shook his head. "Nothing."

She leant slightly forward and with a corner of the sheet started wiping the perspiration from his face and shoulders.

"I wanted to hurt you," he said, his eyes still pressed close. "I lost my way somewhere and I wanted to take it out on you. I'm no better than any ordinary thug."

"Thug. Vagabond. Clochard." She was playing peacefully with these words, a child playing with pebbles. "It's such a friendly word: clochard. I would love to be one."

"You don't know what you're talking about." But there was no harshness left in his voice; it actually suggested something of a new tranquillity that was slowly taking possession of him.

"I know very well," she insisted. "I have often watched them, sitting under the bridges round their drums filled with red coals. And once, it was late one autumn afternoon, I was lying on a bench in the little garden under Notre-Dame, far away from the city, looking up at all the transparent green and yellow and brown leaves above me. I was lying with my head on my arms, my knees drawn up, and I was half asleep, I could vaguely hear the shouting of the playing children. I was imitating the clochards, and it was such a wonderful feeling of absolute satisfaction in my little circle of sunlight, for that one hour. I knew it would soon be dark and I was not sure whether I would have anything to eat – I was very poor then – but I did not care. Because, at that moment, for that hour, I was *there*, lying in the sun, with the leaves and the sky above me, and now and then, very dimly, I could hear the organ play in the cathedral. Perhaps it was just my imagination. But even that didn't matter."

Without opening his eyes he laughed softly; and at the same time he was surprised by his own reaction. "You're a child," he said. "It is easy for you."

"It is easy for anybody."

"I have got myself entangled, Nicolette. *I* can no longer lie in the sun. I have to draw up reports and conduct interviews. It is such important work. Oh, God – !"

"'But do you *have* to?"

"I am a tiny wheel in a very large machine, my little child. And do you know?" His lips formed a cynical smile. "All my life I have been preparing for 'something', for 'one day'. At first I wanted to get past my cadet period. If only I could be Third Secretary, I thought. Or: if only I could be sent overseas. Or: wait till I have a child. And all the time, behind everything else, there was one thought: when I reach the top one day – "

"What about it?"

He opened his eyes. "That is exactly what I am trying to find out now," he said. "Every time I became what I had wanted to be. And now I have reached the goal I have always desired. And what about it? Everything is still the same, exactly the same. A little more responsibility, a little more power, a little less freedom. And what else – ?"

"Isn't that enough?"

"But what *have* I?" he asked. "What am I doing *now* which is really worth while?"

"You are lying with your head on my lap," she said.

He looked up at her small face with the provocative mouth, and the smooth line of her cheekbones and jaws, and her wise, naughty, impossible eyes. His gaze shifted, to her small, high breasts, wide apart like a young girl's, firm and round, and tilted upwards, with little light-brown haloes. Supporting himself on his elbow he leisurely examined her whole lithe body. The tips of her hipbones, and the smooth, tense belly in between. The neat dark triangle, the top line disturbed by a single little curl. The tiny birth mark high up on her right thigh. Her slim, lovely legs with almost boyish knees. And all the time her eyes were watching him quietly and sure of herself, smiling at him, inviting him; and this time it started kindly and leisurely and with much tenderness: at first with lazy, almost tragic undertones, but gradually becoming more intense, as her hands and feet, her arms and legs and breath were coming alive, until her whole beautiful body was moving, against him, close to him, under him. In him, too, elementary reflexes took over, excluding all thoughts, everything except this brief ecstasy. Until the moment arrived when he was flung into a void, a small universe lost in himself, and in her – the paradoxical moment of absolute solitude and absolute togetherness. He became aware of her small teeth against his shoulder, and her fingers clawing into his back, and through her tears and her little bird-like sounds he heard her moan: "Oh God, oh God – !" And long after all movements had stopped he knew, from the almost desperate way she was clutching him to her, that she needed him, that there was *someone* who needed him; perhaps it would be only for a few minutes; but she needed him, now, and perhaps in the future.

He moved his fingers in her hair.

"My little girl," he said. "I love you."

"No, don't." She shook her head, looking at him with her bright, sad eyes. "Don't. It is enough for us to be together. Love is unbearable. I want something I could bear."

123

"I want to protect you, care for you, always," he said.

She shook her head again. Her eyes were anxious, even though her mouth was smiling. Almost sadly he moved away from her. She got up, went to the door to put off the light, and returned to him, snuggling into his arm like a small animal, with her back to him and her hair against his cheek; and in the narrow, uncomfortable bed, on the moist mattress with the hard buttons, she was soon serenely asleep while he was still awake.

The dim, late light of the city was filtering through the wet panes of the window, designing a rectangle above the bed. And caught in this penumbral frame was the shapeless shadow of her little cross hanging from its nail. For no reason at all he repeated the words she had said the other day: *"Agnus Dei qui tollis peccata mundi, miserere nobis. Agnus Dei qui tollis peccata mundi, dona nobis pacem."* And more softly, pensively, once again: *"Dona nobis pacem –"* He could hear her sweet breathing against the pillow. Such a small bed, he thought. And an equally small prayer. And all around them stood the large night. But this he had; this *they* had, and it could not be taken from them.

Without questions, without any thoughts, he was lying next to her, allowing the tranquil osmosis of their bodies to go on and on. And at last the first light slowly came through the window and the low murmur of the city was splintered into the separate sounds of day.

He had to get up, and dress, and go.

Outside it was clear and cold as he hurried to the nearest taxi rank. It was deserted. He hesitated. Then, for the first time, he went down into the metro.

In the course of the day he returned Keyter's report to the Minister, accompanied by a laconic note: *No comment.*

AMBASSADOR

1

How can I speak of her chronologically if she has no chronology?
For she is simply a sort of continuous present tense, a book one
starts reading in the middle and which has no cover, title page,
beginning or end. What I have of her is a confusion of loose
impressions: shreds of conversation, incoherent dream images,
fantasies, superstitions, desires, delightful pagan innocence, lies,
small gestures, passions, long pauses, unreasonable fears and questions, perhaps an attitude of the head, a curling of the lip, a
laugh, an obscene word. Memories of her are never "thoughts"
but sensuous experiences. The sadness of a crumpled wet towel.
An open laundry bag with dirty clothes. The scent of hair sham-
poo. Or an apple – often an apple – on a corner of the table, only
half eaten, with a fresh, clean, sensual white shell pattern of tooth-
marks and tiny, glistening speckles of spit round the bite. I can
see her rolling out of the narrow bed on cold weekend mornings,
screwing her eyes against the colourless light of the window,
wandering through the room aimlessly and naked, not knowing
what she is looking for, picking up a shoe, pulling out a drawer,
stopping for a moment with a stocking draped over her arm, starting to pack away her records, finally making the discovery of herself in the newly bought mirror with the gaudy gilt frame, scrutinising every square inch of her body, piling up her hair on her head
or letting it fall over one shoulder, until, at last, she comes to her
fingernails and starts examining them one by one – and then,
perhaps, she would become slightly shivery and drape an old
blue gown loosely round her. I can see her lying in my arms, her
quiet head sleeping against my shoulder in the legendary innocence
of a girl lost in her deep rest as in water, deeper than water, in a
soundless, still, inorganic layer of existence, beyond dreams.
And I smell her hair, and her cheap or expensive perfume, and
herself: the indefinable *odor di femina*. She walks through the
darkness inside Notre-Dame in a sober dress with a scarf round
her hair. She laughs in a third-rate music-hall, her head thrown
back, her lips and teeth shiny and moist. She stands with a handful of snow in a large white garden with black trees. She leans
against a rail in the metro and, like a puppy, makes friends with
a stranger who is leering lasciviously in her direction. She cries

over a dove nest fallen from a chestnut tree in a rainstorm. I taste her tears. I taste cheep sweets on her lips. I taste the tip of her tongue. In my back I can feel her drawn-up knees. On my upper arm I feel the grasp of her greedy fingers. My cheek remembers the playful touch of her lips. And in my hand sleeps the memory of a small breast. I spell the pretty notes of her name as if that would reveal her to me. But at last my tongue stops on the unpronounced last syllable, just as all thoughts come to rest on what is inexplicable in her. She has the absolute closeness of somebody who is wholly open – glass through which one stares without being aware of it. She is self-sufficient, yet she does not exist in isolation, apart: because through her I return to the past and exorcise all the possibilities which remained for ever unfulfilled; through her I examine my relations with everybody around me; through her I am mercilessly forced back into myself, deeper and deeper, in the hopeless hope that the result would lead me to *her*. For when I think of her, she is a legend, a fairy tale; she is Heloise as well as Francesca da Rimini; and she is also: Pasiphae. But when all is said and done, all that remains is *she* – known, yet unknown. She is so completely herself – a girl, and young – that she has become her own myth.

2

She is lying on her back on the little bed, one knee drawn up high to support the other foot, absorbed in the delicate task of painting her toenails green.

I am standing at the window, satiated with looking at her, watching the window opposite where the young woman of a month ago is removing her necklace and earrings in front of the open curtains. She has already noticed me, because the light is shining; yet, without the slightest hesitation, she proceeds with the strange process through which she undergoes the complete metamorphosis from a sophisticated creature in a coat and tailored two-piece to a pale mother animal with protruding breasts and belly. And all this is taking place without any selfconsciousness or mystery or perverseness: a sober fact. Her husband has entered a moment ago and now he is leading her away from the window, to the bed. It is like a silent movie; but no comedy, because, throughout the entire apparently natural process there is a suggestion of passion and fear in her, which, it seems, she is desperately trying to convey to me, but which remains incomprehensible.

"Can you see them?" Nicolette asks, wiggling her big toe in front of her fastidious gaze.

"Who?"

"The people across the street."

"What do you know about them?" I turn round with an inexplicable feeling of guilt.

"Nothing." She calmly sets to work on the second foot.

She laughs, without looking up.

"How long have they been carrying on like this?" I inquire.

"For quite some time. At first they used to draw the curtains. It's only lately, since they got married, that they don't care any more. She used to live there on her own. From time to time she had a different man with her. Then this one man kept coming back. She got pregnant. And then they got married – at least, that's what I think, for I've seen a ring on her finger."

"Surely that's no reason why they should give free *expositions* to the whole street?"

"I suppose she feels stifled in a closed room."

Her attitude suggests that she would like to say more, that she knows more than she has revealed. But she leaves me with the riddle, continuing, with frowning concentration, her funny work.

"I've told you before that this is no suitable environment for you to live in."

Two green eyes look up at me through loose, light strands of hair. "Why not? People do it everywhere – even in Neuilly or the avenue Wagram." Adding, deliberately: "I've done it there myself."

Does she realise what she is doing to me when she so regularly makes these references to her secret life? Sometimes I wonder, almost dazed: What is the matter with me? What am I doing here with her? What could she – or anybody else like her – offer me? And sometimes I feel the desire to treat her like a child, to punish her, so that she would *know* what she is doing. Above all, there is this despair in me: Here I am with her, but this is not all of her, it is not the whole *she*. There are so many others in this city carrying something of her inside them. More agonising still: every single inhabitant of the city carries her memory in his conscious or subconscious mind, whether he has slept with her, or sold her a pair of nylons, or brushed against her in the metro, or merely stared at her legs. She is not confined to these four walls huddled so closely together under the roof. Like a single cheap grain of bath salts penetrating a large bathful of water, she has permeated Paris: every alley and crumbled wall, every chrome juke-box in cheap little cafés, every old newspaper wrapped round greasy *frites*, every dark church, every clochard, every dented rubbish bin, every stained glass window, every moist black stone along the dirty Seine has something of her – a glance, a footstep, a single hair, a tear, a drop of spit, the sound of a laugh. And what minute part of her belongs to me? Is it not presumptious even to think that I possess anything of her, as if anything about her could be "had"?

She screws the pointed cap back on the varnish bottle and comes over to the window, pressing her nose against the pane. I deliberately refrain from looking at the opposite window and watch her instead. But once she utters a short laugh which forces me to glance outside: The man is standing at his window making obscene gestures in her direction. While anger tightens my jaws, she reacts nonchalantly, smilingly, by pressing the *fica* sign against the window before, with one easy sweep, she draws the curtains.

"Why do you look at them if it upsets you?" she asks.

For a moment I cannot think of an answer.

Then, *à propos* of nothing, she remarks: "You don't get along well with your wife."

"On the contrary, we get along extremely well."

"But you don't need each other."

"What makes you think so?"

"I don't think you want, really *want,* each other."

Without any warning the conversation has reached this point of precarious balance where an answer, however casual, may assume tremendous importance. I have no desire to go on fencing, pretending, playing. It would be senseless; then it would degenerate into one of our "clever" conversations where the only aim is to evade each other conspicuously.

"I want *you,* Nicolette."

For a moment she seems to consider contradicting me. Then, almost demurely, she says: "Yes." And she presses herself against me to kiss and to be kissed, repeating, emphatically: "Yes", as if she is trying to convince something inside herself. And the moment I know or believe, or hope, that she has surrendered completely she remarks neutrally: "She'll come back. And then you will forget all about me. But you mustn't. You mustn't leave me alone again."

"My darling little girl – "

130

She takes my handkerchief from my pocket and attentively wipes her rouge from my lips.

After a while she says: "Come. It's not too cold outside tonight. We are going out."

"Why can't we stay here? It is so seldom we can be together."

"No." There is a nervousness in her eyes. "It's – stuffy inside." And without waiting for an answer she goes to the cupboard, peels off her dress and changes into slacks and two or three jerseys.

"Why do you always want to go out the moment we are together peacefully?" I protest. "It almost looks as if you're afraid of something."

"I want to show you the city."

It always happens like this; and I dare not resist; as a matter of fact, I don't know whether, perhaps, she sincerely means what she says. But even if she does there must be an unconscious motive somewhere. Is it a form of rebellion? – but against what? Or a challenge? – but to do what?

"I'm ready." She throws the ends of a long red scarf over her shoulders. In spite of all the careful attention to her toes her dainty feet are hidden in black furline booties. "Am I pretty enough?"

I smile, and ask: "What for?"

"For the night."

"Yes, you are pretty enough – for the night." Middle-aged, I turn to the door and open it for her. "You'll have to show the way."

She begins to climb down the stairs that are winding their way down into the dark, circle after circle.

Hesitant, still undecided whether I should indeed follow her, I stop after the first few steps.

"Come on!" she calls up to me. "We have a long way to go!"

I have little hope that it would lead to anything. But if I turn back, she will only continue without me. And so, with a little sigh, I follow her down. Reaching the circle of light on the landing below, isolated between darkness and darkness, she glances back before she moves on with the unselfconscious knowledge of her youth. Deep, quiet desire is stirred up in me again. Everything, these days, depends upon such minute, fleeting gestures, ephemeral foam drifting on a dark wind; and yet, for that very reason, it is immensely significant.

She has already reached the third flight of stairs, which has no light. A small dog is barking behind a closed door. "Poor little thing," she says. "He knows my footsteps already. You see, he never gets enough to eat – his owner is too greedy – so I have to bring him food."

I make no comment.

On the edge of the next circle she stops for a moment to ask: "Have you enough money?"

I nod, with a questioning glance at her.

"I feel like spending a lot tonight."

She goes frisking down the next flight. And while I am following her, resigned, I am amused and perplexed by the readiness with which I yield to all her whims. And I remember Erika's regular complaint about my stinginess.

"Be careful!" she calls from the lobby below the last flight of stairs. "The door was open all afternoon and the rain came in. It's a proper swamp!"

In spite of her warning I lose my balance in a slippery puddle, and stumble against one of the rubbish bins. With an infernal clattering the lid rolls on the floor, echoing through the whole building. Nicolette bursts into helpless laughter.

There is an angry shout from the concierge's door, followed by an incredible stream of invective. Then Nicolette, still laughing, takes me by the arm, and we leave him behind in the dark.

We enter an obscure, narrow, silent lane. The noise of the traffic is shut off behind the high buildings. Our footsteps echo against the walls. The little shops and boutiques on the ground floor are all lugubriously shuttered and padlocked. Here and there a lamp post stands meekly in its own circle of light. It is very cold, but there is no wind, and the sky is open, although no stars are visible. The high buildings create the impression that one is walking along deep, subterranean passages.

As we are passing a dimly-lit bistro there is a sudden outburst of noise and violence, with two drunken, tattered women attacking each other like furies. One is pushed through the open door and lands stumbling against us. Hysterical, she staggers to her feet again, swings round and slaps Nicolette. But before the quarrel can turn into a serious brawl – I am aware of Nicolette's clenched lips next to me – a smiling *patron* hurries outside and leads the infuriated hag away. I firmly grasp Nicolette's hand in mine and, much against her will, resume our promenade.

"That man has been sent by heaven," I mutter, not quite recovered from the shock.

To my surprise she begins to laugh.

We follow the gradually widening streets until the parallel lines of the buildings on either side suddenly swing open on the Place Saint-Germain-des-Prés, lying outstretched in blazing light, moving like a thing possessed of its own life. From all sides people are streaming onto the square. Ascetic young men with hollow eyes; girls with stark white bony faces, tousled hair and black clothes, like resurrected corpses; tourists; strollers. And all round the teeming square the lights are burning like so many fires: pale lights enhancing the unworldly atmosphere of the scene; shiny beetles round the open graves of existentialists, living and dead.

It becomes hallucinating, terrifying: this milling around without end or direction; this movement without reason; this heresy against all demands of sense and coherence; this meaningless, aimless rebellion under a heaven without stars, against the doors of the morose church.

And she strolls through it all with so much ease and so much grace, crossing the boulevard against a red light while walls of traffic are dammed on either side, hooting and shouting in a deafening din; students, going berserk, are frolicking among the cars, climbing on bonnets, shouting wise-cracks and abuse. Police are scurrying to and fro to control the traffic, their black cloaks fluttering grotesquely.

"Where are we going?" I shout against the nerve-racking noise.

"Nowhere," she laughs. "We are just walking. Don't you like it?"

I look at her fair hair which has inexplicably come loose round her shoulders; and at the light, swinging movement of her long legs and her big warm coat; and at the little clouds of mist escaping from her mouth with every word or laugh.

We reach the small garden under the church where a few people are forming a thin circle, shivering on hard benches round a cluster of bare black shrubs; in the high branches of the trees badly concealed floodlights are mounted to illuminate the massive tower.

"Last night somebody committed suicide from the tower," I hear her say. "It was after everybody had left of course. How terrible."

In vain I try to find a secret meaning behind her words, but her face is expressionless, half hidden by the thick scarf.

Then there is a scream in the branches above our heads. Nicolette cries out, frightened, catching hold of my arm with both hands. All the heads are turned upwards.

"An owl," murmurs the collar of a shapeless coat.

"I thought it was another crank trying to – " She laughs nervously. "Or a ghost. I've got the creeps. Come, let's go."

Once again we cross the teeming street, find our way through the crowd and, with a sigh of relief, sit down in the corner of a café terrace.

"Satisfied?" I inquire, wryly, when the large cups of mocha are put down in front of us. ·

"Delicious."

"I was referring to the bedlam outside."

"It's the same as usual," she says, emptying four or five packets of sugar into her steaming cup. And the simple gladness kindled in me by her naïve enjoyment of the frothy mocha, together with the warmth that gradually invades my frozen body, change my sullen fatigue to complete relaxation. At one stage I even laugh with her at a bundle of bewildered strangers standing outside, like dishevelled fowls, with protruding necks, gaping at the bedlam.

"Saint-Germain-des-Prés: done," says Nicolette.

Laughing, I banish the memory of how, a few minutes ago, I was standing outside exactly like them: forever on the verge, just outside everything, without understanding.

When I look back at Nicolette the slovenly old man in the brown coat is standing beside her chair. Everything about him is tattered and tired; yet his beady eyes are wrinkled with laughter above his chubby cheeks, covered by a web of red and purple veins.

She leans back, smiling; then turns to me and introduces him: "This is old Brunetto."

The old man grins through his unkempt beard and lifts his hand – whether in greeting or blessing I cannot tell.

I answer with a formal nod, not very encouraging, questioning her with my eyes.

"Old Brunetto is Italian," she explains. "A 'queer'. He used to live in Florence, but after the war he came to Paris. Now he's telling people's fortune in the cafés." She turns to him and repeats something in rapid street French.

He answers in a mixture of French and Italian, which she obviously understands, for she leans across the table to translate: "No ordinary fortune-teller, he says. He is really a prophet."

"And consequently not honoured in his own country: is that why he is here?"

She pays no attention to me. Turning back to him, she stretches out her right hand in his direction, palm upwards. The old man bows to our neighbours, mumbling: "Permette?", removes a chair from their table to ours, sits down heavily and takes her small white hand in his rough, dirty paws. For a few minutes he sits mumbling to himself. Then he begins to "prophesy". Occasionally she translates a few phrases for my benefit. There is great happiness in store for her. A good man. Middle-aged? (He glances in my direction, winking.) He can see a church. And darkness. And an easter egg.

"But what does it *mean*?" she insists. Then, to me: "Every time he sees new things."

"He has to, if he wants to keep on making money out of you."

Ignoring me, they are now discussing his esoteric symbols.

"Now it's your turn," she announces at last.

"No. It's pure nonsense."

"But you *must*! Brunetto isn't a quack! Oh please do."

Grinning patiently, he sits waiting, realising – I suppose – that sooner or later, for the sake of peace, I must concede. When, at last, I reluctantly surrender my hand to his claws I wonder with some amusement: What would happen if one of my staff suddenly looked through a window – ?

He begins to "read".

"He says you're a very important man," Nicolette interprets.

"Thank him for the compliment. But it will not add anything to his tip."

"He says you're engaged in difficult work."

I merely sniff.

"He says there's much happiness in store for you."

"Thank you."

"But he says your own people are going to reject you because they do not understand you."

"I'll take the warning to heart."

"He says he can see a goat walking towards a hill, but without reaching the green grass."

"Is he quite sure it isn't simply an old goat looking for a tender leaf?" I ask, but it does not sound like a joke.

"And now he please wants his money."

"Tell him he is a wise master speaking immortal words." I hand him a ten franc note. "Thank you, Brunetto," I say in French, with exaggerated politeness.

He quickly thrusts the note into his pocket, then lifts both hands to bless us – and to my embarrassment I can see two tears trickle over his flabby cheeks into his beard.

"Brunetto always tells the truth," says Nicolette, with a very solemn air, as the old Italian disappears into the cold night. "I wonder what he could have meant with darkness? Do you think it has anything to do with my dream? Remember, I told you – "

"Come," I interrupt her, upset by the old fortune-teller who has made his appearance like a conscience in beggar's clothes among all these strangers.

And then she leads me into the lanes of another labyrinth: in the direction of the Seine, as far as I can make out from the slight decline. She stops in front of what seems to be an ordinary bistro, but which has a staircase against the back wall leading to a basement from where the muffled noise of voices and shrill music is audible.

"Haven't we seen enough for one night?" I ask wearily.

Her only answer is to take my arm and lead me inside. She seems to know the place, for with a slight nod in the direction of the waiters behind the counter she proceeds straight to the staircase. On the landing hangs a modernistic sign board representing an upside-down clown. Quite apt, I think in passing.

As we descend lower the din increases. And at the turn of the stairs one has a view on a fairly long, narrow room, lit by only two bare bulbs, far apart; for the rest, there is an assortment of phantom-like creatures moving through a whorl of smoke, to the accompaniment of monotonous, oppressing drum and trumpet music from an invisible corner. Occasionally dancing couples make their appearance from the cloud of smoke, nearer to us than the dim figures in the background; shabbily dressed; with white faces and long hair; some of them performing the slow, lazy movements of algae, joined at the pelvis like siamese twins; others moving more jerkily, with groping arms and spastic heads; and as they come dancing past, they turn their heads back wordlessly to stare at us with hypnotic, expressionless, red or black-rimmed eyes.

We find two empty chairs at the end of a long table against the outside wall. Round us is a whirlpool of smoke; visible and invisible surrealist creatures are talking and laughing, sometimes screaming, moving past us, and disappearing again; and in the corner the bodiless drum continues its exorcising beat, working up to regular climaxes and then fading away into the distance, without ever falling altogether silent. We are integrated into the witches' sabbath, temporarily left at peace in our corner – but not for long.

136

"Come, let's dance," says Nicolette. Her eyes are large and excited, with a strange, terrifying expression in them, as if she is moving in a trance.

At first I refuse, but she lays her hand on my arm and makes it impossible not to yield. Tentatively we move into the outer circle of dancers, but as I become more and more aware of her shameless youth so close to me, and of her abandonment to the disturbing, evil heart-throb of the music, I lose all reluctance; and without any effort on my part we are absorbed by the whirlpool, by the entire restless, magical movement. All thoughts, all customary relations lose their significance and disappear; we too, she and I, disappear; pure movement takes over – movement, and the evil primitive rhythm of the invisible drum. And it is only when I become aware of my fatigue again that we drift loose from the throng and return to our seats at the long table. Her hair is damp, but she shows no weariness; I am wet with perspiration, my legs almost numb.

Then a young demon with hair curling round his ears appears at our table and greets Nicolette. She laughs back at him, almost shrilly, and I realise that she is breathing more quickly than earlier in the evening. They seem to be old acquaintances (but where did they meet?) and go on talking for some time without paying any attention to me. Until he suddenly stops in the middle of a sentence, glances at me, and inquires: "And the old chap?" ("Le vieux" are his words.)

"My father," she replies without hesitation.

He extends a bony white hand which I accept. But he seems to be speaking a language infinitely more strange than French, as if we belong to different planets. And after a short moment of hypocritical attention to me he returns to Nicolette.

"Come," he orders.

She looks at me.

He laughs, lifting his hand, pretending to pronounce a magic formula over her: "*Rafel mai amech zabi almi!*" Then takes her hands in his, insisting: "Now you have no choice."

Laughing she gets up, leans over and playfully kisses one of my moist temples; then they are dissolved into the cloud. The drum is moving towards another climax, accompanied by a hysterical saxophone – or is it a distorted human voice? it is difficult to tell – the whirlpool is turning faster, the whole infernal movement is spinning on and on. And somewhere in that cloud is she, Nicolette, lost in the semi-darkness among the many possessed. Sometimes I catch a glimpse of her with her head thrown back, her hair tousled and free, her mouth open, laughing, screaming, or panting; or else I see her subdued, quiet, her head nestled on a shoulder against the pale smudge of an unknown cheek. And the only thought I am aware of is that I have lost her, for a few minutes or an hour perhaps, but irrevocably, because her present is everlasting; and I know that she is young, devastatingly young, wonderfully young; and that I am old, *le vieux*, her father, something from which she had to untie herself before, like the others of her generation, she could lose herself, convulsing in this ecstasy of the void. And it takes place with so much seriousness, even the laughing and cavorting, as if they are all caught in a ritual: a primordial pattern to which one could not react in any conventional way, with any customary emotions. Therefore I am left simply with an experience of dazed anguish, isolated at the far end of the table against the brick-red wall; and yet I am fatally part of the situation. For half an hour, for an hour, for hours I remain waiting, in vain; until the drum is no longer throbbing in the corner but in my own breast, throbbing convulsively, desperately, orgiastically, so that I have to lean back, nauseous, gasping for breath.

Almost panic-stricken I get up and start shuffling along the wall through the smoke while people, chairs, tables, floor, walls are dancing to the tempo of my beating heart. Near the third corner I finally notice a red arrow pointing to a few steps leading further downstairs. Stumbling, I follow the arrow, close a door behind me, and for a few moments remain standing to allow the dizziness to pass, vaguely conscious of the now distant noise. A narrow passage takes me to the inevitable doors marked *Messieurs* and *Dames*. I open the first. Inside it is almost dark, with only the light from the corridor coming through the skylight. In one of the four or five similar cubicles I can hear voices: laughing, panting, groaning. Resigned – nothing can surprise me any more – I pass the row of brown doors to the opposite wall. The third door is wide open and in passing I catch a brief glimpse of the young man and the girl inside standing pressed together, convulsing. On the floor, propped up against a little heap of clothes, is a battery torch, casting grotesque shadows on the back wall, resembling giants with writhing torsos, frantically trying to escape from a well.

When, three minutes later, the automatic door swings close behind me, the giants are still dancing on the wall.

Nicolette is waiting at our table in the *cave*, nonchalantly, as if nothing has happened. Only her pallor and the beads of perspiration on her forehead and round her mouth, suggest the contrary.

"Shall we go?" I ask.

She obeys, without protest. From the staircase I take a final look back. At one of the nearest tables a girl is leaning back, pouring a glass of wine into her open mouth. Even before she has swallowed it all a man next to her leans over and starts kissing her greedily. Then they are shrouded in a whorl of smoke. In the far corner the saxophone resumes its agonised yelling.

Nicolette is already waiting outside in the sudden, clear cold. Above her, inclined over the dark line of the buildings, is the thin sliver of the moon.

We are silent on our way back. There is so little one could say. The streets are almost deserted. Under a lonely lamppost my watch hands reveal an unemotional V – ten minutes to two – but it has stopped: a minute or hours ago. Timeless, we surrender ourselves to the dark streets.

Once she takes a short-cut along a narrow passage without any light. And in this utter, final darkness, without any apparent reason, I think of Keyter. "Do you often come to this part of the city?" he asked his Judas question, weeks ago. I smile wryly in the dark. And yet: would I have been here – "in this part of the city" – if he had not done what he did?

But her hand which touches mine, because she is afraid of the night, banishes all thoughts. Empty, we wander through the city's emptiness, having nothing but each other left.

At last her entrance with the weather-beaten paradise scene appears before us.

"Must I come in?" I sigh.

She nods.

"It was, after all – "

"We are tired," she says, as if that summarises and concludes everything. "Come."

Upstairs, circle after circle, until we reach the little moon shining faintly through the window in the roof. Her step still proves her invincible youth; at the same time there is something infinitely more wise in her than I have ever noticed.

And then: the light of her small room; and our bed.

3

– *and then Naples and Pompeii.* Dolce far niente. *See Naples and die. The great illusion. Naples is a lavatory with a view on the* sea. But I very conscientiously 'did' it all: in Italy one does as the other tourists do. So I dutifully strolled past tumbled walls and loose stones in Pompeii and, being a good tourist, implicitly believed whatever the guide rolled off his smooth tongue as rapidly and with as much meaning as one recites the Our Father.

You may laugh if you wish, but I have also systematically explored a few Neapolitan museums which are usually only mentioned in a whisper in polite company; and in Pompeii all the doors and hatches usually unlocked by a lewd old guide for men only were opened for me. I had to use "influence" of course. Our Embassy had too much red tape (the wretched little Third Secretary, Immelman, is, like Shelley, an "ineffectual angel"), so Annette's Italian in the Foreign Service arranged everything. He probably regarded me as a frigid, frustrated woman in her change of life who was using the opportunity of getting a few artificial "kicks". (Perhaps he was right, although my last few grains of self-respect would not allow me to admit it.)

I am trying to evade the issue. For how could I write about it? How could I force myself to confess that this excursion has brought back so many uninvited, forgotten things? I was not touched so much by the stones or the lava of Pompeii: it was a different sort of pilgrimage.

Twenty-five years of our way of life tend to make one blasé. But I must confess that the sudden confrontation with those statues and symbols and frescoes with their shameless affirmation of sexual delight came to me as a sort of spiritual concussion. At first I lifted my nose and laughed with polite scorn as was required of me. But Paul! one cannot shut oneself off behind a screen if one keeps on wandering among these things for a long time. At first I, too, used to dismiss it all so easily, thinking: What an immoral lot these old Romans were. No wonder Pompeii shared the fate of Sodom and Gomorrah! But make your home on the slope of a volcano, Paul, realising – even subsconsciously – that the lazy smoke of death is curling above your rooftop day and night – and you, too, would take your paint to write on a wall: 'Carpe diem . . . Ergo vivamus, dum licet esse, bene'! But I found that even this is a much too simple explanation for Pompeii. For these people of the frescoes and statues, these calcified corpses which are still being excavated from their beds or streets or diningrooms or baths, these people were NOT leading one long life of bestial orgy. They adorned their walls with the fica and the phallus not because each house was a bordello, but because that was their way of exorcising the Evil Eye, of warding off Invidia. How could

140

they resist the Unknown except by using the essential symbols of life? And this was not merely their answer to Evil, but to death itself. Every grave bears the insignia of Priapus and Venus. There was nothing vulgar or indecent about sex. It was the miracle through which men and women could live openly, purely, in the full freedom of their senses, the only way in which they could share the pleasure of the immortal gods. It became a sort of Mass, a complete transsubstantiation, through which death was changed into life and life into death. The sole paradox which renders life worth while.

And so on.

Don't you think I listened very obediently to all the guide told me? I made notes while he was talking. Point one: sex and Evil Eye; point two: sex and death –

And now they are dead, all of them, all those beautiful people of Pompeii. Did you know that in a prostitute's little room in a bordello they found a basket with charred onions and beans? Take your choice: the immortal delight of the gods – or a basket of onions and beans. And what have I got? I am nearly fifty. (Annette's Italian insists – of course! – that I'm looking younger than forty. Mirror, mirror on the wall – !) I am not even whole any more. I can hardly remember a time when I was whole; and you, I suppose, have forgotten it altogether. I had never been very pleased with the prospect of having a child (after all these years one may as well phrase it politely; but at least I had hoped that I would give birth to her in the normal way, like other women did. And then it was a caesarian. Everyone deeply thankful to doctor and Giver of all. Nobody realised that, suddenly, I was no longer I – bourgeois, if you wish, unimportant, anything, but at least living in a whole body, perhaps even a beautiful body. Now there was the scar, thick and swollen under my fingers at night, a purplish scar, a horrible acknowledgement of my own impotence. I have never been able to "make" anything, to create anything. The only bit of creativity I have ever had, went into the making of this child – and even that I could not do in the normal way. I got used to it, of course. With the years the mark has faded. But it has never disappeared, it is still there. And one day, when they lay out my body, it will still be there: whitish, a line of leprosy.

I can remember the first night, three months after her birth, when you came to me again. How your fingers moved across my belly and suddenly tautened. You didn't say anything. You went through the whole process, step by step according to the prescribed rules, as methodically as you do all your work in the office. But I knew your hands were afraid of that long, swollen scar. I knew, because I, too, was afraid. I tried to dissolve my fear in you, but then I felt your hands move away from the wound and I knew that there was something which could never again be said between us. From that moment neither of us would know me any more: this stranger bearing the mark of Cain – not even on my forehead but, humiliatingly, on my belly. What has become of me, the 'I' with whom I used to live in the whole body? You will have forgotten that night long ago; our nights were never very memorable. But I could not, because it has been branded into me.

I am not blaming you. It is I who never knew, or never accepted, that one could give so much in the dark. I could find many plausible reasons for this: my obedient, carefully planned childhood; the discipline; the boarding school; the holidays at home when I had to 'learn the ropes' with my mother's social obligations – But one reaches a stage where plausible reasons are no longer adequate, and then one has nothing left but oneself.

All this soul-searching merely because an Italian in an immaculate suit has given me a series of lectures on the role of sex in the life of the old Romans, as impersonally as if he was explaining the respiratory system of the frog!

Annette accompanied me on these excursions although I suppose she would have preferred to visit churches. (Are you scowling? This would not be your idea of educating a girl of eighteen!) Sometimes I reproach myself about it. More often I think: That would teach her. But teach what? What is it in me which urges me to shock her, to shake her awake, to force her into something?

But it is not right of me to use my letter to you as a means of solving my own riddles.

I suppose we should be thinking about coming back. It is January already. But it would be senseless to hurry. Those very riddles must be solved first.

Love, Erika.

4

On the last day that chronology mattered, Wednesday 19th December, early in the morning, when I left her after our first night together, I set out quite mechanically for the boulevard Saint-Germain, chilly after the human warmth of her little room. It did not even surprise me to find the taxi rank deserted and as I was going down the metro and walking along the long corridor to the ticket office my only thought (if indeed I had any thoughts) was:

This is as it should be. I joined the queue and bought my ticket. Much to the annoyance of everybody behind me I first stopped in front of the large wall-map to trace my route; then I abandoned myself to the crowd and started drifting through echoing corridors. Despite the early hour it was stuffy inside, with an overwhelming stench of old garlic and feet. Somewhere ahead of me, where trains came clattering past at short intervals, a pair of green gates regularly swung close to stop the crowd. And all the time they were pressing inside, from numerous corridors, down numerous stairs. Sleepy girls with pale faces under their make-up. High coiffures gradually coming undone and stringy in the throng. Preoccupied businessmen in grey overcoats and black hats, reading their papers held in hands outstretched above their heads. Housewives with string bags. Chattering children on their way to school. Serious students with hair curling over their collars. Couples in passionate embrace, kissing with open mouths in spite of the jostling crowd. It was as if I had suddenly arrived there from another planet, looking for the first time at the spectacle of humanity.

I wonder whether I had ever before had the time to stand and watch anything like this? One is generally so much occupied with the mere organisation of life as a *process* that there is no time left for meditation. And what suddenly troubled me was the discovery that everything not experienced meditatively, was worse than inertia: it was regression, because one's faculties of interpreting experience were blunted. And never – not since Gillian and my eighteen months of liberty – had I experienced so much as that previous day. Or: those previous six hours, ever since the door had been opened in her dark building and two voices had come up the stairs singing *Au clair de la lune.* Twelve hours earlier I had been in a taxi on my way to the rue de Condé. At that stage everything had still been oppressively uncertain, brooding, fermenting. And now – ? It seemed no less complex than before. There was no more certainty about the future. But I was no longer working with mere possibilities or hypotheses. Whether I wanted it or not, I was confronted with a *fait accompli.* Nothing was simple; but everything was lucid.

The green gate swung open once again and this time I landed on the dirty platform. A minute later a train came bursting from the tunnel. Having neglected to buy a first-class ticket I was bundled into an already overcrowded second class coach, together with countless others. Forced into a corner with an uncomfortable knob against my back, I stood staring at the moving walls of the tunnel outside.

Was it absolutely necessary that I had to spend a few hours with a warm, fragrant girl on an uncomfortable little bed in order to come to this? But the how and why were scarcely relevant. What mattered, was the simple *fact*. And how elementary it really was! For what could be more natural than that her sort of life had always been there, undetected, on the periphery of my own routine existence? The only difference was that, now, I had also landed on that periphery between two circles, aware of both. Or perhaps: that the previous night had confronted me with the question whether "her sort of life" was not "life itself". Even that was banal. Surely I must have been aware of it all along; I had just shirked the self-inquiry, the conscious analysis which would be the natural result of such a knowledge – because this inquiry so often unearthed nothing but skeletons in one's own graveyard heart: it is so much easier to keep the heart closed. But that would presuppose a possibility of choice; and I no longer had any choice.

The doors slammed shut on the next station, and we rattled on.

Could it all be reduced to this, then? The entire human organisation of state and church, commerce and politics and education, everything: the more laws there were, the more regulations, the more securely one's pattern of existence was predetermined, the easier one could continue without thinking, without the need to think. And all this was kept going for the sole purpose of maintaining the illusion – the illusion that somewhere there did exist a basic pattern of order, that the universe, or "nature", was functioning according to set laws, and that, consequently, society and the individual could also be governed by laws. For this was the only way in which one could maintain the wall between oneself and the terror of the liberty at the root of all things: this passionate life which existed without aim or pattern or direction, this essential chaos. Even something as ordinary as clothes could, apart from obviously practical considerations, be related to an original desire (affirmed by Genesis for those who can believe) to protect man against the terrifying liberty of sex. (Three hours, one hour ago she had still been naked in my arms –)

(Châtelet.)

The doors burst open and I stumbled out with the crowd, trying to find my direction, jostled from all sides. The green gates were already closing for the next train before I finally noticed the sign of the *correspondance* to Neuilly and hurried along to the right platform. I was wet with perspiration, my clothes crumpled. Yet it was all of very little importance. I was moving in a trance.

The journey was resumed.

Within a week the Minister should have my answer. It would be Christmas by then and he would not be back at work before the New Year. Then there would follow the series of Cabinet meetings preparing for the next session of the Assembly. And the Minister would have more than enough to do coping with the consequences of the troubles in November. It would probably be February before he could return to my file. If my knowledge of him could be trusted his first reaction would be to ask for further particulars from one of the senior members on my staff. Provided the matter appeared serious enough – and I felt sure it would – a Commission of inquiry might then be constituted. I did not think they would send anybody from Pretoria. The Minister would much rather appoint a few of my colleagues in Europe. Van Huyssteen in London? – I hoped not. We did not get along very well. Perhaps Saunders in The Hague (he was the Minister's confidànt)? Some time in March – ? Of course, everything could happen much sooner; or it could take even longer – until after the Budget debate in the Assembly. But a date towards the end of March seemed the most likely.

(Louvre.)

It was inevitable, no longer to be denied or ignored: I was standing on the edge of a precipice. Perhaps the only final precipice? – this liberty I had to do both good and evil; to continue either inside or outside my established pattern; to resign myself or to revolt. And also, I suppose: the discovery that neither possibility was, of necessity, more important, more valuable than the other. In an archive file, a hundred years from now, it would really make no difference whether I had quashed Keyter and his affair and continued "doing my duty" as before – or whether I had held on to Nicolette and, with her, through her, broken out of everything as I had done once before with Gillian. And yet: having once become aware of the precipice, having once acknowledged its importance, how could I ever come to rest again, how could I ever be satisfied with anything save the frail, naked, undeniable *being* under the very last veil?

(Tuileries.)

I had three months left. It was as if I had just left a doctor's surgery with the verdict that I had waited too long with cancer. Three months between now and – ? It was not very long. I could barely think any more. Everything which, in the course of my journey so far, had developed in such a logical sequence, distilled in the alembic of the previous night, became clouded again.

I was standing in my crumpled clothes, leaning against a

145

door with a shining handle in my hands, swaying to and fro, and the only thing I could think or hear, the only thing of which I was still conscious, was that one figure: *three*. Even when I tried to remind myself that it was nothing but a hypothesis, I knew that it had long ago, in the secret processes of the mind, been crystallised into a fact.

I was coming nearer to the Embassy. Four stations. I counted them on the map above the door. I started reading the advertisements between the chromium poles above each seat. *Santé sobriété.* Do not drink more than one litre wine per day. *Banania. Vichy.* A ski holiday. (Forget your worries; everything organised beforehand; predestined.)

The train was jerking, swaying. An old woman leaning against a pole lost her balance for a moment. Nobody tried to help her. At the next door stood a young couple in a passionate embrace. (*Carpe diem – !*)

(Champs-Élysées-Clémenceau.)

Three stations. Three months. It had not been "willed" or "ordered" like that: it had simply happened. But this happening was, in itself, unavoidable. That night when she appeared on the threshold of my office, trying to take off her wet coat to bribe me into taking her home – that night had been the beginning. No: by then it had already been under way, as it had been that windy night in Cape Town when I had stopped to pick up Gillian and her large trunk. And it had already been going on for generations the day or night of my birth.

Would it have been better had I *not* known about the three months? Suppose Keyter's report had taken its own course, creating its consequences beyond my existence until, at the very conclusion, I was confronted with the last crisis only? Then I could have lived those three months without knowing. Or would it be better, after all, to know, and live in agony?

Was it even a matter of "better" or "worse" – or was that, too, a purely inescapable fact? Adam and Eve had lived in their garden in the supreme happiness of ignorance. But the fruit of knowledge had to be picked. Not to rebel against God, not to obey the Serpent, but simply because they, *as human beings,* could not conceivably have done anything else. Being human meant desiring knowledge. Without sin there could be no knowledge; nor could there be knowledge without sin. And man could not exist without either.

(Franklin-Roosevelt.)

So they had eaten of the Fruit. What they had thus acquired

was, essentially, the knowledge of their own ignorance and of their own futility: undaunted, never-ending agony. And from the Tree of Life they had been driven before they could pick of its fruit.

So now we were aware of life, but of ourselves we had no life. And this was the terror I had always, without realising it, evaded. But now Nicolette had shown me the garden, the mythological "little garden of Eros", last night; and I could do nothing but look for the way back.

(George V.)

What did a man do who had only three months to live? Would he go on working as usual until, one day, he was carried off on a stretcher? Would he write his memoirs? Or would he become insane? Or would he try to "live"? But would he succeed – after so many years of existing in the passive, of "being lived"?

That I did not know. I only knew that I had three months left. I could not mark time. I could not begin anew somewhere. I could only choose: to live or merely to go on being. I was on the boundary of a limitless, unknown region. It was a country I could explore, an adventure I could experience, a world through which I could travel. There was no necessity, no need to do it: I could remain where I was if I wanted to. Or I could look for a short-cut; or I could find a bulldozer to open up an easy road. But perhaps – Suppose I slung my rucksack on my shoulders and walked straight into the wilderness: what a journey could it not be? Perhaps my equipment would fail me; perhaps I would fall into a river, or down a mountain, and break my legs; perhaps I would wander deliriously across waterless plains. Or else the land itself could be disappointing: a mere wilderness, a desert without end, without beauty, without value.

But was that really important? Even then it would remain the choice between a familiar illusion and an unknown possibility.

(Étoile.)

Almost too late I recognised the name on the blue and white tiles of the concave wall. The train doors were already gliding shut when I quickly jumped out and went upstairs towards the avenue Wagram. The clouds were dispersing. The light was shimmering on wet roofs and branches.

I could see the amazement in Lebon's eyes when he saw me come through the main entrance.

I said: "Good morning, Lebon. It looks as though we're going to have a beautiful day."

As I entered the official residence to change my clothes he was

still gaping at me, with stains of light on his glasses and a froze
drop on the tip of his purple nose.

5

I find that I am returning more and more frequently to Gillian
Perhaps it is simply because, nowadays, I allow my thoughts to
wander at random; because there is nothing I deliberately *exclude*
from thinking or remembering any more. (There may be deeper
reasons too.)

The day I went with her to her father's house. She needed a
dress; we were on our way somewhere and she was not satisfied
with the clothes in her trunk. By that time she had already been
living for some weeks in the room I had hired for her near my flat

It was a very ordinary bourgeois house of the clumsy type which
was then regarded as "modern", with a red roof and bay windows
and a veranda. The garden was in a state of sad neglect: a very
formal, very well-planned garden, all the flowerbeds carefully surrounded by pointed bricks, and a rockery with a cement angel in
the centre.

I was waiting on the stoep for her to unlock the front door,
but as she came up the steps she looked at me with that cynical,
mocking expression of hers and announced: "I haven't got the
key any more. I threw it away."

"What are we going to do then?"

"Break in." Without waiting for an answer she went round to
the back. I followed her, rather disgruntled, but by the time I
reached the kitchen door she had already thrown a stone through
the window.

"Now you can put your arm through and lift the latch." She
was standing with her arms behind her back, whistling.

"You're most irresponsible, Gillian!"

"Oh."

To argue would be useless, so I went to open the window,
climbed through and unlocked the kitchen door from the inside;
but by that time she was already perched on the window-sill.

"Well," she said as she landed inside, her face a bit tense. "It's
looking just the same as usual."

It was slightly musty from being closed so long.

"Now go and get your frock," I said, anxious about her nervous attitude.

148

She did not seem to hear me. Leisurely she walked ahead of me, into the long passage.

"The bathroom. 'Only ten minutes, Gillian. There is no need to bath any longer. Then the temptations of the flesh begin.' " She turned round to me, pale. "And if Gillian has not finished after ten minutes, he comes to see what is happening. The door may never be locked. It is no sin for *him* to look at the flesh."

She went further and opened a door on the left. "Bedroom. This is where my mother died, one night, years ago. With praying and singing and burning of candles."

"Gillian – "

She seemed to be sleepwalking. Another door. I could see her hand tremble on the knob before she flung it open. "Study. This is where the man of God retired to be inspired from Above." She crossed the threshold. There was a large book-case with glass doors against one wall. A smallish desk covered with neat piles of papers, held down by weights. A large Bible. A few straight-backed chairs. On the walls were mainly texts: *God is love. Bless this house. The Lord is my Shepherd.*

"Can you feel the pious atmosphere?" she asked. I have never in my life heard anybody speak with such intense hatred. She went on: "On this chair I had to learn my passages from Scripture when I had done anything wrong. I was first beaten, of course. *'I am the Lord thy God, which have brought thee out of the land of Egypt, out of the house of bondage –'* *'It is a fearful thing to fall into the hands of the living God –'* *'Repent ye therefore, and be converted, that your sins may be blotted out –'* " She was shaken by a fit of trembling and could not continue.

"Come," I said. "We must go." I took her by the shoulders to turn her round. But with amazing strength she forced herself free.

"And there – that's him!" she cried. On the wall next to the door I noticed a row of photographs: forefathers, parents, a faded young woman; and, the largest of all, a youngish man with an ascetic face and forceful eyes, an uncertain, thin mouth, a high forehead.

"Why do you hate him so much, Gillian?" I asked.

"How could you ever understand it?" she asked viciously. "Your father never threw your mother out when she was six months pregnant with you! And in the night, too, she often told me about it, during all those years when we had to look after ourselves, miserably poor. And then she went mad."

She fell silent.

"You have never told me these things," I said, distressed.

149

"Why should I? What difference could it make to you?" Her burning eyes peered at me, then turned away. Quietly she went on: "I saw her go mad. At night I could hear her roaming through the house, moaning and crying. Then she fell ill. I was eight years old. And then he sent for us and brought us back, forcibly, so that she could die decently at home."

"And then?" I asked with an effort.

"And then he wanted to take revenge on me, as if it had been my fault! He used to say that there was a devil in me. I was my mother's child. One day I would go mad like her. Sometimes I thought I would kill him while he was sleeping, but I was too much afraid. Can you understand it? I was afraid."

She became hysterical. Wildly, desperately, she turned round, noticed the large black Bible on the desk and grabbed it. Before I could move a finger she had thrown it at the portrait. The glass was smashed and the splinters were scattered on the floor, but the portrait was still hanging crookedly from its nail.

She shoved me aside, rushed to it and violently tore it from the wall. Her hand was cut by a sliver of glass so that a thin red line of blood came trickling down her palm and wrist. She was crying, soundlessly at first, dropping on her knees beside the portrait, tearing it to pieces. Then she buried her face in her hands and burst into violent sobs.

I stood watching her without moving, caught in a spell. After a very long time she lifted her head and started wiping her face with her hands. A streak of blood was smeared on her cheek. Small red drops were falling from her wrist on to the Bible which lay, open and with crumpled pages, at her knees. It was only after several minutes that she became aware of it, glanced up at me, and returned her distressed eyes to the floor. She picked up the Bible and cautiously wiped her fingers over the bloodstains, as if she could not grasp what had happened.

"He's dead," she said.

Almost solemnly, she began to tear out the stained pages, and as she went on the movement became quicker, more passionate, more deliberate, with sobs still escaping from deep inside her: Genesis, Law and Prophets, Song of Songs, Gospels, Epistles, to the very last prayer of Revelation.

"Gillian! Are you mad?"

She shook her head. Every muscle in her body was taut. She got up. "He always said I would go to hell. All right. I'll go, then. I don't *want* to be good!" She was swept away by her mounting passion. "When the last trumpet sounds and God comes

150

to look for me, I want to say *NO* to Him. I was not made to be good and to say yes. You can go to Heaven, if you want to. But leave me here! Leave me here and let me *live*!"

She turned away from me, resting her head against the wall, for a long time, without moving. Then she went out. I heard her open another door in the passage. But I remained there, trying half-heartedly to shove the mess aside with one foot.

Very much later she returned, wearing another dress – presumably the one she had come for – and with her hair tidied. Her eyes revealed traces of tears, but there was no hysteria.

"Come," she said. "It's time to go."

6

The polite evening of 24th December.

Anna Smith: "What a pity Her Excellency could not be with us. Christmas is the one time of the year one likes to spend with one's own family, don't you agree? Oh, to be back in South Africa: everything here is so very *worldly*, so Catholic. What a good thing our little group can be together tonight."

Our little group. Our little group of strangers in this strange, cold world. (And a mile from here she is waiting for me in her little room.)

Sylvia Masters: "Let's all go somewhere and paint the town red! Would somebody care to fill my glass? Oh thank you *so* much." And she moves about like a hostess, in her dress with its frills and lace and little bows. Somebody accidentally spills a few drops of wine on it and offers an exaggerated apology; she smiles it away with ingratiating charm, but her eyes remain expressionless. And for the first time it occurs to me that she is a dangerous woman, a poisonous woman.

Stephen Keyter: "Why does the church complain about Christmas becoming commercialised? That is the greatest guarantee for its continued existence! The church *wants* to be exploited so that it could preach humility: following the example of Christ, who was, above all, a masochist."

Victor le Roux: "Christmas has lost its meaning. We are left with the trappings – trees and presents and good wishes – but Christ Himself has been reduced to X, the unknown element. We still perform the actions, but nothing more: it is a dancing candle flame without a wick."

And among them all am I, Mr. Ambassador, moving about,

mixing with my staff as it is expected of me, carrying on conversations, looking lonely "because Her Excellency could not be here"; and as soon as I can do so without being impolite, I offer my apologies and depart – a moment before Anna Smith gathers "our little group" under the glittering Christmas tree to sing Silent Night.

I close the door of my one life behind me and walk through the cold into the next: the life of streets and things and people; one person, a girl, Nicolette.

She has been waiting for a long time, wearing a warm cap, a coat and pretty booties reaching up to the middle of her calves; and she is impatient.

"You *promised* to come early!"

"It was impossible. Come. We don't want to be late for Mass." Glancing at my watch I suggest: "Perhaps we'd better take a taxi."

"No," she says stubbornly. "We must walk."

Here and there, from the bistros and caves of the quarter, one hears jazzy music, but the sounds are woolly, muted by walls and drawn curtains. There are few pedestrians about: some clochards on their way to the Salvation Army's reception under the bridges of the Seine; a lonely drunk leaning against a lamp post singing unmelodious carols, occasionally interrupted by declamations: "On earth peace, good will toward men! Hosanna-hic! How about a franc for a poor man?" For the rest, a few tourists looking for something that would make their night memorable; and the sullen, chilly taxi-drivers standing about in little groups at their *têtes de station,* rubbing their hands or sharing a bottle. We walk briskly through the deserted streets. And as we go on the city gradually comes to life around us. The boulevard Saint-Michel is teeming with people. From all directions they come, heading for the river, the island, Notre-Dame. The entire square under the cathedral is swarming with the thousands who, out of habit, superstition, devotion or curiosity, have come to the midnight Mass. All along the rue du Cloître-Notre-Dame the police have constructed barricades in order to control the surging movement towards the doors. The queue, eight or ten abreast, already stretches the whole length of the cathedral. We have to fall in at the back.

We are silent.

At a quarter to twelve the people are becoming impatient. A few barricades are broken down. There is jostling and cursing and shouting. Nicolette uses the opportunity to slip ten or twelve paces forward. I follow her for a yard or so but dare not force my way past a few old women. Far ahead of me I can see her woollen cap, but nothing more. Above us loose clouds are scurrying past the pale stars, creating the impression that the cathedral is falling, and we with it, and the entire unfirm earth.

She worms her way further forward. A few people are shouting abuse at her. Her cap disappears in the throng. She has been looking forward to tonight so much, always with that inexplicable passion in her which I have noticed before when she was speaking of religious matters. (Perhaps this, and the bed, are her only two passions. For the rest, she can so lightly, blithely skim over everything, living with constant irony, untouched by all.)

Another group of people must have been allowed into the cathedral for suddenly we are moving ten, fifteen yards forward. For a fleeting moment I catch sight of her cap again, very far away. Then it disappears and the surge comes to an end, forced against the grim black walls. We have no hope to get inside in time now. Yet we all remain in the queue, stubbornly hoping, believing that a miracle will happen.

The midnight bells begin to peal, ringing loudly, jubilantly from above. All over the city the sound is repeated until the whole world is caught in the shuddering peals. In the Latin Quarter fireworks are crackling. Through the thick cathedral walls we feel the vibration of an organ and listen to the dim gloria of the sopranos.

Slowly the crowd begins to spill across the square. Some are still waiting, but by the time they come inside the Mass itself will long be past. I turn away from the barricaded corridor, trying to find Nicolette. For five, ten minutes there is no sight of her. Then her hand almost imperceptibly slides round my arm from behind and she says: "Come. Let's go back."

"Nicolette – " I put my arm round her. "I am sorry, my darling. You should have come alone."

She shakes her head and makes no answer. When we reach the bridge, light suddenly falls across her tense, cynical face.

"I suppose it just *had* to happen," she says. "It's like my garden – remember? I must always stay outside."

"Now you are exaggerating!" I scold her, more harshly than I mean to. "It's not *so* important after all. And we could go to the Mass tomorrow morning."

"Yes."

It is the sort of acquiescence which infuriates one because it is so entirely disarming.

"Please try to understand, Nicolette!"

"I understand perfectly well. It is not so important after all, like you said."

"Now you're being childish!"

She slips her hand from my arm and walks on ahead of me, alone. (Gillian would have exploded under these circumstances, but Nicolette is different. I am realising it more and more.)

After a while she stops, waiting for me to catch up with her again – probably because the streets are becoming darker now – and in her characteristic way, *à propos* of nothing, she says: "Did you know I've never been baptised?"

I make no answer: because I am still feeling slightly annoyed and guilty, and because I have no idea of what she is aiming at.

"I've never yet received *any* sacrament."

"What do you know about sacraments?"

" '*A sacrament is an outward sign of inward grace'*. I looked it up in one of the booklets one finds on the stand inside Notre-Dame. One is supposed to put the money in a box next to it but I had no change with me so I just took it. Do you think it was sinful?"

"Not unredeemable, I suppose. You are paying far too much attention to the things you read anyway. After all, what difference could there be between a baptised person and an unbaptised one?"

"A hell of a difference," she answers with great conviction. "One who has not been baptised possesses only his natural human life. The baptised one possesses a supernatural, immortal life as well. And don't you think that's important? It you're not baptised, you have to live without grace."

"What grace?"

She shrugs. "I'm telling you just what I read in my little book. And it's true. I know."

I would like to convince myself of her naïvety; of her too ready acceptance of all printed words – from horoscopes to liturgical commentary; of the complete lack of digestion of it all inside her. But to do this would, in itself, be too naïve. She could turn anything from a cobblestone to a chalice into a question (in that she resembles Gillian; but why are they still so many worlds apart?).

"Are you coming with me?" she asks at the main entrance of her building.

"Of course."

She nods and goes in before me. I follow, feeling my way.

"Would you like some wine?" she asks when we are, at last, back in her room. "I'm all shivery." Not waiting for an answer, she goes to the kitchen where numerous empty bottles are crowded into a corner, finds one which is still half full and brings it back to the table in her bedroom. With her head slightly inclined she pours a little into a tin mug. Then she smiles, very faintly, with a hint of relief. Almost solemnly she comes to the bed and starts rummaging through the pile of old illustrated journals she bought along the Seine; after a while she extracts a small black missal from the rubbish and looks up something. Amused, I watch her without any comment. She returns to the table, tidies the cloth and picks up an old crust of bread that has been lying there for a day or two. The light is reflected in the window above her fair head. She has completely forgotten about me, about everything. Her fingers are moving furtively. She is reciting something to herself; only the edges of her lips are moving. (But is it a Sanctus, or a rhyme from Mother Goose?) With her eyes staring intently at her hands, she carefully breaks the little crust into three equal pieces, shaking the crumbs from her fingers. One piece is dropped into the mug.

"Hoc est enim corpus meum."

Her thin hands hesitatingly begin to form a cross, but she does not complete the gesture.

"Hoc est enim calix sanguinis meum."

She looks in my direction, but past me.

"It remains wine and bread," she says quietly. "Do you see?" It is as if she is trying to prove something. But what – and to whom?

Then she turns round abruptly, opens the bottle again and fills the mug to the brim. A few drops spill over the sides. She wipes it off the tablecloth with her fingers and sucks them. Then she quickly gulps down the wine, shudders, refills the mug and brings it to me. In the very corners of her eyes, under the lashes, there is a hint of tears.

7

It is strange, and at times impossible, to think that my "ordinary life" is continuing almost as usual. At first I was, perhaps, more consciously aware of it than before, as if I had to prove to both my staff and myself that one *could* go on. But because no one, not even myself, seemed to find anything strange in it everything in the office has gradually returned to a habit. The mailbag is still delivered on Tuesdays to be opened by a fluttering Anna Smith. Le Roux regularly brings me the French Press cuttings for scanning. The secretaries are writing reports, dealing with consular problems, receiving visitors. There are still telegrams to be decoded and others to be composed. There are telephone calls, interviews, negotiations, talks, receptions. (The only difference is that I tend to delegate more routine work to others; that I am more regularly represented at official functions by one of my subalterns.) There was one week of exceptional pressure when the news of our negotiations in connection with an arms deal was suddenly blurted out in a French newspaper, causing immediate public protests. For a while it even seemed as if the whole transaction would fall through, so that the Secretary of Defence had to pay a quick personal visit to Paris. Then all the discussions with the French Government had to be resumed, practically from scratch. But all of these things are mere ripples on the surface of my days. Often I catch myself smiling ironically at the "importance" of my task, especially as far as the arms deal is concerned. And yet, there is no *essential,* obvious change in my routine, much to my own surprise. (But why?)

Anna Smith still turns up regularly to pour out her heart; once she even burst into tears because Joubert was allegedly maltreating his wife ("such a *dear* woman"). Masters comes in to discuss work; Koos Joubert to fulminate against "the bloody French". Keyter, too, regularly turns up in my office, but relations between us are strained and confined to strict formality. Sometimes I deliberately try to scrutinise his face, but he has always been an enigma. And what would I try to find?

Only once, when he brought me a couple of demands for visas, did he linger on the doorstep for a minute.

"Is there anything else, Keyter?"

"Mr. Ambassador –" After a short hesitation he continued: "Haven't you heard anything –?" For that fleeting moment there was unmistakable tension and uncertainty in his attitude.

I purposely waited for him to complete his sentence, but he changed his mind, his eyes became expressionless again and he concluded laconically: "It's not so important, after all. I beg your pardon, Mr. Ambassador." And he left.

Should I have called him back? But what was there left for either of us to say? So I picked up the visa forms he had left and started studying them.

But in spite of the apparently unchanged routine there is one very important difference: I am almost constantly aware of the fact that I am sitting on this chair, at this desk, occupied with this particular piece of work – almost as if, from an astral plane, I am looking over my own shoulder, an impersonal, detached judge of everything that is done.

I find it impossible to escape from an increasing sense of unreality. Once before, during my eighteen months of wandering, I was sometimes working in my room until very late at night, when I would suddenly look up, for no reason at all, with this same, uncanny consciousness of myself sitting in my pool of light, surrounded by the immense, dark world. I felt like jumping up and rushing into the quiet streets outside, shouting: "I am alive! Nobody believes it, but *I am alive!*" Naturally my reaction at present is not so passionate, not so adolescent. It consists simply of a realisation that everything which is done in this office, is done on behalf of other people – not even "people", but on behalf of an organisation, a powerful machine called "Government", something invisible, something which, perhaps, does not even exist any more (how could I know, isolated in a strange country?), but is kept going by the sheer momentum of so many years.

Sometimes I go down to the reading-room to page through old newspapers. I have read all the news long ago, but now I can judge it not as a daily chronicle of confused events, but as a pile of contemporary history: finished, complete, undeniable, and lacking the personal warmth of something which is still in the process of happening. Rape. Murder. Contravention of the Immorality Act. Sabotage and attempted sabotage. Ministerial comments. Political declamations and demonstrations. Mrs. A. enjoying a few days' holiday in Cape Town. Mr. B. breaking the record for keeping awake. The Rev. C. accused of heresy. Strong southeaster in the Peninsula. Drought in the Free State. Large banana surplus. Readers' letters: "Keep South Africa White." "Farmers need more subsidies." "Nothing wrong with modern youth." "Ban Sunday sport." "Make adultery punishable by law." Photos of V.I.Ps; Grape Queens; Springboks; Ministers' wives at a garden party –

So this is South Africa. These are its interests. These are its people – judging from my pile of newspapers on the dark green leather upholstering of the table in the reading-room. And I know only too well that it is the truth, proved by so many holidays on home leave, once every five years. Each time one sets out with so much enthusiasm; and each time one crawls back, tired and perplexed, disillusioned by visits to colleagues or relatives whose lives have long ago ceased to touch one's own; until, at last, one escapes to the coast, among strangers, to a holiday similar to any other.

And this is the country I have to represent. I have to find support for a policy in which I cannot believe, because it no longer exists in my personal life. I must handle its affairs, although they mean nothing to me. I must buy arms for it, although apart from the personal prestige involved, I do not care whether I succeed or fail. I am no longer concerned with anything which happens there; it has no meaning for me; I have no sympathy with it. I no longer know the people, no longer understand their motives. When I am visited by compatriots, we discuss business for five minutes; ask a few well-meant questions; and say good-bye. When a delegation arrives and has to stay for a few days, we pretend nostalgia for "real South African food", for "good old Afrikaners", for "the splendid old Cape". I doubt whether they believe it any more than I do: but at least they still have to believe in its reality, its inevitability. At least they are involved in it; it is their milieu; it is – perhaps – their *world*.

And – *my* world? It is not there. But it is not here in Paris either. How could it be? – only six weeks ago I started exploring the streets of this strange city for the first time, accompanied by an equally strange, beautiful young girl. Naturally I get along very well with various French diplomats, editors, industrialists (it is in the interests of my work!): but they do not "belong" to me, they do not form part of my world. It is impossible to live in a city for two years and then to think one "belongs" there. I am simply living here, protected by the thick walls of my Embassy, snugly rolled in the cotton-wool of protocol and officialness. And soon – when my three months of grace have expired – I shall not even have *this* left. But God, God, is there no place for me in this world? I am fifty-six years old: I can no longer set out to find myself a place.

I am standing in a very small very dark room with only one high window. Daylight is falling in through it, but I cannot get out – besides, the sun would be blinding. And standing here, I think: man is an everlasting shout in front of his small square of light.

8

Textures: Nicolette lying outstretched on her belly, with delicate brush strokes of light on the fine hairdust between her shoulder blades; the freckledness of her shoulders; the smooth tension of her round buttocks; the threadbare crumpled sheet; the rough blanket with dark shadows in the folds; the silkiness of her hair; the sure modelling of her cheekbones under the skin; and the jewels of her eyes.

9

I had been to a meeting, and when I entered the door of my flat I realised immediately that there was something wrong. I switched on the porch light and waited, listening. There was no sound. But as I was on the point of proceeding to my living-room I heard a muffled laugh from the bedroom.

It was Gillian, lying in my bed, shading the light from her eyes with her hands, peeping at me through her fingers.

"Surprised?" she asked.

I took out a cigarette and lit it, trying to regain my composure. "Not very much," I finally said. "Would you care to tell me *why* you are here?"

"I was afraid of sleeping alone."

"You haven't been afraid for all these weeks."

She shrugged carelessly, sliding up into a sitting position. "You're late."

"And tired. So I'll appreciate it if you would kindly put on your clothes again and go."

She shook her head. I waited for a few minutes, then turned round, closed the door behind me and went to the living-room. I was not quite sure of what she had up her sleeve this time, but I was adamant that she would not have her own way.

As I expected she soon made her appearance in the doorway, casually wrapped in a sheet.

"Aren't you coming to bed?"

"Gillian." I went up to her and stopped, looking into her eyes. "What are you up to tonight?"

"Nothing." There was a hint of warning in her voice. "Do you think I never mean anything seriously?"

It was a dangerous moment. I took her shoulders in my hands. The sheet was slipping off. I could read in her eyes everything she quite shamelessly allowed in them: virginal bravado; provocation; uncertainty; fear. There was no need for her to say more. I *knew*. It was indeed no new game. It was, like everything else she had ever done, an expression of that passion to be free, to break loose, to attempt everything – good as well as bad. It was more than a need: it was a necessity. Perhaps it suggested something unbalanced in her, or an exaggerated adolescent reaction to her past – but I don't think the diagnosis matters so very much. For her, everything was deeply sincere and deeply true. She was no nymph. The very thought would have soiled her. There was nothing uncertain or turbid about this urge in her: on the contrary, like all her other emotions, it was mercilessly pure. It was only a few weeks since the windy night of our first meeting, but I already loved her – or what, at that stage, I knew as love. She was already engaged in the fatal process of attacking everything inside me in order to gain complete possession of me, the way a drowning person gets hold of his rescuer. Why it had to be *me*, I could never explain; nor whether it would have been less fatal had it been someone else.

But here she was standing against me, my hands so violently clutching her shoulders that she had to bite on her teeth, although she made no sound and stared at me unflinchingly. The challenge had changed to invitation, and then to pleading. The sheet fell from her and remained lying at her feet like a large white shell. At that moment we were beyond thought or emotion, hate or love. All was fire. I no longer reasoned in terms of thoughts or images: it had become a much more primitive process, a simple series of impulses in my subconscious mind, like a prism slowly turning against the light.

Then I dropped my hands from her shoulders. I wanted to kiss her, but if I did, I would have no defence left. I stooped, picking up the sheet and covered her with it; then I turned away, trembling. I have no idea why I acted like that. It was certainly no moral scruple. Perhaps I merely sensed that sex, under those circumstances, would be no liberation for her; or perhaps my motives were much less altruistic – simply the fear that I might fail in her eyes, and disappoint her. I desired her, I wanted her, but if I took her, it had to be because love itself had made it unavoidable, not because she wanted to use me as an instrument to prove something to herself. It all sounds so deliberate, so cerebral and so unconvincing in words – even more so today, thirty years after the event. I think I am beginning to realise why I never completed my magnum opus then: I am much too sceptical about the words I use; I have no "gift".

"I thought you loved me," Gillian said.

I made a half-hearted gesture, but could not answer.

"I thought somewhere deep inside you you would at least have something like warmth, like simple human feeling. But you're as cold as ice. You are a robot. You have never been able to feel. You are *afraid* of feeling – !"

"No, Gillian!"

But she was on her way to the bedroom already. Five minutes later I heard her go to the front door. I wanted to speak to her, but she had already slammed the door and I could do nothing but remain where I was. I made no movement. Much later I heard a clock strike twelve. Then I got up and went to my cocktail cabinet and drank two or three brandies and went to bed. But I could not sleep, alternately blaming myself for not having taken advantage of the situation, and wondering whether she had been right after all – that I was, indeed, incapable of feeling.

At two o'clock there was a soft knock on my door. At first I thought it was my imagination. But then it was repeated, very softly. I did not even bother to put on a dressing gown, but went to the door in my pyjamas.

It was she.

"Where on earth have you been, Gillian? What has happened?"

"Nothing."

She came inside, switched on the living-room light, took my cigarette case from the sideboard and lit one – at that time it was still considered unusual; but for her, of course, *nothing* was unusual. Her hand was trembling lightly and the first draw resulted in a violent fit of coughing. She said nothing. I was watching her from the door. There was something tired about her, as if she had wilted slightly. It was visible even in her hair.

I tried to draw her into a conversation, but she ignored me. It must have been at least fifteen minutes before she said in a very neutral voice: "So that's that."

"What's the matter, Gillian?" I felt like shaking her.

"There's nothing remarkable about it really." Her voice was still shallow and calm, but deceptively so. And by that time I knew the expression in her eyes.

"To be quite frank, I found it rather sordid. That's all."

She leant back on the sofa, closing her eyes. After a while she had to press her eyelids very close together, and they were trembling; in spite of her efforts a few teardrops emerged. But there was no sound, no sob.

I sat down next to her and took her hand in mine. It felt cold in spite of the early summer warmth.

"What have you done, my darling? Why didn't you stay here?"

She was breathing deeply, then opened her eyes and sat upright. With a quick movement she opened her handbag and took out a rather soiled pound note.

"Take it," she said and, after some more rummaging, brought out a few half-a-crowns, shillings and two pennies. "This too. I had to pay the rest to the taxi driver."

I was mechanically stroking the note on my knee, not daring to say anything.

161

"Would two pounds be the usual fee – or was the sailor poor?"

"My God," I whispered. "Shut up. Please shut up."

She got up. I could not tell whether she really meant to go. Anyway, she got as far as the door to the porch and stopped there, pressing her head against the wall, her hands grasping the door-post.

"Don't let me go again, Paul. Whatever you do, don't let me go again."

I think it was at that moment that I first began to understand the Christian concepts of "sin" and "guilt".

10

If only one could get rid of this concept of sin and live freely, live absolutely, without the relativeness of the system in which we are entrenched (but *meum peccatum contra me est semper!*). For the moment one frees oneself from this existence, sin lies no longer in the contravention of Jehovah commandments which form the core of the system: after all, if one possesses the freedom to conquer both good and evil by an act of willing, thus transforming it into something *acquired,* something which *is* – irrespective of moral values –, sin could no longer have an existence of its own. Now, theoretically, logically, there could be only two such ways of living which would be entirely free of sin: the absolute negation of Gillian; or the absolute affirmation of Nicolette. But, paradoxically, these ways of life appear to be the very ones in which the concept of sin assumes its most acute (absolute?) form. How else could I explain New Year's Eve? (And it is imperative that I find an explanation, because I desperately need it for my journey through the land of Nod.)

She is standing in front of the ugly mirror, one knee rested on a chair littered with make-up things, pulling faces at herself while she is gracefully underlining her eyes. Her mouth is half open, the tip of her tongue pressed against her upper lip. I am sitting on the bed, leaning against a corner of the cupboard. The sheet is still warm of us, and my body is still remembering hers. But she, it seems, has already forgotten all about it; because what is past – a minute or a year – is absorbed in a free fluid movement deep inside her, secret like a subterranean river.

"Where are we going?" I ask, without much curiosity, even with a touch of resentment.

"I'm going out." She opens her eyes wide and blinks a few times.

"Alone?"

"Mm."

"Where?"

"Out."

"To your nightclub – to sing?"

She quickly glances at me in the mirror. "Mm." Noncommitally.

"But why tonight? All last week you stayed at home."

"I'm only going every second week."

"I want to go with you. I want to listen to you tonight."

She shakes her head and continues with her ritual.

"But it's New Year's Eve," I insist. "I want to be with you."

"No."

But I have already made up my mind: tonight I am going with her. After all, what do I really know about her? I need so much more. I *want* so much more. She is a moth playing round a thin ray of light: she is visible only for the fleeting second when she is caught in the light; often she disappears completely in the dark, leaving no trace, and no promise that she would ever reappear.

It is for no sentimental reason – "our little group"! – that I want to go with her. But there is something so depressing about one year's merging with the next that one feels a need to escape into a crowd. It has nothing to do with the superficial festivity or exuberance: that is merely a civilised mask for the ancient, primitive fear of the unknown, and, perhaps, of death. Even an ordinary midnight (which, occurring every twenty-four hours, ought to be as natural as high tide) retains something of its medieval terror; it is like births taking place in the night, old people dying in the dark, even the act of love – the "little death" – which is performed, preferably, in darkness. How much more true would it not be, then, of this one night, charged by legend and tradition with so much meaning surviving in a collective subconscious that it becomes a sort of spiritual springtide, a culmination of the anguish of being, masked in festivity. Usually one knows – or admits – nothing but the festivity in itself, thus lending absolute value to what is purely relative; but having once discovered the illusion inherent to the "system", one tends to examine the hidden essence of everything. And in this way one experiences, paradoxically, the same catharsis as those who content themselves with the festive surface.

So I wait patiently until she begins to fidget nervously.

"What time is it?"

"Almost half-past ten."

"Then I must go. Honestly I must."

"But not alone."

"*Please* – !" Her cheeks are flushed. "Can't you see I don't *want* to take you with me?"

She goes to the door. I follow her. At the top of the stairs she turns round, opens her mouth to say something, but changes her mind and begins to descend very quickly. We reach the entrance lobby together.

While I am holding the door she makes a visible effort to speak calmly. "You can come with me next time," she says. "But not tonight. Please, you do not understand."

"Why should it upset you if I came along? Surely you're not ashamed of singing in my presence."

"But – " She lifts her hands, then lets them fall back. "It's such a scruffy little place, you may not like it."

"If you don't mind singing there why should I mind sitting there listening to you?"

"But damn it all – !" There is an angry glare in her eyes. She starts off towards the Carrefour. When we reach the corner, she stops; and the argument is resumed.

Why should I not allow her to have her own way? After all, I am just distressing her; and I have no right to her. I must be satisfied with the small segment of her life she shares with me. And yet –

"What time is it now?"

"Twenty to eleven."

There is panic in her eyes. "Please! I am late already!"

I do not answer.

She hesitates. For a moment anything is possible: she may walk on; or she may turn back; she may even slap me. But at last she only shrugs and with a hint of challenge in her voice, she says: "All right then. Come along if you must. But you must find us a taxi and see to it that we're there before eleven."

We hurry to the boulevard and board a taxi. The address she gives to the driver is completely unknown to me. (Not that that is any reliable criterion!) She is sitting on the very edge of the seat, urging: "Vite! Vite! Vite!" Until the driver flares up and snarls something at her. She immediately counters with a word I would never have expected in her vocabulary. His face breaks into a broad grin and the car shoots forward. Relaxed, she leans back. And when we stop at her address she persuades me to give him double the required tip.

For a moment we wait on the dark pavement. Then she mysteriously disappears from my side and only after the initial shock do I notice the narrow entrance behind me. From an illuminated door framed by stained red velvet curtains, somebody is beckoning me. It takes some time before it occurs to me that I have to enter there; that Mademoiselle has gone in at the stage entrance. Somewhat reluctantly I pay him his exorbitant entrance fee – realising afterwards that one is supposed to haggle – and am ushered to a table where a waiter promptly serves me with the inevitable champagne. Nicolette was quite right, I think wryly: I would never have allowed her to come to this wretched little hole had I known what it was like. The boisterous music and the first few items soon confirm my first impressions. Strip: solo. Strip: duet. Strip: en masse. All that changes is the faces of the clumsy girls. Girls – ? There are a few flabby ones who must be nearer to forty than thirty. Some of them have dirty feet. One stumbles over her dress and a man's voice curses her audibly from the wings. The music is deafening. The heavy smoke of many weeks gives me a splitting headache. I try my utmost to confine my thoughts to the present moment, not to anticipate anything; yet, when at last she makes her appearance in her bundle of coloured feathers, I feel no shock – merely sad resignation. There seems to be a stirring in the audience. A microphone shoots up from the footlights and she starts whining a tuneless song into it while slowly, monotonously her feathers fly away until only one is left. But it is not she. I refuse to admit that it is she. It is not that small body which, two hours ago, was moving against mine. I do not know this stranger. It is nothing but a blatant female sex on stilts; and a voice: a cry of rebellion and desire and hate against the low, smoky ceiling, against the audience at their little tables, against *us* at our little tables, against me at my little table with my cheap expensive champagne. And the music, too, is screaming, moaning, cursing, mocking, blaspheming. And all the old men are leaning forward, propped up on their elbows (one of them upsets his glass without noticing it), their mouths half open and slobbering, their gleaming eyes bulging, their gnarled hands moving grotesquely on the tables, like old lobsters. The music grows louder and louder, the voice goes insane and stops at the highest piercing note; and suddenly all the lights on the ceiling are turned on, and she jumps from the low stage and comes dancing among the tables. It is like a wind blowing across a wheat field, the way all the heads turn to follow her so that the greedy eyes can devour her. I cannot look

165

any more. I am sipping my champagne as if it is the most precious drink my tongue has ever tasted. In this way I am trying to ward her off, to keep her at a distance, to exorcise her like an evil spirit to go her way and leave me unmolested. At the same time I know very deeply that there is no way out. She warned me not to come; she wanted to save me from this; she knew what would happen. (How inscrutable are the ways of love –!) But I refused to listen. And now both of us are caught in it, and the unavoidable must happen, *because* of us, *for* us. I do not even consider the possibility of leaving, knowing that if I do not fully experience this last sincerity, this last knowledge, this last agony, everything that has happened until this moment would be valueless. We must first learn to *know*, both of us; and then to live with that knowledge. It is unbearable, but we have passed the stage where we could still claim the mercy of bearableness. And so she comes dancing to my table, and stops, and turns round, and laughs; and turns back to me, and leans over – one of her breasts touching the bottle – and kisses me on the forehead. I can feel the moist, sticky lipstick smudging my skin. The anonymous spectators are applauding, shouting bravo, thumping on the old red carpet with their feet. I realise how they envy me, how some of them will lie awake tonight, peering into the dark with burning eyes, swallowing, remembering this little scene. But I shall go out with the red smudge on my forehead; and long after it has been washed off it will still be there.

And while they are applauding, she is looking at me, and I am looking at her; and I know that she would like to cry, but that she will not, because this moment is beyond such facile emotions; therefore her eyes remain teasing, and mine are teasing back; and we keep on playing our little act to the slobbering audience; caught, both of us, in this loathing which, at the same time, is the most intense communication there has ever been between us. And while we are caught in each other, existing in this strange moment of timelessness, we hear the sudden surge of noise outside, like a dam of sound bursting over us. All the streets, the entire city, come alive with hooting cars, an enormous wave of sound as if, suddenly, there is nothing in the world but sound; as if everything is broken up into neutrons and electrons of sound – not the scream of birth, or the cry of love, or the shout of death, but *mere* sound: the earth and all humanity caught in a siren of distress ringing out against the dark heavens all round.

And then, after the first tremor has passed over us, she goes her way with nimble feet, dances to the stage, throws her arms wide open, crucifying herself against the light, and disappears behind the gaudy curtain

Later a waiter brings me another bottle of champagne. I pay him without looking up or counting the change. Outside the streets have gone berserk. Inside the show goes on. She appears a few more times, either alone or together with others, in an assortment of costumes. Some of the spectators leave and their places are taken by others. My forehead is burning. There is a red smudge on my handkerchief. I am glued to my chair, drenched with perspiration. And it is three o'clock before the thickset manager with his shock of greasy black hair appears on the stage among the naked dancers, slapping one on the behind, to announce the end of the show.

Outside in the cold street I have to wait for a long time before she appears. She smells of cheap soap and cold cream; all her make-up is removed.

"Oh," she said. "You waited?"

"Yes."

"It's cold."

"Quite."

"Shall we find a taxi?"

"Of course."

"There ought to be a few on the Place Blanche."

"All right."

We go to the square, and get in, and drive off.

She is sitting serenely in her corner, now and then turning her face to the window.

At last, when we come to the Place du Châtelet with its rows of sad yellow lamps, she says: "I told you you wouldn't like it."

"You yourself don't like it. Why do you do it?"

"Why not?"

This, I think, is the strangest thing of all: not that we have so few words left in this deep, desolate region we have reached, but that the few we have left are so meaningless. Or is it the contrast with the surrounding silence which makes it more conspicuous?

The old, damp smell of her quarter filters into us as I am holding the door for her. I am firmly resolved to take the same taxi back to my own home, tired of words, tired of questions, tired. But she remains standing in the middle of the street and says:

"Come with me. Please."

Sighing, I pay the driver, close the door and go up the stairs with her. She walks into her little room before me, peeling off her coat, allowing it to fall on the floor. I pick it up and hang it over a chair. It is stuffy inside. She goes over to the window to look out, but it is dark in the room across the street. With a little smile she returns to me.

"Happy New Year." she says lightly.

I merely nod.

"You're angry with me."

"No." It is true.

"Sit down. Over there." She points to the chair at the table. Without a word she takes the top blanket from the unmade bed and carefully drapes it over me, regards it critically, goes to fetch the length of string she uses for a washing-line and ties it round my middle. In the cupboard she finds a rosary which she solemnly places in my lap.

"It is half past three in the morning, Nicolette. What are you up to now?" My limbs are heavy with fatigue.

"We are playing a game," she answers. "I was naughty. I sinned. And now I have to confess. You are the priest."

"No! There's a time for everything. You're being childish."

"It's only a game. I usually play it by myself. But tonight it's more important. Tonight a whole year is past."

With a weary gesture I threaten: "I'm not going to listen to you!"

"You needn't. Priests usually do not listen, I think." And then she kneels down at my feet, her elbows on my knees. "Father," she says, "I hardly know where to begin. I have so many sins."

I close my eyes. I must be dreaming. It is senseless, idiotic. A stupid little game.

"What is there I could forgive you, Nicolette?" I sigh.

"No. A priest never calls one by the name. You must say: My daughter."

"My daughter."

"It doesn't matter whether I am forgiven, Father. It is enough for me to confess."

"All right. Let us begin then." In spite of everything I am a little bit amused.

"Tonight I danced instead of going to the Mass."

"That was very wrong."

"And I danced without clothes."

"That is even worse."

"And I kissed a man."

"Unforgivable. My daughter."

168

It is like a merry-go-round slowly gathering momentum.

"Is that all?"

"No, Father. It is only the beginning."

"But why do you need to confess it all?"

"It is not only I who need it," she evades the question. "But all the others who were on the stage with me. And the *patron,* who fired Jeannine because she had torn her dress. And all those who looked at us thinking we were somebody else. And those who stood at the door selling their second-hand love. And those who bought it. And all the others in the city, in all the other halls. Those who sing and do not mean it. Anyone doing anything without meaning it. I know I cannot sing. I lied to you. But I warned you not to come with me and you did not listen. I should have stayed with you. And I should not have gone to you that night, because you were busy and I disturbed you. And yesterday morning I stole a cake of soap in the Prisunic when they weren't looking. And I hid in the Luxembourg Gardens when it was closing-time but they discovered me and chased me out. Why do they always chase one out? I am not doing any harm there. But I suppose one would get frightened in the night all alone among the trees. I was in Versailles once, in the forest, when they shut the gates, and everything was dark and closed, and when I reached the lake a long line of birds were passing overhead with the most awful cries, it was like dying, and in the end I had to climb over the grilled fence for I was too tired to go all the way back to the opposite side where the gate is always open, and I was too frightened of the black trees anyway, and I tore my dress as I jumped down. Why is it like that? Why do I want to get in when I'm outside; and if I'm locked in I am afraid? Why can I never find rest? I ran away from home to come to Paris, to escape, and I never wrote back. Except once, to ask for money. There were so many things I had to do for money, and sometimes they swindled me and threw me out after – you know – "

She goes on and on; and gradually I get the impression that I am forming part of a fantastic play without beginning or end, with characters appearing and disappearing without aim, laughing and crying without reason, continually revolting against something unknown; and because of the weariness and sleepiness the scene sometimes reels before me, as if I am watching it through water. But when I return to my senses and once again see everything straight, I can hear her voice monotonously going on and on, but becoming more and more tired. Her sentences are becoming muddled, sometimes she repeats the same things over and over, and a few times she lays her head down on my knees, so exhausted that I can hardly hear what she is mumbling. And when at last she remains silent for a few long minutes it occurs to me that she may be waiting for an answer.

"*Ego te absolvo*," I whisper, more for her sake than mine.

"No!" she cries, lifting her head violently. "Why did you say that? Why are you trying to forgive me? You don't even know *what* to forgive! I don't want to be forgiven if I've done anything wrong. I want to be guilty, I want to be punished. What sense could there else be in sinning?"

Determined, I get up and try to pull her up by the arms, but she remains kneeling on the floor.

"You're tired," I say soothingly. "We are both of us exhausted. You no longer know what you are saying. The game is over."

"It is never over." I suspect that she is saying it without meaning it, but she is unfathomable. There is no greater mystery than a person without any mysteries.

"Come," I say. "We are going to bed. That is your punishment."

She smiles, shaking her head, and saying: "No." But she allows me to help her to her feet; and she remains standing before me so that I can undress her. It is the beginning of a new game, a lovely game, a sweet, warm, good game; and, as part of the game, we put off the light and content ourselves with the rectangle of the window, and the shadow of the little cross in its reflection on the wall.

11

I'm not writing regularly enough. But how would you like it if I sat down every Sunday to send you a neat little inventory listed between a loving introduction and a charming conclusion, of all the parties and receptions we have attended in the course of the week, of everything we have bought, of all the places we have visited because we felt we should, or because we wanted to, or merely because there was nothing else to do? The only alternative, it seems, is that each letter becomes a sort of emotional outburst on paper – which is no less unfair to you! What would our friends think of the cool, reserved Erika they knew? You see, I have too much time for rummaging in my own heart. It's like the bottle of bad sherry Anna gave us once, with the dregs at the bottom. If one lifted it too quickly it was undrinkable. Why did we keep it after all? Afraid of "hurting her feelings"? All these sweet, polite little fears! Why didn't we, instead, invite her for a large glass of her own dregs?

But I think this will be the last time you will have to bear with the results of my uncalled-for soul-searching. For we are coming home at last.

The decision came rather unexpectedly. The affair between Annette and her Italian was broken off. By the time I discovered it, it was already three days after the event. Like a good mother I tried to sympathise with my daughter's broken heart, doing my utmost to convince her that it would be for her own good if she confided in me. She refused vehemently. Soon it developed into an unrestrained quarrel in which I accused her of no longer trusting me, of deliberately withholding things from me, etc. "And why shouldn't I?" she asked — our obedient, obliging little Annette! "Why can't I have a bit of life of my own?" And then she started pouring it out, for fifteen minutes or more. Accusing me of always treating her like a tender little plant that has to be kept out of the sun. Of choosing all her clothes. Of prescribing her food, her conduct, her thoughts. And, in conclusion, she insisted that she was sick and tired of it all and that she refused to pay any further attention to me. I could not answer. I was too dumbfounded in front of this stranger who was no longer my child. This scene had been coming for a very long time, I suppose, but I always reassured myself that it was only temporary, that it "would pass". There are so many ways of deceiving oneself!

When I finally walked out, she shouted one last remark: "I won't allow you to smother me any longer with your jealousy!"

"Jealousy?" I asked. That was the last accusation I would have expected.

"Yes! You've always been jealous of me. You merely want to use me because you have no life of your own. And you have always been afraid that Father might take me away from you. And that is what you called love!"

At last I opened the door and went out. Heaven knows through what streets I wandered that long night. And all the time I was thinking, thinking. I remembered how I had resented having a child. It had practically been one of the conditions of our marriage. You couldn't understand it. But could I? Was it a childish way of avenging the humiliation you had made me suffer? — not by staying away for those eighteen months, but by coming back convinced that I was yours for the asking. Why did I so readily yield then? This is what one's renowned "free will" amounts to: I said yes

171

because my mother insisted that I refuse you after the "unfor-
givable slight". And so, because I wanted to rebel against her, we
were married after all. Still, I think I loved you. I know I did. But
God knows there was so much resentment, so much suspicion in
me. How could I give birth to your child before I sincerely wanted
to? But she was born anyway. You were so proud and happy.
How could you know that that frightened me even more? The child
could so easily cause you to cast me away altogether; you two
could become allies against me. What else could I do, Paul? Oh, I
know only too well, now, how adolescent I was. But I thought the
only thing I could do would be to win her as an ally before you
could. And that was what I called love: clinging desperately to a
child I had not wanted, because she was the only thing I could
call my own, and because she could so easily become an opponent.
We were never temperamentally suited to each other, she and I.
And what will happen now? Is it too late to hope for anything?

Whatever happens, we are coming home. I am coming home,
not very proud of myself. I shall have to learn to forgive myself
before I could hope for anything else; but does that come so
easily? And has it any sense? It is not enough to accuse oneself if
one desires to be freed from guilt. So how could it be enough to
forgive oneself? It seems one has no choice but to move away from
oneself to someone or something else, someone less wretched than
oneself. To "confess". Is it a primitive need in one's heart, then,
to confess, to sacrifice? But where does one turn to? The church is
no longer fashionable, it has become an equation incapable of
solving x. But one must arrive somewhere, else one's guilt becomes
too much and too complex, affecting too many innocent people
surrounding the one who has sinned; it becomes collective guilt,
and every generation adds to it, making reprieve more impossible.

You must help me drink my bottle of sherry, Paul. Perhaps, if
one closes one's eyes and swallows very hard, the bottle will empty.

Love: See if you can decipher this word. Erika.

12

With her hair against my neck and her open lips against my
shoulder where, a minute ago, she bit deep into my flesh, she
asks in her unexpected way:

"How does one say in Afrikaans: *faire l'amour* – to make love?"

"One doesn't. There are two sorts of words, but one sounds like
a medical text book, and the other like an inscription on a lavatory
wall."

172

She laughs but her eyes remain serious: "What did *you* use to say then: you and your wife?"

"We never talked about it."

"Oh." She is lying quite still, breathing tranquilly. After a while she comments: "Marc-Louis says: 'Put the devil in hell' – "

"Who is Marc-Louis?"

Her eyes, which have been looking past me, move back to mine. Is she a little bit frightened? Did she say something she never meant to say?

"Just a student," she says, with a shrug.

"How did you come to know him?"

"I know many people in Paris."

"But *him*?"

"Met him in a café or somewhere. I can't remember. He sometimes comes over to chat."

"Just chat?"

"Why do you want to know it all? Does it matter if we do more than chat?"

I dare not answer.

"You're jealous."

"No." I am not. It is the truth. I am merely feeling an immense weariness in me. I have never known that *détresse* – this emotion beyond despair – could be so quiet.

I move away from her.

After a while she gets up and begins to dress while I sit looking down at myself. Marc-Louis: is this the latest name of fate? And all the time while in my new illusion of living I have been feeling that I was moving towards something, he has existed for her, as real as I, and probably even more real in her eyes.

"Just a student – "

Perhaps I sometimes came to her while she was still harbouring his seed deep inside her. And she never showed any sign of it. Why not? Because it belonged to the past, absorbed into her unknown, and therefore forgotten? Or was it, is it, all part of her never-ending game? And how long is it going to last? There is not much left of my three months. And afterwards – ?

She suddenly comes back to me, takes my face in her small hands, forces me to look up at her.

"Why can't you understand?" she asks. "It makes no difference to *us*."

"And 'we' make no difference to *you*, it seems." For the very first time I dare tell her the truth: "Did you know that a commission of inquiry may be sent here soon?"

173

"Why?"

"About us."

At first she looks sceptical; then puzzled. "And then? Will you have to go away?"

"Not necessarily." After a moment I add: "Would *that* make any difference to 'us'?"

She shakes her head but she is no longer looking at me. It is not necessary for her to say anything. For now, at this moment, I *know*.

Yet I insist: "Will you stay with me then, Nicolette?"

Impatiently, desperately, she swings her head back: "I don't know, I don't know, I don't *know*! Why must you go on asking questions? How can I know what is going to happen?"

"So it will be the end of everything between us?"

"Will you be sacked?"

"Does that matter – to you?"

"We are still *here* now," she urges. "Nothing else matters."

I get up and begin to dress.

"Don't go away." She takes me by the arm. "Stay here. Stay with me, always. You must never, never go away."

"Do you love me?"

"What does it *mean*?" she asks in despair. "People say it every day. It's so easy. A word is nothing. What could it *be*?"

"I know. A word is nothing. And to love is nothing. But I love *you*."

I take her in my arms. Over her shoulder I can see delicate snowflakes whirring softly past the window. There is light in the window across the street, but the curtains are drawn.

She must be knowing what I am looking at, for with a little laugh she says: "She is shy tonight. Or perhaps it is because of the snow."

13

I am walking through the city more and more often these days, sometimes with her, sometimes alone. It has become a deep-seated need, more urgent than the simple desire to see as much as possible of the place while I am still here, or an attempt to find, beyond the confusion of streets and buildings, a more coherent pattern of things. It is, really, a daily discovery that everything that has happened, everything that may still happen, has been so predestined by the city itself. It is more than a context for events: it is, in itself, an event taking place with and inside us. And so it is, also, much more than a milieu for her, or a symbol of her: it is,

174

simultaneously, a synthesis of all her elements, and a being with its own existence. The city has its own head, and heart, and belly, and sex. And it seems as though, in the process through which I am robbed of all other convictions, opinions, certainties and possibilities, the city is becoming more and more alive, and a more and more urgent presence.

14

In the mauve of the early evening, while we are waiting for our large cups of coffee in a warm, smoky, pleasant little café, she is absent-mindedly scratching something on the corner of the table with a bent hairpin. It is a single, innocent word which makes its appearance in the old dark wood: *MOI*. And when she catches my eyes on it, she covers it shyly with her hand and drops the hairpin in the cheap green ashtray.

15

Loose thoughts in the serene courtyard of Saint-Séverin:
It is easy to talk about love. She said so herself. It is thinking about love which is difficult. And it happens so often these days, as I am more and more inextricably caught in the web of Erika, Gillian, Nicolette.

For a long time I have succeeded in keeping away all thoughts of Erika, writing polite Sunday letters only. But now that she is coming back, after all her confessions, I have to learn to adapt myself to this inescapable fact.

Long ago, when I returned to her that time, I did not think much about it either. I never regarded it as a problem. Gillian was dead. Something was rounded off, complete, final, without regrets or speculation about the future. It was so *obvious* that I should return to Erika. In fact, it actually surprised me that she did not immediately comply but insisted on first "thinking it over". Not that I had any doubts about her decision: I simply took it for granted that neither of us had any alternative.

The first moment of slight panic came after all the wedding guests had gone and, after hours of driving through pouring rain, we arrived at our destination and were suddenly confronted with each other in the anonymity of the hotel room. She smiled nervously, trying, it seemed, to convince herself of something. But it was no use. What she needed was the conviction of *my* certainty. And, suddenly, I had nothing to offer her. We were desperate to find

175

some sort of preliminary contact before we could proceed to the disconcerting experience custom and circumstances required of us. But at last we switched off the light and put the seal on the night's failure. And although we did "succeed" soon afterwards, according to the prescriptions of medical textbooks anyway, we began to gnaw away at each other's wholeness and security as the years went by. Still, we managed to live together without obvious friction, in strict neutrality.

Sometimes, inevitably, I rebelled, wondering what would happen should I try to satisfy my growing need elsewhere. But I anticipated the cynical expression in Erika's cool eyes, and her voice which would say: "Go ahead, if you must." And I desisted.

Yet she had been carefree and gay earlier, before our marriage, before Gillian. But it was different from Nicolette: Erika was always "proper"; Erika had never been "that sort of girl"; Erika always managed to make me feel inferior.

But how do these things fit in with the woman who wrote those letters from Italy, the woman who is now returning to me? How do they fit in with "us" – the people we have been for almost thirty years? How do they fit in with *now*? I don't know. Is it not presumptuous to talk of "love" if it has never been anything but a dormant possibility?

And Gillian. That, also, would be termed "love". Love? My God: *odi et amo,* a fire which was meant to purify everything and eventually consumed itself. Or was it an exorcism of nothingness, touching, for that very reason, on something essential in love – the urge to maintain *being* in the face of everything destructive, even in the face of itself?

Or is love, really, the most simple answer to the unbearableness of solitude, which makes it a drug? No: it is much too acute for that. Too mercilessly sincere.

And Nicolette? *Lassata, non satiata,* like Faustina: she who can devise, for hours, for whole nights, her delicious games, new positions, intimate little ecstasies: every one of them an act in itself, pure, wholly free from the blemish of thoughts or words. With her love is a never-ending mystery, a quest for insoluble riddles, and for the origin of myths. With her love is a form of bewilderment, because it confronts one with the chaos inside oneself; her body is, indeed, "a wilderness, a true genesis and exodus", a labyrinth from which I could, and would, never escape.

And there is always this irony: love is supposed to "last forever", to be "unchanging" – but our relationship has always, since the very beginning, been ephemeral, calculable within the days and hours of three months – and consequently doomed to futility; and yet there is nothing else I *could* do. In the end even Nicolette will be lost to me; in the end there will be nothing. (And so, *Amare liceat si non potiri licet* – ?) But now, at this moment, while it lasts, she is indispensable: not in any petty, selfish way, but *essentially*.

It seems to me the concept of "rebirth" is merely the Christian interpretation of an experience which is deeply necessary for every human being: an act of renewal, of dissociation from oneself, in order to become aware of the world and the self. And in this sense she has been my rebirth. It is impossible for a man to crawl back into the womb, however much he may try to do so all his life; it is equally impossible to undo this discovery of the world. It is no mirror one can shatter in order to get rid of an image.

Would the mere fact of "civilisation" be responsible for the immense difficulty one has to come to this, and to accept it? Love, after all, is not something civilised, but a primitive need. I do not know. If, indeed, I have unnecessary, unessential "needs" left in me, I shall have to dispense with them as the time grows shorter and shorter. But could this be done voluntarily? Or must one wait for grace? And where does one find *that* – ?

16

The night before it had still been winter. I remember it clearly, for I can still see the misty panes through which we were looking at the people of the window opposite. I can still hear her say: "She can't have very long to go. It must be eight months already." And I can remember her perplexed eyes as she went on: "I don't know *what* I'd do if it happened to me. I wouldn't mind having a child – if it's a girl – but then she must just *be* there, one day, without this sort of thing. It must be like dying; one must feel cornered, smothered. It would drive me mad – "

The snow had melted weeks ago but it was still bitterly cold; at night – and that night too – we gratefully snuggled in each other's warmth against the thin movement of the wind across the slanted roof.

And then, the very next morning, it was suddenly, inexplicably spring. One knew it from the early filtering of the light through the window; and from the new cry of the quarter's brocanteur in the street below; it was visible in the first suggestion of green in the chestnut trees of the Luxembourg Gardens when, later that

177

day, I left my work and went out with her and with hundreds of others to enjoy the sun; it was audible in the laughing of children who had left their overcoats at home; it was obvious in the cafés which had, overnight, shed their glass terraces so that chairs and tables were pushed out on the sidewalks like the foam of a new tide.

"The cold will return," I can still hear her warning. "It's always like this: the false Spring of February – "

But it did not really matter. Nothing had any urgency. The touch of despair which had always been so unmistakable in my clinging to her, had suddenly disappeared; everything was tranquillity. Perhaps that, also, was an illusion like the too early spring. But it was there all the same; it was there to be enjoyed. Those were serene days, quiet and timeless – perhaps the last stillness we would ever know together. But even that did not trouble us. For the first time, maybe the only time, I learned to exist in a continuous present, like her.

I remember –

We are walking on the lowest promenade along the Seine and sit down on stone steps, drowsy of the sun, her light frock pulled up high above her boyish knees, her sandals kicked off, her toes in the dirty water. We are walking hand in hand under the early green chestnut trees, and we sit down at a table in the shade, and drink Coca-Cola. She is wearing peach blossoms in her hair in the narrow path below the Palais de Chaillot. We are standing on the open balcony of an old green bus travelling recklessly to the Bois de Vincennes. She is dancing ahead of me in a flimsy summer dress, with her legs and her body silhouetted against the light like the wick of a candle inside the flame. We are standing together on the Eiffel Tower, on the Arc de Triomphe, on the towers of Notre-Dame: she is afraid of heights – or perhaps it is another form of ecstasy? – yet she insists on climbing every tower. We are sitting in a cheap cinema where she is soaking her little handkerchief with tears.

Often we are talking. She tells me all about herself: a different story every time, but I have learnt long ago not to be annoyed by her lies because every one of them is completely true at the moment of telling. In a few light moments she summarises a whole past of shadows.

Sometimes, more and more frequently, our conversation turns to Erika. Will it not change the relation between us? she asks, quietly, never urgently. And I assure her very sincerely: Nothing could make any difference to us. Nothing could change anything

178

between us. After all, if Erika's return had any decisive effect on what exists between Nicolette and myself, it would mean that our relationship found its only *raison d'être* in the fact of Erika's absence. And it is much, much more complex than that.

Yet all the time I have the secret knowledge that Erika's return will, indeed, make a difference. What it will be, I do not know yet; perhaps it is not even of immediate importance. But it is inevitable that the large, calm, inexorable movement in which we are caught will become more rapid and more urgent when she comes back.

But now, together in this early Spring, everything is still eternally happy.

17

It was on the afternoon of 22nd February that she came back. I went out to Orly to meet her. While Farnham was driving smoothly along the autoroute with its splendid curves and the long rows of lamp posts with gracefully bent heads, I tried to visualise the meeting on the airport, and its consequences, later. How and when would Nicolette make her appearance in our conversation? What would Erika's reactions be? How would it influence the course of events? But something in me was clogged. I could not even think of any *possible* answers; and much to my confusion I could no longer even visualise Erika's face.

But the moment she stepped from the Boeing and moved away from the other travellers towards the special V.I.P. lounge I knew her well enough again to notice that she had lost weight. Not much, but still. That was the only difference. I felt almost disappointed because I had expected that what she had written in her letters would also be revealed, subtly, in her appearance. But even when she reached me and allowed me to kiss her, my eyes eagerly exploring her face, she was the same reserved stranger as before; her hair a few tints lighter than usual; her make-up immaculate; her eyes smiling with calculated friendliness.

"Hullo, Paul."

"Hullo, Erika. Enjoy yourself?"

"Yes, thank you."

"Glad to be back?"

"Of course." With a hint of cynicism in the corner of her mouth. "And how are you?"

"Oh fine, thanks."

Then Annette approached us, as formal and as mondaine, it

seemed, as her mother who looked like her sister; but she was not yet experienced enough to hide a touch of uncertainty: a slight quivering of the mouth, a question in the dark eyes.

"Hullo, Father."

"Hullo, Annette." Our kiss was confined to a light touch of the lips: was she afraid that I might smudge her lipstick, or that I would feel the trembling of her mouth?

"You're lovely," I added playfully. But I meant it.

While Farnham was arranging the luggage we went to the official car.

"Donald and Mary sent their regards."

"Thanks. Did you see them often?"

"Almost daily. No changes in your staff here?"

"No. The Jouberts are going on home leave in two months' time."

Annette was lagging behind, watching a couple of doves. Erika and I reached the car, and stood still, and knew that we were alone.

"Erika – ?"

There was a flickering of her eyelids but she made no answer.

"Are you *sure* you're all right?"

"Of course." She looked into my eyes dauntlessly, and then got in. "Did you long for me?"

It was my turn to answer: "Of course."

Annette was approaching with Farnham and the porter. I stood watching my child intently, discovering to my amazement that she was a young woman. As she reached the door she noticed my gaze, smiled quickly, somewhat embarrassed, and sat down.

We did not talk much on our way back: a few remarks about their holiday, about officials in our Embassy in Rome, about a coming fashion show in Paris.

Once Annette said: "You've grown thin, Father."

"It's your imagination," I answered from habit.

And Erika commented: "It suits you, you know."

With that the tone was struck for the next few days. It came almost as a surprise to see how little difference their presence in the official residence made. We saw each other at breakfast, lunch and dinner and talked about obvious, matter-of-fact things. Perhaps it was just as well. But it could not last; sooner or later it was inevitable for us to come to grips with each other, to talk it all through. This fencing was too deliberate. And it soon became frustrating to find pretexts for going to Nicolette at night. Knowing that they never came to my office, I used "working late" as an excuse for a few times; once or twice I had to visit a colleague for "discussions". But at eleven or twelve o'clock I had to be home; and this lay heavily on the hours I spent with Nicolette. For some time neither of us made any reference to it, but it was obviously beginning to trouble her. And this had to be avoided: the balance was too precarious to be disturbed, the whole too intricate.

About a week after Erika's return Nicolette, for the first time, refused all attempts at lovemaking. And when I insisted to know the reason, she said curtly:

"I'm not a street-girl!"

"But what on earth makes you think that?"

"That's all you want of me nowadays. And we must always finish before a certain time. We are becoming secretive. How long is this going to last?"

That was the final warning. If no occasion for discussing the matter with Erika presented itself naturally, I would simply have to force our conversation in that direction. I felt too tired, too dejected to attempt it that same evening; but I was firmly resolved that the matter would come to a head the next day.

It was with a feeling almost of relief that I entered the official residence and went upstairs. Erika's door was closed, although there was still a thin line of light underneath. Annette's stood open. For a moment I hesitated on the landing. Then the bathroom door was opened and Annette came out, her cheeks glowing after her bath, her fair hair damp. She was wearing a dressing gown of soft yellow towelling, carrying a small bundle of clothes under her arm. And it came almost as a physical shock to see her like that: vulnerable, young, candid, beautiful.

"Oh – good evening, Father!" She smiled in her slightly hesitant way. "Have you just come back?"

I nodded. It was difficult to speak as if our meeting was something ordinary. I had to make an effort to convince myself that she was really my own child. She was indeed a child: a lovely little girl; but at the same time she was a young woman with the soft, free movement of her limbs inside the dressing gown.

She came to me.

"You're working much too hard," she said.

"It's become a habit."

"Would you like a cup of tea?"

"It would wake up the household. It's so late."

"No. It won't take long." Holding her gown with the hand carrying the bundle of clothes she took my hand with the other, still somewhat self-conscious, but adamant.

In the kitchen I sat down on a straight-backed chair, and watched her arrange the cups and boil the water.

"One of these days you'll be nineteen," I said, more to myself than to her.

She looked at me over her shoulder, surprised. "Yes. Why?"

"And this is practically the first time you and I have been alone together."

She went on working, her back turned to me.

I did not know her. How could I love her? Yet that was the very discovery I made, sitting on my white kitchen chair: that I had loved her all along. For she was a child-girl, and therefore she was free. I could exist within my pattern, but she could be free for me. That was the essential nature of a girl; she represented the only absolute things left in my safe, watered down existence. When she had been small I had often watched her through a window, or listened to her laugh. But as she grew up, I noticed her grow into the pattern, become a little hostess, a model child, a well-behaved little tame monkey. I saw her accept it, without resisting. And therefore I closed my heart to her, forgot entirely about her. Which was a negative way of hating.

And now she was with me in the merciless light of the white kitchen, and I made the strange discovery that she was not what I had all the time believed her to be; she was still a *girl*. If I had noticed it earlier – ? But earlier, before her Italian holiday, she had indeed been different. She had been an impersonal statement; now she was a question mark.

She handed me my cup of tea. I took it, and touched her, and held her hand. She glanced up and tried to smile, bewildered.

"What happened in Italy, my little girl?"

I saw her face become tense; for a moment she strongly resembled Erika. "Why do you ask that?" she asked.

"Erika wrote me something about it."

"A bunch of lies, I suppose." She said it without flinching.

"Was it a terrible disappointment, Annette?"

She was struggling against the emotion. Then she began to cry, her head buried in her arms on the table. I laid my hand on her shoulder and made no attempt to stop her. After a long while she said confusedly: "He was in such a hurry. With everything. Always. He just wanted to get married. He just *wanted* me!"

"And you did not love him."

"I did!" She lifted up her head and looked at me passionately. "And I still do." For a moment it seemed as if she would begin to sob again, but she quickly, angrily wiped the tears away

182

with one of her sleeves and continued: "But I was frightened. I do not want to get caught. I do not want to become what you and Erika have become."

I could not answer.

"I went to Erika. She was thrilled. She, too, wanted me to get married. She never realised that I wanted her to *help* me!" Her burning eyes were looking into mine again. "Why have you always left me to *her* care only, father? Why did you never help me? Didn't you know I needed you?"

The clock in the lounge politely struck half-past twelve. She glanced up, almost scared; then, without looking at me again, picked up her clothes and her cup of tea and went to the door.

"Annette."

She stopped.

"We have been living past each other. But perhaps it is not yet too late."

I could see her hesitate. Then she took a deep breath and said softly: "Good-night, Father." And she went out, through the dark dining-room to the staircase.

The following afternoon, directly after work, Anna Smith "just popped in", after a few days' illness, to welcome Erika "back in our midst" and to express the hope that her holiday had been pleasant. "We all missed you ever so much," she said with great conviction. "And poor Mr. Ambassador! He became quite absent-minded lately, the last thing anybody would ever have expected him to be, don't you think so? Now you know me for a frank person, Mrs. Van Heerden, and I want to tell you what an awful admiration we have for your husband. And he's just not the same person when you're not here. Pining away, you might say. Now please don't misunderstand me: of course we are all very glad that you could have had a bit of holiday – "

Erika's ironic eyes looked at me, then returned to Anna.

When we finally came back from the front door, more than an hour later, she said teasingly: "My poor husband. Have you really been so lonely?"

"It's time you and I have a quiet talk together, Erika."

"Talk? That's all we've been doing since I came back."

"No. It has been a clever game of fencing. We never come to anything of real importance."

She remained standing on the threshold of the private lounge, erect, defensive. "And what could be so very important?" she asked.

"All the things you wrote me from Italy. Perhaps you found it just as strange as I did, reading those confessions in *your* handwriting. You have changed, Erika. Why do you refuse to admit it?"

"Oh, the letters?" She moved nonchalantly past me to where her cigarettes were lying on a long low table. "You'd better burn them. They are incriminating evidence. And entirely false, I suppose. I can hardly remember what I wrote." But her calm words were contradicted by her hands holding the packet. "Our French friends would call it *une crise de conscience*. One shouldn't attach too much importance to it."

"There's no need to be evasive, Erika."

She shook her head, blowing out the first smoke. "No. you must remember I was away from my familiar surroundings, away from you. I had more time to think than was good for me. That's all. And now it is past."

"Much of it was true."

"Was it?" Her eyes became narrower, scrutinising me through the smoke.

"But you accused yourself only, forgetting that I have my own share of guilt."

"Please! Not you too," she said, much too quickly. "It was enough that I had to put up with myself. It would be melodramatic if you started too. It's *past*, I assure you. Don't keep on nagging. We have learnt to get along with it."

"So you refuse to discuss it?"

"It's just that I do not believe in the therapy of words." She turned away from me, announcing: "I must see to tonight's dinner. The servants have become very unreliable in my absence."

"I have something to tell *you*."

"Yes?" She turned back politely, but I knew her well enough to sense her irritation. "I am going out again tonight."

She shrugged. "Oh well – "

"I won't be back before tomorrow morning," I said, very calmly, very resolutely.

For a moment she frowned. Then there was a slight change in her expression. "I see." She fell silent, and nodded. "I see. I don't suppose it's entirely unexpected."

"You don't understand, Erika."

"Please don't try to explain." She smiled. "I won't bind you."

There was nothing else for us to say. Only when I turned round to go did she ask: "Was it necessary to tell me?"

But I did not answer.

184

It was only three days later that Erika personally brought me my cup of coffee after work. Her attitude suggested that she had something on her mind, but she evaded my questioning glance and calmly sat paging through a *Marie-Claire* while I was drinking.

Then, almost casually, still flipping over the pages, she said: "She was here this afternoon."

"Who?"

"Your little – hierodoule. Miss Alford."

"Nicolette?" For a moment I was dumbfounded. And yet that was exactly what I should have expected her to do.

"I suppose that is what you would call her," Erika said. Then, with a flickering of her mouth: "And what does she call you? 'Your Excellency'? Or 'Sir'? Or simply 'Uncle'?"

"Now you are childish, Erika."

"I am. I'm sorry. On the other hand, I expected *you* to reveal more adult taste." She seemed to be deeply interested in a few fashion illustrations. "Surely a person in your position could make a better choice?"

"I am not prepared to discuss her with you. Not like this."

"Perhaps it would be better not to say anything, I agree. If that is really your taste it is not much of a compliment for me, is it?"

I put down my empty cup and stood up. "What did she come for?" I asked stiffly.

"She brought some flowers. I wasn't sure whether they were meant for you or for me, so I gave them to the servants. Quite expensive too; this time of the year everything comes from hot-houses, I presume."

I paid no attention to her. But when I reached the door she let down her mask, if only for a fleeting second:

"My God, Paul," she said, "I am ashamed of you!"

Blindly I passed through a few rooms. Was it Erika who had aroused my anger, or Nicolette? I do not know. I only know that it took quite some time before I could force myself to think coolly again: Surely there was nothing else I could have expected? I had made my choice with open eyes. And as I went out to the metro I knew, once again, that whatever happened, nothing could be allowed to come between Nicolette and myself. For that was the only meaningful thing I had left.

But there was still Annette. It is difficult to tell, now, whether she avoided me on purpose, or whether it was the normal course of our lives which separated us during the next few days. But one afternoon I was on my way upstairs just as she was coming down. For a moment it seemed as if she hesitated, wanting, perhaps, to turn back. Then she merely cast her eyes down and swiftly, without a word, came down past me. I could feel a tautness inside me. Strange as it might seem it was as if that moment was filled with much more agony than the two short conversations with Erika.

I called her.

She stopped, but did not look round.

"Where are you going in such a hurry?"

"Just – out."

"What is the matter?"

She shook her head. I thought she would refuse to speak. But then she swung round to me, her hand clutching the rail, and the words came jerking loose from deep inside her: "I thought – in Italy, and the other evening – and you said –" Her voice faltered for a moment but she went on: "And all the time you were doing this! You deceived me! I thought – and believed, and hoped – that everything would be different now. I've never felt so *dirty* in my life!"

Long after the front door had slammed I was still standing there. When, finally, feelings filtered back into my mind, I tried to console myself with hackneyed phrases: The absolutism of youth – Give her time – She'll be more balanced later – But it was useless. And I could not even trick myself into believing that it might help. I simply had to accept that everything which, up to that moment, had been maintained by make-believe was now beginning to fall away from me. I did not know how long the process would last, or where it would land me. I had no power over it any more. I could only go on.

But: my daughter, my unknown child, Annette – !

18

In the early evening, through my office window above the desk with the calendar and a catalogue of French arms, I can see a soundless jet plane gliding into the sky beyond the buildings of the city, writing, like a human hand, white curves on the twilight wall of heaven.

19

It was the first time I had ever seen Douglas Masters flustered.

"Mr. Ambassador," he said. "I know that it would be against the rules to come to you with this, but I find it impossible to do anything else."

"What is it, Masters?" I was struck by the uncommon paleness of his face.

"I have received a letter from the Minister – " He vaguely gestured with a handful of papers. "I simply don't know what to do – "

"What is it about?" It was not necessary to ask the question; I already suspected what was coming.

It was an instruction from the Minister to inquire discreetly into Stephen Keyter's report, of which a copy was attached. He was to reply as soon as possible.

"It seems fairly clear." I looked into his eyes and pushed the documents back towards him.

"But – Surely you realise that this is preposterous, Mr. Ambassador! Why was Keyter not transferred back to Pretoria immediately? Couldn't the Minister have contacted you personally? There could be no justification for this procedure!" He must have been very much upset to lose his customary self-restraint so completely.

"I saw the report in December."

"But why was the matter not crushed immediately?"

"I preferred not to comment."

For a while he gaped at me, not saying anything, not understanding anything. At last he asked, almost pathetically: "But surely it's a parcel of flagrant lies?"

"The facts are correct, Masters. Only the interpretation was wrong."

"But in that case – "

"In the meantime the situation has become somewhat different. In the present circumstances the interpretation would also be correct."

I sat watching him with almost complete detachment, as if the whole matter referred to someone else. He was struggling to master the blow. At last he seemed to make up his mind.

"I cannot be disloyal to you, Mr. Ambassador," he said with taut lips. "I shall not send the Minister any comment."

I shook my head, touched, in spite of myself, by his sincerity. "Unfortunately the matter is not so simple, Masters. I was given the choice either to defend myself or to ignore the request. You have been given instructions which must be executed."

He made no answer, swallowed, arranging and rearranging his papers in a most irritating way. "What must I do?" he almost whispered.

There was something grotesque in the situation.

"I would suggest that you discuss the matter with Lebon. He should be able to report on my movements. You are quite free, of course, to mention that you discussed it with me and that I maintained my attitude."

"But it would be so easy to quash the whole affair." He was practically pleading. "You must realise what it would lead to. We need you here. Mr. Ambassador, this is no time for idle flattery, but surely you realise that you are indispensable to the Government in this position, especially at this stage of the arms negotiations!"

Should I have replied with the obvious cliché that "nobody is indispensable"? That I could not do. I knew only too well what he was offering me. Frankly, had I thought reconsideration could still change anything in the matter, I would have yielded – if more for his sake than mine. But at that stage it was of so little concern, it had become so much of a purely academic problem, that it would have been senseless even to hope that the course of events could still be changed, or that such a change could be of any significance to me.

Therefore I merely shook my head.

"Mr. Ambassador – " But the matter was now beyond the reach of words, and he knew it. I felt sorry for him in this crisis where neither Satow nor all his years of experience could help him find a formula.

"There is only one little thing, Masters," I said. "In Keyter's report you will find the address of the person concerned." I deliberately refrained from mentioning her name. "I don't know whether it would be expected of you to approach her for information as well. But if you could do without it, I shall appreciate it very much."

"Of course!" He was almost pathetic.

But that was not yet the end of the matter. The same evening, as I came back from one of the rare official occasions I had to attend personally, Stephen Keyter was waiting at the main entrance of the Embassy with Lebon, asking to see me for a few minutes. I invited him to the residence, but it seemed he was afraid we might be disturbed by Erika or Annette, so we went up to my office. He was excited, but he remained silent until the door was closed behind us.

"Well, Keyter?"

"Mr. Ambassador." He was fumbling with a cigarette I had offered him. "Mr. Masters came to see me earlier tonight."

"He was here this afternoon."

He was flabbergasted. "So – you know – ?"

I nodded.

For a moment he seemd to weigh everything in his mind, finding it much too heavy to bear; then he suddenly burst out: "Why are they doing this, Mr Ambassador? Why don't they believe me?" Then, impulsively: "You yourself have never believed that I had no personal grudge against you."

"On the contrary. I could not agree with the procedure you adopted. For the rest you did your duty."

"It was more than duty." For a moment he closed up again. His upper lip was twitching nervously. Then he continued very quickly: "I know you will think it idiotic or conceited of me, but my career is the only thing that really matters to me. And tonight Masters said – he was furious – that my whole future might – that he would see to it that – Mr. Ambassador – !" For a moment he was helplessly struggling for words. "I don't think you can understand. Nobody has ever understood. You never find anything difficult. You never do anything which does not succeed. But I – Even when I was a child. My father wanted a son, not a sickly child who often spent more time in bed than out of it. He wanted to make a man of me; that was his one ideal, because in all other respects he was an unhappy, frustrated man. And then I proved to be his greatest failure. I joined the Service because it promised so much for the future. I wanted to arrive somewhere. I *had* to arrive somewhere. And now?" His hands were pressing down on the desk. "What must I do now?"

"Wait. That is all you can do. That is all we can do."

He rested his head between his hands and remained in that position for a long time, his cigarette forgotten on the ashtray, with a lazy spiral of smoke whirling towards the ceiling. I was looking at him as if I had never seen him before. Earlier, I thought, there had been suspicion on his side, and probably hate; resentment and scorn on mine. He had been the one who held the whiphand; I was the one pursued But now, unexpectedly, he was bewildered and had come to me for help; and I could feel compassion for him: this young man who had always hidden his emotions behind cynical intellectualism, and who had now discovered that he could become the victim of his own impulsiveness.

"What did you say to Masters?" I urged.

"Nothing. I told him I first wanted to think it over."

"Why did you come here, then?"

"There is nobody else."

"You are much too young to retire so far into your own shell," I tried to soothe him, upset by his confession. "You must lead a more normal life, with friends, with girls."

"Don't you think I have tried? And every time – "

We fell silent. And it was only after a long pause that I said, without knowing why: "Nicolette."

He looked up at me, shook his head, cast down his eyes again. "But you knew her."

He made no answer.

"She told me herself." Something was urging me on. "The very first night she came to me, last November, after you had thrown her out."

That touched him. He looked up slowly. But his answer came as a surprise: "Was that the first time you met her?"

"Yes. Why?"

"But I thought – " He did not complete his sentence. He seemed to be struggling with himself. "It was a lie anyway," he said after a while. "It was she who left, of her own free will."

"I should have guessed as much."

He did not answer for some time. Then: "Of course. You know her."

I made a movement with my head. How could I answer so that he would believe me: I did *not* know her, nobody knew her?

"I wanted her," he continued unexpectedly. "Perhaps I could have learnt to love her. Perhaps. But it would not have worked out. She always despised me – and she tried to hide it by playing with me." With some self-pity he added: "Perhaps that was what I deserved. I have never inspired confidence in anyone."

"Accusing oneself brings one nowhere, Stephen."

"No, no," he said. "I am merely telling the truth. First there was my mother. She was the only one who ever cared for me. She always took my side. But I did not want her to defend me out of pity. And so I withdrew myself from her too, although she was the one who really needed pity. My father was such a hard man – " He sighed. "Do you see how confused it all is? But how could I trust her after I had discovered that she was a

190

hypocrite, and defenceless clay in my father's hands – ?" And suddenly he plunged into a long, confused narrative about Sunday nights at home, with pious prayers followed by a nauseating scene in his parents' bedroom. "And then she died," he concluded, exhausted. "She used my father's revolver. That is something I could never escape from. I still, often, see her before me. It becomes a sort of poison in one's blood, and it grows more and more until there is nothing else left in one. I cannot bear it any longer. I do not know what is going to happen. And now I have brought this thing upon *you*."

He got up, composed again, as if his last words had frightened him back into himself. "I must go," he said, almost formally. "I have already wasted so much of your time."

"You must not worry too much about it," I said soothingly. "Your report will most probably be accepted. And you can easily convince them of your sincere intentions. I could confirm it."

He showed no reaction. But when we reached the small courtyard below he said: "I am sorry, Mr. Ambassador. About everything. I am terribly sorry."

Our hands touched in the dark. Then he left. I remained in the courtyard, thinking: how strange, how strange that Nicolette, who had once been the gulf between us, was now the only thing we had in common: her game, her lies, her never-ending mystery.

20

The endearing way she has, whenever she is feeling upset or sad, of twirling a little curl on her forehead with one finger, faster and faster, until she is soothed or falls asleep.

21

On Christmas morning she ignores all her expensive presents and puts on an ordinary warm dress and a coat, with an ugly plastic raincoat on top; and her worn-out old brown rosary is carefully arranged round her neck, like a piece of valuable jewellery.

Long before the beginning of the Mass we are waiting inside Notre-Dame.

At first it is merely an expanse of darkness with the distant glittering of a crowd of candles before the Virgin, and the red and blue glow of the stained-glass windows. But gradually one's eyes

191

discover large, heavy columns silent in the dark; and chairs; and clumsy railings round the central block.

In the dusky light of the entrance a couple of small girls are trying to climb up the front, giggling, sprinkling each other with holy water. I can hear Nicolette's sharp intake of breath at this playful blasphemy. Before I can do anything to stop her, she goes to the font and furiously starts slapping the two children. One of them, frightened out of her wits, escapes through the door; the other lets out a loud wail. Nicolette glances round furtively. Then her right hand makes a quick movement, touches the surface of the water, and she hastily crosses herself.

With a slight gesture of her head she beckons me into the dark interior. Her small hands, holding the much-fingered old Missal, are clasped serenely at her breast. I follow her, past chapels with dull mirrors of light on old paintings brown with smoke, round the back of the choir with its fine railing and woodcarving, and back along the opposite wall.

"We must find good places before there are too many people," she whispers.

I nod. But she does not want to sit: she finds a place next to one of the massive columns, where she can lean on the balustrade.

"We can't go in," she explains. "That is reserved for those who are baptised and have received Communion."

"But who would know?"

"You and I."

The organ is vibrating in the high vaults. Her body becomes tense beside mine but she has already forgotten me. It is the introduction to the Mass. And suddenly I feel myself no longer a spectator and a stranger: I want to try, sincerely try, to reach that elusive ecstasy with her.

I never had any dramatic "break" with the church. In my childhood I regularly attended the Sunday services because that was the done thing: without deep conviction, it is true, but also without doubt. Then came Gillian who tore up the Bible and made fun of it as she made fun of all my other conventional beliefs. During my eighteen months in Europe I was never inside a church: once again it was no matter of conviction, and it certainly was no form of rebellion – it was merely unnecessary. It was as natural, then, that I should discard the habit as it was that I should resume it after my marriage. Perhaps it was simply the linear, hygienic nature of Calvinism which never appealed to me: stark, unimaginative, sober, with the miracle of bread and wine reduced to a formula which had long ago lost even its symbolic power.

192

In South Africa going to church was part of the accepted way of life; in Europe it was not. And so, ever since our first transfer abroad the custom was dropped. We merely conformed. It sometimes happens, of course, that I have to attend a service in an official capacity; and then I go without any grudging. It is part of my duties. Or: *was* –

The celebrant, wearing his ceremonial dress, is sprinkling the congregation with holy water. With that the whole intricate pattern of the Mass begins, at first carefully, almost with hesitation – *In nomine Patris, et Filii, et Spiritis Sancti* – and once again I become aware of her reaction: no discernible movement, barely a gesture, but, rather, a slight quivering, as if she is trying to reach out of herself, beyond the balustrade separating us from the faithful, beyond all barriers, to a wider expanse, a purer form of existence, a salvation; and I can feel my own urge growing with hers, because, in this present chaos, it would give meaning to so many things if I could once more reach a state of certainty in which I could know, and say, without faltering: *here; and now; and this* –

The altar is incensed, and then the bishop. It is the transition to prayer, the existence between heaven and earth, the eternal yearning.

The slow movement of a little while ago is becoming more urgent and more mysterious.

Kyrie eleison.
Christe eleison.
Kyrie eleison.

The bishop spreads his hands across the altar, brings them together again; and then the walls start trembling: *Gloria in excelsis Deo* –

Only her wrist makes a little movement to turn over a page of her Missal.

In the large liturgical movement of prayer, reading, and song, in the reaction of the congregation – standing up, crossing themselves, sitting down again – I try to determine: is *this* what she has come for, to form part of this rhythm and certainty, this unchanging pattern – the very things Gillian wanted to escape from?

Credo in unum Deum – Everything lucid, fixed in the unequivocal words of the Latin text. Why could not all our words and experiences be so charged with essence – ! Where did the watering down begin of everything which has once been indispensable?

Da nobis per huius aquae et vini mysterium – Once, in another

193

existence, she said these words sitting next to me in an official motor-car. I thought, then, that she pronounced them without any seriousness; it will never be possible to make that mistake again.

At the beginning of the Sanctus she closes her eyes. I want to touch her in my desperate desire to accompany her into that unfamiliar realm she has seemed to reach. But it is no longer possible. Somewhere I have lost my way. I can hear the hosannah in my ears, but it is nothing but sound, sensory perception, superficial melodic joy. And so, when the bishop commences the same little ceremony she has performed before me in her little light room, last night, I am a mere spectator.

Hoc ist enim corpus meum.

It is very silent now. Every word and gesture is pure symbol.

Is this the only way in which we can really exist – through an endless series of symbols? For every thing is unique; the smallest event can never be repeated; even last night's emotion is absent today with the repetition of the same ceremony. And because it is utterly impossible for two experiences to be wholly similar the only solution is a never-ending search for common denominators, symbols which would render the chaos intelligible, livable. We cannot go on without them. Yet this very habit keeps us away from essentials, from truth, from the heart of things!

Pater noster qui est in caelis –

I am forced to listen, trying, in my own language, to find the miracle which would change the wine of every separate word into blood, a minute Mass on its own.

Et ne nos inducas in tentationem. Sed libera nos a malo.

It comes so unobtrusively, a liturgical necessity; yet the moment the phrase is pronounced by the congregation, and by Nicolette beside me, it becomes a key to many things. *Sed libera nos a malo.* Deliver us from Evil. It is not for the Mass that she has come here today, not for the bread and the wine and the burning of incense: the true reason is this phrase. This is why she is satisfied to stand outside the railing, listening to the words alone. *Libera nos* – God, as God, is hardly important. Surely Nicolette desires no eternal life. She merely wants to escape from the fear that liberty could also be evil; and that she might destroy herself if she remained in it. And so she takes refuge here, in this beautiful pattern which would, as surely, destroy her if she got caught in it.

And I? Is this the reason why I am here? *Libera nos* – But I have already broken out of one pattern; I have already chosen the unknown we term evil because we dare not explore it: how could I, then, desire to be freed from freedom? What could that offer me? "Salvation". The beauty of the ritual. Faith manifested in the Church: the enormous organisation, the infallible remedy for all troubles, the answer to all questions (*Come to Me – !*) But, surely, that would bring me back to Genesis: the choice between happiness without knowledge, and agony with knowledge. Is not the foundation of all religion the maintenance of the illusion that the Paradise still exists? Its image remains alive in us because we could not otherwise bear to wander eternally in Nod. We know the angel with the sword is guarding the entrance to the Garden, so we plant our own little garden and try to convince ourselves that this is Eden.

Ite, missa est.

22

It was the last time, although I was not yet aware of it, that all the inhabitants of my pretty, ordered world came together.

The delightful ritual of courtesy. Erika and I standing at the front entrance (Annette refused to appear in public), she elegantly dressed in one of her Italian outfits, every little wrinkle removed by hours of conscientious preparation. Third secretary Harrington, a Don Juan with a small black moustache, accompanied by his attractive wife with her bleached hair. Koos Joubert, formidable and smiling, a few yards ahead of his wife who is dressed in the clothes she wears to all formal occasions. Stephen Keyter, thin and polite, and Victor le Roux with his unkempt forelock. Douglas Masters, clean shaven, combed, brushed, oiled, with a little bow to Erika and several convincing excuses for the absence of his wife. Anna Smith, draped in purple silk, with green beads, a strong aroma of Chanel and a hat trembling with multicoloured flowers. Colonel Kotzé, the Military Attaché, short and erect beside his plump, motherly wife. Herman Verster, the Commercial Attaché, with his large, soft goat's eyes behind thick lenses, accompanied by his bony, angular wife. Some acquaintances from other Embassies. A few people Erika had met at esoteric social functions.

Then drinks, and the first conversations which gradually began to flow more smoothly as the customary groups drifted together out of the conglomerate mass. White, unobtrusive waiters moving about with trays. Laughing. Talking.

"You should have seen it. It was absolutely – "
"Hutchinson has been transferred to Copenhagen from – "
"The bowling at Lords – "
"Now surely – "

O

"It has not yet reached the Committee stage – "

"I can't see how Britain could possibly – "

"Do tell us all about Italy – "

Almost without any specific signal, as if everything had been planned in advance, the movement was directed towards the dining-hall. Anna Smith landed within earshot and, leaning forward, started off on a detailed description of how she made her own hat. On my left a Canadian woman repeatedly told me, each time in different words, how delighted she was that her husband had just been transferred to sunny South Africa. On my right French policy in Europe was criticised. Then someone complimented Erika on the main dish; in well-chosen words this was duly re-affirmed by all the other guests.

Each with his predestined part in the hierarchy. Each with his well-proven set of opinions and convictions, reiterated at every opportunity: like information punched on a card, so that each time the correct key is applied the same original formula is conjured back.

I did not know whether anyone really believed in it any longer, but nobody would, even for a moment, consider any alternative, because this existence was so well-proven, so harmonic, so successful. Life had become a Mass without transsubstantiation; yet we went on drinking the wine, eating the bread, making the required gestures – else we would go mad. And so: come fill the cup. To-morrow, thank God, we die. *Et après nous –*

After the long meal the movement flowed back to the reception hall. The ladies sat down in a corner, on chairs and settees; the men formed little standing groups. I had a conversation with Kotzé. Then with a British diplomat. After a while I took my empty coffee cup back to the special table which had been placed near the archway to the dining-hall.

Behind the archway there was a small group of men. And I heard Koos Joubert's annoyed remark: "But what the hell, let the man have his fling if he wants to! Why not? That's what women are there for – "

They did not notice me. I carefully placed the empty cup with the rest, and turned round, and went back to the nearest group.

"I've always maintained that the French – "

"But you have to consider – "

In the background: "What a pity all the good old Afrikaner traditions are disappearing – "

"I still prefer living in Paris to – "

"Such an up-and-coming young man – "

It needed an effort to continue; the light amusement with which, earlier in the evening, I had played the game with them – and I mean *played* – was no longer adequate. But it was going on and on:

"But don't you think – "

"Surely it's preposterous that – "

At half-past ten the first guests left.

"Are you sure you wouldn't like to stay?"

"It was absolutely – "

As we were coming back from the front door Stephen appeared in the doorway of the reception hall. In spite of Erika's polite arguments he insisted that it was time to leave. They exchanged compliments. Then I accompanied him to the front door.

Suddenly, without premeditation, there was an opportunity to escape.

"Are you in a hurry?" I asked.

He seemed surprised. "Not particularly – "

"It's so stuffy inside. A bit of fresh air would be welcome. Could I go with you for a little way?"

"Of course," he said. "I came by metro anyway."

Lebon opened the main entrance and saluted. One side of his collar was turned up.

Silently we walked along the deserted sidewalk. Perhaps he was waiting for me to speak. Perhaps it had been naïve of me to come along. But the heart pays no attention to propriety.

"It has been – a pleasant evening," he said after a while.

"You need not be polite, Stephen."

He made no answer.

"The cat is out of the bag," I said at last, purposely, when we reached the rue de Tilsitt and had to wait for a stream of traffic.

He looked at me quickly.

"I heard Joubert talk about the report," I explained.

"I didn't say anything!"

"I never thought it was you, Stephen."

For a while he was silent, probably trying to judge my expression. Then he said: "I heard a rumour that Sylvia Masters blurted out something."

That would explain her absence. I could imagine her affected voice: "You'll have to tell them I couldn't come. I just can't face it. To think that all this time – "

"It must have been an ordeal for you."

"It was merely a bit unexpected. I'll have to get used to it."

At the metro entrance he stopped: "Wouldn't you like a liqueur in my apartment?"

"Thank you."

We spoke very little on our way to Les Sablons. There we went up to his apartment and in silence we sipped from the little glasses.

"It's a very pleasant room. You have good taste."

"It's not homely enough."

"One needs people for that. Not that it always helps, of course."

He merely nodded. After a while, looking intently at his glass, he said: "Nicolette stayed here once while I was away on holiday. You should have seen the place then."

I smiled. "I can imagine it."

"Sometimes she came here to have a bath, during office hours. And one night – " He took another sip, leaving the sentence unfinished. A minute later he said: "She came back one evening just before Christmas."

I looked up, holding the glass very tightly, waiting.

"She made as if nothing had ever happened. I was not very companionable, I'm afraid. If only she would say something, make the slightest gesture, to prove that she felt sorry, or guilty. But she had come merely to tease me. She always wanted to see how far she could go with me – and then she would merely laugh. She told me very spitefully, that night, that she was having an affair with you – " He looked down at his restless hands, "I told her I didn't care a damn with whom she flirted or what she did. To crown everything, she showed me a tie she had bought you and asked me whether I thought you would like it. I opened the door and told her to go. And she went."

"I see." I accepted it as if I had known it for a long time.

Like the previous time it was she who caused our conversation to flow more easily. Not that we talked much, but it was unhurried and not strained. And at last he went downstairs with me.

"It is beautiful outside," he said.

"It's a night for walking."

It was slightly cool, with a breath of wind, and the suggestion of a crescent moon delicate behind flimsy clouds.

As if it had been agreed between us we started walking, away from the metro, without any definite direction, along the dark lanes of the Bois de Boulogne. Now and then one of us spoke. But most of the time we walked along in silence, leisurely, each wrapped in his own thoughts, yet gratefully conscious of the other. Fifteen minutes, half an hour, an hour. Later time no

198

longer mattered. And when we returned at last the metro was closed and I had to take a taxi.

"Good-night, Mr. Ambassador."

"Good-night, Stephen. Thank you."

It had all been so completely natural. And why not? For in the new emptiness in which I was finding myself, he had become, without either of us anticipating it, the only person with whom I could talk.

And I sat gratefully thinking of him in the taxi on my way home, back to Erika's cool displeasure about my "neglect of duty" and the "affront" to my guests.

23

In spite of the mystic spell in which the Church holds her I often notice, whenever we pass a priest or a nun in the street, that her right hand forms the sign of the horns against the Evil Eye.

24

We came down the mountain together, late in the summer afternoon, hand in hand, with an empty rucksack on my shoulders, Gillian moving beside me with nimble feet, untouchable in her happiness, with sun on her hair and in her eyes, and a rare serenity on her face. There was nothing, during that whole long day, against which she had to rebel. Early in the morning we had climbed to the top along an easy route, made fire among the speckled rocks, lay on our backs high above the sea under the scattered clouds, desiring nothing more.

"Everything is so confused so often," she said as we came down. "Tomorrow, perhaps, it will be so again. But when all is quiet, like today, I know I love you. And I do not want it to be different again."

It is not often that one makes important discoveries so suddenly that they need not mature inside one but simply *are* there, complete and whole and undeniable. That was what happened that afternoon, when she said those words. I saw the wind playing with her dark hair, and the casual way in which she would, occasionally, sweep back the loose strands. And I knew that that happiness was too impossible, it could never last – and that it *would* last was the very thing she expected of me. She *demanded* it. And if I did not succeed not only I, but everything would be destroyed for her. She had fastened herself to me like a sucking shell, in the desperate faith that I would help her. But I could not. My heart was too accustomed to small, ordinary things, I relied too much on habit.

And when I left her that evening, I started calculating with almost uncanny calmness, how much money I had saved for my wedding with Erika; I made an inventory of all my possessions; the next day I sold everything I would no longer need, booked my passage on a boat, and a week later I left. I was not trying to escape. It was the only thing I could do if I wanted to give her this last opportunity, however improbable, of finding something, somewhere, which could save us both from the precipice. I did not know whether she would find it. But there was a chance, and that was all that mattered. And I had to withdraw from everything she had broken down around me, and try to find something which would still have relevance and meaning.

25

It is not only for the sake of completeness that I must also relate this, but because it is, indeed, indispensable. What was strange was not that it happened, for I had been prepared for it, but that it took such a long time to happen.

Anna Smith came sobbing into my office that morning: "I don't know *what* to do," she said. "I refused to believe it. I would have believed it of anybody else but not of you. And to think how I trusted you with all my personal problems, all my secrets – !"

It was rather difficult to tell what that had to do with the whole matter, but it would be useless to interrupt. She insisted on knowing what my plans for the future were, whether I intended going on with my work as if nothing had happened.

"I don't think there is any alternative, is there?" I asked.

"Then I'll have to resign," she sobbed. "You must realise that I cannot go on like this. I have to consider my reputation. What will my people say if they knew that I've been working in the same office with you all the time?"

Comical, grotesque – undoubtedly. But at the same time I realised that these judgments and condemnations of others would, in the future, be a constant threat to the significance of my relationship with Nicolette.

With the exception of Masters, who came to give me his formal assurance that after serious consideration he felt convinced that our personal relations could continue unaffected by his unqualified resentment of the professional immorality of my conduct, none of the others discussed the situation with me personally. But I knew that for a long time it would be the main subject of all their conversations. And I could easily imagine their respective reactions:

Harrington: "It's normal, isn't it? Most men of his age get an itch. It's nothing but hormones – "

Colonel Kotzé: "Shocking. A man in his position should have enough self-restraint – "

The typists, giggling: "It's naughty but it's nice – "

Once I happened to overhear Victor le Roux warning: "I do not think we should be so ready to judge – " But when, shortly afterwards, we reached the main entrance together, he merely said good-bye, like any of the others, and went his way. Not, I presume, because he felt resentful or embarrassed, but simply because there was no earthly reason why he *should* do anything else. We had nothing in common.

26

Oh you girls of Paris – !

With your high hair and slim brown legs and your spring buds of breasts, black eyelashes, sappho lips, with string bags in your hands or books under you arms:

joking gaily and self-consciously with the gendarme at the Luxembourg gates in the dusk when the park must be closed –

leaning, crushed and swaying in the metro, against pale young men with fanatic eyes and eager hands, ignoring the crippled old women stumbling to their seats –

walking across the bridges of the Seine where once there were markets and fairs, with acrobats and fortune-tellers, swinging your narrow hips and sometimes, in despair, flinging yourselves into the dark green water under the high cathedral –

playing the old love-game against the fences of parks, metro rails, shop counters, old doors, or dirty walls, with more or less abandon, more or less sincerity, more or less joy – and every one, every one of you, carries, like her, between your smooth thighs the *gouffre* of Baudelaire!

27

I realised all the time how much was demanded of Erika to continue with everything as if nothing had changed, but I knew, after so many years, her formidable willpower and I expected her to keep up appearances until the very last. If ever she referred to the subject again, I thought, it would be in the same sarcastic, condescending terms as before.

Therefore it came as a surprise when, one afternoon while we two were alone at table (Annette was somewhere in the city attending an art lecture), she asked: "How long do you intend going on like this, Paul?"

I looked up. Her eyes were calmly watching mine. "I thought we had settled the matter," I said. "We need not interfere with each other's lives."

"Surely you must have realised it wouldn't work out that way."

"It was you who suggested it."

"There's no sense in blaming each other, Paul. Besides, the matter is no longer as simple as it was a week ago."

"It is exactly the same."

She shook her head. "No. It is no longer a private affair. It is not even confined to the Embassy any more. I had tea with the wife of the Dutch Ambassador this morning. There were quite a few people. Nothing was said directly, of course, but enough was implied to make me realise that it has become one of the sauciest little bits of gossip in 'official circles' at the moment."

"Sooner or later it had to become known, I suppose." I spoke as neutrally as possible.

"But don't you understand, Paul? It is no longer a matter of you and me. What about your position? There are responsibilities you dare not ignore. You are bound by certain obligations."

"Don't you think I have considered everything a long time ago? It's not easy, Erika. But I was not caught unawares."

"And what about *us*?"

"Us?" I had no idea what she meant.

"You and I. I am no longer sentimental or idealistic, Paul. When I came back from Italy I did not think we would be able to start all over again. But at least I was prepared to *accept* certain things. And now – "

"We have been married for almost thirty years. Where did it bring us? Have we ever shared one single thing? Still, we tried. You cannot deny it."

"But what do you want to *do* then?" She made no effort to maintain her composure.

"Exactly what I am doing now. It will not last very long. What is going to happen afterwards, I don't know. I am trying not to think about it. Even at this moment I have very little, almost

202

nothing. But it's something. And it is more than I have had for all these years."

"Yet it was you who came back that time and insisted that we get married, even though I was uncertain."

"I did what I considered the 'right' thing. That is what I have always done. Now I know better and I am not trying to deny my guilt. But how could it possibly improve matters if I discarded the only valuable thing I have left and tried to convince myself of a new lie – knowing that it is a lie?"

"In other words I do not count any more."

"There is nothing I would like more than to see you happy, Erika. But that could never happen by playing blind man's buff together. It will be unbearable – for both of us."

She got up. "It is beyond repair, then?"

I nodded and did not answer. If only I could put out my arms to her to help her, but it was no longer possible. The years behind us had been too sterile. Both of us had contributed to it. I knew only too well how guilty *I* was. But was it not she who had written, in her last letter from Italy, if I remembered correctly: "It is not enough to forgive oneself, just as it is not enough to blame oneself – ?"

If only she could learn to accept it, with me. But there was something new in her, a hopelessness, a lostness I had never known, a desperation of which I would never have thought her capable. And it led up to the evening I would have liked so sincerely to forget, however necessary it was for everything which still had to happen.

When I came into my bedroom from the office to change for the evening, she was sitting on my bed in her dressing-gown. Her hair was tousled, presumably from her bath.

Surprised I stopped on the threshold.

"Erika! What are you doing here?"

"Is it so unusual to see your wife in your bedroom?" She laughed shrilly.

That, and her way of speaking, warned me: she had had too much to drink. It was the first time since her return from Italy.

"Are you feeling ill?" I asked with clinical objectivity.

"No, I'm fine. That's why I'm here." She clumsily tugged at the loose lapels of her gown. "Or don't you want me here?"

It was like a slap in the face. But I controlled myself, not wanting to lose my temper while she was in that state. Nevertheless, I spoke hurriedly, almost harshly, when I answered: "This is no time for pretence, Erika. What are you trying to do? You

203

have never given yourself to me willingly. Not even the first time!"

She got up, reeling slightly; but her voice was sober: "How could I? You never freed me so that I could give myself. And I wanted to. I *wanted* to. That first night I lay praying, pleading all the time: 'Dear God, please let him succeed. Please let us succeed. Please let something *happen* between us!' But it didn't." Her words were becoming confused and jumbled. At last she fell on her knees, almost sobbing: "But it is not too late yet. We can still try. We cannot let everything slip away from us!" Exhausted, she lay forward, resting her head and arms against the bed.

"Please stop it, Erika! We have already discussed everything. You're drunk."

"Drunk?" Another laugh, her head falling backwards. "Now I am drunk. But I *want* you! You are not going away tonight. You're going to stay here, with me, because I want you!"

I clenched my jaws, took her under the arms and picked her up. "You must go to bed, Erika. Come, I'll help you."

She tried to slap me, but stumbled. If I hadn't caught her, she would have fallen.

"Leave me alone!" For a few minutes she remained standing, swaying on her feet. And all the time she kept on mumbling: "You are staying here tonight. You are staying with me – "

I turned round to go out.

"You don't even know about the doctor!" she cried suddenly, almost triumphantly.

"What about the doctor?" I no longer knew what to expect.

"I am going to have an operation. He told me even before I went to Italy. And after the operation it will be too late. You'd better stay here *tonight* – !" And she flung open her gown and remained standing, trembling and white.

I felt sick. If it was inevitable for all this to happen, why couldn't one be left with a little dignity? Was *this* necessary?

She was reeling dangerously. I caught her as she fell and took her to her own room. Then I telephoned the doctor. Before he arrived Annette turned up from the city's secret heart. She did not greet me.

"Please go up to Erika," I said without moving.

She went upstairs. A minute later she called from the landing: "What has happened? What have you done to her?"

"Stay with her." I ignored her questions. "The doctor is coming."

If only I could say: 'It is not my fault.' But she would not have believed me. Perhaps I could no longer believe it myself.

The doctor arrived and gave her an injection. Over-excitement; nothing to feel worried about, he said. It was symptomatic of her condition. He would advise us not to postpone the operation for much longer.

"I never knew about it before tonight," I was forced to admit. "Is it anything serious?"

"It could become serious. It is, of course, a very common complaint at her age."

After he had left, I went up to her room. She was sleeping. Annette was sitting at her bedside but she did not look up.

I went out. I could not go to Nicolette in that state of mind. I did not even want to talk to Stephen. So I had dinner in a restaurant and went to my office to work until past midnight, as often in the past.

The next day she seemed to be quite normal again, although she was still tired.

Just after lunch, Annette having gone up to her room, she said in her old, calm way: "I am sorry about last night's scene – "

"You were not normal. Please forget about it."

"Sometimes one is normal when it looks least like it. But it was rather disgraceful. It will not happen again."

"Of course."

"I mean: I am going away."

I searched her eyes.

"To South Africa. I should have gone there in the first place, instead of to Italy. It's the best thing I could do."

"But there is nobody in South Africa you could go to."

"I know. That is why I am going. I am not trying to escape. On the contrary, I am trying to act in a responsible way – as you would prefer."

"But is it necessary?"

"Don't you think it is?" Her eyes had a very wise expression. And I had to admit that it would, indeed, be the best solution – for the moment. I would have preferred it not to happen at that stage, but her considerations were more important than mine. And why should I try to save the face of our marriage if neither us nor anybody else still believe in it?

Less than a week later I took her and Annette back to Orly in the official car. Because I had previously arranged everything through the Embassy there was no delay at the customs. In a formal little luxury lounge we sat together for the last few minutes.

205

We talked about the magnificent airport building. The infallible flight schedule. The friends she would meet in London before proceeding to South Africa in three days' time. Annette did not take part in the conversation.

Then their flight was announced by the loudspeaker. I accompanied them to the last glass door.

"Good-bye, Erika."

I kissed her.

At the very last moment her fingers bit deep into my arm. "My God, Paul – !" she whispered.

"As soon as everything is settled, I'll probably return myself," I said, simply because something had to be said. "Then we'll see each other again. Perhaps it will be very soon, a few weeks from now."

"Do you really think it could be as simple as that, Paul?"

"We'll see. In the meantime – good luck."

She nodded and started walking towards the illuminated corridor which led to the tarmac.

"Annette – ?"

My daughter was standing before me, looking at me; but without kissing me, she went away. She was crying.

I turned back. I did not want to go up to the top. Somewhere outside, very far from the colossal building, I finally came to a standstill, and leaned over a balustrade. Before me was the vast, dark expanse of the airfield. It had started to rain. But I remained standing, watching how the gangway to the plane was driven away. Listening to the deafening scream of the engines. Seeing the monotonous blinking of the wing lights while the tyres were screeching on the wet concrete as they moved away in the dark. After a few minutes they disappeared behind other planes. Still I did not move. The rain was pouring down. At last, in the distance, I heard the increasing roar of the engines. And very far away a tiny red light started moving horizontally past me, then described a graph into the air. It was not visible for very long. It was raining too hard. Cold and drenched I returned to the waiting car.

The weather was changing, I thought. Nicolette had been right: the early Spring of February was unreliable. The cold was setting in again.

NICOLETTE

One cannot bath in a basin. I had to learn to get used to it, for there was nothing else I could do. I bought my little white basin in the Monoprix the first week I was here and took it with me wherever I went. It is getting rather old and worn now. It was much too expensive, really, but I didn't know any better then and I still had some money, because it was before I had to sell my coat. It's not *bathing* at all. It merely keeps one's feet warm. And the old crippled man is always looking through my vasistas from his balcony across the street and there's nowhere else for me to stand. Perhaps he has no other place to stand either and it doesn't really matter, for in my turn I look at the people of the window opposite, and they look at the old Hungarian couple who are always sunbathing on their little balcony on the third floor of my building, and I suppose they have someone else *they* could look at, and so we zigzag across the street until we reach the ground. I wonder whether he ever goes down the street with his crippled leg. He's always on his balcony when I look out. Perhaps he has disappeared by now. I must go back and have a look. Usually I do not stay away from my room for so long, unless I leave Paris, of course. But I seldom do that nowadays. I used to do it very often. I've been here for days, it must be four or five already. And here I'm lying covered by warm water in the large white bath with the steam against the roof and walls trickling down the tiles in shiny tears. I've been lying here for more than an hour already. It doesn't matter, of course, I can lie as long as I like, for here's nobody to bother me. The one servant who tried to be cheeky left yesterday. I'm glad. I don't know why there should be so many of them in an Embassy. I love the green bath salts although I think I used a bit too much today. His wife must have left it behind. Or his daughter. I keep forgetting that he has a daughter as well. She wasn't here when I brought the flowers. Only she. She was very friendly, except her eyes, and she invited me for a cup of tea. She wanted to know all about me. I can't remember what I told her. Not that it matters. Why do people always want to know? Stephen too. I used to have my baths in his apartment, in the morning when he was away. And one evening.

I like it most with my head resting against the edge and my feet on either side of the shining taps. He never told me whether he liked my legs. I wish they were a bit thicker. But fortunately my feet are not bony. It's a funny thing, a body. And this one little curl here. Marc-Louis never tires of playing with it even when he's half asleep. Nicolette-à-la-houppe he calls me. And *minette* is what he calls that. *Faire minette.* He can go on all night. Not the Ambassador. He gets tired more quickly, or else he thinks he ought to stop. I wonder whether he is shocked by the games I make him play. He is so serious. But I know he thinks I'm merely a sort of little circus animal doing tricks. A funny child. Someone who amuses him. And one of these days he will get tired of me and drop me, I'm too unimportant for someone like him. He sometimes talks about trouble coming, but it's only to make me get used to the idea so that it won't hurt so much when it happens. Why should he really care about me? My hair is getting wet, lying like this, but it's all right. Mother always scolded me. Daddy didn't mind. He always washed my feet for me. He had to, else I kicked up a row. The Ambassador comes to sit on the edge of the bath sometimes, especially when I'm having a shower. I love it even more than bathing, with the tiny drops stinging one's shoulders while one stands without moving, your hair getting soaked, until it feels as if you are all water yourself. One should have an apple to eat under the shower. Yesterday there were no apples so I tried to smoke a cigarette but it soon became soggy between my fingers. I used to have apples in the garage too, those days. The dusky garage always smelling of fresh straw, and somewhat musty, and of tar or oil or something. And the whispering voices of the boys. I was the only one who laughed, softly, munching my apple. Stupid, lying like that with one's dress pulled up so that they could look. But I never did it for free. They did all my homework for me, and brought me apples, and sweets, and pocket-money of course, anything I asked for. Pigeons too, commons and pedigree homers, they made me a big cage for them. But I never liked pigeons in a cage and so they flew away in the end. It feels like two small doves breathing in his hands, the Ambassador says. He likes them like this. I think they're a bit too small. I can remember how I once stuffed cottonwool in there and how shy and proud it made me feel. He's got beautiful hands, the Ambassador, perhaps a bit too broad, but they're kind and soft. Daddy's were thinner and not so strong. We always went for a walk at night and on the first corner there was the honeysuckle growing wild in the hedge of the vacant lot. I can remember the smell of those evenings. And when it rained on the hot tar. Sometimes he put a few of the flowers in my hair. And mother was angry if we stayed away too long. It always happened. She scolding us, or him alone. Until he couldn't bear it any longer and went away. I wonder whether she likes lying in the bath for so long too. I don't think so. She doesn't look like it. I like pretending that it's really my house now, and that I'm living here now that she has gone away. That's why Francine left, said I ordered her around too much. I ask you. All these rooms and the carpets and the tapestries on the walls. It's like a museum. But I suppose they have to make do with what they get. Stephen's is pleasant and homely, I wonder whether he planned it all by himself.

This bathroom is as big as my whole bedroom. I must go back there. I want to see what is happening to the people opposite. It can't be long now, a couple of weeks, or even less. I never knew one could get as swollen as all that. I once saw a cow that got bloated, it must have been when I was out with my father somewhere. They had to cut a hole into her belly, just like that, with a knife. Green lucerne or something. But it was no use, she died anyway. They're not doing it so regularly these days. She's crying often. And I hate tears. I'd rather jump into the Seine than let that happen to me. I wonder what it would feel like? The water is so green and deep. As long as one doesn't put up a struggle. You must abandon yourself to the stream so that it takes you away, and slowly turns you in a circle, until you remember less and less, and care less and less, and feel how death takes you, not in a hurry, but slowly, passing under all the bridges of the city, under the misty sky which grows darker and darker until you can see no more, hearing a singing in your ears, singing everywhere, dying, dying splendidly, just as you feel when there is someone inside you and the small feeling grows wider and wider, at first it is there only, deep inside you, with his voice in your ears, softly, and speaking words you cannot understand, with his hands round your shoulders or in your hair, until it spreads all through you, your belly and legs, your breasts, your arms, your fingers and toes, with a throbbing in your head, and your eyes pressed tightly closed, with your voice crying in your own ears, crying and pleading and sobbing and praying, not praying with words, but becoming prayer, being prayer, all of you, the you which is so much more than the ordinary you, until, beyond the last darkness you awaken in terrible light and slowly come back again, to darkness first, to dusk, to quiet light, and you open your eyes and you smile slightly, wearily, with your mouth still against his shoulder, but it is a smile which is neither joyful nor sad. I have died so many times. But every time it is only my own voice praying. Never a priest's. *Dies irae, dies illa.* I always go to burials whenever I can. Sometimes I go with the relatives in the black bus of the municipality. They all think I am one of them. Or else I wander through *Père Lachaise*, especially in summer when one can escape from the sun under the heavy green trees among the tombs. Sometimes I take flowers with me. There are so many graves without flowers. But I do not want to *be* dead. Dying is different. You know you are going. But once you're dead you don't even know you're dead. You're just lying there under your stone. *Pie Jesu Domine, dona eis requiem.* It sounds like the fairytales he told me on our walks at night, with all the magic words and rhymes one could not understand although they made the stories more beautiful. It's strange to think of him and mother. But they must have done it, else I wouldn't have been here. And the Ambassador and his wife. But they had separate rooms later. One can understand that, for I don't think she really knows what it is like to *feel*. And I suppose when she looks at herself she will feel ashamed, thinking it must have been a mistake, the way one sometimes leaves a slit in a doll or a bunny where one has stuffed in the cottonwool. That's why he is really like a boy who doesn't exactly know what to do. And he says thank you each time. It's as if he's searching for something in me, but what have I got to give? Marc-Louis is different. He is almost violent when he wants me, and he hurts me if he wants to, and it's wonderful, it's what I *want*. He is so sure of everything that one could go to him to hide from the world, and from loneliness, and from cruelty, and from uncertainty. Yet, when I am with the Ambassador, and he is so gentle, he is like my father would have been, I think, then I want to be everything for him he wants me to be; and for me he is hands, and a voice, and sometimes a face. With Marc-Louis I go mad, everything starts tumbling around me, as if the building is falling in, and the earth, falling, falling through the night. He opens something inside me and lets me out, sure of myself, of everything, of all the world. And yet, with the Ambassador I really feel more. And when it is past and we are sleeping together, it is almost unbearable. I also feel free, but I'm alone in the night, with nothing I can recognise around me, and all I know is that we are there, together, alone, and that I need him more and more because I can no longer find my way in the dark. I must not allow him to use me like this, as a plaything. But in the beginning it was I who wanted to play with *him*. And now there's nothing else I could do. Would that be sinful? Why do I always know about sin when I'm with him? It is nothing I *am*, nothing I *do*. I don't know. Neither does he. On New Year's Eve he didn't know why I wanted to confess. He thought it was just another game. And what I really wanted to ask was simply: Dear God, forgive me for loving him, but it's like my father, and what we are doing is like the little flowers he used to put in my hair at the corner of the vacant lot in the evenings, and like the washing of my feet when I had my bath. Forgive me for *knowing* that he will leave me and for pretending not to care; forgive me for not knowing what I did wrong and for only knowing that he *thinks* I have done something wrong. It is not my fault; forgive me for that also. One becomes so confused when one is praying. Sometimes I do not pray, for then I am not dying while it is happening, as with Stephen. With him it was just like going to the dentist. Or like the last time in the garage when the neighbour's boy said the ugly word and I got up and dusted my dress behind and went away. I never did it for anyone of them again, not even when they put all their pocket-money together one week and brought it to me. For Stephen I was just a little adventure, a hill he could climb, a body. Not even a body, just an *organ*. He wasn't looking for anything with me, and so he found nothing, and then he thought it was my fault. If only he knew.

It's a pity they put the mirror on that wall. In a bathroom one needs a large mirror right opposite the bath, leaning over, so that one could see oneself. I could never understand why some people are so ashamed of themselves. Could it be true that the nuns in convent schools do not allow the children to bath without clothes? If I had to have a house built I would cover all the walls with mirrors, especially round the bed. Each time you move your head, you must see yourself a hundred or a thousand times, from all angles. When I was small I used to lock myself up in my room and lift the long mirror from the hooks of the dressing-table and look at myself for hours, wearing all sorts of clothes, or naked. I pulled faces, and I stood up, and sat down, and bent to the left and to the right, and looked over my shoulder, and stood on all fours, and sometimes I sat down on the mirror. The day after my eleventh birthday the mirror slipped from my hands just as I was putting it back on its hooks. I've never seen a thing break like that. Suddenly I was lying on the floor all round me: here a nose and two eyes, there a leg, there a hand, there a part of my body, there eyes, and there eyes, and there eyes, eyes everywhere. I tried to pick up the bits and cut my hand, and got scared and ran away. I didn't come back before it was dark. If it hadn't been for daddy I would have got a hiding. He took me in his arms and comforted me, and then I started crying for the first time. Not because of the mirror and the eyes, but about the seven terrible years ahead of me. And it worked out exactly like that. It was only a week or so later that he went away and never came back. Mother didn't want to keep me with her and sent me to boarding-school. I ran away. Then another school. Later she sold the house. We never lived in a place for more than a year, often for only six months. Usually in hotels. Our suitcases were always packed. We never settled anywhere. It went on like that until the day after my eighteenth birthday. Then I knew the spell was broken, the seven years had passed, and I could start doing what I wanted again. Mother was having an affair with someone, as usual. Charles or something, I can't remember his name. There were so many of them. But she wanted to marry this one and I would be in the way. So I went to him and borrowed money from him to come here. I never paid it back. I will, one day. The trouble is, I honestly never have enough. I don't know how it is. Sometimes I lose it. I suppose I'm giving too much to beggars. And every now and then I'm in hot water. The Ambassador can't understand it, he is so precise with everything. He gives me a lot, whenever I ask for it, just like daddy did; but it's no use. It lasts for a day or so and then I'm broke again. That's why I stripped in the club, but now he's forbidden me to do so. What difference could it make to him? It's only every second week and it seldom goes on later than two or three o'clock in the morning. I undress in front of him. Why not in front of others? I do not belong to him, I belong to nobody, I was made of nobody's rib. But men always want to *possess* one. As if they haven't got enough as it is. But I suppose that's the way it should be, and perhaps it's a good thing. For it turns one into a sacrifice each time, whether one wants to or not. And that is necessary. It's not superstition, it's the truth. When I was small there was a terrible storm one night. I was sure it was the end of the world. The next morning I decided to bring a sacrifice so that there wouldn't be another storm. I found a frog in the garden and put it on top of a lot of old papers on a pile of stones and cut off its head. It was terrible, terrible, the blood all over me and the frog kicking and wriggling in my hand. I don't think I've ever been so afraid in my life. By the time the frog was dead I was crying almost hysterically. But I knew I simply *had* to do it. I lit the papers and ran away and for weeks I never came near the place again. It was years before there was another storm like that. And once daddy got ill, quite seriously: at night I was lying in my bed listening to the footsteps in the house, and the doctor's voice, and there was light under my door. That was the first time I got scared of death. And again I knew that only a sacrifice would help. I couldn't face a live thing again, but I took my prettiest doll and chopped off her head and burnt her. It almost broke my heart. I got an awful hiding and I deserved it, of course. My mother would never have been able to understand that I didn't do it because I hated the doll but because I loved her. And daddy got well again. Later, with the boys, I sometimes asked them to tie my hands. Then I lay there with shivers running down my spine, just because I felt so deliciously helpless, being sacrificed. And that was the same feeling I had the first time it happened here, in Paris. I can't even remember the room or the man. I haven't the faintest idea in which part of the city it was. It was just somewhere. Somewhere with a weak, bare bulb. And I was helpless. And it hurt. But even that made me feel a bit glad, because I knew I was being sacrificed against my will – to something, I didn't know who, or what, or even why. I only knew it had to, sooner or later, and I was glad it could happen. And it has always been like that ever since, always. Sometimes it was nothing but a dreary little Cain offering, all smoke and no fire. But sometimes it was quiet and happy. I suppose Abel must have felt like that, with the wide blue sky and the smoke almost invisible, without a quiver, straight up to heaven, like a transparent little tree growing before one's eyes. Some sacrifices I brought willingly. Others were taken with force. But each time I felt relieved afterwards. Not that I can remember any particular occasions. Only one night. For that was the only man, I think, whom I have ever wholly loved: so much, that when he was inside me, I begged him to take my throat in his hands and to press more and more tightly, and to kill me. It was on the way to Chartres, in the early Spring, soon after I first arrived here, a sort of pilgrimage of thousands of young people from Paris. It took a few days to get there, I can't exactly remember how many. We were walking. It was a peculiar feeling: this one surging movement of a whole crowd of strangers, all around one, and I in the middle, going somewhere. We formed little groups and ate food from our rucksacks. At night we slept in the open, under the cloudless sky. It was chilly, but not cold. And I thought about the cathedral at the end of our pilgrimage. Nothing has ever meant so much to me as that unknown cathedral to which all of us were going. It seemed to me I was walking in a trance, alone among all the others. Some sang. There were a few with guitars. At night there was sweet and sad music in the distance. I knew nobody and I was glad I didn't, because now there was no one I had to talk to, unless I really felt like it. And I was free to say what I wanted, because they were strangers who wouldn't remember what I had said, and even if they remembered it would not matter. There were no ties. Nobody expected anything of one. It was just one streaming movement like a river in flood, further and further. And then, that night. It was late, past midnight I think, and it was very quiet, except for one little guitar very far away. There was a sliver of a moon and one could barely see one's own hand in the dark. I was awake, lying with my arms under my head, looking up. Vaguely I could make out his figure standing against the sky. Then he squatted down. I asked him why he was not asleep. He started when he heard my voice beside him. Why wasn't *I* asleep, he asked. We started talking, whispering so as not to disturb the others. About all sorts of things, our pilgrimage, and the cathedral which he knew well, and the weather, and the wonderful night. And then we talked about Easter and Holy Week, anything, everything. Except about ourselves. We did not matter. Later he lay down beside me and his voice became even softer and his hands moved to the buttons on my breast, leisurely, as if it was the most natural thing in the world. And then his voice stopped and only his hands went on whispering, and mine began to wander across him, shyly at first. His body was smooth and young. And he was so unhurried. There was no need to hurry, for I knew it had all been predestined, and the night was long and kind. I think I even fell asleep once, and started dreaming. But at last I could feel him on me, and inside me, and everywhere, and then, I think, there was nothing but the dream. When he got up at last I remained lying, unmoving, empty and filled, thinking over and over: *Hic est enim corpus meum.* His hand touched my cheek ever so softly. And then he was gone, disappeared into the night. And I began to recite the Pater noster but I fell asleep before I had finished. I do not think there was any other man I have ever known better, although I never even asked his name or saw his face. I loved him so much because these things were so utterly unnecessary. He wanted nothing. So I could give him everything, and he me. Why couldn't it always be like that? Why couldn't Stephen be like that? Why was he always in such a hurry? Why did he always want to *force* me? Didn't he know –

This is very special soap he gave me and it smells like expensive perfume. I think I shall remember the soap best of all when I am back in my room, or when he has become tired of me and left me. It's always like this. I can no longer remember the neighbour's boy, even though it was he who started the game. But I remember the smell of the garage. And I can smell it still, every time. And the apples, half sweet, half sour, in the dark. They say it was not an apple Eve gave Adam. I wonder what it really was, and why they lied to me. And the honeysuckle of the vacant lot. Daddy's face, too, has disappeared; and the little photo I had of him was forgotten in one of the pockets of the coat I had to sell. I could never find it again. It's strange that something which has been one's very own could disappear so completely. But I can still remember the vague, sad smell of his jackets. And his hands after one of our long walks. Like those of the man in the night, but it is really the grass I remember, and the damp ground. That, too, is slightly sad. The Ambassador's office clothes are dry-cleaned too often, they only smell of benzine. But in his wardrobe I found a few old jackets which I go to smell every day when he is away. Something of tobacco. Something of shaving cream. Something of perspiration. And something of himself. If he finds out about it, he will laugh again, and perhaps run his fingers through my hair as if I am a funny child. He never knows how worried I often feel about him when he is away, or how afraid I am that he may find something about me he doesn't like. I want him to like me. He must like everything about me. He mustn't think I am too thin or my legs are too long or my breasts are too small. He mustn't think I am bad or ungrateful. He must *understand*. He must believe everything I say, and trust me, and he must not laugh at me. I wasn't sure what would happen the night I rang the bell outside and told the concierge a lie and went up to his office. All the way from Neuilly I was merely thinking about how I could take revenge on Stephen, how I could hurt him, how I could land him in trouble. I was so *mad* at him. When I reached the Arc I suddenly remembered that the Embassy was very near there, and I thought about the Ambassador. I decided to come to him and to tell him all sorts of things about what Stephen had done to me. But when I reached his office door, the only one which had light underneath, I saw him sitting inside in the light, writing, the way daddy used to sit with his poems at night. I always sat curled up in the big armchair smelling of cats, watching him while he worked. So I thought I would only ask him to take me home. He looked tired. I think it gave him a fright to see me so unexpectedly. And I was afraid he would turn me out and let me go home alone. All the way in the Avenue de la Grande Armée I was not afraid at all. Why should I? I've been *everywhere* in Paris at night. But then, there, I was afraid of going further alone, in the rain and the dark. And I *was* tired. He frowned, and I thought he would scold me. I suddenly wondered what he would do if I started taking off my clothes. Perhaps I wouldn't have resented it if he took me there, in his office. Afterwards he could take me home, or give me some money for a taxi. But he didn't. He felt sorry for me. If he had taken me as I wanted him to, I would never have come back to bother him. But because he was good to me when it was not necessary for him to be good, there was nothing I could do except come back. And I had to do so every time, again and again, until he would start *liking* me, so that I could know that his goodness was not just charity. When we stopped at my building he wanted to come with me. I said no, although I was sure he wouldn't listen to me. No man would. But he did. I suppose he thought it would frighten me if he came along. And I stood in the rain with his jacket over my head, wanting to plead with him to come inside to my room and sleep with me. For then it would have been *done.* Then I would no longer owe him anything for his goodness. But he believed me again when I said no for the second time. I did not want him to be good to me. It binds one just as much as being bad. René was like that. It went on for months. He beat me and shouted at me and hurt me. He was often drunk and then he didn't care what he did to me. Many times he threw me out of his room after he had taken what he wanted of me. He didn't care whether it was cold or raining outside. Some nights I thought I would die of cold. But every time I went back to him to be shouted at and hurt. In the end he grew afraid that someone else might take me away from him and he started treating me better. Then I was free again and I left him. They've got no right to bind one like that. Every time I tried to provoke the Ambassador, to dare him to do something. I *wanted* him to take me. Yet, if he had taken me then, the first time he came to my room, I would have resented it. It's all so confused. He *had* to do it, but if he did, he would no longer have been good to me and then I could no longer stay with him; and if he did, he would have done so merely because I had provoked him, and then he would have thought, and known, that I was bad, and I could not bear that from him. Perhaps I would have jumped into the Seine then. For then I would have been free, but soiled. I do not want to be bound to him, yet I cannot bear being freed from him, unless he could let me go without losing his goodness, and surely that is impossible. Oh, I don't know. I really don't. And then, at last, he did come to my room and took me. He pulled the blanket from me and threw me on the bed. And *took* me. But that, too, he did because he was good, not because I had lured him into it. And with that he really tied me faster to him than ever before, because *that* had not been between us earlier, and two who once have lain together are forever almost one. That was the night Marc-Louis was with me. In the *cave*, first, and then in his room, and then he brought me home and it started all over again. He was tipsy. We woke up everybody with our singing, our voices echoing through the whole building as we climbed the stairs, and people shouting at us from their bedrooms. *Au clair de la lune.* We always sing it. But it is not "our" song. It is *mine.* It became mine on my very first day in Paris when I heard an old clochard sing it in the garden of Saint Julien le Pauvre. It was as if he himself was the poor old Lubin of the song, wandering through the streets in the dark, asking Pierrot to open his door and to bring some light and a pen for him to write with. What on earth would he want to write in the night? And Pierrot refuses to open, he is too snug in his bed. It's like the bridegroom shouting at the poor girls with the empty lamps to stay outside, they may not come in to the party. And so old Lubin goes to the girl next door. But all this wandering in the dark has made him crafty. He no longer says: Open, for the love of God. He says: Open, for the God of love. And together they start looking for a candle and a pen, and while they are searching, the door closes behind them and then it doesn't matter any longer whether they find something or not. It's different from my dream, for the dream never ends happily. It never ends. It's like after daddy had gone away and I started sleep-walking, in the house at first, but one night outside. When I came to my senses, I was in a strange street. It was pitch dark. I had no idea where I was and I started running without knowing where to go. I heard a clock strike twelve and got terribly scared, for that was the time the ghosts came out, gnashing their teeth and crying like wind or like owls. There was a park with a high hedge. The trees were swaying in the wind. Behind every tree something was hiding, waiting to jump on me as soon as I came past. I began to cry and I ran faster and I hurt my feet on the hard asphalt. I could not get away from the darkness. I couldn't go on any longer. And then a car stopped. It had to, for I was right in the middle of the street. I heard the screeching of the brakes and I thought: Now they've got me. And when I woke up again I was at home in a hot bath and then in bed. I must have given them my address. That was the only time my sleep-walking took me so far from home. But the dream remained, and it is still with me, except when he is sleeping with me. He also likes the song and sometimes he hums it with me. He doesn't know why I

219

sing it, of course, for him it's just a little song, and perhaps, if one thinks about it, *everything* is just a little song, with some sadness in it, and some joy, not that it really matters, but I suppose it's better if it could end happily. Stephen merely got annoyed when I sang it and one night he said: "I wish you would stop wailing this idiotic little tune!" I would have liked to explain to him, but Stephen is so impatient. He can't stand me. He can't stand any woman. Sometimes I wonder whether he isn't a queer. But I don't think so. I hope not.

It has started raining against the window. Now I'll have to lie a little longer, else it'll be cold getting out of the warm water. One feels so snug and quiet and protected here, one cannot even hear the street noises, it's like a womb. Yet I like rain, and walking in it. It's such a delicious feeling of sadness and aloneness, like my first days in Paris when I didn't know a soul and had nowhere to go. I can walk through the streets for days on end. I love the Champs-Élysées and the Opéra quarter and the fashion centre around the rue François I. Perhaps these are my favourite streets. Not quite, though. I think I really prefer the dirty little streets near Les Halles and the rue Saint-Denis and all those cul-de-sacs, especially at night when the lorries are unloading vegetables and things. Or the streets between the rue Monge and the rue Claude Bernard, of course. And the whole quarter around the Place des Vosges. Perhaps I like it because it makes me feel scared. Nobody pays attention to you when you're walking along those streets, but there are always invisible eyes peering at you through the holes of the doors and from the nooks of the old buildings. There are voices belonging to nobody. And stray cats. I hate cats. And the old buildings must be supported by scaffoldings else they'll fall in. Like some of the old clochards who cannot stand alone any more. They spend their days sitting under their bridges, their hands trembling. The D.T.s, I suppose, or old age, or illness. I wonder what happens to them when they die. I suppose they've got a special cemetery somewhere, like dogs. Or else they're cremated. I'd hate that, it's like hell. It would be much better to throw them into the river. After all, they spend all their lives on its banks. If I were a clochard I'd love to be carried away by the river when I'm dead. And if I knew they were going to burn me, I'd lie on the edge of the water and roll in just when I'm going to die, in the night, so that they won't find me. I told Stephen I'd love to be a clochard. But that was not quite true. For I am one already. I don't stink like them, and I'm not old or ugly, and I don't drink very much, and my clothes aren't so worn, but I don't think it depends on what one looks like to be a clochard. I don't think one could really *become* a clochard. One is born like that, the way some kittens are alley cats even when they're born in a beautiful house. It's like an illness inside one. Only, it's *not* an illness, because it's not bad, it's not something one hates. Or perhaps some people wouldn't like to be clochards? But does it matter whether one likes it or not? One hasn't got any choice. Stephen is a clochard. He doesn't know it, of course. He'll never know it, because he doesn't want to. He'd always struggle against it. But he is one, all the same. Therefore he and I should –

I was here in the bath that night, using his wife's green bath salts, or his daughter's, when he came back from Orly. It was later than I thought. I had begun to wonder whether he would come home, after all. Perhaps he'd gone to my room. But I *knew* he wouldn't. Perhaps I had done the wrong thing coming here, because I knew he would be feeling miserable. But he needed me. He never said so, but I had known it even before he took his wife to the airport. He was angry when he came in and found me here. He wanted me to get out of the bath and dry myself and get dressed and go away. He wanted to be alone. I laughed at him, although it ached. I knew it would make him even more mad at first, but I had to. Else he would never have been able to forget his wife. I'm not jealous of her. I don't think it has ever been necessary. But if I hadn't come here that night, he might have started longing for her, thinking all sorts of impossible thoughts. And I had to help him. Men are like that. He's even more clumsy than most. Sometimes I feel very much older than him. He thought it was one of my games when I asked him for an apple, and lay here in the bath eating it. I splashed about in the water, and soaped myself before him, and dared him to wash me, and whistled while I was drying myself, and asked him to make me warm because I had left my clothes in his room. He first picked up the towel I had dropped on the floor, and looked at the rim in the spotless bath: it must have been the first time this bathroom had ever looked so untidy. But then he had to pick me up, for my teeth were chattering, and he took me to his room. He left the light on for he wanted me to dress. Even at that moment he still wanted me to go. But I took off his jacket. And then he knew there was nothing else he could do if he wanted to get rid of his loneliness. And he took me, in his bed. After a while his body began to jerk. He was crying. And he stayed inside me. It was the most passionate of all his nights with me. And when we fell asleep at last, as it was getting light outside, it felt as if we were dead together, and we were happy together. And after we had slept for a while he moved and whispered against my cheek: "Stay with me, Nicolette." And I smiled and tried to answer, but I was too tired, and we slept on. He has forgotten all about it, I'm sure. Of course, he meant it when he said it. But when we were awakened by the sun, he was no longer my lover of the night, but the Ambassador, and I was his child, his pick-up child, his plaything child, his funny child, of whom he would soon tire. If only it would last until Easter. I don't know why I wish it so desperately. But I *do*. He must go to High Mass with me. It doesn't matter what happens afterwards. Why did He allow them to crucify Him? He should never have become a human being. It was unworthy of God to do that. It must not be necessary always to bring sacrifices. It makes one guilty. If only I *knew* whether the bread really changes into His body, and the wine into blood. It would make everything so much easier. It will make everything worth while. But now I don't know. And I'm afraid. I do not want to go to High Mass alone on Good Friday when all is black and the altar bare. I can't do it any more. Not another year. And yet I dare not stay away. He must come with me. We can stand beside the column again. It will be easier if he comes with me. Stephen never wanted to. He scoffed at me and said I was pretending to be a little nun. He thinks I'm a hypocrite. He never even wanted to come inside to look around. He doesn't believe in anything. But I don't think he really means it. I think he is afraid. He got angry when I said so. He cursed, and I had to cross my fingers. Why didn't he come with me? Perhaps he really wanted to, but was too shy. Perhaps he'll still come with me one day. If only he could learn to believe in *me* –

My hair is absolutely soaked, but I don't care. I love rubbing it dry, and there's a fire downstairs where I could go and sit. I felt shy when he came to me the night I was washing my hair. Not shy for myself, but for his eyes. But I didn't put on my clothes. I did it on purpose. I *wanted* to shock him, I *wanted* to hurt him, I *wanted* to provoke him, so that he could take me and become just as bad as he thought I was. And he tried to provoke *me*, by asking me about all the other men I knew. What does it matter to him? I *know* no other men. They're simply there, that's all. Sometimes they come to me, and it's good, and it's necessary, and it's wonderful, and then it's past. And all the time I wanted to beg him to stop, and perhaps he wanted to beg me to stop, but neither of us could. And then Stephen came to my door and he was furious with me. He thought it was Marc-Louis or someone, and he wanted to come in, but I wouldn't allow him to. I wanted him to *admit* that he was jealous, and to tell me *why* he was jealous. But he only warned me that I was playing with fire. Did he think he could scare me with that? He turned round and went away. I followed him to the railing. When he reached the landing just below mine, I called to him – softly, so that the Ambassador would not hear. But he pretended not to hear me, and went on. I almost ran down behind him, to ask him to wait for me. If he would give me two minutes to dress, I would go with him wherever he wanted, I would do whatever he wanted. I could no longer bear the conversation in my room. If it went on much longer, something would give way. Then the Ambassador would get angry and take me, as I dared him to do. And then I wouldn't have any feeling left for him. He was already losing all his respect for me. And I didn't *want* him to. Stephen had to take me away before that could happen. But he mustn't become over-anxious again. Or perhaps I wouldn't even have minded if he did that night. But he had already gone, and I had to go back. A few minutes later the Ambassador left anyway. For the last time, I thought. But it was Stephen who made me ache inside.

Oh dear, now I've splashed too much water on the floor and the lovely magazine I've been reading an hour ago is all wet. I still wanted to cut out my horoscope. Not that it's really necessary, I suppose, for I know it by heart already. But I keep it every month. *Unexpected change of residence.* Would that mean the couple of days I've been living here in the Embassy? But the horoscope month only begins today. So it must mean my going back to my room, for I'm leaving tonight. He wouldn't mind. Perhaps he'll feel relieved, for my presence may embarrass him, although I hardly poke my nose outside the door. *Excellent month for money matters.* I could always do with that. And then: *Your love problems solved at last.* That's the one which puzzles me. I haven't got any problems that must be "solved". Unless it means I'm going to give Marc-Louis the sack. I think I should. I like him very much. He's a wonderful lover, but I'm getting too used to him. And he is beginning to get used to *me*. That's the way it turns out time and again. There was Roger; I used to pose for him. At first it was a hell of a struggle to sell his photos, for he was unknown and had to compete against all the famous ones. I was inexperienced too. Then some big shot or other saw one of the studies Roger had meant for himself. A couple of them were published. The very next week he got a few important contracts. The wheels started rolling. And then I left. I didn't discuss it with him, for he wouldn't understand. But it was getting us both down. The work and the success and everything. We were no longer free. There was no uncertainty left, no adventure, no freedom. We no longer mattered to each other. O.K. So I quit. Same thing in the *Grande Chaumière*. I modelled for the art students. There were quite a few of us and it was a struggle to stay in demand. Then suddenly they wanted no one but me. At the same time they didn't really *care* about me, the inside me. I quit again. And Claus, the German student. He worked himself half to death, night after night. Studying, and writing too. I kept house for him. Copied his notes. Washed and mended his clothes. We lived very chastely together. I enjoyed it, as long as he needed me. But then he, too, started taking me for granted. So *voilà*, off I went again. Always, always. Everything comes to an end. Nothing *lasts*. I suppose one gets used to it and learns to accept it. If only, this time, it would last until Easter. It's not so long, only a few weeks. Yes, I think I'll talk it over with Marc-Louis. Stephen doesn't believe in the stars. I once read him his horoscope. *Gemini.* He said it was balls. We had quite a row about it. If only Stephen would listen. If only there was *something* he would believe in.

It's getting time to get out and dry myself with the large new white towel he gave me. Or with his. I think his. And then I'm going to dress. He had some clothes sent again this morning for me to choose from, I tried them on for hours. I don't know how I'll possibly manage to send anything back, but it will be greedy to take them all. I love clothes. I love wearing them and looking at them in the mirror and going out in them and feeling them against my skin. That especially. Every dress is like a lover folding you in his arms. But I also love being naked. It's all right to wear clothes for looking beautiful or for feeling warm, but it's not as *necessary* as being naked. That's the way one *is*. One has to breathe and feel and laugh with one's whole body. But it's impossible here in the city. I went to one of the nudist clubs once, but with them being naked is just like wearing different clothes. Everyone is too conscious of it, too proud of it. One should be naked *without* thinking about it You must simply *be* like that. Stephen tried to peep at me the night I was having a bath in his apartment. Why didn't he come in? I wanted him to come in. I wanted him to see me, to be glad about me. That's why I went there. And I specially put on my red panties, my tiny, ridiculous, beautiful red panties. I wanted him to see it, and to know what it meant. But he never even looked at it. He only wanted me, *wanted* me! The way one holds something in one's hand, a bird or something, when you're small, until it stops struggling and is dead and no longer beautiful. He didn't realise how unnecessary it was to bind me to him. He already *had* me. Not because he was good to me; not because he was bad to me. But because I loved him. I tried not to believe it, because it's too much to bear. One can't live with it. It's not *right* for people to love each other, for then they *need* each other, then they can no longer live without each other, and that kills one. And I don't want that. And I want that. For I love him. I want him. I want him to want me. Not to use me, but to know me the way I know him. And then he *may* use me. Then he must. Then he must do nothing but use me. Then I want to be a body to him, I, the whole I, his. I have so often tried to tell it to him, but he never understood, never wanted to understand. Before Christmas I went back to him to show him that I love him. And I took him an expensive Jacques Fath tie with a rough texture which would go well with his charcoal jacket. But when I showed it to him, he said: "I suppose that's for the Ambassador? Take away the bloody thing!" And so I said: "Of course it's for him." But I didn't mean to say it. I told him about the Ambassador, thinking he would be jealous and try to take me back. But he merely laughed at me and made me feel as if I had betrayed the Ambassador. Why must everything make me feel guilty? Why can't he understand? How could I go to him and tell him in plain words that I want him? For if I did that, it would be vulgar and no longer true. And it must be true. It is true. That is what the stars meant. It must be what they meant.

No. I am not going to dry myself with his towel, but with mine. My clean, clean, white one.

CODA

1

The first telegram, *en clair*, arrived on the morning of 3rd April while the Ambassador was busy copying Nicolette's laundry list from a crumpled bit of paper on a stiff white sheet with the Republican crest at the top.

After Harrington, who had brought him the telegram, had gone out again, the Ambassador sat looking at it for some time as if he tried to memorise the contents. Then he carefully put it aside, under a paper-weight in the form of a springbok head, completed the laundry list, underlined it neatly and added the date at the bottom. He folded the sheet and shoved it under a corner of his blotter to be handed, later in the day, to one of the servants at home who would take Nicolette's bag to the laundry which normally did the washing for the official residence. Then he checked his watch, picked up the telephone and asked the girl at the switchboard to ring Keyter.

"Mr. Ambassador?"

"Could you come up to my office for a moment, Stephen?"

"I'm coming straight away, Mr. Ambassador."

With his hands folded on his clean blotting paper, the Ambassador sat waiting without any sign of impatience until the young man knocked on the door.

"Come in."

Keyter stood in the doorway, waiting for the Ambassador to speak; but as nothing was said, he asked: "Was there something you wanted me to do, Mr. Ambassador?"

"No. No, nothing." He moved the telegram across the desk towards the Third Secretary. "Only – this. It has just arrived."

Keyter tried to read something in the Ambassador's face – discouragement, hope, satisfaction, anything – but after a short hesitation he came nearer, took the telegram, glanced through it, nodded.

The Ambassador was waiting for his reaction.

But Keyter merely asked: "May I keep it?"

"Of course."

"Did you want to – Have you – "

"No, that was all, Stephen." He leaned forward, almost reluctantly, but said nothing more.

229

Keyter put the telegram into his pocket. "How long is 'immediately'?" He asked without looking up.

"A week. Two at the utmost."

"I see." There were tiny beads of perspiration under his nose.

"You needn't be upset by it. I'll send the Minister a telegram to explain that your services are needed here at the moment." He got up to lend more emphasis to his words: "There is no reason why you should be afraid of anything, Stephen. At the very least we shall be able to delay your return to Pretoria for a couple of months. Whatever happens then will be mere routine. It need not have any influence on your career. I shall see to it that the telegram is dispatched without delay."

"No, Mr. Ambassador."

Puzzled, the older man looked at him, leaning forward on his hands. "Why not, Stephen?" he asked. "I can still protect you. And you know it."

"It is so easy to destroy a person," Keyter said quietly. "It's not so easy to save oneself. But that is what I have to do now. There are other senior officials in Pretoria who might be willing to pull some strings for me. I had them in mind when I was drawing up the report. But now I know something I did not realise then: That I could only live with my own conscience if I am willing to bear all the consequences, alone."

One didn't say these things in a crisis, the Ambassador thought. It was all too well reasoned out, a recitation learnt by heart. It sounded well. It was "honourable". It was the way one ought to react. But it was not Stephen Keyter. He had learnt his recitation too well, however, and no one would be able to get round it.

Keyter was looking at him as if he expected an answer. But then he turned back to the door.

"I am sorry, Stephen," the Ambassador said behind him.

"Sorry?" He swung round. "Why? Please, you mustn't be noble now. There was nothing noble in what has happened. It's no use trying to fool each other. It just makes it more difficult."

The Ambassador did not answer. Neither of them moved.

"It's all so petty, really," Stephen said at last. "Some jealousy. Some ambition. Not much more."

"It's not as easy as all that, Stephen." He said so, he felt, merely in an attempt to force his way through the cool façade of bitterness in the young man's attitude. "It's not so easy to diagnose anything," he repeated.

"It's not true," Keyter answered. "That is the very reason why everything went wrong. We have always been looking for 'difficult' diagnoses, even when we talked about Nicolette. And all the time it was so terribly simple. As simple as love and hate."

"Why must you mention her again?" the Ambassador asked, tired.

"What else is there to talk about?" After a moment he added almost accusingly: "A few days ago I saw her coming from the official residence."

"She is back in her room," the Ambassador said.

Their words were drawing lines across each other; it was no conversation of questions and answers, but a series of jumbled remarks, as if each had memorised some lines from a different play and was now reciting them.

"She came past me, whistling, and ignored me."

"She had been in my house for a few days."

"At the front door she stopped to talk to Lebon. I heard them laugh."

"She came after Erika had left."

Only then did Keyter ask the first question: "Is she back in South Africa, or still in London? – Erika."

"She's in Johannesburg. Or she was when she wrote her letter. It came yesterday. You must visit her when you get back –" He repressed a feeling of anguish and went on hurriedly: "She will be lonely, I think. Annette left her and went to Cape Town. She wanted to be on her own."

"It would do her good."

"I suppose so." Then: "The divorce will be settled soon."

"I didn't know – "

"We never discussed it before she went. She wrote it in yesterday's letter. Not that it came as a surprise, of course."

"No. Still – "

"It will be difficult for her to adapt herself to the country again. One loses all contact. She should appreciate it if you visited her occasionally."

Keyter nodded. "And the operation – ?" he asked.

"Soon." With almost polite interest: "Did she mention it to you then?"

"Yes." He looked at the Ambassador's averted face, and said softly, reluctantly: "Did you know that Erika and I – ?"

Painfully, silently, the Ambassador's eyes turned to him. "Was it necessary to tell me this, Stephen?"

"I can no longer hide it from you."

"I understand."

"Please don't think – Nothing ever *happened* between us. It was

231

just that, in one stage, we needed each other." Adding almost angrily: "It makes it sound cheap to talk about it. But it was not."

"Everything sounds cheap in words. But sometimes – you were right – one has to say it, in spite of all. We must learn to live with cheapness too." Once again composed, he asked: "Have *you* heard from her lately?"

"No. I think she avoided me ever since she came back from Italy. And I avoided her."

"Because of me."

"Because of everything. It could never have lasted anyway. And now I have caused you this, too."

The Ambassador shook his head.

"And I could have saved you from it by saying nothing. Why is one always driven to confession? Why couldn't one learn to bear what is laid on one? Why is one always forced back to some sort of religion, to a God, just to get rid of one's burdens? It is humiliating. It is *unworthy*. And because I could no longer bear it, I had to unburden it on you, which is even more disgraceful. Why couldn't one be strong and pure and free? Free of *guilt*. There was no guilt while it lasted. But now, now that I tried to get rid of what happened, because I could no longer bear it inside me, *now* it is there. And it was the same with the report. I believed I was doing the right thing; and perhaps it was right – up to the moment when I began to put it in writing, to *confess*. Then the whole idea became a miserable, clumsy piece of work before my eyes. But it was too late to stop. Everything was suddenly so intricate. And it had been so clear before."

Almost with a smile, but wearily, the Ambassador said: "You should have been my son, Stephen."

The young man looked at him, amazed, but without resentment.

"I don't know what I would have made of you," the Ambassador said. "But God knows, a man needs a son. He must put his small hand in yours and walk beside you and ask neverending questions. You must rediscover the world through his eyes. You must make him kites and catapults. He must swim naked in a water hole and come to you for comfort and praise after he has shot his first bird. He must bring you the fish he has caught. And the first little girl who makes his head turn."

"It doesn't work out like that."

"No. Nothing works out. But if it *could*!" Almost apologetically he remarked: "That is what age does to one, you see?"

232

Stephen turned back to the door. When he reached it, he laughed wryly, as if something had suddenly struck him, and said: "So I am going back."

"When do you want to leave?"

"I could get everything in order in a day or two. There's nothing which binds me. Nothing."

"If there's anything I could do – "

"Thank you, Mr. Ambassador," he said formally.

The door was closed.

The Ambassador picked up the telephone. "Mrs. Smith," he said, "I do not want to be disturbed by calls or visitors."

"But you have an appointment with the managing director of the arms firm – "

"He could talk to Col. Kotzé today. Or come back tomorrow."

"Yes, Mr. Ambassador," she said aggressively.

He leaned back against the high back of his chair. Outside there was quiet sunshine and the distant noise of the streets. All round him were the musty corridors and offices of the Embassy, alive with the inscrutable activity of invisible people. Upstairs, somewhere, Le Roux, he presumed, was busy going through the day's newspapers looking for reports on South African affairs, and jotting down notes of piquant events which might be used in his writing. Verster was preparing statistics for the following week's commercial conference in Brussels, and trying to make up his mind whether his son should go to a French school or to a boarding-school in South Africa. Colonel Kotzé was studying a catalogue of French aircraft. Mademoiselle Hubert, in the Hellschreiber's office, was typing Le Roux's report about a scheme of cultural exchange between France and South Africa; coming down to the toilet at regular intervals to readjust her hair. In the office next to his, Masters was systematising particulars in connection with French policy in Africa; on a memorandum sheet next to him lay the times of arrival and departure of the plane with which Sylvia intended going to London for her next shopping spree. Joubert, in his office, was discussing his forthcoming home leave with a South African visitor. Harrington was working on a financial memorandum, fretting about the fact that as a result of inadequate French contraceptives he would be a father in six months' time. The Registry Office was noisy, with constant coming and going, as Anna Smith and her typists and clerks were looking up files, typing letters, criticising the latest plays, comparing France and South Africa to the everlasting detriment of the former. In the reading-room downstairs the messengers were calculating the staff members' postage expenses for the month and comparing their most recent amorous experiences with divers men and women. In the first basement office the typists were preparing for the lunch break which was only forty-five minutes away. And behind the next door Keyter was working on visa forms; or perhaps he was looking at his telegram through a cloud of smoke dancing upwards from the tip of his untouched cigarette.

And here he was sitting in his beautiful chair behind the desk with the calendar which still showed the dates of January; in the still heart of all the activity in the concentric circles around him; isolated from it; alone; looking down at the folded laundry list on his blotter.

He noticed the apparent calmness of his hands with the fine dust of hair on his fingers shining in the light from the window. He made no effort to take up one of the pens from the heavy silver inkstand, or to open one of the files piled up near his right elbow. He remained sitting, motionless, while the watch hands on the wall followed their circular course round the timeless centre, until all sounds and suggestions of life had disappeared from the building, as water would drain from a bath. At one o'clock he got up, put the laundry list in his breastpocket and went through the empty building down to the dull sunlight on the grey cobblestones of the courtyard. At the main entrance Farnham and Lebon were chatting with a bored gendarme. They greeted him as he came past. He nodded, then crossed over towards the avenue Wagram where he often had his meals. While he was waiting to be served, he casually paged through a journal he had bought at the kiosk outside. On the last page the week's horoscopes were summarised in neat columns. With a faint smile he started reading the forecasts for *Scorpio* and *Leo*. There was not much in common between them. He took his knife and carefully tore out the page so that he could give it to Nicolette when he saw her again. Then he put the journal on his lap, ate his food, paid the bill, and returned to the Embassy. He went into the official residence and up to his bedroom. There he opened Nicolette's laundry bag on the bed to compare the contents with the list. As he had expected, she had omitted some items and he carefully made the necessary alterations. There was something melancholic about the heap of crumpled washing on the bed. It must have been several weeks' clothes, for they were damp with the heat of her little kitchen and there was a tired smell about them, somewhat clammy, a past tense smell, pathetically personal. Inexplic-

234

ably an old broken sandal and a few crumpled bits of paper had found their way into the bag. He took them out. The papers were covered with budget reckonings. One scrap contained the undecipherable second half of a word followed by an exclamation mark. The Ambassador scrutinised everything very closely before he dropped the scraps into a waste-paper basket. At last he put her washing – including some sheets from the official residence he had given her – back into the bag, with the list on top, and took it down to the servant who would deliver it to the laundry.

Using the sandal as a pretext he went to the rue de Condé, but Nicolette was not at home and after half an hour's fruitless waiting he turned back and sauntered aimlessly towards the river. For a long time he stood leaning over the wall looking at the lazy movement of the long flat-bottomed boats gliding under the bridges. Later he went to a bistro for coffee. But before he had emptied his cup, he discovered that he had forgotten her sandal on the river wall. It upset him unreasonably. Without finishing his coffee he hurried back to where he had stood. But the little sandal was gone. Perhaps it had fallen over the side, and drifted away, or sank. He felt as if he had lost something of infinite value.

He walked back to the rue de Condé with a heavy heart. But she had not returned yet. In the boulevard Saint-Michel he entered a smoky cinema where a sentimental American film with an almost inaudible French sound track was being shown. Infidelity. Tears. Everlasting love. Suicide. Miserable, he sat looking at it, feeling dull resentment against the lie of it all. For life was not like that, he thought; he *knew*. Or was it true after all: was everything, essentially, a melodramatic tale, badly constructed, filled with clichés, full of sound and fury? And every anonymous little actor played his part, convinced that he was indispensable, contributing something important to the unintelligible whole; and in the evening, his costume – his wedding garment – stripped from him, he would drown his few dollars in a bar, and curse, and stumble over a loose stone on his way home, and get lost in the dark.

He had a headache by the time he came outside again. Taking a short-cut to the rue de Condé, he found her at home at last, showing no traces of her day's mysterious wanderings through the city.

They had dinner together, and talked for some time; but he felt cornered in her little room, thinking of Keyter all the time. Everything had been so confused that morning. They had to come

235

together again to discuss everything leisurely. She soon sensed that he had something on his mind, but knowing that she hated the sight of Keyter, he did not tell her about it. She became slightly irritated. And both of them felt relieved when, towards eleven o'clock, he suddenly make up his mind and departed. For it had become a need in him to *speak*. And there was only Keyter he could go to.

As he entered the building in the rue Jacques-Dulud, he became almost unpleasantly aware of the total absence of smell in contrast with Nicolette's dwelling-place. The anaemic light lay quietly on the floor, the brown railing of the staircase, the narrow red carpet.

On the fourth landing he knocked on Keyter's white door. All was silent, and there was no light under the door. He could smell something, though. He sniffed, but could not place it. He knocked again, with some hesitation, realising that if Keyter was asleep he should rather not wake him. It was almost half-past eleven. Perhaps it would be better just to leave a note, and go. The smell was becoming unpleasant.

As he was tearing a page from his notebook he heard voices downstairs and leaning over the railing he could see a middle-aged French couple coming up, probably on their way back from a theatre or a concert. He wrote Stephen's name on the outside of the small folded page. The man reached the fourth landing a few steps before his mink-wrapped wife, and started looking for his key. Apparently they lived in the apartment right opposite Stephen's. The woman stopped on the last step, with lustreless light on her dyed hair. She sniffed, scowling.

"What's the matter? her husband asked, unlocking his door and stepping aside.

"Gas," she said, bringing her right hand, with its large topaz ring, to her nose. "Did you forget to put off the stove again?"

He sniffed too. "It's not coming from our apartment," he said and turned towards the Ambassador. "Somebody has not perhaps left the gas on, Monsieur?" he inquired.

"I was not inside," said the Ambassador. "I have just arrived here, but there's no one at home."

"These young people," the woman said. "Always going out and leaving the gas on. They never think of the neighbours." She came to Stephen's door and gave a few delicate sniffs. "There's no doubt at all," she declared, pressing a perfumed handkerchief to her nose. Without waiting for comment she started rapping on the door with her ring.

236

There was no answer.

Annoyed, she looked at the Ambassador: "Well?" she asked. "What are you going to do about it?"

"Nothing," he answered icily. "Mr. Keyter will turn off the tap when he comes back, I presume."

"In the meantime we may be asphyxiated!"

Without answering he went to the staircase. But when he reached the first landing he realised that he was still holding his note for Stephen in his hand. He stopped. At that moment, for the first time, he was struck by the absurd, alarming thought: what if Stephen was *not* out? It must have been that afternoon's melodramatic film which made him think such outrageous things. But whether his sudden anxiety had any foundation or not, it had now become imperative to find out what was going on. He hurried downstairs.

There was no light in the concierge's glass door when he knocked. But he heard a bed creak and a few minutes later the door was opened a few inches. "What d'you want?" a woman's voice inquired. She was wearing a thick brown coat over her night dress, with curlers in her hair.

"I am sorry to disturb you, Madame, but there is gas leaking on the fourth floor and there doesn't seem to be anyone at home."

"*Merde!*" she cursed and came out, buttoning her coat. With a single reproachful glance at the Ambassador, she started climbing the stairs, muttering various remarks about the condition of her heart. He followed calmly. On the fifth floor there was a long and heated argument with the middle-aged couple, accompanied by sniffing and loud hammering on Keyter's door, which, in turn, caused various other occupants of the building to shout for silence from their respective apartments.

"Why don't you *do* something?" the woman in mink kept on asking.

"What could I do?" the concierge answered. "I haven't got a key for the door. *Merde!*"

Whereupon the mink woman turned round to her husband, demanding peremptorily: "Are you going to allow this person to insult me?"

In the meantime a few other people had also come upstairs and were adding their opinions to the general confusion. Only the concierge's curlers were visible in their midst, while regular *merdes* indicated that she was still involved in the argument.

"Wouldn't it be better to telephone the fire brigade?" the Ambassador suggested at last, not without irritation.

237

This led to a new discussion about whose duty it was to telephone, and whether it was the fire brigade which had to be summoned, or the police. But finally the concierge forcibly opened a way through the crowd and hurried downstairs, her coat flapping round her knees, her terrifying head bobbing.

And fifteen minutes later they all heard the braying of the fire brigade van outside, followed by the reappearance of the concierge, accompanied by two officers. Her attitude of solemnity was ridiculously out of keeping with her appearance.

The door was opened. A sickening wave of gas rolled on to the landing. One of the two officers turned round briskly and motioned the spectators to stand back. With their faces protected in their sleeves, they disappeared inside. A light went on. Almost immediately one of them reappeared.

"Get a doctor," he called. "And the police. There's someone inside."

For a moment they were all too dazed to react. The concierge started sobbing hysterically. The middle-aged man of the apartment opposite Stephen's led her away. The others started pressing forward. The fireman had disappeared again. A moment later both of them came staggering out, carrying something between them. They all crowded together.

"Stand back!" one of the officers ordered, pushing the man nearest to him out of his way. The body was carried into the opposite apartment. The Ambassador followed them.

"Stay outside!" one of the officers snarled at him, trying to slam the door in his face.

Hurriedly the Ambassador explained the matter. The officer still glared at him suspiciously, but allowed him to enter. The door was closed. The mink woman had already telephoned the police and was trying to decide which doctor to call. Without asking her leave the Ambassador took the telephone from her hand and dialled the number of the doctor who usually attended the Embassy staff. While the woman stood muttering rude remarks beside him, he laconically explained to the doctor what had happened.

The firemen were already applying artificial respiration. The concierge was sitting wide-eyed on an Empire chair, with eight fingers in her mouth, mumbling alternatively, and at regular intervals, *"Mon Dieu!"* and *"Merde!"* Occasionally she removed one hand from her mouth to cross herself.

"And that in our apartment!" the mink woman said, glaring at the Ambassador.

Her husband tried to calm her down, but she snarled at him so he resumed walking to and fro in the room, his arms behind his back.

Ten minutes later, while the two officers were still kneeling on the Persian carpet beside the inert body, the doctor arrived. The Ambassador opened the door.

Afterwards he retained only a very confused memory of the hours that followed. The police. The trip in the back of the ambulance to the American hospital in the boulevard Victor Hugo. Waiting in a sterile corridor, oblivious of time. The doctor, at last, exhausted and matter-of-fact: "I am very sorry, Your Excellency. There was nothing we could do." The trip – by taxi, or in the doctor's car? – to Masters' flat in the avenue Malesherbes, through deserted streets with yellow traffic lights flickering monotonously on and off. Sylvia's aged face without make-up, hideously distorted while she sobbed: "Oh, I've always known something awful was going to happen – !" Douglas Masters in his blue striped pyjamas with the top button missing, revealing his white, hairless breast. The yellowish light inside a *mairie* where they tried to persuade a sleepy policeman to withhold the details from the press. Masters taking him to the Embassy in the early grey dawn, trying to say something, but changing his mind. The chill air on the sidewalk under the skeleton chestnut trees black against the empty sky. The thought: "He is blaming me for it all – " The sensation of ice cold perspiration on his face. And, when he put his hand into his pocket to find a handkerchief, the crumpled journal page with the horoscope he had forgotten to give to Nicolette. (*Brilliant success in all spheres this week. Make full use of your opportunities. The world is smiling at you.*)

With a short, angry gesture he threw the page into the gutter. Then he turned round to the heavy, lugubrious entrance of the Embassy and pressed Lebon's bell to be admitted.

2

After Gillian had broken down everything in me – my convictions of morality and convention, my belief in tradition and religion and social institutions, and an existence devoid of all surprises – there was only one thing left: life itself. This small, indispensable fact, I thought, even she would not be able to deny or transcend. But she risked this as well, as recklessly as anything she ever did.

Or was it, the first time at least, merely a dangerous game of which she knew that it would not be pursued to the end? It arose from a triviality: a quarrel which started when she sat next to me in a concert and kept on talking aloud until I got angry and told her to shut up; she jumped up and went out; I followed. In the large empty foyer I tried to hold her back with force, but she broke loose. Outside on the broad steps she broke into a violent fit of cursing and screaming and blaming and abusing while I tried in vain to calm her. At last she cried: "Why can't I talk if I want to? Are you ashamed of me? But why can't I be *me*? Nobody ever leaves me alone. I am sick and tired of you and your dainty little manners. I'm sick and tired of everything!" Concluding melodramatically: "I want to be dead! I'm going to kill myself!"

"Don't be foolish, Gillian!"

"You don't believe me!" she cried. "All right, I'll show you – !" And she ran off into the dark.

Go to hell, I thought. But after a while I began to feel uneasy. I realised how easily, in an inconsiderate moment, she could do something desperate. She had already defied everything my way of life represented in her eyes; who knew but she would get it into her head to defy life itself?

It was after midnight when I reached my room. There was light inside and the door was half open.

"Gillian!" I called. But there was no answer.

I hesitated, and went in. She was lying diagonally across the bed, fast asleep, still wearing her concert clothes. Something in her attitude scared me. It was no ordinary sleep. I went to the bed quickly. Under her shoulder I found the empty tablet bottle. I called out her name, tried to lift her, slapped her cheeks to wake her. But with barely a moan she slept on. I wasted no more time but ran to the telephone in the entrance hall.

There was a tense hour. The doctor said: "She is out of danger now. We were damned lucky to get to her so soon."

I sat at her bedside all night, watching her pale face, listening to her deep breathing.

"But why did you do it, Gillian?" I asked the next day. "Don't you realise what could have happened?"

"I knew you would come," was her only answer. And whether she teased me or was serious, I did not know.

That was the first time, and it had no grave consequences. But perhaps I realised, even at that early stage, that it had been nothing but a warning, a preparation for what was to follow. And when many months later, in Arles, I received the letter with the casual reference to her death, I knew immediately and almost with resignation: this was inevitable, and so it had happened. I never found out how it had come about: whether it had been an accident, or illness, or whether she had indeed taken her own life. I could not trace anybody who had known her during her last months when she had been living in Durban, among complete strangers.

I can only remember that on the very first day after my arrival in South Africa I took the bus from the city to the terminus where one boarded the small bus to the Stellawood cemetery. It was full; and everybody had flowers, except me. I spent more than thirty minutes in the caretaker's office at the entrance trying to trace the number of her grave. I had so little information. When I found it at last I discovered with a shock that she had already been buried three months before I had received the letter.

An annoyingly jovial driver took us past the blocks of graves. Hers was right on top of the hill, where one could look out on the bay of green and grey sea. There was a gusty, chilly, unpleasant wind. A few wretched seagulls were tumbling in the hazy sky high above the city, uttering their forlorn cries.

There was no stone, nothing except the number I had found at the office. How could I know that she was really lying there? *She?* My only proof was a blotted inscription in an official book, and a number. How could I even know that she was dead? Everything she had ever done had been a defiance of life, a way of living in another dimension. All I knew was that she had denied our ordinary form of life, shedding it the way a snake crawled from its useless old skin, leaving it to others, to people like me, who could satisfy themselves with it. It was my first confrontation with death: the sober fact of *not being*. I could not even rebel against it. And I could do nothing to comprehend it. I would simply have to learn to be satisfied with the very existence she had taught me to reject. Perhaps it was worthless; but it was all I had. That, and her memory. But the memories I carefully kept away. And it is only these last few months that I realise they have never left me completely. She has always been with me, like the number of her grave, waiting, a riddle to be solved, an answer to be found.

3

It was on the morning of Tuesday, 9th April that the second telegram, this one in code form, was delivered on the Ambassador's stinkwood desk.

241

4

She had just had her bath and was brushing her teeth when I arrived. She quickly opened the door to let me in, then darted back and went on with her brushing, her feet in the small basin filled with tepid water, with puddles all over the floor, her smooth body and arms and long legs glistening in the light of the kitchenette's bare bulb, while her right arm was moving rhythmically back and forth. I took place on a straight-backed chair beside the gas stove. Talking was out of the question. Even if she heard me, which seemed improbable with all the noise she made, she would not pay any attention to me – she was much too deeply absorbed in what she was doing. It lasted fully five minutes. Then she rinsed her mouth, gurgled noisily, washed her toothbrush under the tap and started drying her face with a flurry of towel movements.

At last her two green eyes peeped through the loose strands of hair over the edge of the wet towel, and she laughed, and said: "Hullo!"

"I brought your laundry." I pointed to the bag she had given me the previous week.

"Thanks. Will you put my things in my cupboard for me? I won't be long."

I went to the cosy confusion of her bedroom, emptied the bag and packed the clean, anonymous, sterile stack of washed clothes into the wardrobe, as neatly as was possible in that chaos.

"Where are we going tonight?" she called after a few minutes and came dancing in, threw down the towel on the bed and began to hunt for clothes.

Remembering the macabre result of another, similar evening, I asked: "Must we really go out?"

"Yes." She was struggling with her head inside a jersey. "It's beautiful outside."

"We're not going to a *cave* again."

"No," she laughed. "No, tonight we'll look for *light*. We can stroll around wherever we find light."

"The Champs-Élysées?"

"Yes. We can start at the top." She closed a zip. "At the American Drugstore" She went on prattling, dressing, brushing her hair, applying make-up to her eyes, trying on one pair of shoes after another.

"I brought you some money," I said, placing the notes I had put aside on the table.

"Is it all for me?" she asked, amazed. "Why?"

"You need it more than I do. That's why."

Holding one shoe in her hand, she hopped towards me and kissed me. I smiled into her happy eyes, but it was slightly strained, because I knew for what reason I had really brought the money, what I really tried to compensate for, what I really desired –

"Come!" She skipped to the door and opened it.

Outside the tired old building the evening was young and cool, with a hint of Spring. Light, low clouds reflected the city's light, lending everything a phosphorescence in the dusk. We took a taxi along the Seine to the Pont Alexandre III. The Louvre, the Place de la Concorde, the Madeleine on the opposite side of the river, the Assembly on our side, the Invalides, the bridge – everything was floodlit; the Eiffel Tower fingering the clouds with its rays of light; and in the streets, wet after the afternoon's shower, everything was reflected brilliantly, blindingly, fantastically: the entire city transformed into a carnival of unearthly splendour. Along the avenue Alexandre III we reached the Champs-Élysées with a fluid movement of car lights gliding past us from the direction of the Arc. It seemed as if we ourselves lost all substance and became part of the one immense flood, everything dissolved into streaming movement, into white, shining light. And from the sidewalks came music: here a few street musicians, there a group of hilarious students, or a clochard with a merry flute, and once a whole bus of singing children; piano or orchestral music from all the cafés and the wide open windows on the higher floors. She was leaning her head out of the window, her hair streaming in the wind, her eyes opened wide to allow the light to flood into her. Once she looked round at me, blinking, laughing, the lights reflected in tiny specks in her eyes.

"It blinds one to look so long," she said. "It's like looking into the sun. Now I'm seeing dots everywhere!" And she turned her head back to the window and gazed out again, while I sat watching her, so light and young beside my heavy years: a little Beatrice.

At the Étoile we got out, crossed the endless avenue of light between two waiting walls of traffic, and began to saunter down the opposite side towards the Drugstore. In front of an illuminated window a beggar in a moth-eaten tailcoat was playing sweet, nostalgic tunes on his fiddle. But suddenly he switched to something else as a nun was approaching from the opposite side – I first noticed it when Nicolette's hand formed the sign of the horns

R 243

– and started playing *Ave Maria*, his tiny eyes wise and twinkling in his wrinkled, bearded face. The nun passed him with down-cast, disapproving eyes. But Nicolette stopped and urged me to give him something. And as we went on she sang softly to the accompaniment of his thin melody:

"Sancta Maria, Mater Dei, ora pro nobis peccatoribus, nunc et in hora mortis nostrae –" But her voice was playful, without the sombre melancholy I had sometimes noticed in it. And she stopped abruptly when we reached the Drugstore.

"Look!" she said, pointing to the sky. "The moon is out!"

For a minute it gleamed through the clouds. Then the city lights were once more reflected from an even, silvery ceiling, and I opened the glass door and we stepped into the bright, neon-lit interior. It was crowded, but we found an empty table and ordered enormous méringues. All round us were chromium, and loud jazz, and a horde of strangers. And once again, as so often in the past, I was amazed by the fact that I could feel relaxed and happy merely because she was with me, even in surroundings which would normally have grated me.

"Do you think it was wrong of the old man with the violin to play *Ave Maria* when the nun came past?" she asked suddenly, with white crumbs on her lips.

"He got the tip he wanted, whether it was wrong or not. And I suppose that's all he cared about."

"I hope he's not going to be punished for it one day." She shut her eyes, swallowing a large mouthful of ice cream. "Do you think it's true – *really* true – that one is resurrected after one's death?"

"It's possible." Thinking back to it now, it sounds so incredibly naïve; but at that moment it was, all of a sudden, so simple to believe anything, to see clearly into the heart of everything which was normally incredibly complex. And I could believe again what had already become impossible: that it was irrelevant, really, whether there existed any hereafter, or God, or something-more-than-human; it simply depended upon whether one could *believe* it, because it was the creative act of faith in itself which mattered. And for that short while I *did* believe, because I was prepared to accept anything while she was there with me, in that gaudy interior with its too many lights.

She had finished before me, but the meringue was too sweet for me anyway; and because I did not want to bore her we left immediately to resume the night's pilgrimage of wonder and discovery.

We crossed the Champs-Élysées again to look at the étalages

opposite; and leisurely we strolled down as far as the Lido. We did not go down to the nightclub – it was much too early anyway – but merely followed the arcade past the luxury boutiques surrounding the central café. I admired the clothes and jewellery at which she pointed, but most of the time my eyes were fixed on *her*. It must have been the artificial light which made her look so different, with an almost unworldly beauty, as she gazed, enraptured, at the expensive, subtle wares aimed at feminine irresistibility. But those were only the first few steps into the little world of Venus. From there we went towards the Rond-Point, turning left in the rue du Colisée with its gigolos and pimps waiting on the illuminated sidewalks; past a nightclub with photos of breathtaking artistes posted at the door – 'girls' who, in the process of stripteasing, would be transformed, shockingly, into men.

Nicolette's only – laconic – comment was: "Angels are like that too, aren't they? So what's wrong with it?"

We walked to the rue du Faubourg Saint-Honoré where we boarded a bus to the Opéra. Arriving there, she first took me to the metro entrance in the centre of the square to show me the dazzling spectacle of all the concentric circles of light; then we walked right round the opera building, catching unexpected, exhilirating snatches of choir and orchestral music coming from the inside, until we arrived back on the brightly illuminated square.

I was beginning to feel tired. For the first time my thoughts went back – why? – to Stephen, to what had happened six nights before. She did not even know about it yet and I did not want to upset her with the news: I knew it would be a shock to her, even though she had detested the man. And the little time we had left was too precious, too vulnerable for any risks.

I thought about the days of feverish activity behind me: there had been so many things to arrange before the body could be returned to South Africa; then had followed the inevitable waiting, for I had known very well that the Minister's main reason for recalling Stephen had been to obtain first-hand information before the final move. And now –

But it was no time for thinking about that. Stephen's name, above all, had to be banished from my thoughts.

She took my hand to lead me further on our way. I looked at her, and smiled at her, and felt my momentary unrest ebb away. What did anything else matter while we two could still wander through the celestial city? It would end soon. It had to. But at that moment everything was still precious and present.

We stopped at the Italian Travel Agency to look at the colourful posters. There was an immense imperial eagle representing Rome. Rome – My thoughts threatened to start wandering again, but she was at my side, and I looked at her intently, urgently, seeing the reflection of all the lights around us in her beautiful eyes, and repeating, in my mind, the words she had sung so lightly, earlier in the evening: *"Ora pro nobis peccatoribus, nunc et in hora mortis nostrae – "*

We wandered on, from light to light, window to window, poster to poster.

"It's so beautiful," she sighed once. "I must go travelling, everywhere, seeing everything, travelling, travelling without end – "

I listened in silence, thinking: *She is even more beautiful now than earlier tonight.* But as I became more and more tired I realised more and more acutely that our journey must soon end; it was a predestination to which I had to resign myself.

We had a cold drink on a café terrace, resting for a while, staring at all the people passing us in the luminous night. When we landed in the metro, fifteen minutes later, it was like a temporary blindness after all the lights. But it was most welcome. The train was almost empty, so we could sit down, only half conscious of old men with open newspapers like huge, sensational moths; and workmen in blue overalls, with lecherous eyes.

At the Cité station she got out, without explaining why. But I soon discovered the reason, for when we came round the corner of the Préfecture de Police, Notre-Dame was in front of us, floodlit, drifting weightlessly against the dark. And when we reached the bridge there was also the slightly rippling reflection of the old cathedral in the water before us, more beautiful than I had ever seen it, a crown of light on a night of light. She was very quiet beside me as if her ecstasy had become more and more introverted until, at last, it was burning like an unflickering candle inside her.

"M'sieur-dame – ?"

From somewhere in the night the gnarled old woman had made her appearance. Nicolette said nothing. It was strange, since she usually reacted so quickly, urging me to buy something. She was merely waiting quietly, almost piously, as if words were entirely unnecessary. I gave the old woman a note, but took only one rose in exchange: a white one, almost a bud still, with very tender petals. And I handed it to my little guide, who lifted herself on her toes to kiss me, still saying nothing. The old woman had already disappeared. We set out on the last stage of our journey to her room.

246

There she carefully placed the rose in a glass with water and put it on the table. While she was busy, she casually glanced through the window and, looking back over her shoulder, said: "Did you know the people opposite – "

"No." I went to her and put my hands on her shoulders. "Forget about them. They're not important now. Nothing is important. Except you. Except us."

She nodded serenely and made no protest when I began to unbutton her jersey. I turned her round so that she could lean with her back against me.

"Do you remember: once, before I had been with you for the first time, you said – "

"I remember."

She stood listening to my hands. She came with me to the virginal little bed. And together we set out on a new journey, through a new little universe, the ancient journey, but a new one, unhurried, filled with discoveries and beauty, loneliness and comfort, despair and faith, just she and I, just us, with our single shadow trembling on the wall. And at last, after a very long time – but time did not matter – I said:

"You must believe me. I love you."

"Yes," she said. That was all: "Yes."

That was enough for the moment. But the rest, I knew, had to follow inevitably. And I had to announce it as calmly as I could: "The telegram came today."

"Which telegram?" She was tenser now, no longer soft and lazy.

"The commission will be here the day after tomorrow. Or tomorrow, rather, for it is almost morning."

She did not answer.

"There's no reason why it should make any difference, Nicolette."

Her head moved, but whether she shook it or nodded, I could not make out.

"Whatever happens, we remain the same. What could it be to you what they decide about my work?"

"It will be before Easter," she said at last.

"A day before Easter. Why? What does that matter?"

"Nothing. I was only thinking."

I made no movement, waiting for her to explain, but she said no more. If only I could take her shoulders very tightly in my hands, and hurt her, and *force* her to believe that nothing would make any difference to us. But it was like Christmas morning at the Mass, when she had entered into a dimension where I could

247

not follow her. I could only remain lying next to her, hoping that this, at least, would last. But she was no longer tranquil and I had to let her go to put off the light. For we did not need it any longer: the early dawn was already coming through the window, greyish and young.

She returned, and lay down beside me again; but we did not sleep. At last I got up and dressed. She made no movement.

When I reached the door I said: "I shall come back tonight."

She nodded.

"Early."

"All right."

And then I went out. The concierge's wife was on the first floor, scrubbing the steps, and muttering a curse as she had to stand aside to let me pass. Outside on the pavement the rows of rubbish bins were waiting patiently to be picked up by the municipal lorries.

5

It was almost like before, the way in which the Ambassador did his work in his office that Wednesday. Not that he could hope to get through everything that had piled up during the previous weeks, but that was not so important. He merely wanted to keep himself busy in order not to think again about the things which had been thought out and resolved so long ago. He worked in strict isolation, having instructed Anna Smith not to allow any visitors or telephone calls, and refusing even to see members of his own staff.

The telegram of the previous morning had supplied only the most essential information, omitting even the names of the commission members. But late in the afternoon he was informed that there would be a telephone call from London at eight o'clock that evening. That gave him a clue.

The call was unexpectedly delayed, however, and by the time he and his colleague had arranged about the commission's time of arrival at Orly the next morning, it was much later than the Ambassador had foreseen.

When, at last, he knocked on her grey door, out of breath from climbing the stairs too quickly, there was no answer. He knocked again, calling her name, and waited; but there was not the slightest sound inside. He was puzzled and upset. Surely she would have waited. She had known that he would come. It was impossible that anything could have happened. He knocked again, although he already knew very well that she was not at home.

He went downstairs, not even bothering to put on the light which had gone out long ago. By this time he knew his way. Outside, he walked round to the opposite pavement of the rue de l'Odéon to make sure that there was really no light in her window. For a long time he remained waiting there, lighting a cigarette once, waiting, looking up every now and then, smoking, waiting. The window remained dark. He was still warding off all thoughts. Perhaps she had just gone somewhere to buy food, or a magazine, or something to drink. At last he stamped out his cigarette with his shoe and walked back towards the Carrefour de l'Odéon. For a moment he considered going up to her room again, but he decided against it and went to the rue de l'École de Médicine instead, to a bistro they had sometimes visited. She was not there, and the *patron* could not recall having seen her earlier in the evening. The Ambassador left and went to the next possible place. She was not there either, nor had she been there. At last he ended up in the boulevard Saint-Michel where he meticulously entered every single bistro and restaurant, even those where they had never been together. Most of the waiters to whom he put his question treated him curtly; a few grinned knowingly, or winked; but all the answers were the same. He went as far as the Luxembourg Gardens, and even crossed the boulevard to the newspaper and peanut stalls in front of the closed gates in case she would be there, hidden in the sauntering crowd. She was not. He went to the high, black fence of the park, his back to the crowd, trying to peer inside. The first few yards were dimly illuminated by the street lights, but further on it was dark, with the heavy mass of trees an impenetrable screen against the sky. One must feel desolate inside there at this hour, all by oneself at the pond in the sunken garden in front of the palace. The green chairs would be stacked in heaps under the silent statues. Perhaps the dim glow of the night sky would be reflected in the pond, but all around it would be dark, an endless night which would isolate one completely from the people and the traffic, and the city itself. Yet it was almost with yearning that he peered into the dark towards that invisible pond beyond the black trees. But the park gates were shut.

He shrugged slightly and began to walk back, trying all the bistros on his side of the boulevard, until he reached the river. And all the time he had the impression that she could not be very far; that he would only have to walk a few more yards to see her fair head bent over a glass of Coca-Cola (or red wine to-night?); or to catch a glimpse of her legs in the crowd; or to hear her laugh or her voice. But he could not go on wandering like this. Perhaps she had already gone back home and was waiting for him. So he returned to the rue de Condé, and, refraining on purpose from looking at her window from the rue de l'Odéon first, went up the high staircase to knock on her door again.

There was still no sound inside, and no light.

Without waiting any longer he pressed the bell which rang on the landlady's side. He could hear her shuffling footsteps approach the door. A sliver of light fell across the landing.

"Who's there?" she asked.

The Ambassador went to the door so that she could recognise him.

"Oh, it's you," she remarked in an ingratiating tone of voice. "No, she isn't here. She's gone."

"Perhaps you could open up for me again, then I could wait for her inside."

"I said she was *gone*. She's not coming back."

He could not immediately grasp it. "But she – "

"I can't stand here all night," she snarled. "Don't you understand French? She's gone, she left with bags and baggage, boots and all, this afternoon. Her place is empty. She paid me for two weeks in advance: she would have diddled me if I wasn't careful. And where am I going to get another lodger? People are so damned fussy these days."

"But she can't be gone," he said quietly, interrupting her. "Didn't she leave an address or a message?"

"Why should she?"

"But we arranged that – "

"That's no business of mine. Perhaps she wanted to get away from you. Fancy a young girl like her going with such an old man anyway. I never liked the idea."

"I am not interested in your opinion, Madame," the Ambassador remarked sharply.

"So now you want to insult me. What are you doing here so long? I'm sure *I* can't help you." She began to close the door.

He abandoned his reprimanding tone. "Couldn't you let me go in just for a minute?" he urged. "Perhaps she left a message there."

"There's nothing. I've swept the floor and all."

"But surely it couldn't do any harm just to let me have a look."

"There's nothing, I tell you." The door moved further.

He quickly took a note from his wallet. It was a preposterous tip to give her, but he had no change, and he did not care.

"Monsieur!" she exlaimed, shocked. "I will have nothing to do with bribery!" For a moment she stood leering at him. Then, with a flick of her plump hand she grabbed the note, slipped it into her apron pocket, took a bundle of keys from a nail in the wall and waddled past him with an attitude of offended dignity. She unlocked the opposite door, pushed it open, switched on the light and stood back.

"Now you can see for yourself!" she said.

He looked at her, but her eyes were averted. So he went in without waiting any longer, through the little lobby to the bedroom. There were four bare walls with the plastering coming off in shreds in one corner. A scrubbed brown table with old ink and cigarette marks. A rectangular, heavy brown cupboard with one door hanging open obliquely. It was empty, the shelves and drawers covered with old newspapers. A couple of chairs. An ugly little bed with a bare striped mattress with old brownish stains. The mirror with the gilt frame was lying on the bed. The floor was swept, as she had said. It was a strange room where he had never been before. Not even a room: a little bare cage filled with junk.

He went to the window to compose his thoughts. A light opposite caught his attention. Absently, he looked at it. The room was empty. But while he was still standing there, the young woman made her appearance from somewhere deep inside, wearing a loose faded gown, carrying a baby in her arms. She came to the window to make sure that it was closed; but she made no effort to draw the curtains. Sitting down on the side of the bed, she opened her gown, took out a large, swollen breast and forced the nipple into the child's mouth. Then, oblivious of the sucking baby, she looked up, out of the window, to the outer darkness, and to the man opposite.

He turned away, leaving the strange little room, and went to the kitchenette. The old blue gas stove stood primly against the inside wall, the grating blackened and greasy. In the corner, at the window in the slanting outer wall, was the washbasin, anaemic, impersonal. On the floor stood the little white plastic basin.

She was away, then. And there was nothing left of her. Not a scent, not an empty lipstick, a crescent toenail, an old toothpaste tube, the core of an apple, a hairpin. Not even the question mark of a little hair curl on the side of the basin. *Nothing.*

251

It seemed as if she herself had never been here. All he had left, were a few memories. And how could he even be sure of these? Everything was so essentially *unsure*. And it was a shock to him, this discovery that he felt the *need* of a sign of her existence. Was it imperative, then, for one to leave something behind in order to have being? Was that, really, the only way one could exist, through signs, algebraic symbols representing unknown quantities – ?

The landlady called from the front door: "What on earth are you doing? How long are you going to keep me waiting?"

"I'm coming," he answered absently, continuing his frantic search. But he found nothing.

He went back to the bedroom to start all over again, looking even on the cupboard and under the bed. Nothing; nothing. And when, at long last, he stood up wearily and saw the landlady's impatient face appear in the doorway, he was aware only of the slight, faded pattern the little cross had left on the wall; even the nail had fallen out.

"I found the cross under the bed," the landlady remarked, adding with a sneer: "What on earth could *she* want it for, I wonder. I've got much better use for it."

For a moment the Ambassador held out his hand toward her, half open. Then it fell back to his side

"Come on," she said irritably. "I'm not going to wait any longer."

He merely nodded. Without looking out at the window opposite, he went past her, aware only of the bewilderment in his heart about the girl: somewhere in this wild city, tonight, without her cross. How could she exist without her little set of faiths and superstitions and myths? Or would she simply go to the Flea Market at Clignancourt the next week-end and buy herself another little cross? But could it really be so simple – even for her?

He waited outside until she had closed the door behind her. "Good-night, Madame," he said, "And thank you."

He went downstairs. He waited until the heavy door with its weather-beaten, beautiful old carvings banged behind him. Then he went away, aimlessly. Even familiar streets would be strange to him tonight. He went on walking merely to keep moving, wandering through the labyrinth, avoiding people and light. At last he reached the river near the Pont des Arts, went up the steps to the deserted bridge and stopped in the middle, leaning over the railing, his face towards the illuminated cathedral. He remembered another night on this bridge. And all the times she

252

had spoken of the river, and of the desperate creatures who flung themselves into it. She herself – ? For a moment he felt scared, paralysed, exhausted. Even that he did not know. He could merely believe, or hope, that it had not happened to her. But he would never have believed it of Stephen either. And exactly one week ago –

Would that, in the end, be the simplest, perhaps the only way out? What else was there left? Tomorrow the two members of the commission of inquiry would arrive. It need not take long, perhaps a single day would suffice. Before Easter everything could be completed. And then? What, what indeed, did he have left? Not even a little cross.

For a long time he remained standing there, his hands clutching the bridge railing. Then he turned away deliberately and crossed over to the opposite side, away from Nicolette's bank, back to his own. Perhaps he would regret this moment's decision in the days or years to come; and it would never again be possible to come this far. But now, and for this moment, he had decided. There was still an irrational *lex humana* he had to respect.

He passed behind the Louvre and lost his way in the new maze around Les Halles; later he landed in the boulevard Sebastopol, but turned away again, towards the narrower lanes beside it, the dark, dingy quarter where the young street-girls were initiated. All round him in the night the invisible human activity was going on. He could hear his footsteps echo against the walls. Now and then, on the vague periphery of a circle of lamplight someone or something slinked past. From an open window came the wailing notes of a cheap jazz tune with dark, undisguised lust. A man went in at the door of an obscure hotel accompanied by a prostitute. On the curtains and blinds of the windows above were dancing shadows. How many people within the boundaries of this one city were not, at this very moment, occupied with love? It was night; it was the hour of love. All the world was caught in it. And through it all, aware of it all, he was continuing on his long journey. *Amare liceat si non potiri licet –!* Endlessly the city stretched out around him, circle upon circle, teeming with all its natural and unnatural lusts: those of Sodom as well as those of Pasiphae.

Pasiphae. This beautiful name was suddenly caught in the web of his thoughts. And he held on to it, grateful to have *something* to occupy his mind. Pasiphae. Mother of both the Minotaur and Ariadne; source of the Fall, and of salvation; an archetype, representing Eve as well as Mary. And without being aware of the transition, he thought: she, the false heifer, had landed him in the labyrinth; but had she not made it possible for him to find the thread which might lead him out of it as well – ?

On a street corner under a lamppost a young girl stood looking at him, waiting for him. He was so wrapped up in thought that he saw her too late to cross over to the other side as he usually did. She was thin, and wearing too much make-up, her mouth too large, painted too red. Her dress was tight and very short. She was smoking with apparent sophistication, cynically; but when he came to her he noticed the uncertainty in her eyes and her swift gestures.

"Bonsoir – ?" she said, wavering.

His first reaction was to walk on without answering, but he was troubled by her embarrassment. He stopped reluctantly.

Her lips formed a grateful little smile.

"Vous voulez – ?" she asked.

He resented his own weakness. But he was touched by her youth.

"You shouldn't be here, my child," he said, uneasily and not paternally as he had meant to.

Her face tautened. She half turned her back on him, trying to blow out the smoke casually through her nose.

My God, he thought, she could not be older than seventeen.

He felt an urge to talk to her, but he knew it would be impossible to penetrate the screen of resentment and that it would merely make it more painful for both of them. And so, although he was acutely aware of how futile and even abhorrent his reaction was, he took his wallet from his breast pocket and gave her all the money he had left. She opened her mouth, trying to say something, but she did not.

He waited no longer, but walked away stiffly. Perhaps she was laughing at him. But he could not look back. He could only go on.

Because he had given all his money to the girl, he had to walk all the way. It was like a penance. As he went further, the streets around him grew wider and more desolate. But he was hardly aware of fatigue, of anything but the city itself which was surrounding him like a sacred wood. And, paradoxically, he felt that it was absorbed into him as well, with cathedrals and brothels, light and dark streets, everything.

Only when he finally pressed the bell at the main entrance of the Embassy did he become conscious of his utter exhaustion.

He had to wait a long time for Lebon to open, wearing a crumpled black overcoat over his pyjamas.

"It's the last time I shall disturb you at night, Lebon," the Ambassador said sympathetically. "You've had a hard time lately."

"That's nothing, sir," Lebon said complacently, almost fraternally. "I understand. If only women would appreciate what we have to sacrifice for them, that's what I always say."

The Ambassador smiled wearily. "One can't always have things the way one would like to," he said.

"For such a cute little dish like her, though – " The concierge made a vague, but eloquent gesture. "She's got beautiful eyes, sir, don't you think so?"

"She has."

"Unusual, like. The colour: one doesn't see it often." Closing the door behind them, he apologised: "I don't want to keep you from your sleep, sir."

"Not at all," the Ambassador said, still lingering, as if he could not bear going on alone; and yet he knew the concierge must be sleepy.

"She was here this morning," Lebon said suddenly.

"She?"

"Yes. We chatted for a few minutes."

"What did she come for?"

"She didn't say. I think she forgot, because after a while she went away again without coming in."

"Didn't she – say anything?"

"How d'you mean, sir? We were just chatting. You know what it's like."

"Was that all?"

"Yes." Lebon scratched his head. "And I talked to her about Mr. Keyter. I thought she knew about it."

The Ambassador nodded slowly. "What did she say to that?" he asked quietly.

"Nothing much. She stood looking at me for some time. Then she seemed to get angry, and she asked: 'What about it? Why did you tell it to me? What made you think I would like to know?' And then she left. I'll never understand women, I tell you. No two of them are alike."

"I must go," the Ambassador said.

"Good-night, sir." Lebon saluted. Then he thought of something: "I heard about to-morrow's business, sir – "

The Ambassador stopped.

"If there's anything I could do for you – "

"Thank you, Lebon."

255

The Ambassador walked along the driveway, past the official residence, into the courtyard of the office building.

Behind him he heard Lebon bolt the door and disappear into his own quarters, whistling. There was something familiar about the tune

Of course –

The Ambassador took out his keys to unlock the door. This was where she had come in, that first night. *Donna m'apparve –,* he thought with a little smile.

As he tried to find the right key, he stood humming Lebon's little tune, Nicolette's little tune:

> *"Au clair de la lune, on n'y voit qu'un peu.*
> *On chercha la plume, on chercha du feu.*
> *En cherchant d'la sorte, je n'sais c'qu'on trouva,*
> *Mais j'sais que la porte sur eux se ferma –"*

He unlocked the door and entered the dark reading-room. Behind him the door clicked shut again. Without putting on the light he went upstairs to his office.

There was still work to be done.

November 1962—August 1963.